Braywatch

ROSS O'CARROLL-KELLY

(as told to Paul Howard)

Illustrated by ALAN CLARKE

PENGUIN BOOKS

PENGUIN BOOKS

UK | USA | Canada | Ireland | Australia
India | New Zealand | South Africa

Penguin Books is part of the Penguin Random House group of companies
whose addresses can be found at global.penguinrandomhouse.com.

First published by Sandycove 2020
Published in Penguin Books 2021
001

Copyright © Paul Howard, 2020
Illustrations copyright © Alan Clarke, 2020

The moral right of the copyright holders has been asserted

Typeset by Jouve (UK), Milton Keynes
Printed and bound in Italy by Grafica Veneta S.p.A.

The authorized representative in the EEA is Penguin Random House Ireland,
Morrison Chambers, 32 Nassau Street, Dublin D02 YH68

A CIP catalogue record for this book is available from the British Library

ISBN: 978-0-241-98477-2

www.greenpenguin.co.uk

For my nephews, Christopher and Wayne

Contents

Prologue

I honestly haven't seen the old man this happy since the day Seán FitzPatrick was cleared of, I don't know, whatever it was he was *accused* of doing? I mean, who even remembers any more?

He runs his hand through his hair slash wig and goes, 'It's a day for the ages, Ross! Quote-unquote! Children will read about this in their history books!'

'*Our* children,' the old dear goes, trying to manoeuvre her mouth into something resembling a smile but failing miserably. She ends up just grimacing – like a focking baboon with thrush.

He takes her hand in his. 'That's right!' he goes. 'All one, two, three, four, five, six of them will be born into a world where they will truly know the meaning of the words *macte virtute sic itur ad astra*! Excellence is the way to the stors – eh, Kicker?'

I'm there, 'Seriously, stop holding hands, it's making me want to vom.'

Hennessy smiles to himself as he stares across the river at the Four Courts. '*Datum perficiemus munus*,' he goes.

Pissed. The two of them.

'*Acta est fabula, plaudite!*' the old man fires back. 'Exclamation mork! Exclamation mork! Exclamation mork!'

Kennet looks over his shoulder. He's like, 'What's the stordee, T . . . T . . . T . . . T . . . Teashocked? Are you w . . . w . . . w . . . w . . . wanthon me to thrive up and down the quays wooden mower toyum?'

'I don't know!' the old man goes. 'How long have we kept the chap waiting?'

'It's an . . . n . . . n . . . n . . . n . . . n . . . hour, Teashocked.'

'An hour! No, I think that should be sufficient time for the famous Michael D. to reflect on the momentousness of the occasion! And hopefully tell the staff to get the good cognac out! I should think the day calls for it!'

Yeah, no, we're in a limo heading for the Phoenix Pork, followed by a cavalcade of black Mercs and Gordaí on, like, motorbikes with their *sirens* wailing? The old man is about to be sworn in as the leader of the country. And I've come along mainly just to rip the piss.

'I probably should tweet something!' he goes, whipping out his phone.

Charles O'Carroll-Kelly √ @realCOCK – 3m

On the way to Aras an Uachtarain to receive my seal of office to become Ireland's fifteenth Taoiseach! A new beginning for our country! #COCKforTaoiseach #irexit #fockEU

Reply 870 Retweet 3.8k Like 13.2k DM

I'm there, 'I hope something goes wrong. And I mean that genuinely. You trip going up the steps and break your neck. Something.'

The old man totally ignores this. He goes, 'Give me the list again, Hennessy, old scout!'

And Hennessy's there, 'W.T. Cosgrave.'

'A pious bore!' the old man goes.

'Éamon de Valera.'

'A raving madman!'

'John A. Costello.'

'A weak fool!'

'Seán Lemass.'

'A blithering halfwit!'

'Jack Lynch.'

'A coward and a traitor!'

'Charles Haughey.'

'I liked him! You know, I think I even loved him! I wish he were alive to see this day!'

'Garret FitzGerald.'

'A well-meaning buffoon!'

'Albert Reynolds.'

'A gombeen and a back-stabber!'

'John Bruton.'

'A man utterly devoid of personality and charm! I remember sitting beside him at a dinner in the RDS one night and falling asleep with my face in my soup!'

'Bertie Ahern.'

'Ah, Bertie! Dear, dear Bertie!'

'Brian Cowen.'

'Moving swiftly along!'

'Enda Kenny.'

'An idiot geography teacher!'

'Leo Varadkar.'

'An airhead – minding the class in the absence of a grown-up!'

We reach Heuston Station and Kennet takes the right turn over the bridge. That's when the old man's *phone* all of a sudden rings? He looks at the screen, then answers it.

He's like, 'Fyodor, how the hell are you? *Dobroye utro*, my friend! Yes, I'm on the way to the Pork now! Thank you very much! You're too kind! Yes, I'd be absolutely delighted to sit down with you and your chaps to discuss my Programme for Government! I'll call you tonight! *Do vstrechi! Do vstrechi!*'

He hangs up.

I'm like, 'Why isn't *he* here?'

'Who?' the old man tries to go.

I'm there, 'Er, your *Russian* mate? You know, seeing as *he* rigged the election and everything?'

I watch him exchange a look with Hennessy. Then he goes, 'I've no idea who you're talking about, Kicker! No idea whatsoever!'

We wait for the filter light to change. Eventually, it turns green and through the Pork gates we drive.

The old man's there, 'I'm going to do wonderful things for our country! Yes, I'm going to make *all* my children proud of me! And that includes you, Ross!'

I put my two hands together as if in prayer and I go, 'Oh, Thathy, I'm alrethy proud!' doing an impression of Christian's eldest, Ross Junior. 'I'm tho proud, I feel like my horth ith abouth thoo burtht!'

We arrive at the gates of the Áras. Some dude in an ormy uniform approaches the cor on the driver's side. Kennet opens the window. 'I've the T . . . Teashocked in the back,' he goes.

The dude's like, 'You know you're an hour late?' which is pretty ballsy of him, it *has* to be said.

The old man ends up just roaring at the dude. He goes, 'I am the democratically elected *leader* of this country! I will arrive when I choose to arrive! Open these bloody well gates this instant – you insolent clock-puncher!'

The dude does as he's told, then up the driveway we go.

'The first item on your agenda,' the old man goes, '*as* my Attorney General, Hennessy, will be to find out who that chap is and sack him from his job!'

The actual gaff eventually comes into view. It's some pile of bricks, in fairness to it.

The old dear crosses her legs and runs a hand up and down her stockinged thigh like she thinks it's *sexy* or something? It does very little for me.

Fock-all, in fact.

She goes 'Why does *he* get to live here anyway, Chorles?'

'Who?' the old man goes. 'Michael D.? Well, Dorling, the Áras is traditionally the home of the President!'

'But who says it *has* to be?'

'Well, I don't know! It's in the Constitution, isn't it, Hennessy?'

'I'll have to check,' Hennessy goes. 'I haven't read it since I was in college.'

The old dear's there, 'I'm just wondering does he really *need* all of these rooms? We've got six babies on the way. And six surrogates who are going to be looking after them for the first year of their lives.'

'Excellent point!' the old man goes. 'I'll have my new A. G. read this famous Constitution, then I'll call the chap in a week or two and tell him to sling his bloody well hook!'

'*We* should have the nicest house, Chorles. I mean, *you're* the leader of the country. And the President doesn't really *do* anything, does he?'

'Not as far as *I* can see! Yes, I think, on balance, he and Sabina *would* be a lot happier in a little flat somewhere!'

'They can fock off back to Galway for all I care.'

We pull up in front of the gaff. There's, like, hundreds of people standing around outside – most of them journalists and photographers. Kennet gets out of the cor and opens the back door. The old man gets out first, followed by the old dear, then Hennessy, then the Rossmeister General.

The air is suddenly filled with the sound of cameras clicking and questions being shouted. It's all, 'Charles, what message do you think this election result will send out to the rest of Europe?' and 'Charles, do you stand by your statement during the campaign that global warming wouldn't be such a bad thing if rising sea levels result in Cork being wiped from the map?'

Hennessy goes, 'You'll have plenty of time to hear the Taoiseach speak after the Warrant of Appointment is signed.'

We stort walking towards the gaff. Except the old man looks suddenly, I don't know, *concerned* about something?

'Where the H, E, double hockey sticks, is he?' he goes. 'I'm talking about the aforementioned Michael bloody well D.! Shouldn't he be standing at the front door waiting to greet us?'

We reach the doorstep – except the door stays *shut*?

The old dear goes, 'What does he expect us to do – knock?'

I'm there, 'It serves you right for dicking him around by arriving deliberately late.'

The old man's there, 'Kennet, knock on the door, will you?'

Which is what Kennet ends *up* doing? About thirty seconds later, the door is opened by some random dude in a suit. He steps out of the gaff followed by two – again – *ormy* dudes? He's got, like, a solemn expression on his face – like he's about to be the bearer of bad news.

And – hilariously? – it turns out that he is.

'You, em, haven't received a call?' he goes.

The old man's like, 'A call? What the hell are you talking about? Where is the President? I want him here this instant!'

I'm there, 'This is genuinely hilarious, by the way!'

Hennessy's phone all of a sudden rings. He answers it, listens for about sixty seconds without saying a word, then just hangs up. He's just, like, staring into space like a man in basically shock.

'Well?' the old man goes. 'Are you going to tell me what in the name of Hades is going on?'

'The result of the election has been suspended,' Hennessy goes, 'due to allegations of widespread electoral fraud.'

I look at the old dear. She's standing there with her mouth open – like a focking salt pig with lipstick on the rim.

The old man's like, 'Widespread electoral fraud?' at the top of his voice.

And the reporters all hear it, because they're suddenly going, 'Did he just say widespread electoral fraud?' and *their* phones stort ringing then?

'Apparently,' Hennessy goes, 'eight individual returning officers have reported serious irregularities with the voting register and have refused to declare results in a total of sixteen different constituencies.'

The old dear goes, 'How dare they? How *dare* they?' like she did when Tanqueray started putting their gin in child-proof bottles and I had to drive to the house at seven o'clock one morning so she could have her first straightener of the day.

Hennessy's there, 'The High Court has agreed to a request from the clerk of the Dáil to suspend the result of the election pending an investigation.'

The old man looks up at one of the top windows. He can see Michael D. and Sabina looking down at him. He storts screaming at them, going, 'Come down here now, Mister so-called President! Do your Constitutional duty and sign my Warrant of Appointment! This! Bloody! Instant!'

The old dear's shouting up at him as well. She's going, 'How *dare* you? How *dare* you do this to us?'

Hennessy goes, 'Chorlie, it's not going to happen today. Let's get back in the cor,' because the press are obviously *loving* it?

I hear the David Davin-Power dude go, 'Will you appeal this decision, Charles?'

But the old man doesn't answer him. He just shakes his fist at Michael D. and shouts, *'Ab abusu ad usum non valet consequentia!'* before Hennessy manages to bundle him into the back of the limo.

The old dear is still standing there on the gravel driveway, swaying like the last man in Grogan's on Holy Thursday night. She's shouting up at Michael D., giving it, 'You two had better stort packing up your things! As soon as this misunderstanding is cleared up, you can fock off and find somewhere else to live!'

Then Hennessy shoves *her* back into the cor as well.

Five minutes later, we've driving back through the Pork gates again.

I'm there, 'I'm so glad I came. I'd be *actually* kicking myself if I'd missed that.'

The old dear goes, 'I don't understand what's happening, Chorles! I bought this outfit especially for the big day. I'm not going to be able to wear it again because everybody's seen it now.'

No one else will forget it either. She looks focking raddled in it.

The old man is red in the face. It's like he's going to have another hort attack. He goes, 'It's an attempt to subvert the will of the Irish people, Dorling!'

I haven't seen a man this angry since the time I spotted Seán O'Brien going into the passport photo booth in the Stephen's Green Shopping Centre and I stuck my penis through the gap in the curtains because I thought the dude would find it hilarious – except it turned out not to be Seán O'Brien at all, just a heavy-set man who worked for Holland & Barrett.

He goes, 'Put more simply, Fionnuala, what you have just witnessed here this morning is a *coup d'état!*'

Ireland's Fascist Family

Sorcha says she loves the smell of brand-new school books. That's an actual quote from the woman. She goes, 'The night before going back to school was – oh my God – *always* my favourite time of year? As in, I wouldn't be able to actually sleep. I'd have, like, butterflies in my tummy, just thinking about all my books! Their spines yet to be broken! All that knowledge inside just waiting to be consumed!'

What a focking sap, I think – although I do manage to resist the temptation to say it? The thing is – right now? – I'm *kind* of the man of the moment around here, having pulled Sorcha out of the wreckage of her old pair's Shomera after a tree fell on it. Yeah, no, we've had sex literally three nights in a row since then. I haven't seen the girl this horny since the time in college when she developed a weird fetish for tradesmen and used to get me to put on heavy-duty work pants and a Dewalt tool belt before doing it on the floor of the utility room while her old pair were out at their couples watercolour workshop in Harold Boys' School.

That was the Celtic Tiger, I suppose – we *all* did a lot of crazy shit.

'Yeah, no,' I go, 'it's whatever you're into, I suppose.'

Honor is supposed to be storting secondary school tomorrow – in other words, *actual* Mount Anville? It's one of those landmork days in the life of a South Dublin girl, which is why Sorcha has spent the entire evening covering her school books with Cole & Son's Woods and Stors wallpaper at one hundred snots per roll.

'Just *look* at these titles!' she goes. '*Religious Beliefs in Our World . . . Bienvenue en France . . . Be the Difference: Civil, Social and Political Education for Girls Whose Parents are Loaded.* .. Oh my God, I'd love to be Honor right now, setting off on her voyage of discovery! What I wouldn't do to relive it all again! The Ernst & Young Profiles in Ethical Leadership Conversation Series! The Sleep-Out to End, I don't know, *Poverty*? The skiing trip to Pinzolo.'

I'm there, 'She's not going, Sorcha.'

'Of course she's going. Don't be ridiculous.'

'Er, you heard what she said at dinner. She doesn't want to *go* to Mount Anville.'

'Oh, that's just nerves, Ross.'

'Nerves? The kid has balls like Owen Farrell.'

'Look, it's just because she didn't have the best of endings to her time in the junior school. I think she's possibly worried that some of the parents still blame her for ruining the Confirmation day.'

Yeah, she told the Bishop that the Bible was all horse shit, then walked out of the church, lobbing fock-bombs over her shoulder. You bet your focking life the parents still blame her for ruining the Confirmation day.

I pick up her brand-new school diary with the Mount Anville motto on the front: *Oderint dum metuant.*

In other words, *Let them hate me, so long as they fear me.*

I'm there, 'Maybe she'd be better off storting school somewhere else – as in, somewhere nobody actually knows her.'

The door is suddenly thrown open and Leo comes chorging into the kitchen with a rugby ball tucked under his orm and his two brothers in hot pursuit. He's shouting, 'Ruuugggbbbyyyy!!!' at the top of his voice. Brian tackles him to the ground, knocking the Brabantia bin over and spilling rubbish across the floor. Sorcha screams. Johnny is first to the loose ball. He picks it up and kicks it back across the kitchen, narrowly missing his mother's head and finding touch on the kitchen counter, where it knocks over and smashes the mug she bought on a visit to the United Nations while on her J1.

'Boys, you *know* the rules!' she goes. 'No rugby in the house!'

That's Sorcha's rule, by the way. It's not mine.

I'm there, 'Did you *see* the contact that Johnny just made with the ball, though?'

Sorcha goes, 'They should be in bed, Ross.'

So I'm there, 'Upstairs and put your pyjamas on, goys. I'll be up in a minute to read you a story.'

I'm reading them *Becoming a Lion* by a certain Mr Johnny Sexton. Might as well stort them off on the classics.

The boys chorge out of the kitchen, going, 'Ruuugggbbbyyy!!!' and Sorcha just smiles at me.

She's there, 'You're *so* good with our children, Ross.'

And I'm there just letting the compliment sit when she suddenly adds, 'You'll talk to Honor, won't you?'

I'm like, 'Me?'

'Please, Ross. You're the only one she listens to.'

'I'm not sure she does, Sorcha. Plus, I'm worried about her off-loading on me. I've got that interview coming up for the Head Coach job in Pres Bray and I can't afford to have my confidence rocked right now.'

She's like, 'Ross, I'm begging you,' and then she smiles at me. 'It's just that everything is going so well at the moment – including between us.'

Yes, that's the unmistakable sound of sexual intercourse being dropped onto the negotiating table.

'Hey,' she goes, 'do you know what I found in the attic the other day? Do you remember that toolbelt we used to mess around with when we were younger?'

I'm like, 'Er, vaguely.'

'Remember we'd pretend that you'd come to replace the float switch on the dishwasher when Mom and Dad were out at their life-drawing class?'

'I thought it was a watercolour workshop?'

'Will you talk to her, Ross? Please?'

And, being too nice for my own good, I end up saying yes.

So up the stairs I trudge, already dreading all the nasty shit that the girl is going to say to me about my weight, my rugby career and my lack of brains.

I knock three times, then I push the door open slowly and I stick my head around it. She's lying on her bed, her nose buried as usual in her phone.

I'm there, 'Okay, Honor, please don't say anything hurtful. I don't want my head filled with doubts – especially when I'm about to return to coaching. Look, your old dear has asked me –'

But then I suddenly stop talking – because I notice that the girl is crying.

She tries to deny it, of course. She doesn't like people seeing weakness in her. She puts her phone face-down on the bed, quickly wipes her tears away with her hand and goes, 'Have you never heard of focking knocking?'

I'm there, 'I did knock. Honor, what's wrong?'

'Nothing's wrong.'

'Is this about Mount Anville?'

'No – because I'm not *going* to Mount Anville.'

I notice her brand-new uniform spilling out of the bin in the corner of the room. I'm just glad her mother isn't here to see that.

I'm like, 'So what are the tears about?'

She picks her phone up off the bed and she shows me the screen. She goes, 'This!'

And I'm like, 'This? What's this?' and I take the phone from her.

'It's a video of a polar bear,' she goes.

I press Play on the thing, then I actually laugh. I'm like, 'Look at him swimming there! He's gas!'

'He's looking for food,' she goes, 'for his cubs.'

'I didn't actually *know* that polar bears could swim?'

'He's been swimming for, like, six hours – non-stop.'

'You'd have to say fair focks.'

'But now he's exhausted. And there's nowhere for him to stop and rest because –'

I'm like, 'What, Honor?' because I can see her eyes suddenly filling up again.

'Dad,' she goes, 'all the focking ice has melted.'

I'm there, 'Er, bummer.'

'Do you not understand what I'm saying? The next place he could rest is, like, miles away. And he's already gone too far to go back.'

'So, like, what happens to him? Don't worry about spoiling it for me.'

'He focking drowns, Dad.'

Jesus Christ, *I* suddenly fill up with tears then. I'm like, 'What? This dude?' because he's, like, a beautiful, beautiful animal. Big paws on him and everything. 'No way!'

'Way!' she goes. 'He's too tired to carry on swimming – and he focking drowns.'

I end up losing it then – as in, *I'm* suddenly bawling my eyes out. Honor goes, 'And it's our fault, Dad.'

I'm like, 'Ours? I hope you're not including me in that?'

'I'm including everyone in that. This is the result of what we've done to the planet – as in, like, global *warming?*'

'Global warming? I didn't think you were interested in that kind of thing.'

'I'm not. I don't give a shit about it. But I'm allowed to be sad about a polar bear that drowned.'

I honestly don't know what to say. She can be so sweet sometimes. She hands me a tissue.

'Here,' she goes. 'I'm sorry, I didn't mean to make *you* sad as well.'

I wipe my eyes.

I'm there, 'Hey, it's cool, Honor. I only came upstairs to ask you if you'd hopefully changed your mind about going to Mount Anville.'

She goes, 'I'm not going to Mount Anville. End of conversation.'

'Are you doing this to get back at Sorcha for wrongly accusing you of trying to poison your brother –'

'He's my *half*-brother?'

'– and then packing you off to Australia for the summer?'

'I don't give a fock about that. I had a great summer.'

'I know you did. Hanging out with your auntie Erika and little Amelie. So why don't you want to go to Mount Anville? It's one of the most expensive schools in Ireland.'

'Because it's *her* dream for me to go there – not *mine?*'

'But you have to go somewhere, Honor.'

'I want to go to Loreto Dalkey?'

'Jesus.'

'What?'

'Nothing. I just don't know how Sorcha is going to take that.'

'Fock her.'

'Look, Honor, you know I'm *always* on your side – irregordless. I'm just asking would you not maybe give Mount Anville a chance – even for, like, two or three weeks? I mean, you and me are mates, aren't we?'

'Yeah. So?'

'*So* . . . if you don't want to do it for her, then do it for me.'

She just, like, stares at me, saying nothing.

I'm like, 'Just think about it, will you?'

Then I tell her goodnight and I tip out onto the landing. I'm about to head next-door to read the boys their bedtime story – I'm at the bit where Sexton scores his try for the Lions in the third Test against Australia – when I suddenly hear voices downstairs. Voices I instantly recognize.

Yeah, no, it's Sorcha's old pair.

For fock's sake, I think – they were supposedly moved out. I pretty much chorge down the stairs, then I burst into the kitchen, going, 'What the fock are you doing in my house?'

'Ross, don't be rude,' Sorcha goes. 'I told my mom and dad they were welcome to call in any time.'

'I didn't think you meant that literally. Two focking knobs.'

They've moved into an oportment, by the way, in – hilariously? – Smithfield. Good enough for them, I say.

I'm there, 'So how's the new gaff working out? Shit, I hope.'

Sorcha's old dear goes, 'It's a bit on the small side. But it's big enough for just the two of us.'

Her old man tries to change the subject then. He goes, 'Is Fionn home?' thinking it'll bother me.

But Sorcha's there, 'No, he's teaching tonight.'

Yeah, no, he's back working four nights a week in the Institute.

Sorcha's old dear goes, 'Oh my God, *look* at all these school books! Honor must be *so* excited about storting in Mount Anville tomorrow, is she?'

And I'm there, 'No – because she's not focking going.'

Her old man's there, 'What do you mean, she's not going?'

'Not that it's any of your focking business, but she's thinking in terms of Loreto Dalkey instead.'

Jesus Christ. From the looks I get, you'd swear I'd said she was thinking of going on the game.

'She will not be going to Loreto Dalkey,' Sorcha goes.

I'm there, 'There's nothing wrong with Loreto Dalkey. Helen Curran went to Loreto Dalkey. Helen Curran off the weather.'

'Your daughter needs psychiatric help,' Sorcha's old man goes – he literally *says* that?

I'm there, 'What, just because she doesn't want to go to Mount Anville?'

Sorcha's old dear goes, 'She's being offered the chance to go to one of the most expensive schools in Ireland – and, what, she's going to just throw that away?'

'Anyway,' Sorcha's old man goes, deciding to change the subject, 'I haven't come here to discuss that girl. There are far weightier matters at hand – matters of state!'

God, he's a knob.

He goes, 'You heard the result of the election has been suspended, I presume?'

Sorcha's there, 'Yeah, no, Ross was in the Pork this morning – when Chorles and Fionnuala were turned away from the Áras.'

'Well, did you hear about the latest development? The Dáil and Seanad have been undissolved! All outgoing TDs and Senators have been recalled!'

'Er, only while the investigation into possible overseas *election* meddling is going on?'

'Well, that could take anything up to a year. They're talking about appointing a Senior Counsel to investigate.'

'Dad, stop it.'

'Stop what? You're still a sitting member of the Oireachtas, Dorling!'

'I'm not interested in politics any more.'

'A year, Sorcha! You could make *twenty* speeches in that time!'

'About what?'

'Our democracy is under threat – from dork forces.'

17

'And the last thing the world needs right now is more speeches.'

He goes, 'This is your opportunity to finally make a name for yourself. What's the matter with you? Every time you're offered a chance to make something of your life –' and then he makes a big point of looking at me, then going, '– you throw it away.'

I'd love to deck him. The only reason I never have is out of loyalty to my wife – although it'd nearly be worth chinning the focker and asking for forgiveness down the road.

Sorcha goes, 'Dad, I've told you before, the most radical political thing that people of my generation can do for the world now is to teach the next generation to know better.'

It's at that exact moment that the kitchen door opens and Honor is suddenly standing there in the doorway, wearing her full Mount Anville uniform, albeit crumpled from being stuffed into the bin.

When Sorcha sees her, it's *her* turn to burst into tears? She puts her hand up to her mouth and goes, 'Oh my God, Honor, I've dreamt of this day from the moment you were born!'

That's an actual understatement. She had her name down for Mount Anville about fifteen minutes after she got the two lines on the pregnancy test.

'Oh my God,' she goes, 'the colours really suit you, Honor!'

And Honor just looks at her mother, weeping tears of pure pride, and goes, 'It's going to need to be focking ironed.'

It's, like, four o'clock in the morning when my phone rings, suddenly waking me up. I check the little screen and it ends up being Ronan, ringing from – I'm *presuming*? – Vegas, where he got himself hitched to Shadden three days ago.

The focking idiot.

I'm like, 'Ro, how the hell are you?' and I don't bother saying congratulations because I genuinely don't see it as something worth celebrating. I'm a lot of things, but I'm not a hypocrite. 'What's the weather like over there?'

He goes, 'Rosser, Ine just arthur heardon the news!'

I'm like, 'What news?'

'About me grandda – it was odden CNN, Rosser. Thee said they're arthur over-toordening the resudult of the edection.'

'Yeah, no, it's true – there's going to be, like, an *investigation*? They're appointing, like, a Senior Counsel. That's according to Sorcha's old man.'

'An investigashidden into what, Rosser?'

'Into possible Russian interference. I was actually there when they told the old man to fock off. It was genuinely one of the funniest things I've ever seen.'

'The doorty Judasing fooks. Pooer Cheerlie.'

I laugh. He genuinely can't see any wrong in my old man and I don't want to be the one to burst his bubble.

But then I just think, fock it, I might as well burst his bubble.

I'm there, 'Ro, you know it's all true, don't you?'

He's like, 'What's throo?'

'My old man and the Russians. He's been in bed with them for years now. That mate of his – as in, Fyodor? He rigged the election.'

'Me boddicks.'

'Dude, Erika found out all about it. The old man basically agreed to give them all of Ireland's natural resources, we're talking oil and gas and – I think I'm right in saying – *trees*? That was the deal if they put him in the Taoiseach's office.'

'That dudn't sowunt like the Cheerlie I know, Rosser.'

I go, 'Yeah, no, a fine judge of character you are. Speaking of which . . .' and then I let it just hang there.

He's like, 'What?'

'Yeah, no, I believe congratulations are in order?'

Okay, it turns out I *am* a hypocrite?

He goes, 'Ah, you heerd, Rosser.'

I'm like, 'Yeah, no, I saw the photos on the family WhatsApp.'

'It's joost you nebber reployut – to say feer fooks.'

'No, you're right, I didn't.'

'Shadden's arthur putting a load mower pitchers up odden her Instagraddem.'

'Yeah, no, I can't wait to see them.'

'If your thalken to Rihatta-Barrogan, make shurden tell her that she looked beaurifuddle as a flower girdle.'

'Yeah, no, I'll, er, make sure to mention it. So you got married in a Hooters, huh?'

'Yeah, the Happy Ebber Arthur Chapoddle.'

'What were you, pissed?'

'Soddy?'

'Yeah, no, pordon me for trying to understand what the fock is going on in my son's head. I mean, you broke up with Shadden – you were happily playing the field.'

'I wadn't happy, Rosser.'

'Give over. You were riding everything with a body temperature in UCD. How could you *not* have been happy?'

'It was alt the riding that helped me readize that Shadden was the wooden I really lubbed, Rosser. She's the mutter of me thaughter and I wanthed to make a seerdious cobbitment to her.'

'Dude, you were married by an Elvis impersonator.'

'Ah, that was oately a birra fudden.'

'Wedding's are fun, Ro. Marriage is work. Trust me. A focking *Elvis* impersonator, Ro!'

He's quiet for a moment then. I think he expected me to be a lot happier for him than I actually *am*?

'On the plus side,' I go, 'hopefully it won't be legally binding.'

And he's like, 'I bethor go, Rosser. Ine taken me wife and thaughter to Caesar's Padace to see Madiah Keerdy.'

'Who?'

'Madiah Keerdy.'

'Okay, say that one more time.'

But he doesn't. Instead, he just hangs up on me.

Honor is quiet in the back of the cor. Sorcha asks her if she's okay and she says she's fine. Well, she actually goes, 'Will you stop focking asking me that? And stop telling me that it's all ahead of me as well.'

'Well, it *is* all ahead of you,' Sorcha goes. 'Diversity Week! The Saint Madeleine Sophie Barat Prayer Circle! Antiquing classes!'

'For fock's sake.'

'The Pop-Up Gaeltacht!'

The old man's voice suddenly comes on the radio. Yeah, no, he's telling *Morning Ireland* that what we witnessed in the grounds of Áras an Uachtaráin yesterday was nothing less than the theft of our country by shadowy forces who want to silence the will of the people.

He sounds totally unhinged.

He's there, 'IT'S AN OUTRAGE!' and he basically roars it. 'AN OUTRAGE! And we all know who's behind it! The same people who are trying to stop Brexit! The same people who are trying to hound Donald Trump from office! The same people who want to keep our country trapped within the Euroreich!'

I go to switch it off, except Sorcha goes, 'No, don't. I want to hear what he has to say.'

'You keep referring to shadowy forces,' it's, like, Rachael English who goes. 'Can we discuss –'

But he's there, 'I make no apologies for describing them thus! The result of a democratic election is to be the subject of a, quote-unquote, investigation – by a member of the Law Library, no less! If you heard about it happening in South America, or even Africa, you probably wouldn't be surprised! But in Western Europe? In Ireland? You'd think, no, they'd never dare try it here! But they're doing it! Right now! In front of your bloody well noses! In front of RTÉ! In front of the rest of the world! They are stealing the election!'

'Granddad!' Leo pipes up in the back of the cor. He's sitting on Honor's knee, suddenly all excited. 'It's focking Granddad!'

'Focking Granddad!' Brian and Johnny stort shouting. 'Focking focking focker!'

Sorcha goes, 'Shush now, boys. Mommy wants to hear this.'

Rachael English is like, 'Can we discuss the issue at the heart of yesterday's – I think it's fair to say – *unprecedented* events? And that is the issue of alleged interference in the democratic process, possibly by overseas agents. Some of the details of these alleged electoral irregularities have been published in this morning's papers. In Carlow–Kilkenny, where the New Republic candidate topped the poll, there are claims that as many as five thousand votes may have been cast by people who were dead.'

'*Allegedly* dead!' the old man tries to go.

'In Cavan–Monaghan, where New Republic took three of the five available seats, there are reports that as many as seven thousand people *with* voting cards may have been turned away from polling centres because their names had mysteriously disappeared from the voting register.'

'Oh my God,' Sorcha goes, 'I really love your dad, but he is, like, *so* corrupt.'

Rachael English is like, 'Charles O'Carroll-Kelly, do you have – or have you ever had – any links with Russia?'

'Yes,' the old man goes, 'I sat on *Moscow Flyer* during a guided tour of Jessica Harrington's yord – a privilege, I'm happy to say, I paid for at a charity auction in Delgany Golf Club! Look, all these questions are designed to deflect from the real issue, which is that New Republic received an overwhelming mandate from the people of Ireland to govern! And now that mandate is being overturned by a sinister plot aimed at keeping us in the European Union against the wishes of the people! That is why I am asking every man and woman in this country –'

She goes, 'Charles O'Carroll-Kelly, are you aware of a plot by Russian interests to influence the result of the 2017 General Election with the intention of further weakening European unity?'

'LET ME FINISH! I'm asking every man and woman in this country who cares about freedom to turn up at my Rally for Democracy outside the Dáil tomorrow morning.'

She's there, 'Charles O'Carroll-Kelly –'

And that's when the old man ends up suddenly losing it with her. He goes, 'YOU WILL ADDRESS ME BY MY CORRECT TITLE! WHICH IS TAOISEACH!'

But Rachael English is like, 'You're not the Taoiseach, though, Charles O'Carroll-Kelly. The thirty-second Dáil was recalled last night and Leo Varadkar will continue to act as Taoiseach until an investigation has been carried out.'

'That's it!' the old man goes. 'If you're not going to address me by my proper title, then this interview is terminated!' and the next thing you hear is the sound of him removing his microphone and storming out of the studio, shouting, 'A classic, old-style putsch! That's what this is!'

'Oh my God!' Sorcha goes, switching off the radio. 'Oh! My! *Literally?* God?'

I'm there, 'He's focking lost it in a big-time way.'

'A rally, though! I wonder will many people turn up?'

I'm there, 'Who knows? Who even cares?'

Suddenly, I'm taking the left turn off the Stillorgan dualler onto Trees Road Lower and we're very nearly there.

Sorcha goes, 'Oh my God, I can't believe how *nervous* I suddenly am? I can't tell you how many times I've thought about this day, Honor, and imagined how it would go!'

Honor's like, 'Don't get your focking hopes up. I promised Dad I'd give it two weeks. If I don't like it, I'm going to Loreto Dalkey.'

'I hope you're not saying that just to upset me.'

'I'll learn to smoke and talk like a focking skanger.'

I'm there, 'Helen Curran doesn't talk like a skanger. Off the weather. I don't *know* if she smokes, though.'

'Oh my God,' Sorcha goes, 'you are obsessed with Helen Curran off the weather.'

'I'd hordly say I'm obsessed with her!'

'Okay, *how* many times have you Friend Requested her on Facebook?'

The answer is nine – but I don't bother responding.

A bit like Helen herself.

Yeah, no, instead, I keep driving and soon the traffic storts to slow down. We're suddenly port of a long convoy of mostly black, mostly four-wheel-drive vehicles covering the last few hundred yords of the Mount Anville Road. It's technically a school run but we actually look like we're invading a country.

'Oh my God,' Sorcha goes, 'just driving up this road is bringing back *so* many memories for me. Honor, do you know is the Calcutta Municipal Dump Virtual Immersion Experience still a thing?'

Honor's like, 'Don't know – don't *give* a fock?'

'Sister Bénezét used to turn up the thermostat really, really high, then she'd take a bag of refuse from the bin store and use an electric fan to blow the fumes into our faces, while telling us all to close our eyes and pretend our parents had no money.'

'Yeah, *great* story, Mom!'

'Ruuugggbbbyyy!!!' Leo roars, just randomly, like I sometimes do. 'Focking rugby!'

I go, 'Good point, well made, Leo,' just to let him know his daddy is proud of him.

I pull into the cor pork and I kill the engine. Sorcha unclips her seatbelt, opens her door and goes, 'Okay, are we ready?'

Honor's like, '*Excuse* me?'

'We're going into the school with you, Honor.'

'Er, no, you're focking not.'

Sorcha laughs. She goes, 'Yes, we are. Oh my God, it's Orientation Day, Honor – it's a special day for, like, First Years *and* their parents?'

'You are not coming into the school with me. Dad, talk to your focking wife.'

But there'd be no point. There's no way in the world that Sorcha is going to miss this. So we *all* end up having to get out of the cor. I take the boys out of the back seat while Honor grabs her school bag and her viola case from the boot and goes, 'Oh my God, you two *better* not focking embarrass me.'

I look around. All the other moms and dads are getting out of their SUVs with their kids as well. And that's when I pick up on a definite atmos. From the looks we're getting, it's pretty obvious that a lot of them are surprised that Honor has even shown her *face* today?

And no one – and I mean *no* one – comes anywhere near us. As we're walking towards the school, I notice Currer Bell Whelehan's mom giving Honor an absolute filthy.

'The fock are you looking at?' Leo ends up shouting at the woman. 'Focking face like a well-slapped orse!' which, I have to admit, is a line he probably got from me.

What makes matters worse is the fact that the school building is locked. Yeah, no, we're all expected to wait around outside until nine o'clock on the actual button, which means we're standing there on our Tobler with all these other parents giving us serious daggers and talking about us out of the corner of their mouths.

Yeah, no, it's obvious that the Confirmation hasn't been forgotten.

Eventually, Mallorie Kennedy – as in Courage Kennedy's mom – decides to be the bigger woman and tips over to us to break the ice. She's there, 'It's lovely to see you, Sorcha. And little Honor. Can you believe it, Sorcha? Our daughters – *actual* Mounties!'

Sorcha's there, 'I've been telling Honor from the time she was born that this is one of *the* landmork moments in a girl's life – along with her wedding day, her sweet sixteenth –'

'And her Confirmation,' Mallorie goes. 'Sorry, that's not me being a bitch. I just thought it was best to make a joke out of it. If you don't laugh, you'd cry – isn't that right?'

Sorcha's there, 'Well, I hope my daughter won't be defined for-ever by that one episode, Mallorie. I think her storting in the senior school is an opportunity for everybody to draw a line under what happened that day.'

I'm thinking, you must be focking kidding me! These women have memories like Warren Gatland.

Finally, after making us wait around for, like, twenty minutes, they decide to open the doors and we all shuffle into the entrance hallway, where the Mount Anville School Choir are waiting for us with their big, bleached-white smiles.

One of the girls, in this really over-the-top, Disneyland Paris voice, goes, 'Hold your breath . . . make a wish . . . count to three . . .' and then they all launch into a version of 'Pure Imagin-ation' from – seriously? – *Willy Wonka and the Chocolate Factory*.

It's like something off the *Late Late Toy Show*.

'Fock's sake,' Honor goes under her breath. 'Focking spare me, would you?' although I think it's actually pretty good. I even make a point of putting my hand over Brian's mouth when he storts shouting, 'Shut your focking holes, you pack of bitches!'

When it's over, we all end up clapping, then Sister Consuelo – the Principal – steps forward and welcomes all of the new First Years to Mount Anville and the stort of what she knows will be a wonderful journey of learning for them.

'A journey of learning!' Sorcha goes. 'Oh my God, that's the exact same phrase I used to my dad last night!'

I spot Roz Matthews – mother of the famous Sincerity – across the other side of the room. I give her a wink, but she turns her head – not impressed – and then I realize I must have accidentally given her the kissy lip as well and it's not cool to do shit like that these days.

When Sister Consuelo is finished talking, the breakfast tapas are produced – we're talking Nutella mini pancake kabobs, we're talking avocado and salmon sushi rolls, we're talking battered pineapple skewers. You can say what you want about Mount Anville, but they know how to cater an event. If they'd been in chorge of the Last Supper, it would have been a Butler's Pantry, seven-item finger buffet and no one – not even Jesus himself – would have looked miserable in the paintings.

The school orchestra then storts playing a medley of tunes, including 'A Moment Like This' by – I think – Kelly Clorksen and 'Unwritten' by – definitely – Natasha Bedingfield, while everyone just, like, mingles.

Sorcha goes, 'Honor, will we go and look at some of the pictures on the walls? There's one somewhere of me with Mary Robinson.'

'No, thanks. I'm going to go and stab Sincerity Matthews in the head with this wooden focking skewer.'

Of course, what Honor doesn't know is that Sister Consuelo is standing right behind her. The woman clears her throat just to let us know she's been busted.

Sorcha ends up nearly passing out. She goes, 'S . . . S . . . S . . . Sister Consuelo – oh my God, hi!' but it's obvious from the woman's expression that she heard every word of what Honor said.

As Rhett Butler's footman said after answering the door, 'Scorlett for you!'

The woman goes, 'Your children aren't shy, are they?'

I'm there, 'We've always encouraged them to express themselves.'

Yeah, no, I forgot to mention, Johnny is trying to see how many bacon and waffle sliders he can stuff into his mouth at once, while Brian and Leo are punching him in the stomach, trying to make him spit them out onto the floor.

Honor goes, 'What the fock business is it of yours, you busy bitch?'

You can see that Sorcha is morto. She tries to change the subject. She goes, 'Sister Consuelo, I haven't seen you since our ten-year reunion. Do you know is the Calcutta Municipal Dump Virtual Immersion Experience still a thing?'

Sister Consuelo just, like, stares her down until Sorcha ends up having to look away.

'Your daughter made quite a name for herself in the junior school,' the woman goes and she obviously doesn't mean it as a compliment.

Sorcha's there, 'She made mistakes, Sister Consuelo, which she's hopefully *learned* from? I hope that won't be held against her in the future. And I'm saying that as a former Head Girl, as well as a founding member of the Peace and Justice Committee and the Events Convenor for the inaugural Diversity Week.'

The nun actually laughs. I'm guessing it's a rare enough occurrence. She goes, 'Held against her? Let me tell you something, your daughter is on the thinnest of thin ice.'

Honor just goes, 'Fock this shit. I'm going to Loreto Dalkey.'

And that's when Sister Consuelo really opens up on her. She goes, 'Loreto Dalkey won't take you! There isn't another school in Ireland that *will* take you, you horrible little girl!'

She is one scary lady when she's angry. The ground seems to actually tremble. Johnny spits a hordened cricket ball of chewed-up bacon and waffle onto the floor and I watch a stream of piss run down the inside of poor Leo's trouser leg.

I'm like, 'Er, can we all just calm down here?'

Honor looks at the wooden skewer in her hand and – I swear to fock – I can tell that she's trying to decide where she's going to stab Sister Consuelo with it. If I know my daughter like I think I do, it'll be through the focking hort. But Sister Consuelo is too quick for her. She grabs Honor's hand and squeezes her little fingers. Honor howls with the pain and eventually lets go of it.

'Oh! My God!' Sorcha goes.

I'm like, 'Whoa!'

Sister Consuelo grabs the skewer and holds the shorp end up to Honor's chin. She goes, 'You listen to me – you will *not* be giving *me* a nervous breakdown like you did poor Sister David last year! I am going to be keeping a tight leash on you! First thing every morning, you will come to my office and you will show me your homework! If you step out of line even once, I will make sure that every day you spend in this school will be a living fucking hell!'

Everywhere, jaws just drop. A nun!

Honor just nods. She's in too much pain to even talk. And all the other moms and dads and their little Mountie girls burst into a round of applause.

'Good,' Sister Consuelo goes. 'Welcome to Mount Anville. I'll see you tomorrow morning – bright and early.'

'Mariah Carey!' I go.

The woman behind the counter in Elvery's is like, 'Excuse me?'

'Yeah, no,' I go, 'that's what my son was trying to say yesterday.'

She looks at me like she's no idea what I'm talking about. Mind you, there's no reason she should.

I'm there, 'He's from Finglas, you see – sometimes it takes me a few days to figure out what he was trying to say. Once or twice, it was weeks before the penny dropped. Sorry, I'm just thinking out loud here.'

She goes, 'That'll be €52.50.'

Yeah, no, I'm buying a Canterbury thermoreg hybrid jacket because I want to look the port for my upcoming interview in Pres Bray. Dress to impress. That's the best piece of advice that the great Jamie Heaslip ever gave me – along with 'Never order ribs on a first date' and 'If you indicate left when approaching a roundabout, you will be correct for at least a portion of the journey around.'

I hand the woman my plastic.

'Mariah Carey,' I go. 'Definitely random.'

Five minutes later, I'm leaving the shop and my phone all of a sudden rings. I whip it out – I'm talking about my phone – and it ends up being my old man. Of course, like an idiot, I end up answering it.

He goes, 'Ross, where are you?' and it's obvious he's been drinking.

I'm like, 'I'm in town – not that it's any of your focking bee's wax.'

'Ah, you came after all!'

'Excuse me?'

'I said to your godfather, "I'd be very surprised if Kicker shows his face today! You know my son, Hennessy. He's such a strong proponent of democracy, he'll be terrified that his anger might bloody well boil over!" The last thing we want today is violence, Ross?'

'What the fock are you even talking about?'

'It's the Rally for Democracy – outside Leinster House! Hennessy and I are just having a couple of straighteners in Buswell's while I arrange my thoughts about what I'm going to say! The bloody well *gall* of these people, thinking they can steal an election and no one will stand up and say, "No, no – not here! Not in this country!"'

Then he hangs up on me.

I decide to swing by just for the laugh. Although I end up having to Google the words Leinster House because I've forgotten where it even is – a strong proponent of democracy, my hole – and it turns out it's on Kildare Street, which is on my way to Fitzwilliam Square, where I happen to be porked anyway. So I stort walking in that general postcode.

Two other pieces of advice Jamie Heaslip gave me are 'A Mortini should be drunk in three mouthfuls' and 'A man who wears a bum bag is only four-tenths of a man.'

I'm always telling him he should stort a podcast.

When I reach Kildare Street, I can't actually *believe* the size of the crowd? There must be, like, ten thousand people there. And there's a really nasty atmos. People are waving their fists in the air and they're shouting abuse at the Gords and they're chanting, 'CO'CK for Taoiseach! CO'CK for Taoiseach! CO'CK for Taoiseach!'

I manage to get only about halfway down the actual street. That's how thronged it is.

All of a sudden, I hear my old man's voice coming over the speaker system. Then again, there might not *be* a speaker system – his regular talking voice is loud enough to be heard over the crowd in the Aviva Stadium.

He's there, 'Ladies and gentlemen, as the lawfully elected leader of this country . . .'

There's, like, roars of approval – it's pretty much *deafening*?

'. . . as the lawfully elected leader of this country,' he goes, 'I am deeply, *deeply* moved by the size of this turnout today! It is encouraging to know that there are people in this country who still believe in the principles of democracy and the rule of law, notwithstanding the efforts by vested interests to subvert the expressed will of the Irish people!'

There are boos from the crowd.

'Because, make no mistake about it,' he goes, 'that is the objective of these people who would so publicly and so flagrantly attempt to cancel the result of the election! Last week, the people of this proud nation went to the polls and faced a choice! They could vote for the same old tired élite who have run this country, mostly badly, since Independence – or they could vote for change! People, in their hundreds of thousands, backed my vision for our country! And now you, the people of Ireland, are to be denied the Taoiseach you voted for because an unelected, faceless élite think they know better than you!'

A chant goes up of 'We want CO'CK! We want CO'CK! We want CO'CK! We want CO'CK!'

He goes, 'Unfortunately, you're not allowed to have CO'CK! Yes, my friends, CO'CK has been removed from the menu!'

There's, like, loud boos.

He's like, 'Let's not mince our words here! If what happened in our country this week happened in Central America or the Middle East, we would call it what it is – an attempted *coup*! You *might* be tempted to think, No, they'd never try to get away with that! But you'd be wrong! They are doing it – and they're doing it right in front of you! THEY'RE STEALING THE ELECTION!'

There's, like, more boos. The next thing I hear is the sound of, like, glass smashing. People are obviously breaking windows.

'And when I say *they*,' the old man goes, 'you know who I'm talking about! The same people who forced us into accepting a so-called bailout deal, with terms every bit as punitive as those forced on Germany in the Treaty of Versailles! A bailout deal that continues to suck all of the money and all of the energy and all of the entrepreneurship out of our economy and will go on doing so for decades, if not centuries, to come!'

The chant goes up again: 'We want CO'CK! We want CO'CK! We want CO'CK! We want CO'CK!'

The old man goes, 'Oh, here they come! Our friends from An Gorda Síochána are making their way to the front!'

There's, like, more boos from the crowd.

He goes, 'I wondered how long it would take! You see, people, you sent the Establishment a message last week! You said it's no longer business as usual for people like them! We've wised up! And this, my friends, is their response! To simply set aside the result and tell you that it's all an, inverted commas, Russian plot! Well, what are we going to do about it? *What are we going to do about it?*'

Suddenly, out of nowhere, I hear the sound of shots – actual *shots?* – being fired. I shit you not. There's all this, like, screaming, then I notice people sort of, like, scurrying away, looking over their shoulders with fear on their faces.

'The Gordaí are firing tear gas!' I hear the old man go. 'They're firing tear gas, ladies and gentlemen!'

And that obviously panics the crowd. I hear more screams and people stort moving faster, pushing each other out of the way, trying to get the fock out of there.

'These are the lengths they will resort to in order to steal the election!' the old man goes. 'To stage a *coup d'état*, of course, it's necessary to have the police and the army on your side!'

I hear two more shots and then more screams, even *louder* this time?

I look back and I notice one woman emerging from the crowd,

holding a scorf up to her mouth, with tears streaming from her eyes.

Then I notice an elderly man being helped away by two men, who are holding an orm each. They manage to get him halfway up Kildare Street, then the man stops, doubled over, and storts spewing his guts up on the road.

My old man is also throwing up. I can hear him through the microphone. Then he stops – mid-puke – and goes, 'They've got the batons out now! Disperse, everyone! For your own safety! Look at them, they're beating their own people!'

And that's when the *real* panic storts. People stort running and I end up having to run with them or else get caught up in the crush. It's like the running of the bulls in, I don't know, wherever-the-fock.

Some dude running beside me is just going, 'The bastards! The focking bastards!'

And as I'm rounding the corner next to the Shelbourne Hotel, the last words I heard my old man say are, 'This is what it means, my friends . . . to live . . . in a fascist state!'

I end up feeling bad about what I said to Ro. So – yeah, no – I decide to give him a ring. It turns out he's just got off the plane from Vegas.

I'm there, 'Look, Dude, I didn't mean to piss on your parade.'

He's like, 'Ine moostard, Rosser – doatunt woody abourrit.'

'It's just, you know, I still say you're too young to be married. You've still got a lot of seeds to sow. You're going to hopefully ride a lot more women in your life.'

'Me hooerding days is wed and throoly oaber, Rosser.'

'I'm also worried about you marrying into that family. The Tuites. Pack of focking scumbags. Focking animals.'

Ronan's there, 'Er, I hab you odden speaker phowun hee-or, Rosser.'

For fock's sake! He tells me now?

I hear Shadden go, 'Howiya, Rosser?'

And I'm like, 'Er, hi, Shadden.'

And Rihanna-Brogan goes, 'Howiya, Rosser?'

'Hey, Rihanna-Brogan. How was Vegas?'

'Ah, it was amazing,' she goes.

'And how was Mariah Carey?'

Ro's there, 'She puts on suddem show, Rosser. You'd wanna see the seats we got – oatenly thoorty rowuz from the fruddent – werdent we, Shadden?'

I'm like, 'Thirty rows? Yeah, no, fair focks.'

'You'll hab to cub oaber to look at the wetton pitchers.'

I try to come up with an excuse, but I don't have enough time.

He's like, 'We're godda hab a few thrinks in the gaff tomoddow neet, Rosser, joost to cedebrate. Ine godda get Buckets and Nudger rowunt – then moy ma and Shadden's ma and da and her brutter and her sistodder.'

I'm like, 'Yeah, no, whatever.'

'I'll see you tomoddow neet, Rosser.'

He hangs up.

I'm sitting at the kitchen table, by the way, scribbling a few notes in the Tactics Book, trying to come up with a few good lines for my interview in Bray next week.

I check the old man's Twitter feed. I just want to make sure the dude is okay after the pretty much riot outside the Dáil yesterday. It turns out he tweeted a selfie of himself and Hennessy with tears streaming down their faces and some Gorda dude in a crash helmet pointing his truncheon at them.

Then he's like:

Charles O'Carroll-Kelly √ @realCOCK – 1d

An SC will investigate #GE2017 result. But who will investigate Gordai who used tear gas and batons to break up a peaceful rally in Dublin today? A fascist police force protecting a fascist Euroreich! #COCKforTaoiseach #irexit #fockEU

Reply 2,231 Retweet 9.1k Like 19.3k DM

All of a sudden, Fionn walks into the kitchen, carrying little baby Hillary. He's there, 'Hey.'

And I'm like, 'Yeah, whatever.'

Things are still majorly awks between us, even though I've agreed to let him carry on living here. There's a little bit of me that will never get over the fact that he rode my wife and made her pregnant. Or that he let Sorcha pack Honor off to Australia for supposedly poisoning his son.

He goes, 'Sorcha said you're prepping for your interview. Pres Bray, huh?'

I'm there, 'Yeah,' and I can actually *hear* the defensiveness in my own voice. 'So focking what?'

'Hey,' he tries to go, 'I was only making conversation.'

And I'm there, 'Well, there's no actual need. Just because I let you carry on living here doesn't mean we're going to be bezzy mates.'

He goes, 'Fine,' and he switches on the radio.

I'm there, 'I'll never forgive you for what you did, okay? We're never going to be friends again.'

He's like, 'I'm, er, just going to get Hillary his breakfast.'

'Hillary's breakfast' being the milk of my wife's breasts straight from the fridge. I doubt if I'll ever get my head around how focked up this entire situation is.

Honor walks into the kitchen then and goes, 'Who left the focking landing light on?'

Fionn's there, 'Er, I think it may have been me, Honor.'

And she goes, 'Can we all maybe switch *off* the focking lights when we leave a room?'

I laugh. I'm there, 'That put you in your box, you four-eyed freak. No better woman – eh, Honor?'

But then she turns around to me and goes, 'And will you stop leaving the focking bathroom taps dripping? Do you even give a shit about the kind of planet that you're going to leave to me and *my* children?'

And before I get the chance to ask the obvious question – what the fock does a dripping tap have to do with the state of the planet? – the news comes on the radio. And the first item just, like, shocks me to my core.

The dude goes, 'Gardaí have denied that any of its members

were involved in attacking protesters at a so-called pro-democracy rally in Dublin yesterday. A spokesman claimed that subversives dressed in Garda uniforms were responsible for setting off tear gas and using batons to disperse the rally. He described the development as "deeply sinister".'

Ronan hands me a can of – I shit you not – Galahad Export and I stare at it like I've no idea what I'm supposed to even do with it.

I mean, I'm hordly going to *drink* it?

'Look at the b . . . b . . . b . . . b . . . b . . . bleaten face on him,' Kennet goes. 'He's toordening he's nowuz up at the thrink you're arthur g . . . gibbon him, Ro.'

Shadden goes, 'Ine soddy we've none of them beers you usuaddy thrink, Rosser. Are you wanton a slippody nipoddle?'

A slippody focking nipoddle. Jesus of focking Nazareth, I can't believe I'm now related to these people.

'*I'll* hab a slippody nipoddle,' Dordeen – Shadden's so-called mother – goes.

Tina – Ronan's old dear – is there, 'I'll hab one as weddle, Shadden.'

Shadden's sister, Kadden, goes, 'Yeah, gimme wooden of them.'

Shadden puts the bottles of Baileys and Sambuca on the coffee table and tells everyone to just 'help yisser fooken selves'.

A second or two later, there's a rattle on the letterbox. Ro goes out to answer the door and in walk Nudger and Buckets of Blood, along with Blodwyn, Nudger's girlfriend – a former conquest of mine – who I notice is up the spout again.

I'm like, 'Nudger, Buckets, how the hell are you?'

And they're like, 'Alreet, Rosser,' because they're major fans of mine.

'And Blodwyn,' I go. 'Congratulations. What's this, your third?'

She's like, 'That's rait!' because she's Welsh. 'Fooken laahst as well, if I've any say in it!'

And we all laugh. I don't know why. Possibly fear.

'Hee-or,' Kennet goes, 'd . . . d . . . d . . . d . . . ditn't you and Rosser there have a thing w . . . w . . . w . . . w . . . w . . . woodence befower?'

Blodwyn picks up one of the Aldi miniature spring rolls that are laid out in bowls on the table. 'Yeah,' she goes, 'this is what his prick was laik!'

Kennet finds this absolutely hilarious. He goes, 'D . . . d . . . d . . . d . . . d . . . did you hear that, Dadden? The geerdle said Rosser theer has a m . . . m . . . m . . . m . . . mickey on him like wooden of them spring r . . . r . . . r . . . r . . . rowults, look.'

He's absolutely hammered. I can see that even Shadden, Kadden and Dadden are embarrassed by him – and the Tuites would have a pretty high embarrassment threshold in *normal* circumstances?

I'm like, 'Are we looking at these wedding photos or not?' because I just want to get the fock out of here.

Ronan hooks the laptop up to the TV, then calls Rihanna-Brogan downstairs. She walks in, gives me a big hug – loves her granddad – and sits down on my knee. Then ten seconds later we're watching a slideshow of their trip to Vegas, while Shadden, Ronan and Rihanna-Brogan give us a running commentary.

'That's where we stayut the foorst tree nights,' Shadden goes. 'The Bedaggio. Wait'll you see the fowun tiddens, Ma.'

She's trying to say 'fountains'.

Rihanna-Brogan goes, 'The wather daddences to the music, so it does, Rosser.'

'M . . . M . . . M . . . Moy Jaysus,' Kennet goes, 'that's b . . . b . . . b . . . bleaten mad, so it is.'

Shadden's like, 'And theer's the food cowurt. You could hab litoddy addyting you wanthed and as mooch as you wanthed ob it – chips, pizza . . . What else, Rihatta-Barrogan?'

Rihanna-Brogan goes, 'Chips.'

Jesus Christ, the next three hours end up being the longest three hours of my life. It's like watching *The Lord of the Rings* all over again, except the ring in this case came from Argos rather than the Dork Lord of focking Mordor.

'Ah, this is the neet arthur the wetton,' Shadden goes. There's a photo of her and Ro in what looks like a tattoo porlour of some description. 'We got each utter's nayums tattooed on eer botties as a soyun of eer lub for each utter.'

The next shot is of Shadden's shoulder with the word 'Ronan' on it in Celtic writing, then there's one of Ro's left tit with the word 'Shadden' tattooed on it just above the nipple.

I look at Tina and she doesn't look pleased – even *with* three pints of Baileys and Sambuca swilling around inside her.

'I lub the way that's writ,' Dadden goes. 'Ine godda get "Bohiz" in the sayum writing – except on me back.'

'Hee-or, Shadden,' Kennet goes, 'if you th . . . th . . . th . . . th . . . think that Ronan habbon your nayum tattooed on he's tit is godda s . . . s . . . s . . . s . . . s . . . stop him hooerding arowunt, you're v . . . v . . . v . . . v . . . veddy mooch mistakidden.'

Ronan's there, 'That peert of me life is oaber, Kennet. Ine arthur making a cobbitment to the geerdle.'

'Feer fooks to you,' Buckets of Blood goes. 'That reet, Nudger?'

And Nudger's there, 'Yeah, feer bleaten fooks.'

'No more r . . . r . . . r . . . r . . . r . . . r . . . r . . . riding young woodens,' Kennet goes. 'Especiady when you go back to that UC bleaten D.'

Ronan's there, 'That's alt behoyunt me, Kennet.'

'It'd bleaten bethor be. Utterwise, me and Dadden theer will break yisser fooken legs. Am I reet, Dadden?'

Dadden goes, 'You're bleaten reet, Da.'

'Dadden bought a g . . . g . . . g . . . g . . . gudden in Lanzer Dotty. We'll thrun you in the b . . . b . . . b . . . boot of Cheerlie's keer and we'll b . . . b . . . b . . . b . . . b . . . beddy you up the Dubbalin Mountiddens.'

Darren bought a gun in Lanzarote. Jesus Christ. I'm just like, 'Toto, I have a feeling we're not in Kansas any more!' except no one laughs.

Dordeen has some advice for her newly married daughter then. 'You get yisser self pregnant as soowun as you fooken can,' she goes. 'Anutter little babby to feeyut – that's the oately thing that'll tie him dowun.'

'That's reet,' Kennet goes. 'W . . . w . . . w . . . w . . . woorked wit me – that reet, Dordeen?' and he blows her a kiss across the room.

I can't focking believe my son has agreed to spend the rest of his life around these people.

Ronan goes, 'Hee-or, Rosser, you nebber toawult me about the bleaten riot the utter day.'

I'm like, 'You didn't hear the news? The Feds are saying it was fock-all to do with them. I presume they were all *your* mates dressed up as Gords, were they, Kennet?'

'F . . . F . . . F . . . Fook alt to do with m . . . m . . . m . . . me,' he tries to go.

'That's all fake newuz,' Ronan goes. 'It was the bleaten Geerds what did it – thee toordened on their owunt.'

Yeah, no, that's the old man's line. Last night, he tweeted:

Charles O'Carroll-Kelly √ @realCOCK – 1d

Gardai attack pro-democracy protesters – then claim it was the work of 'sinister forces'! Wake up, people! THEY are the sinister forces! #COCKforTaoiseach #irexit #fockEU #TheyStoleTheVote

Reply 1,566 Retweet 7.2k Like 16.1k DM

Ronan goes, 'What they're arthur doing to him is wrong, Rosser. People voted for chayunge – not mower of the sayum.'

I'm there, 'Ro, the election was rigged. Kennet there will tell you. He's been driving him around for these past two years. He knows all about Fyodor and all the rest of it.'

But Ronan just shakes his head. He goes, 'Ine godda spend some toyum in the libroddy, reading up odden the law. Ine godda foyunt out if what they're doing is eeben legal.'

'You're only encouraging him, Ro. He's carrying on like a dope. And him about to bring six *kids* into the world?'

'Six?' pretty much everyone in the room goes, and I know they're trying to figure out how much that adds up to in children's allowance money.

'How much childer dodden's allowance would you get for six babbies?' Dordeen goes.

Told you.

Kennet's there, 'B . . . B . . . B . . . B . . . B . . . Be a lot of muddy – that's all's I know.'

Dordeen's like, 'Fair fooks to her, so!'

I'm like, 'Yeah, there are more reasons for bringing children into the world than just money, you know?'

And they all just stare back at me like they're waiting for a list of examples.

Ronan looks around him. 'Hee-or,' he goes, 'speaking of kids – where's the boyuz?' because – yeah, no – I brought Brian, Johnny and Leo with me.

I'm like, 'They're out in the back gorden, throwing the ball around. I didn't want them in here, breathing in second-hand cigorette smoke. Plus, they're very focking annoying.'

At that exact moment, the door opens and Brian, Johnny and Leo come chorging into the room, going, 'Rugby! Rugby! Rugby!'

Brian and Leo jump straight into my lap. But then I watch in horror as Johnny sort of, like, wobbles across the living room, then falls sideways onto the floor.

I'm like, 'What the fock?' and I run over to him and pick him up. I look at his eyes and they're, like, glassy.

I'm there, 'Oh my God – he's focking drunk!'

'Th . . . th . . . th . . . th . . . thrunk?' Kennet goes.

I'm there, 'Look at him. He can hordly focking stand.'

Shadden goes, 'Will I do him a froy-up?' like it's the most natural thing in the world for a child to be off his tits like this.

I'm like, 'No, I don't want you to do him a fry-up, Shadden. I want you to tell me how my five-year-old son has ended up shit-faced in your focking house.'

Kennet just shrugs. He goes, 'He m . . . m . . . m . . . m . . . m . . . musta had a slug ourra the b . . . b . . . b . . . b . . . bottoddle of vodka I left on the table out theer.'

'What?' I go. 'So *you* think it's okay to just leave booze lying around within reach of children?'

39

'Doatunt be gettin' bleaten obstreperdous wit moy Kennet,' Dordeen goes. 'You shoulda been supervisin' yisser childor, not leabon them rudding arowunt where there's thrink evoddy wheer.'

I'm gently slapping Johnny's face, going, 'Come on, Johnny, sober up, Dude,' but the kid is as shit-faced as Junior Cert results night.

Kennet goes, 'It's no bleaten heerm lettin' kids hab a thrink or two in addyhow. In Itoddy, thee let kids hab red woyun with their didders and thee grow up to respect addlecohol. Or maybe it's the French that does it.'

It's no good. Johnny is totally out of it – he's like a rag doll in my orms.

Ronan goes, 'Ine soddy, Rosser.'

But I go, 'It doesn't matter,' and I carry the kid to the door. 'Come on, goys, we're out of here.'

I ring the old dear and I'm like, 'Where the fock are you?'

She goes, 'The girls and I are enjoying a day of pampering.'

I'm there, 'How many have you had?'

'Not *that* kind of pampering. I'm in Brown Sugar.'

Yeah, no, I forgot. Tuesday afternoon is when she gets her aggressive facial hair removal done. She hates missing an appointment. I've seen her when she's skipped a week – she looks like Brendan focking Gleeson.

I'm there, 'Have you had your shave yet?'

'I'm not having a shave,' she tries to go. 'If you must know, I'm having my hair done. And don't be ghastly to me, Ross. Will you *please* think about my condition?'

'What condition? Alcoholism?'

'In case you've forgotten, I'm about to become a mother.'

'You're not even pregnant. You've got six surrogates carrying the focking things for you.'

'Those *focking things*, as you call them, are going to be your brothers and/or sisters.'

'No, they're not.'

'Yes, they are, Ross – whether you like it or not. Now, as I said,

I'm trying to enjoy a day of relaxation to mork my entry into my second trimester.'

And she ends up hanging up on me.

As it happens, I'm actually on Grafton Street. I'm supposedly meeting Oisinn for a couple of cheeky afternoon pints in The Bailey, except I'm actually early. So I decide to swing around to – yeah, no – Brown Sugar to rip the piss.

So, like, five minutes later I'm walking through the door of the place – and, at the top of my voice, I go, 'Make sure you leave enough hair to cover the 666 on the back of her head!'

And that's when I cop something definitely unusual. When she said she was enjoying a day of pampering with the girls, I just presumed she meant Delma and all her golf club mates. But she meant the actual surrogates.

Yeah, no, they're all sitting in a line in front of the long mirror – we're talking Szidonia, we're talking Roxana, we're talking Loredana, we're talking Brigitta, we're talking Lidias I *and* II – and they're all having their hair blow-dried.

This scene actually *throws* me for a second or two? Because I just thought – yeah, no – they all *hated* my old dear's guts? Except, no, they're all, like, laughing and eating chocolates like it's some big – like she said – girlie day out.

The old dear is telling one of her boring anecdotes at full volume. She's going, 'So I said to this policeman person, "Oh, you want to breathalyse me, do you? Why don't you focking breathalyse *this*!"' and she sticks up her middle finger.

Now, I've heard this story about a hundred times before – her speech at the Irish Cancer Society's Daffodil Day Ball, her eulogy at the funeral of a former honorary secretary of the Foxrock Tidy Towns Committee, and in Dún Laoghaire District Court when she lost her driving licence for failing to comply with a test to determine her blood alcohol level – but this time it's the *response* that's different?

Everyone in the room actually laughs.

And Roxana is like, 'Oh, Fionnuala, you are so funny!' in her – whatever it is – *Moldovanian* accent.

I'm there, 'What do you mean by hanging up on me? Do you know how rude that is, you horrible focking hogbeast?'

She doesn't answer me. She doesn't get a chance to, because Lidia I suddenly turns on me.

She goes, 'Do not speak to your mother in this way! You must show her respect!' and the others all nod their heads in agreement.

I totally ignore her and I go, 'She's big enough and ugly enough to stand up for herself.'

I swear to fock, Szidonia suddenly stands up from her chair, points at me and goes, 'If you speak to Fionnuala like this again, I will slap your face – do you understand what I say?'

The old dear goes, 'It's quite alright, Szidonia. That's how Ross expresses his affection for me.'

Szidonia sits down, except she keeps glowering at me in the mirror.

I'm thinking, what the fock? As in, when did things suddenly change? I could have sworn that they definitely, definitely hated her. And she treated them like actual slaves. It can't be that I'm mis-remembering all that shit about her making them sign contracts and putting them on, like, diet and exercise plans.

So I end up coming straight out with it. I'm there, 'What's going on? As in, I thought *they* focking hated you?'

Roxana goes, 'Hate Fionnuala?' all – yeah, no – wounded innocence. 'This is not true, Ross.'

I'm there, 'You were all miserable. She treated you like – I don't know – slaves.'

The girls all laugh.

'Slaves?' the old dear goes. 'Ross, we all get along famously. And why wouldn't we? They're wonderful girls who are helping me and your father to have the family we've always wanted.'

'And we are being paid very well for it,' Lidia II goes.

'Slaves, indeed!' the old dear goes.

They all laugh again.

I'm there, 'But I heard you giving out yords to them for not, like, sticking to their diet and exercise plans.'

Szidonia goes, 'Yes, your mother was angry with us because she finds out I am secretly smoking and Loredana secretly is drinking and Roxana is not doing her exercises. But this is because she wants the best for us and for her babies.'

I'm like, 'What? Seriously?'

'At the beginning,' Roxana goes, 'we did not behave very well. But now things are good.'

Obviously so, because Lidia II puts her orm – I swear to fock – around the old dear's shoulder and goes, 'Fionnuala, you are so good to us!' and then she plants a kiss on her cheek.

And Loredana smiles at her and goes, 'We are so lucky that it was us you choose.'

But then I just happen to look at Szidonia in the mirror and I notice that she's, like, staring at me really intensely and, at the same time, gesturing with her eyes, trying to draw my attention to something on the ground beside her. So I look down and I notice that – oh, holy fock! – she's written something on the floor in hair clippings. It's two words.

And it's just like, HELP US.

2.

Bray Dream Believer

The secretary goes, 'Did you have any trouble getting here today?' and I end up nearly laughing in the woman's face.

I'm sorely tempted to tell her the truth. I drove thirteen times around the Loughlinstown roundabout, trying to persuade myself to take the turn onto the N11, then spent another twenty minutes in the hord shoulder just after the turn-off for Old Conna Golf Club, asking myself what the fock I was doing.

The woman's like, 'You're not *from* Bray, are you?'

And I go, 'Jesus Christ, no,' possibly sounding a little bit *too* disgusted? 'I live in, like, Killiney? Have you heard of the Vico Road?'

She pretends she hasn't heard of the Vico Road.

She goes, 'Bray is actually really lovely at this time of year. Did you see the heather on Bray Head on the way in?'

That's one of the things I hate about Bray – the way the locals are always trying to sell you on the merits of the place. I actually went on a few dates with Laura Whitmore back in the day and she was forever at it – cutting me off mid-rugby anecdote to point out that Bray was named the nineteenth cleanest town in Ireland in a 2011 Irish Business Against Litter survey and that the aquarium on the seafront has the largest collection of clownfish anywhere in Europe, excluding a place in France, another in possibly Greece and – she thought – one in maybe one of the Scandinavian countries. It did my focking head in. It was what broke us up in the end – well, that and her finding out that I was married with kids.

I'm like, 'Er, no, I didn't notice the heather. I might check it out when I'm leaving – that's if I think of it. Anyway, I'm here to see a, er, Mister O'Brien?'

She goes, 'Do you mean Brother Ciaran?'

I'm there, 'I don't know. I've got Mister O'Brien written down here.'

She's like, 'Can you tell me what it's in relation to?'

And I go, 'It's in relation to rugby,' and I love the way the words sound when I say them.

'Rugby!' Leo goes. 'Focking rugby!'

Yeah, no, I forgot to mention, I've brought the boys along *with* me?

'Then it's definitely Brother Ciaran,' she goes.

Suddenly, the door behind her opens and standing there is an old dude in his – I'm *guessing*? – mid-seventies, with grey, side-ported hair and big, red, jolly face.

He goes, 'You must be Ross O'Carroll-Kelly.'

And I'm like, 'Oh, I'm Ross O'Carroll-Kelly alright!' just trying to keep it light. 'And these are my boys. Leo, Brian – and that little one, with the ball in his hands, is Johnny, the future Leinster and Ireland number ten – isn't that right, Johnny?'

'Rugby!' Johnny goes.

I'm like, 'They take after me. The day the Six Nations started this year, my wife said to me, "You were saying *Rugby!* in your sleep last night, over and over again. And I was like, "I wasn't asleep."'

He has a good chuckle at that. I can be very funny.

He walks with the aid of a stick, I notice. He shakes my hand and he goes, 'Ciaran,' and then he goes, 'I've heard a lot about you,' but I don't ask him what he means in case he's talking about some of the shit I've said about Bray on social media, especially some of the memes I've put up involving pictures of war and famine.

He's there, 'Let's go for a walk, will we?' and me and the goys follow him outside.

We walk through the cor pork towards the main rugby pitch.

'So what do you know about Bray?' the dude goes.

I'm there, 'I know the aquarium on the seafront has one of the lorgest collections of clownfish anywhere in Europe.'

It's a new one on him.

He's there, 'Is that so?'

'Yeah, no,' I go, 'I dated Laura Whitmore back in the day. That'd

47

be my main link with Wicklow. And then, another time, when I drove down to Aughrim after Shane Byrne offered to wash my cor with his brand-new, sixteen-horse-power water jetter. It nearly blew the thing off the focking road.'

Ciaran has another good chuckle. I can tell that he likes me. I'm tempted to say, what's not to like?

We keep walking – him limping just ahead of us. We walk onto the pitch, as far as the 22, then he stops.

'Bray,' he goes, looking around him, 'is a fabulous place to live.'

I'm like, 'Yeah, no, keep talking – I'm still listening.'

'It's a fantastic town with wonderful people. But do you know what Bray suffers from, Ross?'

'I'm going to take a punt and say lead poisoning?'

'It's lack of confidence.'

'Oh. Right. Okay, forget I said that.'

Johnny boots the ball high in the air – he has *some* right foot – and Brian and Leo go haring after it.

'I see it all the time,' Brother Ciaran goes. 'The people in this part of the world have so much to offer, but they just don't believe in themselves. Every year, I tell the new First Years, "You are every bit as good as the boys in Blackrock College."'

I'm like, 'Jesus, steady on.'

'It's true.'

'I'm just making the point – Alan McGinty wouldn't be happy with you putting that about. You might even get a solicitor's letter.'

'They have as much potential as any boy in any of these famous *fee-paying* schools.'

'Okay, even supposing that's true – and I'm letting a lot go here – where's this conversation heading?'

'When Katie Taylor won her Olympic medal, I saw a change come over this town. Everyone walked taller. Everyone was filled with a sense that here, at last, was something that Bray could lead the world in.'

'Women fighting.'

'Boxing, Ross. It galvanized everyone. For that summer, Bray was a community that believed in itself. And we need something like that to bring us together again. A success story that the town can really get behind.'

'And you think that might be –?'

'Rugby.'

'Then you're talking to the right man.'

Brian has the ball tucked under his orm, I notice. He's got his head down and he's heading for the try line. But then Leo appears out of nowhere and absolutely creams him.

I shout, 'Great tackle! Now, help him up, Leo! That's it! No, don't kick him in the balls, Brian! Shake his hand and compliment him on the tackle! Good boy!'

I'm giving Brother Ciaran a little glimpse of what I do.

He's there, 'You come highly recommended.'

'I'm not fishing for compliments,' I go, 'but I'd be genuinely interested in knowing who's been blowing my trumpet?'

'Richie Murphy, the IRFU skills coach, was a student here at Pres.'

'Yeah, no, Richie tried to persuade me to sign for Old Belvedere back in the day. But I was too much of a pisshead at the time. I'd consider him a friend.'

'He said Joe Schmidt had read your Rugby Skills Book.'

Richie is getting a high-five the next time I see him – whether he wants it or not.

I'm like, 'Yeah, no, it's a Rugby *Tactics* Book? But continue.'

'And he thought you might have something to offer,' he goes, 'as a coach. We're playing St Michael's in the first round of the Leinster Schools Senior Cup.'

I'm there, 'Yeah, no, I literally Googled the draw on the way here today,' because I want him to know what an unbelievable *competitor* I am?

'And I think we could really make Bray feel good about itself,' he goes, 'if we could, you know, keep the score low.'

Suddenly, I can't believe what I'm actually hearing.

I'm like, 'Excuse me?'

He goes, 'They beat us by sixty points two years ago. I was thinking, if we could reduce that to, say, twenty this year, it'd be a wonderful thing for the school and for the town.'

I just, like, glower at him.

I go, 'You're wasting my focking time. Come on, goys, let's go – back to the cor,' then I turn on my heel and I stort walking away from him.

He storts hobbling after me on his stick, going, 'What's wrong? What did I say?'

I turn back to him and I'm like, 'What's wrong? Jesus Christ, no wonder the people of Bray don't have any confidence.'

He's there, 'What are you talking about?'

'I thought you were hiring me because you were interested in winning the Leinster Schools Senior Cup.'

His jaw goes slack. Oh, he wasn't expecting that.

'Winning it?' he goes. 'You mean winning the whole competition?'

I'm like, 'Yes! I mean winning the whole competition!'

He laughs. He goes, 'It's just we haven't won the Leinster Schools Senior Cup since, well, I don't *know* when.'

I'm there, 'I do. It was 1932. I looked it up on Wikipedia – because that's what you get when you hire a coach like me.'

'I don't want to give the boys unrealistic hopes.'

'Then why are you telling them that they're just as good as the kids in Blackrock College?'

'Well, I meant that academically.'

'But not in terms of, like, rugby?'

'I don't know very much about the game.'

'Clearly not – if losing by twenty points is the height of your ambition.'

'Please, stop walking. Just wait a minute. Are you saying you think Pres Bray . . . can *win* the Leinster Schools Senior Cup?'

'I don't know if Richie Murphy mentioned this along with all the other good stuff he obviously told you about me, but I'm a born winner – like my boys there. I don't set out to *lose* by any score. I set out to win. So you can either hire me on that basis or we can get back on that N11 and we'll write this off as a daytrip to the focking seaside.'

He doesn't know what to say. He's obviously never met anyone like me before in his life. He just stares at me like he thinks I'm insane.

I'm there, '*Your* decision, Brother Ciaran.'

He goes, 'Okay. If that's what you –'

I'm like, 'I want to hear you say it. I want to hear you say the words: we can win the Leinster Schools Senior Cup.'

He's there, 'We can win the Leinster Schools Senior Cup,' but it ends up sounding pretty weak.

I'm like, 'Louder.'

'We can win the Leinster Schools Senior Cup!' he goes.

I'm there, 'Dude, I want you to say it so that the, I don't know, heather on top of Bray Head there can hear it.'

At the top of his voice, he goes, 'WE CAN WIN THE LEINSTER SCHOOLS SENIOR CUP!'

And I'm like, 'Congratulations, Brother Ciaran, you've just hired yourself a Head Coach. Obviously, pending the agreement of a salary and expenses package. I'll email your secretary with my, I suppose, *demands*?'

'Focking rugby!' Leo shouts.

And I go, 'Damn right, Leo! Damn focking right!'

'Oh my God,' Sorcha goes – this is while she's getting dressed – 'you'll *never* guess who I'm meeting today.'

I'm like, 'Yeah, no, who?'

She goes, 'Claire!'

I'm there, 'Claire? As in Claire from Bray of all places?'

'Yeah, she's back from Canada.'

'What, for good?'

'Yeah, no, her visa ran out. And you'll never guess what.'

'What?'

'She's opening that organic bakery she always dreamed about.'

'Which one? Wheat Bray Love?'

'Yeah, except now it's going to be, like, a hipster café instead. I'm actually calling out to see her this morning.'

I'm there, 'Is *he* with her?' meaning Garret.

Focking Garret.

'No,' she goes, 'he's still travelling around Southeast Asia. Although they're back in touch with each other again.'

I'm like, 'Seriously?'

'Yeah, no, she Liked one of the photos he posted on Instagram of, like, a Buddhist temple somewhere in, like, Thailand. Then *he* gave *her* a Like when she posted a picture of the Wheat Bray Love sign going above the door of the shop. Then they've been talking to each other on, like, WhatsApp ever since.'

'What a lovely story. I'm in focking tears here.'

'Ross, don't be mean. Claire says they're talking about possibly getting back together when he comes home.'

She's quiet for a moment then, as if she has something on her mind. It turns out she *does* have something on her mind.

She goes, 'Ross, I spoke to Claire and she swore to me that nothing happened between you two.'

It turns out that Claire is a liar.

I'm there, 'Nothing did happen. It was all in *his* head.'

It turns out that I'm a liar as well – although that much we *already* knew?

She goes, 'So you're saying you definitely *didn't* have sex with her?'

I'm there, 'Come on, Sorcha, I've got higher standards than that.'

I don't have higher standards. I don't have any standards.

'Even though that's why Garret left her?' she goes.

I'm there, 'The dude's paranoid, Sorcha. Paranoid and a prick.'

'Swear to me, Ross. Swear on our children's lives.'

'I'll do better than that. I'll swear on my mother's life.'

'Okay,' she goes, smiling at me, 'I believe you. I just wanted to get that straight in my head before I met her. I don't want to find out later on that something did actually happen.'

I'm there, 'You won't. I can guarantee you of that.'

She finishes getting dressed, then goes into the en suite to do her face.

'Oh my God, speaking of Bray,' she goes to me through the door, 'how did your interview go?'

I'm there, 'Yeah, no, I'm taking my first training session tomorrow.

It'll be interesting to see the standard. I'm slightly worried that I may have promised too much at the interview. But we'll see.'

'I'm sure you'll do amazing,' she goes.

It's a nice thing for me to hear – even though she knows diddly focking squat about the game.

She steps out of the bathroom.

'Okay,' she goes, 'I'm going to go and wake Honor and the boys and then make them their breakfast.'

I'm there, 'Er, cool,' even though I'm wondering why she's telling me.

She goes, 'I have to say, Ross, I am so, so proud of Honor.'

I'm like, 'Proud of her? What's brought this on?'

'It's just the way she's settled into Mount Anville. We haven't had *any* complaints about her.'

'Yeah, no, that's something to be proud of, I suppose.'

'I almost don't want to say it out loud in case I *jinx* it? But she seems to be getting on – oh my God – so well. She's doing her homework every night and she's showing it to Sister Consuelo every morning.'

'Yeah, no, I'm *saying* fair focks.'

She's like, 'So what are you doing today?'

And I'm there, 'I thought I'd have a possible lie-in, then go through the old Tactics Book to come up with one or two pearls of wisdom for the goys tomorrow.'

It's a lie, of course. I'm actually going to drive out to the old pair's gaff to find out what the fock is going on with the surrogates. That message that Szidonia sent me in Brown Sugar has, like, freaked the shit out of me. I need to get her on her own, which is tricky enough because the old dear hordly ever lets them out of her sight.

But Thursday is when she usually has lunch with Delma and the rest of her crew. So I know she'll definitely be out from around 1 p.m.

So I go back to sleep for a couple of hours, then I get up, throw on my clothes and tip downstairs.

I end up running into Fionn in the hallway – he's got Hillary in a focking papoose – and he actually tries to make conversation with me.

53

He goes, 'Did you see that message on the Castlerock College WhatsApp this morning?'

I'm there, 'What message?' walking straight past him towards the front door.

'It's just a reminder that it's Father Fehily's birthday next week.'

'Yeah, I know when Father Fehily's birthday is, Fionn.'

The twenty-eighth of September – every year, without fail.

He goes, 'So there'll be the usual Mass in the school. He would have been a hundred this year.'

A hundred? That's a pretty good innings, I think – even though he obviously died years ago.

I'm there, 'Fascinating,' refusing to even look at him.

And then he has the actual balls to go, 'He would hate to think of us fighting like this, Ross.'

And that's when I finally look at him and I go, 'Don't even, Fionn. Don't. Even.'

Twenty minutes later, I pull up outside the old pair's gaff, except her cor is still in the driveway. Yeah, no, I'm possibly too early. So I sit there and I check my old man's Twitter feed. It turns out the Government has appointed some Senior Counsel – a total randomer called Roderic Grainger – to investigate the result of the election. And the old man is not a happy bunny.

This morning, he tweeted:

Charles O'Carroll-Kelly √ @realCOCK – 2h

Ireland has no honours system. But we DO have appointments to tribunals and investigative committees! Roderic Grainger is a FAILED BARRISTER and an FFG lackey who will deliver the result the establishment wants! WAKE UP, PEOPLE! THEY STOLE THE ELECTION! #COCKforTaoiseach #irexit #fockEU

Reply 1,112 Retweet 8.6k Like 17.8k DM

I hear a cor engine stort. I look up and I watch the old dear drive away.

I let myself in using my key. I stand in the hallway and I shout out, 'Hello? Is anyone home?'

Ten seconds later, one of the Lidias – it's actually Lidia II – appears at the top of the stairs. She goes, 'Oh, it is you!' and then she calls Szidonia, who, a few seconds later, appears on the landing beside her.

I think I'm on the record as saying that she looks like Alexis Ren – except obviously four months pregnant.

I'm there, 'I got your message,' meaning the one she wrote on the floor.

She goes, 'What message?' and of course I'm suddenly doubting myself. Yeah, no, I'm sort of, like, semi-dyslexic? And now I'm thinking, okay, did I just *imagine* seeing those words?

I'm like, 'Er, the message you sent me last week? In, like, Brown Sugar?'

She ends up pretty much flipping. She goes, 'You think I want to have the sex with you?' and she storts coming down the stairs towards me in what would have to be described as an *unfriendly* manner? 'This is what you are thinking?'

I'm like, 'Errr,' genuinely thrown by this unexpected turn in the conversation. 'I just thought you were trying to tell me –'

She goes, 'You think *this* is something I find attractive? A fat rugby man who is balding and sweaty?'

I'm sweating because I had the heated seats on – it was like focking Fiji in the cor.

I'm there, 'You definitely sent me a message – unless I very much misread it?'

She reaches the bottom of the stairs.

'Oh, you very much misread,' she goes, pushing me backwards through the hallway.

I'm there, 'I apologize,' backing away from her. 'I'm semi-dyslexic. Which is possibly down to – like you said – rugby. They still don't know what the long-term effect of all those collisions is going to be.'

'You come here and you stand in your mother's hallway with your penis in your hand . . .'

I'm like, 'Whoa, wait a minute!' and I end up looking down – just to double-check.

She goes, '. . . and then you say to me that I am sending you messages.'

I'm about to say something – 'What the fock?' seems to cover most of the bases – except she puts her finger to her lips, then, using her eyes, she indicates towards the door of the downstairs toilet.

I'm like, 'Excuse me?' totally confused now.

She grabs the handle, then she pushes open the door and sort of, like, bundles me inside so that I'm standing with my back to the sink. She closes the door. She reaches behind me and switches on the taps.

Then she whispers, 'We must be careful – Fionnuala has recorders.'

I'm like, 'Yeah, no, she had the whole place bugged that time she was convinced her, I don't know, Bulgarian cleaner was stealing from her. Drinking in the afternoon makes her paranoid.'

'Shut up,' she goes. 'You must help us.'

I'm there, 'Okay – and when you say help, what are you talking in terms of?'

'You must help us to run away.'

'Run away? What, all of you?'

'All of us.'

'But I just thought when I saw you that day in Brown Sugar, you all seemed to be getting along like – I don't know – cheese and biscuits.'

'It was all acting.'

I just nod. I'm there, 'Yeah, no, I should have seen through it. Her anecdote about giving the finger to the dude who was trying to breathalyse her – no one could find it that funny.'

'We make plan,' she goes. 'We say we will act like all is good. And when she is not expecting, we will run away.'

I'm there, 'Run away – as in, where?'

'Home to Moldova.'

'Jesus – before you've even *had* the babies?'

'Your mother is crazy lady.'

'Hey, you're preaching to the choir there, Szidonia.'

'She should not have six babies. She should not have even one baby.'

'But, like, they're hers. And my old man's. As in, *her* eggs and *his* – I hate saying the word but you've backed me into a corner – *jism*?'

'We carry babies. You think this means nothing? We have no rights?'

'I don't know. I've seen stories like this covered on the likes of *Hollyoaks* and *EastEnders*. Surrogates who, like, bond with the babies they're carrying. I never know whose side I'm on, although I usually end up in tears no matter who gets the baby in the end.'

'I see your face. You do not want your mother to have these babies.'

'Yeah, no, I'm dubious – like you. She's focking seventy years old.'

'She is crazy lady.'

'She's head-in-the-fridge bonkers. I'm not denying it.'

'So you will help us to escape?'

'I don't know. Why do you even *need* my help? Could you not just walk out the door now and head for the airport?'

'She has our passports.'

'What?'

'In the safe. In your father's study.'

'Fock.'

'Do you know code for this safe?'

Oh, I know the code alright. It's 2, 5, 0, 5. Seán FitzPatrick's birthday. But I'm not going to tell her that because I know what she's asking here. She's asking me to betray – even though I *hate* them? – my old pair.

I'm there, 'I don't know the code, no. They keep that very, very secret.'

Szidonia goes, 'She is not fit to be mother.'

And I'm suddenly thinking back to my own childhood. The old dear showing me where she kept the turpentine just in case there was no vodka for her first Mortini of the morning.

I was five years old.

'My little borman!' she used to call me. And I'd be thrilled – just to have her even acknowledge my existence.

I'm there, 'I don't know, Szidonia.'

She goes, 'You must. She cannot be trusted with children. You know this.'

I push Szidonia away and I reach for the handle of the door.

I'm there, 'I'm sorry, Szidonia. I'm not sure I could *do* it to them?'

I leave the bathroom and I walk up the hallway towards the front door. Szidonia shouts after me, purely so the old dear's bugging equipment will pick it up.

She goes, 'I cannot believe you come here for sex! You filthy animal!'

So – yeah, no – I'm sitting in the cor pork of Pres Bray, flicking through my Tactics Book, looking for an inspirational quote or two to offer to the members of the Senior Cup team this morning.

Two *immediately* catch my eye? 'No one can make you feel inferior without your consent,' which is Eleanor Roosevelt – who I've obviously never heard of – and 'There is no elevator to success – you have to take the stairs,' which is Kourtney Kardashian, who I obviously *have*?

I think I'll possibly use them both.

I'm just about to get out of the cor when my phone all of a sudden rings. It ends up being the old dear. And I don't know why I end up answering.

She goes, 'Ross, can I speak to you about something? It's rather delicate.'

I'm there, 'You haven't shat yourself in the Merrion Tree Bistro again, have you?'

'Ross, I want you to stop going to the house and bothering the girls.'

'Excuse me?'

'A little *birdie* told me that you went to the house yesterday and made certain *advances* towards Szidonia.'

'Little birdie, my hole. You've had that house bugged ever since you accused Irina the Cleaner of stealing from you – *wrongly*, as it turned out.'

'Ross, those girls are pregnant with *my* babies. I don't know if that gives you some sort of Oedipal thrill –'

'Er, *how* many Bloody Marys did you have for breakfast?'

'– but there are millions and millions of women you could have sex with who *aren't* carrying your mother's child.'

I'm there, 'Ring me back when you're sober.'

But she just goes, 'Goodbye, Ross,' and she hangs up on me.

I check the time. It's, like, one minute to nine. I get out of the cor and I head for the rugby pitch with my famous Tactics Book tucked under my orm. It's a cold and crisp September morning – one of those mornings when you can see your breath in front of your face.

Suddenly, I spot them – the twenty or possibly twenty-five members of the Pres Bray senior rugby squad. They're, like, gathered in a huddle, waiting for me. And I'm having instant flashbacks to standing in a similar huddle all those years ago, waiting for Father Fehily to arrive and tell us that *this* was going to be the year that Castlerock College made every other school in Leinster, plus Roscrea, eat their words.

I'm literally buzzing as I walk up to them and introduce myself.

I give it, 'Hey, goys. I'm Ross O'Carroll-Kelly. And I'm going to be coaching the Pres Bray Senior Cup team this year.'

No one says shit. They don't cheer. They don't punch the air. They don't stort jumping up and down and screaming like *X Factor* contestants when they find out who their *mentor* is going to be? They don't even go, 'Hey, Ross, it's an honour to have a legend of the game passing on his knowledge to us.'

They all just look at me with blank faces. Although I'm aware that this might just be a Bray thing. I decide to offer them something hopefully inspirational.

I'm there, 'This morning, all of you are emborking on a journey – the same journey I emborked on, which led to me lifting the famous Leinster Schools Senior Cup.'

One of the kids – a tall, red-headed kid who's definitely going to be one of my second rows – goes, 'When was this, like?'

I forgot that about people from Bray. They say 'like' at the end of their sentences instead of in the middle like ordinary people.

I'm there, 'Excuse me?' because – yeah, no – there's definitely a bit of hostility in his voice when he says it.

He goes, 'When did *you* win the Leinster Schools Senior Cup, like?' and he makes a big point of looking at my Ned Kelly.

'It was in 1999,' I go.

Instantly, they all laugh.

'Are you serious, like?' this other tall, red-headed dude goes – I'd be shocked if they're not twins. 'Sure, that's eighteen years ago, Boss Man!'

And that's when it suddenly dawns on me. These goys weren't even born when I lifted the famous tin pot back in the day. They know nothing of the Rossmeister's reputation.

Now, I know I can do one of two things here. I *could* open the back pages of my Rugby Tactics Book and show them some of the things that have been said about me by players they *have* heard of – the likes of Johnny Sexton, Joey Corbery, Jordan Lormour – sometimes in interviews, sometimes to my face, sometimes on social media and sometimes to third porties who then reported the information back to me.

But then I think, no. Telling them that Robbie Henshaw referred to me as 'one of the greats' when I saw him coming out of Massimo Dutti on Grafton Street one day, or that Tadhg Beirne called me – and I quote – 'a legend', then followed it up with a high-five emoji, then a medal emoji on Twitter, might come across as a bit braggy slash desperado.

I'm there, 'Okay, I'm accepting that, to you goys, 1999 might seem like a long time ago.'

'Meaning the last century,' the first of the two red-headed boys goes in that uppy-and-downy way that people from Wicklow talk.

I just go, 'Goys, what I'm interested in finding out today is your basic skills levels. So what I'm going to do is ask you to divide yourselves into forwards and backs, then we're going to run some drills and I'm going to hopefully identify your strengths and weaknesses.'

They stort to separate into two groups. There's, like, one or two waverers, but what I end up with is, like, fifteen or sixteen big dudes on the left, and fifteen or sixteen smaller goys on the right.

'Okay,' I go, 'who's your kicker?'

This dude puts his hand up – a pretty boy, I can't help but notice, not unlike my good self!

I'm like, 'What's your name?'

'Barry,' the dude goes. 'Barry Austin, like.'

I'm there, 'Okay, Barry Austin like! I can already tell that me and you are going to get on like a house on fire! Maybe spot a few balls there and let me see what you can do with the boot. Forwards, we're going to improvise a few scrummaging and lineout situations. Backs, for the moment, I'm just interested in seeing your basic handling abilities.'

I clap my two hands together and I'm like, 'Okay, everyone, let's play some rugby!'

It wouldn't be an exaggeration to say that I am – *literally?* – *fizzing* with excitement? Unfortunately, though, the feeling doesn't last very long. Because one thing becomes obvious very, very quickly.

They're no focking good.

And when I say that, I'm actually being *kind* to them? The forwards couldn't push over my old dear at one o'clock in the afternoon, when she's ready for her first drunken nap of the day. And the two big goys – yeah, no, they're twins alright – can't actually jump. The backs can't string together three passes without dropping the ball or knocking it on. And as for Barry Austin, the dude couldn't kick a pig in a toilet cubicle. He doesn't even know how to strike the ball properly and he's missing kicks from directly in front of the posts.

I walk around, offering advice where I can – 'Come on, front rows, put some intensity into it!' and 'Barry, maybe don't close your eyes as you're making contact with the ball!' – but one thing is already blindingly obvious. I totally oversold myself at the interview stage.

And – oh, fock – that's when I suddenly spot him. We're talking Brother Ciaran. He's hobbling towards me on his stick with a humungous smile on his face.

He holds out his hand to me. 'Ross,' he goes. 'You're very welcome to Presentation College, Bray.'

I'm there, 'Yeah, no, thanks, Brother Ciaran.'

'Ciaran,' he goes. 'Just call me Ciaran.'

'Ciaran, then. Can I just double-check with you – this is definitely the *first* team, is it?'

'Yes, that's right.'

'Okay – and this isn't one of those hidden camera shows, is it?'

Oh my God, that might actually be it! Richie Murphy is a good friend of mine, but he is one sick focker when it comes to practical jokes.

Jesus Christ, I'm suddenly wondering is *Anonymous* still on TV, then I'm thinking, what if Brother Ciaran is actually Richie Murphy in a latex mask? They can do incredible things with make-up.

Look at Kendall Jenner.

'Hidden camera show?' he goes.

And I'm like, 'Forget it. Just my imagination playing tricks on me.'

He goes, 'So how are they doing?'

And I'm there, 'Yeah, no, it's been an, em, interesting morning.'

'Interesting?' he goes. 'I take it that's a good thing?'

Seriously. He *actually* says that.

I'm there, 'Yeah, it's a good thing alright. I just wanted to assess their basic, I suppose, *skill* levels?'

'So do you still believe it?' he goes. 'Do you still believe they can win the Leinster Schools Senior Cup?'

Jesus Christ, these goys couldn't win the Leinster Schools *Junior* Cup. They'd probably have a better rugby team if they went co-ed.

I'm there, 'Dude, I wouldn't say it if I didn't one hundred percent believe it.'

And then I hear one player turn around to another and – again, in that uppy-and-downy voice – go, 'Here, how many points do you get for a try, like?'

Sorcha shakes me awake at – admittedly – eleven o'clock in the morning.

She goes, 'Ross! Ross!'

I'm like, 'Helen Curran.'

'Ross, wake up!'

'What? What? What's going on?'

She goes, 'Ross, we have to go.'

I'm there, 'Go? Go where?'

She picks my clothes up off the floor and just focks them at me. She's like, 'Sister Consuelo just rang. She wants to see us.'

I swing my legs out of the bed and stort getting dressed.

Sorcha goes, 'I'll go and put the boys in the cor.'

Fifteen minutes later, we're on the Stillorgan dualler and I'm finally waking up. Sorcha is doing a hundred and twenty Ks and driving through every orange light on the way.

'You're driving like a mad bitch,' Johnny goes.

And he's not wrong, in fairness to him.

I'm there, 'Do we know what this is even in relation to?'

And Sorcha goes, 'Isn't it obvious, Ross?'

'Er, not to me.'

'You heard Sister Consuelo that day, Ross. She had it in for Honor before she even arrived at the school. So every time something happens, *she* is going to be blamed and *we're* going to be summoned to the school. Well, I'm not going to stand by and watch her being victimized. *I'm* going to be an advocate for our daughter, Ross – even if *you're* not?'

Jesus.

Fifteen minutes later, we pull up into the Mount Anville cor pork. I let the boys out of the cor, then into the school we trot.

Yeah, no, we're sitting there, waiting to be called. Johnny is just, like, mindlessly ripping up all the magazines on the table in the waiting room, while Brian and Leo are standing on chairs and gobbing into the fish tank.

Sorcha doesn't like the way Sister Consuelo's secretary is looking at her – or maybe the way she *imagines* she's looking at her – because she goes, 'Sorry, do you have kids yourself?'

The secretary's like, 'Er, no, I don't.'

And Sorcha goes, 'Well, maybe you can spare us the judgy looks until you *actually* do?'

Sister Consuelo sticks her head out of her office and goes, 'I'll see you now.'

I take a deep breath. Sorcha might not be scared of Sister Consuelo, but I am.

We follow her into her office – first Sorcha, then me, then Brian, Leo and Johnny.

'Please,' Sister Consuelo goes, 'sit down.'

'Look at the focking head on her!' Leo goes, pointing at the woman. 'Bet with the ugly stick!'

He clearly has no fear either.

We all just pretend we didn't hear it.

Sorcha goes, 'Do you mind me asking what is this in relation to? Because it's only the middle of September and you're *already* complaining about our daughter. I know she came to this school with a reputation – and maybe some of that was possibly justified – but this is beginning to feel a bit like bullying.'

But Sister Consuelo says something that knocks her back on her heels. She goes, 'Honor is an absolute joy to have in this school.'

Me and Sorcha both look at each other.

I'm there, 'An absolute joy? Are we talking about the same girl here? I'm Ross O'Carroll-Kelly and this is Sorcha Lalor.'

She goes, 'I've actually come to look forward to our meetings each morning. Honor brings me her homework, I look over it and we have a little chat. She's good-humoured, respectful and polite.'

I'm like, 'Really? Jesus, you couldn't take these three off our hands, could you?'

'Fock you,' Brian goes. 'You focking prick with ears.'

I'm like, 'You're the prick with ears, Brian.'

Sorcha's there, 'Did you say that you and Honor have . . . *chats*?' because one thing our daughter has *never* been is a chatter.

Sister Consuelo goes, 'That's right. She's been educating me.'

I'm there, 'In terms of?'

'In terms of the planet.'

Sorcha's jaw – I swear to fock – just hits the floor. 'The planet? Honor doesn't care about the planet.'

'On the contrary. She's *very* concerned about it. She showed me a video – of a polar bear.'

'Was that the one that drowned?' I go. 'Yeah, no, she showed it to me as well. And then she storted giving out shit about people leaving lights on and taps dripping, although I honestly couldn't see the connection, which is why I sort of, like, mentally checked out.'

Sorcha's there, 'Oh my God, I was trying to get her to watch that polar bear video for, like, six months. I'm *always* talking about the environment, aren't I, Ross?'

'Yeah, no, you never stop.'

'The Lalors were the first family in Ireland to have a dual-flush toilet – and that was down to me constantly explaining to my mom and dad the importance of *water* conservation?'

'She's very upset by what happened to this poor polar bear,' Sister Consuelo goes. 'So she said that she and one or two of the other girls wanted to set up a Climate Justice Committee.'

'Oh! My God!' Sorcha goes. '*I* tried to set up a Mount Anville Environmental Action Committee twenty years ago. But then Sister Bénezét told me I should address my concerns about the well-being of the planet directly to God through the Saint Madeleine Sophie Barat Prayer Circle.'

'Well, I think it's clearer now that the Lord is challenging us to fix this problem ourselves. And Honor is absolutely determined to do that. She marched into the staffroom one morning last week and started lecturing the teachers about their carbon footprint. As a result of her little outburst – and we won't say anything about her language – the teachers have agreed to ban disposable cups from the staffroom.'

'Single-use coffee cups was the subject of my maiden speech in the Seanad – wasn't it, Ross?'

'Well,' Sister Consuelo goes, 'it sounds to me like you've raised quite the little activist. Anyway, I just wanted to check with you – as her parents – whether she has your blessing to set up this Climate Justice Committee?'

'Oh my God, yes!' Sorcha goes. 'A thousand times, yes! A million times!'

Sister Consuelo smiles. She's not nearly as scary all of a sudden.

'Like you said,' she goes, 'Honor came to this school with a reputation and some of the staff – myself included – were perhaps a little too quick to judge her. You should be very proud of yourselves as parents.'

'Fock you,' Leo goes. 'Focking face like a monkey's minge.'

Twenty minutes later, we're back in the cor and we're driving home again, this time at a *normal* speed?

Sorcha's going, 'Did you hear what she said, Ross? She said we're amazing, amazing parents! I knew that constantly reinforcing the message about being conscious of our own individual environmental footprint would pay dividends in the end. We're not going to say anything to her, though.'

I'm there, 'Er, why?'

'You know what she's like, Ross. If we give her our approval, she'll probably lose interest just to spite us. No, let's give her space – she'll talk to us about it when she's ready.'

It's an incredible feeling. I'm talking about going back – as in, driving through those famous black gates with the words *Castlerock College* written above them, and then underneath, *Pecunia non olet*, meaning, 'Money has no smell'.

It would *not* be an exaggeration to say that I've got, like, *literally* goosebumps?

The good feeling doesn't last long, though. As I'm tearing up the long, gravel driveway towards the school, I automatically look to my left to check out the rugby pitch – the famous hallowed turf where me and the goys performed our magic back in the day. Except the posts, for some reason, have disappeared. And then I see something that forces me to slam on the brakes.

The pitch is full of – I shit you not – *vegetables*.

Now, I know that line will generate a laugh or two among my critics in Blackrock – not to mention Michael's, Belvedere and Clongowes – who'll be no doubt thinking, 'It always *was* full of vegetables, Rossmeister!' But I'm talking about *literally* vegetables? There's, like, rows and rows of cabbages and – I don't know – whatever *other* types there are? And next to the pitch, I notice a massive sign that just says *Morket Gorden*.

I can feel my blood storting to boil.

There's no rugby in the school any more, ever since we were stripped of our Leinster Schools Senior Cup title for – yeah, no – doping. But to actually dig up the pitch and use it to grow carrots and focking turnips? It's, like, beyond the beyonds.

I'm in an absolute rage as I swing the cor into the teachers' cor pork. I pull into the space next to the one morked 'Principal' and I know *exactly* what I'm going to do before I do it. I open the door of the A8 and I make sure to give McGahy's cor a good belt with it.

He's driving – I'm not making this up – a Fiat 500 in Tiffany blue.

It's actually the cor, as much as the vegetable gorden, that ends up pushing me over the edge. Not content with banging the side of it once, I actually stort kicking the inside of my door, four or five times in fact, to make sure that I put a big, massive dent in his door, all the time going, 'I'll give you . . . morket . . . focking . . . gorden.'

Then I examine my handiwork. Yeah, no, I've made absolute shit of his cor – good enough for him – and I'm actually chuckling to myself thinking about the job he's going to have trying to match that paint.

I tip up over to the church, feeling suddenly better about things.

The place ends up being rammers – we're talking two or three hundred past pupils crammed into the place – even though Mass hasn't even storted yet. I spot Christian and JP sitting halfway up on the right. They're holding the entire row for the stors of the 1999 Leinster Schools Senior Cup team.

I'm like, 'Hey, goys, how the hell are you?' and it ends up being high-fives and bear hugs all round.

JP goes, 'Happy birthday, Father Fehily, huh?'

And I'm like, 'Yeah, no, hord to believe he would have been a hundred today. So how's the Vampire Bed business going?'

JP's there, 'Yeah, it's absolutely flying.'

He invented a bed that allows you to sleep standing up, so that it takes up exactly half the space of a regular bed. Christian is Head of Morkeshing for Europe, the Middle East and Africa.

'We've also been invited to showcase it,' Christian goes, 'at the Deportment of Housing, Planning and Local Government's Big Homelessness Think-In at the K Club before Christmas.'

I'm like, 'Whoa! That's, like, major!'

JP goes, 'Yeah, we're hoping so. There's, like, ten thousand home-less people out there – and counting. That's a hell of a lot of orders.'

I'm there, 'I'm delighted for you, goys. I genuinely am.'

I decide to change the subject to more important matters. I'm like, 'Did you see our old pitch, by the way? Goys, it's got focking cabbages growing on it.'

'Yeah, no,' Christian goes, 'school allotments are apparently the new thing, especially with the whole, like, climate emergency. Castlerock have apparently won awards for their sugar-snap peas.'

I'm there, 'We used to win awards for our focking rugby.'

'Hey, I'm not defending it,' Christian goes. 'I'm as pissed off as you are about it.'

JP laughs.

He goes, 'Tell him what you did, Dude.'

Christian looks at me with a big, cheeky grin on his face.

I'm like, 'Go on, let's hear it! What did you do?'

He goes, 'I threw my cor into McGahy's porking space!'

Oh, fock.

'Yeah, no,' he goes, 'I saw that it was free and – you'll love this – I just thought, What would Ross do in this situation?'

I'm suddenly remembering that Lauren drives a Fiat 500 in Tif-fany blue. I decide that it's probably best to say fock-all, though.

Oisinn, Magnus and Fionn show their faces just as the actual Mass is kicking off. I give Oisinn and Magnus a high-five each, although I make sure to leave Fionn hanging. He pretends that it doesn't bother him.

We're listening to Father Reddin do his thing – Holy Mary and all the rest of it.

Out of the side of his mouth, Oisinn goes, 'I believe congrats are in order. I hear you're coaching Pres Bray now?'

I'm like, 'Yeah, no, it's all true – every word.'

'What was it you used to call people from Bray?'

'What, mouth-breathing funfair people?'

'That was it.'

'Dude, I've got to stort somewhere. I mean, Joe Schmidt storted off in Kawakawa. That hordly sounds like an end-of-the-rainbow sort of place.'

Magnus goes, 'So Presh Bray ish a good team?' because he knows fock-all about rugby, being from obviously Finland.

I'm there, 'No, they're focking terrible. But now I've got a problem.'

'What's that?' Oisinn goes.

'I may have given the Principal the impression that we could win the Leinster Schools Senior Cup.'

Oisinn laughs. 'You told him Pres Bray could win the Leinster Schools Senior Cup?' he goes. 'Pres Bray, Ross?'

I'm there, 'Yeah, no, I don't know what happened. I sort of got carried away by the sound of my own voice.'

'This is the word of the Lord,' Father Reddin goes.

And we're automatically like, 'Thanks be to God.'

He goes, 'Now, I'm going to invite Tom McGahy, the Principal of Castlerock College, to say a few words of appreciation about Father Denis Fehily, whose one hundredth birthday we celebrate today.'

Fionn goes, 'He doesn't look happy.'

JP's there, 'That might be because Christian stole his porking space!'

Oisinn laughs. He goes, 'That's the kind of thing Ross would normally do!'

And I'm like, 'Yeah, no, I'd definitely do something in that ballpork alright. Definitely in that ballpork.'

Fionn – utter dick though he is – is right about McGahy. He looks like he'd rather be performing root canal surgery on himself than doing this.

'Ladies and gentlemen,' he goes, 'thank you for coming here today, the day of the year when, according to tradition, we remember the late and – to some of you – lamented former Principal of Castlerock College, Father Denis Fehily. Denis was an interesting man in many ways. His teaching methods were unusual – some would say that they had no place in a modern school classroom. I know he meant a great deal to some of you but, as the current Principal of the school, I've made the decision that his one hundredth birthday will be the last time we celebrate his life in this way.'

There's all this – all of a sudden – muttering in the church. I end up jumping to my feet straight away.

I'm there, 'You're a focking disgrace.'

Everyone turns and looks at the Rossmeister.

McGahy tries to go, 'How *dare* you?'

But I'm like, 'No, how dare *you*! You've always had it in for him – and rugby.'

'Rugby brought nothing but shame to this institute of learning.'

'Presumably that's why there's cabbages and focking porsnips growing on the twenty-two-metre line out there?'

There are literally gasps from the rest of the, I don't know, congregation. It's news to them. They obviously didn't drive through the staff entrance like some of us.

I'm there, 'That's right, everyone. He's turned the old rugby pitch into a focking morket gorden.'

There end up being *more* gasps?

'In keeping with our mission statement to set our students a good example in regard to environmentally sustainable living,' he tries to go.

I'm there, 'None of us came here today to listen to you bang on about environmentally sustainable living – you focking knob-end. We came here today because we loved Father Fehily – yeah, we loved him, even for all his faults. He wasn't an *interesting* man. He was a focking great man. He was rugby. He was his quotes about life and his Hitler 45s and the smell of whiskey you caught off him if you happened to walk past his office at, like, eleven o'clock in the morning! He was a leader! Unlike you. You were a shit teacher and now you're a shit headmaster.'

It's a genuine mic drop moment. And that ends up getting recognized by the crowd because they all stort clapping and going, 'Well said, that man!' and 'Porsnips? It's a focking disgrace!'

But I'm not even finished. I'm there, 'You say rugby brought shame on this school? I say that's focking horse manure. I don't want to come across as intellectual, but rugby taught me everything I know about friendship and brotherhood and loyalty and – I'm just going to come out and say it – love. You say this is the last time we'll ever celebrate his birthday. You're wrong – because we'll go on celebrating it.'

'Not in this school,' McGahy makes a big point of going.

I'm there, 'Then we'll do it somewhere else. You won't stop us. And you won't wipe out what Father Fehily means to us. So fock you, McGahy – and a plague on your morket gorden!'

That gets an actual round of applause.

'Fair focks!' people are suddenly shouting at me. 'Fair focks!'

I stand up and step out of the – I want to say – *pew*? It just feels like the kind of line I should leave on. And, in view of what I just said about friendship and brotherhood and loyalty, it'd probably be wise for me to move the Audi before Christian finds out it was me who made shit of his wife's Fiat.

I'm like, 'Dude, what's *your* name again?'

'Steven Nagle,' he goes. 'Except they call me Nailer, like.'

Yeah, no, it's my fourth training session with Pres Bray and – I'm going to be honest here – they're even worse than I originally thought. But the money's good. Or certainly good enough to keep me coming back.

I'm there, 'Let me ask you something, Nailer – who taught you how to throw a rugby ball?'

The only reason I'm asking is because he's *supposed* to be my scrum-half?

'Who *taught* me?' he goes, like it's the most ridiculous question he's ever been asked. 'No one taught me. I taught meself, like.'

Yeah, no, I thought as much.

I'm there, 'The thing is, Nailer, passing a rugby ball is very much a *technical* skill?'

He goes, 'I just fuck it as far as I can, like.'

'Yeah, no, I can definitely see that. But you're never going to get

71

any accuracy throwing it that way. And you're not going to put any speed on it either.'

Useless as they are, I can see more than a few ears prick up. Who am I kidding pretending that I'm doing this for the shekels? I'm doing it because it's what I was born to do – in other words, *teach*?

I'm there, 'One of the most important jobs for a scrumhalf is to get a fast ball to his number ten. Think of Peter Stringer and Ronan O'Gara.'

'Who?' I hear one of our forwards – some fat dude – go.

All the other players have storted to gather around me now, obviously hungry for any scraps of knowledge I might throw them.

'Er, Peter Stringer and Ronan O'Gara?' I go – and I'm met with this sea of just, like, blank faces.

Nailer's there, 'Who are they, like?'

I actually laugh. I can't wait to text the two goys later on and tell them that no one in Bray knows who the fock they are.

I'm there, 'It doesn't matter. Look, I'm going to show you how to pass the ball. Can someone hold my Rugby Tactics Book?'

One of the tall, red-headed twins – they're called Dougie and Lenny, by the way – takes the book from me. He's there, 'I'll look after it for you, Boss Man!'

Then I ask for a ball and someone tosses one to me. God, I love how it feels in my hands.

I'm there, 'Okay, passing is – like I said – a skill that has to be worked on, over and over and over again. Father Fehily, my old schools coach, used to say that perfection is repetition, plus repetition, plus repetition – then he'd keep on saying it for anything up to ten minutes. Which *I'm* not going to do because we've only got, like, ten minutes of our session left. Okay, where's Barry?'

'Which Barry?' Nailer goes.

I'm there, 'Er, Barry Austin – as in, like, your number ten?'

'He's not in today,' someone else goes. 'He's at an Engineering Open Day in UCD, like.'

I'm like, 'Excuse me?' because I can't believe what I'm actually hearing. 'What the fock is he doing at that?'

'He wants to do Engineering in UCD next year, like.'

'What I mean is, why is he prioritizing his academic career over his rugby?'

It ends up being shrugs all round. I just shake my head and decide to proceed with the lesson irregordless.

I'm there, 'Okay, I'll be the number ten for this drill. Let's just say it's something I know a thing or two about! Nailer, which hand are you strongest passing off?'

He goes, 'What do you mean, like?'

'As in, are you more comfortable throwing with your left or your right?'

'Like I says to you, I just get it in me hands and I fuck it, like.'

'Well, are you left-handed or right-handed?'

'Right-handed, like.'

'Okay, hold the ball. That's good. Now, when you're passing off your right hand, you put your left hand here – that's right – underneath the ball, to keep it steady. Now, you're going to use your right hand to spin the ball –'

'Why do you need to spin it, like?'

'Er, to give it distance and *accuracy*?'

'Keep doing it the way you're already doing it, Nailer,' a voice goes. It's the fat dude, whose nickname seems to be Ricey. 'If it's not broke, don't fix it, like.'

I'm there, 'What do you mean, if it's not broke? It *is* broke! I'm telling you it's broke!'

'My da's a member of Woodbrook. Played off a twelve handicap, like. One day, a fella in the club says to him, you've a glitch in your swing. So me da went off and had lessons – with a pro, like. Now he swings the club like Tiger Woods, but he plays off a handicap of twenty.'

'Two totally different things,' I go.

'How are they different, like?'

'They just are, Ricey, okay?'

Nailer makes an attempt to throw the ball the way I showed him, except it only travels a few feet before hitting the ground like a shot seagull.

'Told you,' Ricey goes.

But I'm like, 'Nailer, just trust me. It'll feel weird at first, but after a while –'

And that's when I suddenly hear laughter. Either Lenny or Dougie – they're impossible to tell aport – has my Tactics Book open in his hands and he's obviously found something in there that he finds, for some reason, *hilarious*?

He goes, 'Listen to this one, like,' and then – I swear to fock – he storts reading out some of the things that famous players have *said* about me? '*Ross O'Carroll-Kelly had the natural talent to achieve everything that Brian O'Driscoll achieved in the game – and more. Victor Costello to Denis Hickie, overheard by JP, in 3fe on Sussex Terrace.*'

They all crack their holes laughing.

I'm there, 'Yeah, no, you lot can afford to laugh alright. You've got Michael's in the first round of the Leinster Schools Senior Cup the second week in January and your scrum-half doesn't even know how to throw a focking rugby ball.'

I snatch the book out of his hands.

He's there, 'Sorry, Boss Man!'

But I'm like, 'Forget it. Let's just call it a day.'

No one even objects. They all just stort making their way back to the dressing room. I go back to the cor, feeling totally deflated. I'm thinking – yeah, no – maybe I won't bother my hole coming back again.

I stort the engine and I'm just about to pull out of the cor pork when I spot Brother Ciaran hobbling towards me on his stick. I have no choice but to wind down the window.

'I have the most exciting news!' he goes.

I'm thinking, okay, please tell me that the players were only *pretending* to be shit?

I'm there, 'News? Yeah, no, what is it?'

He goes, 'I've arranged a friendly for us next month, Ross. After mid-term.'

I'm tempted to point out the obvious to him – that it's rugby and there's no such thing as a friendly. That's why we call them Tests. But I don't.

Instead, I'm like, 'Who's this match against?'

And – I swear to fock – he goes, 'Blackrock College.'

I end up actually laughing in his face.

He goes, 'Is that okay?'

I'm there, 'Blackrock College? Are you focking serious?'

'Well, you did say that we were capable of beating any team in the country, didn't you?'

'I, er, did say that, yeah.'

That was before I saw them play.

He's there, 'It's all arranged, Ross. They've agreed to play us here – the first week in November!'

I smile at him and I go, 'Yeah, no, that *is* exciting news,' while inside I'm just thinking, Fock-a-doodle-doo!

So we're in, believe it or not, Dunnes Stores in Cornelscourt – yeah, no – doing the weekly *supermorket* shop? We're, like, standing at the checkout – we're talking me and Sorcha at one end, putting all of our items onto the conveyor belt, and Honor at the other end, packing everything into the old Bags for Life.

Sorcha suddenly turns around to me with a look of, I don't know, *something* on her face?

She's like, 'Ross, look!'

Honor is – I swear to fock – removing all of the plastic packaging from the pears and the croissants and the porsnips and the whatever else and she's just, like, dropping it on the floor. Then the boys are just, like, kicking it away.

It's not long before the checkout girl – who isn't great, by the way – notices what's happening and goes, 'Sorry? Can you please stop doing that?'

And Honor – no better woman – is like, 'Excuse me?'

'You have to take the packaging with you,' the checkout girl goes.

Honor goes, 'Why?'

'Because it comes *with* the item.'

'No, it doesn't. It's totally focking unnecessary. Did you know there's, like, an island in the middle of the Pacific Ocean made up entirely of discorded plastic – it's, like, twice the size of the state of Texas? And if we all left our unnecessary packaging behind for *you*

75

to dispose of, then supermorkets would think twice about using it in the first place. You stupid focking bitch.'

Sorcha goes, 'Oh my God, Honor, you have no idea how proud I am hearing you talk that way.'

'Focking bitch,' Leo goes, imitating his sister. 'Stupid focking ugly fock.'

'So, so proud,' Sorcha goes as she's sticking my credit cord in the chip and pin machine.

The woman's like, 'You let your kids talk to people like that, do you?'

'With the future of our planet hanging in the balance,' Sorcha goes, 'I would never censure any of my children for speaking truth to power.'

Truth to power? The poor woman is probably on shit money and a zero hours contract and she's having to take abuse from my kids.

Sorcha takes the cord and the receipt and then pushes the trolley away as Honor walks on ahead with Brian, Johnny and Leo. I roll my eyes at the woman, sort of apologizing, then I follow them back to the cor.

'Why didn't you tell me?' Sorcha goes, as we're loading the bags into the boot.

She's obviously decided that *now* is the time for the big chat?

'Tell you what?' Honor goes.

'That you and I have a common interest in our concern for the future of the planet – of this planet we call Earth.'

This planet we call Earth. Focking spare me.

'The fock are you talking about?' Honor goes.

Sorcha's there, 'Sister Consuelo told us everything. About you setting up a Mount Anville Climate Justice Committee – very similar to the Environmental Action Committee that I very nearly set up when *I* was in the school?'

Honor's like, 'It's not only me,' like she's being accused of doing something wrong. 'Sincerity Matthews is involved in it as well. And Currer Bell Whelehan.'

'But she said you were the one who walked into the staffroom and storted lecturing the teachers about single-use coffee cups!'

Sorcha goes. 'Can I just ask you, Honor, was that because of my Seanad speech?'

'Everything doesn't have to be about you, you know?'

There's, like, silence between them then. Honor puts the last bag into the cor and Sorcha closes the boot.

Sorcha's there, 'You know, it's okay to care about things, Honor.'

Honor looks away – all sad. For a second, I think she's actually going to cry. She's there, 'I don't know why I'm so upset. It was only a focking polar bear.'

Sorcha goes, 'Are we talking about the polar bear in the video I sent you?'

'Mom, can you stop trying to make it about you?'

'I'm sorry, Honor. It's just that, well, this is the first time I've ever felt that we're on, like, the same page.'

'He just, like, gave up and let himself drown. I got upset. And then I storted going on all these websites about, like, global warming. And they said that if we keep going the way we're going for another five years, the damage we'll have done to the planet will be, like, *irreversible*?'

I decide to try to ease her fears.

I'm there, 'You don't want to believe that, Honor. It's all horse shit.'

Sorcha's there, 'Oh my God, Ross, what are you doing?'

'Er, I'm trying to put our daughter's mind at rest?'

'What, by telling her lies?'

'They're hordly lies. According to my old man, climate change isn't even a thing.'

'Oh my God, you don't *genuinely* believe that, do you?'

'Why would he say it if it wasn't true?'

'Because, Ross, his political porty is being bankrolled by shady Russian business interests who want to go on extracting fossil fuels from beneath the surface of the Earth, including Ireland.'

'And your argument is, what – that that would be bad for the planet?'

'It's not *my* argument, Ross – it's, like, irrefutable, scientific fact.'

What Honor doesn't seem to realize is that I'm on *her* actual *side* here?

She goes, 'The reason the planet is focked is because of people like you, Dad.'

I'm like, 'Me? The fock did I do?'

'Er, it's actually what you *didn't* do? People have known for, like, fifty years about the damage we were doing to the Earth. But people like you refused to change your behaviour.'

'Hey, I'm only just finding out about all of this now, Honor.'

'Your generation created this problem – and it's up to *my* generation to fix it.'

I watch Sorcha's eyes fill up with tears. I haven't seen her look this proud since a borman in House asked her for ID on the night of her thirtieth birthday.

'Honor,' she goes, 'I'm – oh my God – *so* proud of you!'

Honor's there, 'I'm not saying this shit so you'll be proud of me.'

'I know you're not – but I am anyway!'

'So what are *you* doing about it?'

'About what?'

'Er, about global *warming*?'

'I'm doing loads, Honor. I recycle. And our house was the first in Ireland with – again – a dual-flush toilet.'

'I'm talking in terms of our corbon footprint. I'm talking about us making the kind of drastic lifestyle changes that will actually make a difference to the emissions that we, ourselves, are responsible for?'

Sorcha's like, 'Well, what do you *want* us to do, Honor?'

And Honor – I swear to fock – goes, 'I want us all to go vegan.'

I'm there, 'Okay, let's not lose our sense of prospectus here.'

But Sorcha's like, 'Oh! My God! *Goosebumps?* I was going to suggest we tried it for the first few weeks of the New Year. I read an orticle in *The Gordian* about it. They're calling it Veganuary!'

Honor goes, 'I'm not talking about the New Year. The damage that dairy forming does to the biosphere through the emission of methane is killing the planet, hour by hour. I'm talking about doing it now.'

I'm there, 'I am not giving up meat, Sorcha.'

But Sorcha goes, 'Er, we are, Ross! And we're giving up dairy as well!'

Lauren has barely opened the front door to us when Sorcha puts one of her size five Gucci Brixtons in it.

'Oh my God, Lauren,' she goes, 'what happened to your cor?'

Yeah, no, I did a serious focking number on it. Out of the corner of my eye, I can see that the entire front door on the passenger side is mangled to shit.

Lauren's there, 'I've no idea. It happened last week when Christian was at that Mass for that priest.'

That priest? She's talking about Father Fehily. Again, zero rugby knowledge.

Of course, Sorcha refuses to let it go. 'Oh my God,' she goes, 'Ross, *you* were at that Mass as well, weren't you?'

It's like being married to Vincent Browne.

I'm there, 'Maybe we should drop the subject, Sorcha,' then I hand Lauren the bottle of Marqués de Riscal that we brought and I make sure to mention that it wasn't cheap. I go, 'You'll notice that's none of your screw-top, petrol-station plonk, Lauren,' just so she doesn't throw it in with the Châteauneuf-du-Topaz that everyone else no doubt brought.

We're supposedly here for Ross Junior's birthday, by the way, but we're still standing in the focking gorden – in the middle of focking Booterstown.

Sorcha's there, 'I'm just wondering, Ross, did you notice anything suspicious?'

And I go, 'I'm just making the point that maybe it's something Lauren is too upset to talk about. You're going to have a hell of a job matching that paint, Lauren – and that's not me being a dick.'

Lauren just shakes her head. She goes, 'Christian thought it would be a good idea to pork in the *staff* cor pork?'

Sorcha's there, 'Oh my God, why would anyone do that?'

Seriously. Once a Sixth Year Prefect, *always* a Sixth Year Prefect.

I'm there, 'Are you not even going to invite us in?'

Lauren looks down at Brian, Johnny and Leo, straining at

the – quite literally – leash. They're going, 'Rugby, rugby, rugby, rugby . . .'

'Oh,' she goes, unable to hide her disappointment, 'you brought *them*.'

Sorcha's there, 'I hope that's okay. We promise we'll keep them on their lead at all times.'

'You're going to have to. It's just that Ross has his anxiety issues, as you know. I don't want anything triggering him – especially on his birthday.'

Triggering him. Fock's sake.

The girl finally invites us in. She goes, 'You haven't brought the other one, have you? No offence.'

This is how she refers to my children.

Sorcha goes, 'Oh my God, no offence taken, Lauren. Yeah, no, Honor decided to stay home. She's on the Internet, reading stuff about – believe it or not – the climate emergency and the uncertain future of our planet. We've gone vegan, by the way!'

Lauren doesn't comment on any of this shit one way or the other. She just opens the door and lets us in. She leads us down to the kitchen, where the porty is in full swing. It's full of kids and their parents.

The boys are going, 'Rugby, rugby, focking rugby,' and I notice a certain – I'm going to use the word – *nervousness* cross people's faces when they see that we've arrived. Everyone would want to seriously lighten up. I let the boys off their leash and tell them to go mingle. 'Focking rugby fock!' Leo goes. 'Focking rugby focking fockers!'

I stort mingling. I end up talking to Chloe and Sophie. Chloe is talking about a girl she knows who's put on so much weight since she went back on the pill that the facial recognition software on her phone doesn't work any more.

Sophie's like, 'No! Way!'

But Chloe's there, 'Way!'

And Sophie goes, 'That's, like, Oh! My God!'

A few seconds later, Ross Junior comes over to me.

'Hi, Roth!' he goes. He talks like the kid with the big glasses out of *Jerry Maguire*. It's pretty cute, although I'd say it *could* get annoying after an hour or two. Like, I'm sure that even Tom Cruise had moments on the set when he wished the kid would just shut the fock up.

I'm like, 'Hey, Ross – happy birthday!' and I hand him the present we brought him.

He's there, 'What ith it?'

And I go, 'Why don't you open it and find out?'

He opens the wrapping paper, being careful not to tear it, then he takes out the box. Yeah, no, it's some kind of giant Stor Wars action figure. He looks at it, absolute confusion on his face.

Christian tips over then. He goes, 'Hey, Dude, how the hell are you?'

I'm like, 'I'm all good, Christian. I'm *all* good.'

Ross Junior goes, 'What ith it, Roth?'

And Christian's there, 'It's Kylo Ren, Ross. From *The Force Awakens*.'

It clearly means fock-all to the kid.

Lauren has to stick her hooter in, of course. Across the kitchen, she shouts, 'It doesn't have flashing lights or make loud noises, does it? I mean, you focking *know* my son has his anxiety issues.'

But that's when something totally unexpected happens. Christian ends up *turning* on her? He goes, 'Yeah, Ross was kind enough to buy our son a present, Lauren. It might be nice to say thank you before you stort looking for the focking gift receipt.'

Of course, every conversation in the kitchen ends up stopping.

Lauren just, like, glowers at him. It's obvious that she's still pissed off about the cor. But, like I said, I've never heard Christian speak to her like that before.

I have to say – I like it.

Christian hands me a glass of wine – the shit stuff – and indicates the back door with a nod. I follow him outside to the gorden. We sit at the picnic table.

'Here,' I go, 'this isn't the wine *I* brought, is it?' except he doesn't answer me. I decide not to make a big issue out of it because I can see that he's got shit on his mind.

I'm there, 'I thought you two had sorted your problems out?'

He just shakes his head. He goes, 'We're, er, not seeing eye to eye on things at the moment. Someone's bullying Ross.'

I'm like, 'Whoa!' pretending that it comes as a major surprise to me. It doesn't. Even *I* get the urge to bully him and I'm his supposed godfather. 'Have you any idea who?'

'He won't tell us,' Christian goes. 'I presume someone at school. We were watching TV the other night and I noticed he had this bruise under his eye. I asked him who did it, but he wouldn't say. Then Lauren wouldn't let me press him on it because she's afraid of him having –'

'An anxiety attack?'

'Exactly. She says he'll tell us when he's good and ready.'

'So, what, her answer in the meantime is to let him keep getting the shit kicked out of him?'

'No, her answer in the meantime is to apply to become a Teaching Assistant in the school.'

'Excuse me?'

'A Teaching Assistant. In his actual class. Just so she can be around him all day, every day.'

'Over-mothered,' I go. 'I've said it before and I'll go on saying it – although not within earshot of *her*. Especially after the way she reacted the last time.'

The back door opens and – speak of the devil – Ross Junior steps out into the gorden. He goes, 'Mommy thaid you have to come in becauth Granthad ith here!'

Christian shakes his head, then throws his eyes skyward.

'Hennessy,' he goes. 'That's all I focking need.'

Back into the gaff he goes. Ross Junior goes to follow him, except I call him back. I'm like, 'Ross, come here for a second, will you?'

He's there, 'What ith it, Roth?'

'I'm hearing rumours on the old grapevine that someone is bullying you.'

He makes a butterfly with his two hands and places it on his chest. Then he closes his eyes and storts trying to, I don't know, regulate his breathing.

I'm there, 'There's no need to do that, Ross. Look, I'm not going to ask you who's kicking the shit out of you. I just want to show you how to deal with bullies – as your godfather.'

He opens his eyes. Oh, he's interested.

I'm there, 'Do you know how to throw a punch, Ross?'

He shakes his head. He goes, 'Mommy thayth that violenth ith never the anther.'

I'm there, 'With respect, your mother's talking out of her hole – although that's obviously off the record. Come here, I'm going to teach you how to throw a punch.'

I hold up my right hand.

I'm like, 'Hit me as hord as you can.'

He goes, 'Mommy thaid –'

'Forget what Mommy thaid. Mommy knows fock-all about raising boys. Come on – make a fist and hit me as hord as you possibly can.'

He makes a fist, but he sort of, like, flicks it at my hand, like he's swotting a fly with a newspaper. I'm going to be honest, I barely feel a thing.

I'm there, 'Come on, you can do it horder than that, Ross!'

He does it again, a little bit horder this time, but it's still not great.

I'm like, 'Dude, you're sort of slapping me with your knuckles there. You need to *properly* hit me – with this port of your fist here. See it?'

He nods.

I'm there, 'And throw it like you're trying to drive your fist through my hand and out the other side.'

He tries it again. Oh, that's better. He's actually pretty strong for such a weedy kid.

I'm there, 'Put your entire body weight into it, though. Remember, a punch actually comes from the shoulder. And twist your fist on impact – like this. It does more damage that way.'

He tries it again.

I'm like, 'That's better.'

And again.

I'm there, 'Okay, you're getting it now.'

And again.

I go, 'See? *That's* how you deal with people who give you shit.'

It's an actual miracle because suddenly he can't *stop* throwing punches? He's, like, red in the face and he's pretty much screaming as he absolutely pounds my hand. It's like he's getting rid of years and years of pent-up frustration and I end up having to eventually tell him to stop because I'm scared he might do me an actual injury.

'And that,' I go, 'is how you deal with pricks who take liberties.'

I knock back the rest of my wine and I head back into the gaff, leaving Ross Junior in the gorden, throwing punches at imaginary enemies. I feel genuinely great about myself.

Kylo Ren is obviously going back to the shop, by the way, because I hear Sorcha telling Lauren that she's really sorry and she'll get me to dig out the receipt. Hennessy, I can't help but notice, has brought a brand-new rugby ball for Oliver, Ross Junior's little bro.

Christian goes, 'Yeah, you know it's not actually *his* birthday, don't you?'

And Hennessy's there, 'The other one,' which is obviously his pet name for Ross Junior, 'has no interest in the game. And if that's not your fault, I don't know whose fault it is.'

And Christian – I swear to fock – goes, 'Oh, you're going to give me a lecture on parenting now, Hennessy, are you? You being a focking expert and everything?'

I have never heard Christian stand up for himself like this before. It's like suddenly having money again has restored his confidence and he's in no mood to take S, H, One, T from anyone.

Yeah, no, there's hope for his son yet.

Hennessy gives him one of his looks – like he's trying to figure out how much weight it would take to drag his body to the bottom of the sea.

Sorcha tries to break the tension by going, 'Oh my God, Lauren, if you need a referee for the Teacher's Assistant job, you can definitely, definitely put *my* name down?'

'Me too,' Claire goes – as in Claire from Bray, of all places.

I'm like, 'Look who it is. I heard you were back from Canada.'

She's like, 'Hi, Ross,' and she says it in a really defensive way.

'I was just telling Claire,' Sorcha goes, 'that we've seen a huge change in Honor since she storted in Mount Anville. She's definitely less of a bitch – *and* she's set up a Climate Justice Committee!'

I'm there, 'I heard you might be getting back together with that focking dope you married.'

'We're back talking again, Ross – although just on WhatsApp.'

'And he believes you now, does he? That me and you never –'

Sorcha's like, 'Ross!'

And I'm there, 'I'm just saying, if they get back together when he comes home, I want an apology from him for accusing me in the wrong.'

Randomly, I notice that Lauren has put our bottle of Marqués de Riscal – twenty-two snots, by the way – on the sideboard, separate from all the other drink. She'll feed us piss all day and then drink that tonight when she's watching – I don't know – *The Good Wife* on Netflix. What a focking mug I was. Lesson learned.

Hennessy is still glowering at Christian. He's obviously not loving this new version of his son-in-law.

He goes, 'What happened to Lauren's car?' because he bought it for her as a birthday present.

Christian's there, 'Somebody obviously hit it with their door.'

'Repeatedly,' Hennessy goes. 'You know what kind of a job I'm going to have matching that paint?'

'Yeah, no,' I go, 'that's the point *I* keep making, except I keep getting totally ignored.'

I think I'm possibly a bit pissed.

He goes, 'Lauren said you were driving it at the time.'

He's still talking to Christian.

Christian's like, 'Yeah? What's your point, Hennessy?'

I nearly feel like saying fair focks to him.

'His point,' Lauren goes, 'is that it wouldn't have happened if you hadn't porked in the teachers' cor pork.'

There's suddenly what would have to be described as a commotion at the other end of the kitchen. I hear one or two parents go, 'Oh! My God!' with genuine concern in their voices, then I hear Sorcha literally scream.

She's there, 'Ross, it's Johnny! He's collapsed!'

I push my way through the crowd of kids and their parents and I see Johnny lying face-down on the kitchen floor.

I'm there, 'It's nothing to worry about. I think he's possibly just drunk again.'

'Drunk?' Sorcha goes. 'Again?' because I didn't tell her what happened that night in Finglas.

I'm like, 'Yeah, no, he had a few drinks when we were in Ronan's. He's obviously developing a real taste for it now,' making him sound like a serial killer.

Sorcha goes, 'Oh! My God! I am *so* embarrassed!'

I'm like, 'Put him upstairs in one of the bedrooms to sleep it off. Although make sure you roll him onto his side.'

She's there, 'No, Ross, we're leaving. Oh my God, Lauren, I am *so* embarrassed.'

She picks up our drunken son and carries him to the door, going, 'Bring the boys, Ross – we're going home.'

I grab Brian and Leo and put them on their leash. Then I grab our bottle of Marqués de Riscal – there's no way I'm leaving it – and I follow her to the door.

Christian walks with me.

'Already a pisshead,' I go. 'He definitely takes after me.'

Christian's there, 'Jesus Christ, Ross, is he going to be okay?'

I'm like, 'Dude, this is called parenting. It's all ahead of us. By the way, I really admire you for standing up to Hennessy the way you just did.'

He smiles and goes, 'What I haven't actually told them is that me porking where I did might actually turn out to be a *good* thing?'

I'm there, 'As in?'

Christian goes, 'There's CCTV cameras in the teachers' cor pork,' and I feel my body turn instantly cold. 'I'm going to ask McGahy if he'll let me look at the feed.'

I'm there, 'I don't know, Dude. I think you should hopefully let the whole thing drop.'

He goes, 'No way, Ross. I'm going to find out who totalled Lauren's cor.'

3.

Do You Remember the Good Old Days before the Goatstown?

Jesus, I'm weak with the hunger. It's been, like, three days now without meat – without milk, without butter, without cheese – and I can nearly feel myself wasting away. Dinner today – we're talking *Sunday* dinner? – was a mushroom risotto that looked and smelled like a baby's sick. And for all I know, that's what it was.

I tip downstairs. Sorcha and Honor are sitting at the kitchen table with Fionn and they're talking about a thing called – I shit you not – urban *density*?

Honor's there, 'I read this statistic that, like, two per cent of the world's land surface is occupied by cities – and they consume, like, seventy-five per cent of the world's natural resources.'

Sorcha's like, 'Oh! My God! I'm going to remember that statistic! What was it again? Ninety-five per cent?'

'Seventy-five per cent.'

'Seventy-five per cent. I'm going to definitely, definitely remember that.'

Of course, this is Fionn's favourite type of conversation – full of facts and focking figures – and he can't resist throwing his thoughts into the mix.

'I've actually just finished reading a book on the rise of the megacity,' he tries to go. 'In other words, cities with a population of more than ten million people. In 1950, there was only one in the whole world – obviously New York. In 1990, there were ten. Now, there are thirty-one. And, like you say, Honor, big cities mean higher consumption lifestyles.'

'I'd love to read that book,' Honor goes.

I'm like, 'Seriously? Is that how you want to spend your time? Focking reading?'

Fionn's like, 'Hey, I'll give it to you, Honor,' and it really pisses me off to see *him* – the focker who accused my daughter of trying to poison his son – now trying to be her bezzy mate. 'It's really great that you're taking an interest in this stuff.'

'God, I'm so hungry I'm seeing spots,' I go, shuffling over to the fridge. I open it and look inside, but there's fock-all in there that would fill the hole in me. 'I said I'm seeing definite spots before my eyes.'

Sorcha's there, 'Oh my God, Ross, will you *stop* being so melodramatic?'

'I'm sorry,' I go, 'you're going to have to tell me again, Honor. How is me having a cheeseburger bad for the actual planet?'

Honor sighs like she's sick of explaining it to me – which she probably *is*, in all fairness?

She goes, 'Livestock accounts for, like, thirty-two billion tonnes of corbon dioxide which is released into the biosphere every year.'

I'm there, 'And that's, like, cows opening their lunch, is it?'

'Basically, yes. Cows, sheep and pigs breaking wind produces more greenhouse gas emissions than, like, all the planes, trains, cars, buses and trucks in the world *combined*?'

'So what we *actually* need – bear with me here – is *fewer* cows, sheep and pigs, right?'

'I know what you're going to say, Dad.'

'So by eating them, I'm kind of doing my bit to reduce the numbers – aren't I?'

'Yeah,' Fionn tries to go, 'that's not how it works. To save the planet, we're unfortunately going to have to let a lot of these animals go extinct.'

And I'm like, 'Yeah, I was talking to my daughter – not you. Maybe you should stop sticking your focking beak into my family's business.'

'The point that Honor is trying to make,' Sorcha goes, 'is that there are far more pigs, cows and sheep on this Earth than nature ever *intended* there to be? The biosphere can't cope. That's why it's going to take something radical like the entire population of the world switching to a vegan diet – like ours! – to save the actual planet. I have to say, I'm – oh my God – *loving* being vegan. I've actually lost two pounds in, like, less than a week.'

I'm there, 'I have to say, Honor, I liked you more when you were a bitch.'

Sorcha's there, 'Ross! That's a horrible thing to say!'

Fionn stands up. He's like, 'I'll go and get you that book, Honor,' and he focks off upstairs.

I'm there, 'Him and his books. I'm surprised at you, Honor, showing an interest.'

And that's when Sorcha's phone suddenly rings. She answers it and goes, 'Hi, how are you?' and then she listens very carefully, going, 'Oh my God . . . calm down . . . oh my God . . . yes, he's here. Just give me a second and I'll buzz you in.'

She hangs up, then dials the number on her phone to open the front gate.

'The fock's going on?' I go. 'Who is it?'

And Sorcha's there, 'It's Lauren. Did you do something to upset her, Ross?'

Oh, fock! Her cor! Oh, fockity, fockity, fock-fock-fock!

I'm like, 'Er, no – what's your reason for asking, Sorcha?'

'It's just that she sounds really angry,' she goes. 'And then she asked me if you were home.'

'Maybe tell her that you made a mistake and I've gone out after all.'

'Why? Do you know what this is about?'

'No, it's a genuine mystery.'

There's a ring on the doorbell, followed by the hammering of the knocker.

I'm like, 'Maybe don't answer it.'

Sorcha laughs. She goes, 'She knows I'm here, Ross. I just buzzed her in.'

Then she tips out into the hallway to open the door.

Honor goes, 'Oh my God, what did you do?'

And I'm like, 'Nothing,' trying to calm myself. 'You know Lauren. She flies off the handle for sometimes no reason at all.'

The next thing I hear is her voice in the hallway. Oh, she's pissed off alright. She's going, 'Where is he? Where is that focking prick you're married to?'

Then – *Críost* on a focking *rothar* – I hear Christian going, 'Calm down, Lauren. Let's hear what Ross has to say first.'

And I'm suddenly thinking, okay, there's a possible chance I might be able to sweet-talk my way out of this. So I step out of the kitchen and I go, 'Lauren, Christian – how the hell are you?'

Lauren goes, 'I am going to rip your focking head off with my hands,' and she comes chorging towards me, with Christian and Sorcha following closely behind her, trying to calm her down.

I'm so terrified for my own personal safety that I end up breaking the most valuable rule that my old man ever taught me: never admit or deny anything until you've been actually accused – and, even then, keep denying it way beyond the point that everybody stops believing you.

'Look,' I end up going, 'I didn't know it was *your* cor, Lauren, even though I knew you drove a Fiat 500 in Tiffany blue. Yeah, no, I thought it was McGahy's, because Christian threw it into McGahy's porking space. That's the only reason I ended up smashing the shit out of *your* door?'

Christian and Lauren are just, like, staring at me with confusion on their faces. Christian goes, 'That was *you*?'

And I'm there, 'Yeah, no, I presumed that was why you were here. You mentioned that there was, like, CCTV in the teachers' cor pork.'

'McGahy wouldn't let me see it. He said it served me right for porking in his space.'

I'm there, 'So why are you *actually* here?'

Lauren goes, 'Did you teach my son how to throw a punch?'

Oh, fock.

I'm like, 'Er, I'm just racking my brains here, Lauren. It definitely doesn't *sound* like me?'

I hear Honor go, 'Oh! My God!' because she hates Lauren as much as *I* nearly do?

Lauren's there, 'He said you did – unless you're calling him a liar.'

'Okay, then, I'm admitting it – yeah, I did teach him how to throw a punch, the little focking squealer. And it's fine, by the way, you don't have to thank me.'

'*Thank* you?' Lauren goes, her voice absolutely dripping with disgust.

I'm there, 'He was being bullied, Lauren. He was getting the shit kicked out of him.'

'It was Oliver who was picking on him,' Christian goes. 'That's why he didn't want to tell us.'

I actually laugh. I'm there, 'Oliver? His little brother? Jesus Christ, that's even worse. That's even more reason to teach him how to stand up for himself.'

'Well, he certainly did that this afternoon,' Lauren goes. 'He punched his brother in the face – and he broke his focking nose.'

'Oh! My! God!' Sorcha goes – yeah, no, *she's* only making it worse for me by overreacting.

I'm there, 'Lauren, if it's any consolation, Oliver will certainly think twice before ever focking with him again.'

It's definitely the wrong thing to say. Lauren makes a sudden grab for me – we're talking both hands clamped around my throat. Then she storts pressing down hord on my Adam's apple with her two thumbs, trying to choke the basic life out of me.

Christian storts trying to drag her off me. He's going, 'Lauren, you're going to kill him!'

And Lauren's like, 'I focking know I am – just leave me to do it, will you?'

Sorcha is going, 'Oh! My God! Oh! *My* God!' and not even bothering her hole to *help* me, by the way?

I'm actually storting to feel faint, like I might lose consciousness any second, although that might also be the hunger.

Somewhere in the hallway, I hear Honor go, 'Hill! Air!'

But then, somehow, Christian manages to get Lauren to release her grip and she ends up turning her anger on *him* then?

'That's it,' she goes, 'take *his* side. All rugby boys together, isn't that it?'

He's like, 'This has nothing to do with rugby, Lauren.'

And she's there, 'It's always to do with rugby. If it's a choice between me and your wanker teammates, I always come off second best.'

It all escalates very quickly after that. Suddenly, the conversation isn't about me any more, it's about their marriage. And it slowly dawns on me that I'm actually witnessing the final moments of it.

'Do you know what your problem is?' Christian goes.

Lauren's like, 'What, Christian? What do you think my problem is?'

'You're a bully – just like your old man is a bully.'

He's talking about Hennessy, bear in mind.

She goes, 'My dad is twice the man you are.'

He's like, 'Yeah? So why have you spent fifteen years in counselling talking about what a shit father you had growing up?'

'Fock you.'

'You're messed up, Lauren. And you've messed our kids up as well.'

'We're finished.'

'Too focking right we're finished.'

'I want you out of the house tonight.'

'I'll be glad to go.'

'Oh my God,' Sorcha goes, opening the bedroom window, 'the *smell* in this room!'

I'm there, 'Yeah, no, I can't help it. It's all that green shit I'm being made to eat. I'm rotting from the inside out.'

'I'll go and put some dry herbs into a muslin bag.'

'What, for breakfast?'

'No, it's a really good eco-friendly air-freshener.'

See, it says a lot that I had to actually ask.

'Poor Lauren,' she goes.

I laugh.

I'm like, 'Poor Lauren, my hole. I know she's a friend of yours, Sorcha, but she's a serious head-wrecker. All *I* tried to do was teach her son how to stand up for himself.'

'Do you think it's definitely over?'

'It certainly sounded like it, didn't it?'

'By the way, there was a message on the Mount Anville Moms WhatsApp last night. The balance is due on Honor's school trip. It's, like, three grand.'

'Three grand? Where the fock are they going? The moon?'

'They're going skiing – in, like, January.'

'It's the first I heard of it.'

'Ross, the annual ski trip to Pinzolo is, like, a rite of passage for Mount Anville girls. Pay it today, will you?'

I'm like, 'Yeah, whatever,' throwing back the covers and hopping out of the bed.

Sorcha goes, 'You were shouting, "Fock Blackrock College!" in your sleep last night. Were you having that nightmare again where you're in Riverview and Brendan Macken is laughing at the sex noises you make when you're using the elliptical trainer?'

I'm there, 'Not this time,' throwing on my training gear. 'I was thinking about this match we've got coming up. I was originally nervous, but suddenly I'm thinking, hey, if anyone's capable of turning Pres Bray into a winning team, it's me.'

I pick my phone up off my bedside table and I dial Brother Ciaran's number. He answers on the third ring.

'Ross!' he goes. 'I didn't know if we'd ever hear from you again!'

I'm there, 'Meaning?'

'Oh, it was just your face the last day. I thought I'd frightened you off with the mention of Blackrock College!'

I'm like, 'Frightened? Of Blackrock College? You obviously don't know who you hired, Dude.'

He's there, 'Will we see you on Thursday, then? For training?'

'No, you'll see me today.'

'Today?'

'I'll be there in one hour.'

'It's just that the boys will be in class.'

'So get them out of class.'

'Well, obviously I'd have to, em, clear it with their teachers first.'

'Okay, who's the actual Principal of that school?'

'I am, of course, but their education is very important –'

'Dude, you don't beat Blackrock College by training once a week. We're going to need to increase it to two or three times.'

'I'll talk to their teachers.'

'Be quick about. I'll be there in one hour. I want them waiting for me out on the pitch.'

I hang up on him and I smile. God, I love the feeling of being a coach. This is what it must have been like for Joe Schmidt storting out.

Sorcha goes, 'I'm actually going to Bray myself this morning!'

I'm like, 'Jesus! Why?'

'Claire wants to show me her interior design plans for Wheat Bray Love.'

'So what kind of muck is she going to be serving in this place?'

'Oh my God, she was telling me about some of her ideas, Ross. She's going to be doing this, like, Deconstructed Caesar Salad that *she* actually invented? And she's also going to have this thing where, between 2 p.m. and 5 p.m., coffees and teas are free – instead of paying for your actual drink, you pay five cent for every minute you're sitting down.'

'People will take the piss.'

'I don't know, Ross, people from Bray are very supportive of their own. That's according to Claire.'

'They will take the piss – trust me.'

Jesus Christ, I've squeezed out another one and this one smells like a focking gas leak.

Sorcha goes, 'Maybe get some chorcoal tablets, Ross – they're good for flatulence.'

Five minutes later, I'm hopping into the cor and I'm pointing it in the direction of Bray. I'm actually looking forward to spending the morning with my players, sharing my wisdom and hopefully persuading them that Blackrock College aren't exactly the All Blacks. They are actually beatable.

The goys – I'm relieved to see – are all waiting for me on the pitch as per my instructions. They don't look too happy to have been pulled out of their classes. I'm definitely going to have to change the culture around here.

I'm there, 'Okay, goys, let's train.'

Either Dougie or Lenny – I don't think I'll ever be able to tell them apart – goes, 'Train? In the rain, Boss?'

Yeah, no, I forgot to mention that it's absolutely pissing it down.

I'm there, 'It's not a summer sport, my friend,' and I'm really pleased with myself for coming up with the line on the spur of the moment.

I've got, like, a bag of rugby balls. I tip them out onto the ground, then I stort throwing them *to* them?

Barry Austin – the focking Engineer – goes, 'It's just we're supposed to be in *class*, like?'

And I'm like, 'There are more important things in the world than the focking Leaving Cert – Mister Don't Bother Showing Up for Training Because I'm Going to a UCD Open Day.'

He looks confused. He's there, 'I'm just thinking about me future, like.'

And I go, 'There are more important things in the world than your future. You want to beat Blackrock College, don't you?'

'Blackrock College?' Ricey – the prop – goes. 'I thought we had Michael's in the first round, like?'

Un-focking-believable. Brother Ciaran hasn't even told them yet.

I'm there, 'We're playing a match against Blackrock College. First week in November.'

'A friendly, like?' Ricey goes.

I'm there, 'No, a focking *Test* match, Ricey.'

Nailer – my so-called scrum-half – goes, 'Blackrock will hockey us, like.'

I go, 'Not if we put in the work beforehand,' and I feel like I'm storting to really grow into this role.

'They've an unbelievable team this year,' Nailer goes. 'They call them the Dream Team, like.'

I'm there, 'What if I told you that we could beat them?'

Oh, that grabs their attention.

'Beat them?' either Dougie or Lenny goes. 'Beat Blackrock, like?'

I'm there, 'Yes, beat Blackrock, Boss. What if I told you I had a plan? What if I told you that the answers are all written within the pages of my Rugby Tactics Book?'

I can see them all looking at each other, obviously thinking, is this goy for real?

I'm there, 'What do *you* think, Ricey? If I told you that, in just a few weeks, I could teach you enough so that you would have nothing to fear from the Blackrock front row – would you be interested?'

He goes, 'I suppose, like.'

I'm there, 'What about you, Barry Austin? If I told you, that between now and the first week in November, I could turn you into a kicker in the mould of, say, Joey Corbery, would you be up for it?'

He goes, 'I suppose I could get all the Chemistry notes from one of the lads in the class, like.'

All the Chemistry notes. I can tell I'm going to have trouble with this goy.

I'm there, 'And what about you, Nailer? If I told you that I could turn you into an Ireland Schools standard scrum-half, would you be interested?'

He goes, 'I don't know. I probably would, like.'

That's all I need to hear.

I'm there, 'Okay, let's get to work. Nailer, I want you to practise throwing the ball the way I showed you a few weeks ago.'

He goes, 'I've been thinking about that. I think I'm going to stick with just fucking the ball as hard as I can – it works for me, like.'

I end up letting a roar at him. I'm there, 'You will throw the ball the way I tell you to throw the ball! And you will practise it over and over and over again until you're doing it in your basic sleep! If you don't want to do it, I can always find myself another scrum-half! And that goes for the rest of you if you don't want to put in the work!'

And they all just nod, because they know that the time for horse-play is over.

What the fock?

That's number one, two and three on the list of questions I want to ask Christian. But it's, like, two weeks before he even returns my texts, then he agrees to meet me for a pint in Kielys of Donnybrook Town.

He's standing in our usual spot when I arrive, drinking – yeah, no – a sporkling water. I expect him to look like shit, except he doesn't. He looks great. Like a load has been genuinely lifted.

I'm there, 'Dude, what the fock?' because – like I said – it's a question that covers pretty much everything. 'I've been texting you, like, five times a day since that little scene in my hallway.'

He goes, 'I just wasn't ready to talk about it.'

'You have to tell me, Dude – is there another woman?'

'*That's* why you were texting me five times a day?'

'No, obviously I wanted to know that you were okay. Here, it's not Lisa McGrew, went to Holy Child Killiney, is it? Because she works in Orthur Cox and I know she still has a thing for you.'

He takes a sip of his fizzy water and he stares into the distance. He goes, 'Me and Lauren were never really suited,' and I'm thinking, fock, it looks like we're taking the scenic route here. 'Maybe as boyfriend-girlfriend, but not as, like, husband and wife – and definitely not as parents.'

I'm there, 'You let a hell of a lot go, Dude. The patience of a saint and blah, blah, blah. Just tell me, is it Carolyn Ansboro? I met her in Fade Street Social a few months ago and she asked after you, which I thought was definitely random at the time.'

'We should have never got back together after we broke up that time. We were just delaying the inevitable. Whatever we felt for each other was long gone.'

'Carolyn Ansboro pulled me off one night in her old dear's Opel Vectra while she was supposed to be giving me Biz Org grinds. I'm just putting the story out there so there's no awkwardness later on.'

'Ross, it's not Carolyn Ansboro!'

'Okay, that's a definite relief. She milked me like a focking Friesan. I jipped all over her old dear's seat covers.'

'There's no one else, Ross. Our marriage just didn't work out.'

'So there's no going back? It's, like, definitely over?'

'We've agreed that's it. We're going to separate and then, when the time comes, we're getting divorced.'

'Heavy.'

'It's not. It's amicable. Or we've agreed to make it amicable for the sake of the boys.'

He pulls a face like he smells something bad. He does smell something bad.

I'm like, 'Sorry, Dude, that was me. I've been eating a lot of – again, randomly – vegetables.'

Jesus Christ, I'm rotten.

He's there, 'I don't think there was a single day of our marriage when me and Lauren didn't have a row. She always had to have her own way.'

'She was no fan of mine,' I remind him. 'She made that very much obvious.'

'And she doesn't let things go. She stores up grievances.'

'I'd say she's still banging on about me making shit of her cor, is she? And Ross breaking Oliver's nose. Although I do feel a little bit responsible for that one.'

Christian just shakes his head. He goes, 'Hey, I think they'll both benefit, long term, from the experience,' which is a nice thing for me to hear. 'Oliver's minding his manners around Ross now. And Ross has realized what happens when you stand up to bullies, which is no bad thing either.'

'Well, just to let you know,' I go, 'I've had no thank-you call from Lauren and I won't be holding my breath.'

A waitress walks past holding a plate with a sirloin steak, onion rings and pepper sauce and I'm suddenly salivating. I catch Mary's eye and I go, 'Can I get the Kielys burger with, like, bacon and cheese, then obviously chips?'

And she's just like, 'No.'

Literally that.

I'm there, 'Er, okay, what about the sirloin steak? You definitely have that because one just went by.'

'Ross,' she goes, 'you're supposed to be off all meat.'

I'm like, 'What? Who told you that?'

'Honor rang here.'

'Fock's sake.'

'She said if you asked for meat, I wasn't to give it to you.'

I don't actually believe this. Mary has been more of a mother to me than my *actual* mother. I mean, she practically reared me.

I'm there, 'Mary, you know there are other boozers I *could* drink in?'

'Yeah,' she goes, 'she's phoned all of those as well.'

'What?'

'I know she rang Paddy Cullen's. I know she also rang the Merrion Inn.'

'Un-focking-believable.'

'We'd a lovely chat. She's very intelligent, isn't she?'

'Okay, why does that surprise people?'

'She said that livestock causes more air pollution than all the planes, trains, cars, buses and trucks in the world combined.'

I turn back to Christian and I'm like, 'I honestly preferred Honor when she didn't give a fock about anything or anyone.'

Christian smiles. He thinks I'm joking. But it's not long before the conversation swings back to him and his broken marriage.

He goes, 'I mean, when Lauren found out that I invested in JP's Vampire Bed idea, she went absolutely apeshit. But, of course, now that it's a success –'

'I'm presuming she's changed her tune?'

'She never said sorry, Ross. She never said, "Christian, you backed your instincts on this one and you were proven right."'

'The least you were owed was a fair focks.'

'You'd think so, wouldn't you?'

'A simple fair focks.'

'But no.'

'Dude, I used to watch the way Lauren treated you and I used to think – no offence – but a girl would need to be a hell of a lot better looking than Lauren for me to put up with the kind of shit she gave you. All the same, I have to admit, I had no idea how unhappy you were.'

'Ross, I'm an alcoholic.'

'Well, I'm still dubious about whether you're an *actual* alcoholic or whether you were just murder for the sauce.'

'Er, I was miserable in my marriage and I was using alcohol to *anaesthetize* myself from it?'

'Hey, I'm not judging you.'

I catch Mary's eye and order another pint. Jesus, I knocked that last one back in, like, three mouthfuls.

I'm there, 'Here's to freedom, Dude!'

And Christian goes, 'By the way, you owe her three grand for the damage to her cor.'

I end up seeing a massive, massive improvement in the Pres Bray goys over the course of the next few weeks.

For instance, my outhalf – we're talking Barry Austin – has stopped closing his eyes when striking the ball, which is an obvious plus. Johnny Rice is really putting his back into it at scrum-time and is storting to look like a half-decent hooker. And Steven Nagle – the famous Nailer – has stopped just focking the ball anywhere when it pops out of a ruck and has storted actually *passing* it?

I think he's genuinely shocked by how much distance and accuracy he's managing to put on the thing.

Overall, I would say I'm greatly encouraged by how much they've come on. The goys are enjoying their rugby and they're very much responding to my coaching methods. I'm not exactly shouting it from the rooftops, but I'm beginning to feel quietly *confident* about next week?

So – yeah, no – I'm sitting at the dinner table, drawing a few diagrams into my Rugby Tactics Book, just ways in which I think we could genuinely hurt Blackrock, utilizing *our* strengths against *their* hopefully weaknesses.

'Ross,' Sorcha goes, 'we're supposed to be having dinner,' because I'm like Dustin Hoffman in *Rain Man* here, lost in my own little world.

I'm like, 'Dinner?' suddenly snapping out of it.

It's couscous, in case you're wondering, with mashed cauliflower, saffron and crispy shallots.

I'm there, 'Yeah, no, that's a joke. And by the way, I forgot to thank you, Honor, for ringing Kielys and telling Mary not to serve me a burger.'

Sorcha goes, 'Oh my God, Ross, what is it about a thirteen-year-old girl caring about the planet that you find so triggering?'

I'm there, 'She rang The Bridge as well, Sorcha – and poor Dave Kearney happened to answer the phone. He sent me a text telling me that my daughter gave him a serious bollocking and there'd be no more pulled pork flatbreads for me. The entire staff got a memo.'

Honor refuses to get into it with me. She just goes, 'Oh my God, Mom, that book Fionn gave me is, like, *so* good.'

I'm there, 'You better not let it out of your sight, because I'll put it straight in the focking bin, just like I do *all* books that I find lying around that aren't about rugby.'

'Did you know,' she goes, 'that ninety per cent of cor journeys are less than a single mile in length?'

Sorcha's there, 'Oh! My God! Are you *actually* serious?' although I'm not as easily impressed as my wife.

I'm there, 'What does that even prove?'

'It proves,' Sorcha goes, 'that we are more reliant on our cors than we need to be!'

This coming from the girl who drives down to the front gate to collect the post if she doesn't want to get her Uggs wet.

I could mention it, but I decide not to go there.

'Plus,' Honor goes, 'two out of every three cor journeys involve a single occupant.'

Sorcha's there, 'Are you listening to this, Ross. That's, like, oh my God!'

I'm like, 'Yeah, this coming from the girl who drives down to the front gate to collect the post if she doesn't want to get her Uggs wet?'

Fock it, I decided to go there after all.

'Yeah,' she goes, 'this coming from a man whose dad thinks he should be the next Taoiseach, even though he's on the record as saying that global warming is a hoax?'

Honor's there, 'I was telling Sincerity and Currer Bell that we need to come up with an idea that just, like, focuses everyone's attention on climate justice – and gets people to change their everyday behaviour.'

'What about making an amazing, amazing speech,' Sorcha goes, 'at assembly, including some of those statistics you just quoted. I could help you with it. I could also show you some of the speeches I made on the subject during my time in the Seanad.'

Johnny stands up from the table, having cleaned his plate. Him and his brothers are letting me down in a major way, by the way, eating everything that's put in front of them with no complaints.

Sorcha goes, 'Johnny, come back to the table. We're going to have some dairy- and egg-free ice cream with foraged berries.'

Except Johnny doesn't seem to *hear* her? He keeps walking, then for no apparent reason he veers to the left, bumps into the wall and hits the deck.

Sorcha screams and we're both straight up off our chairs and across the kitchen to make sure he's okay.

'Focking dope!' Leo goes. 'Focking dopey prick!'

I pick him up and I'm like, 'What the fock is going on? Jesus, was he at the booze again?' because he's turning out to be a bigger pisshead than his grandmother. 'Who the fock is giving our son alcohol?'

Honor goes, 'Don't look at *me*!'

I'm there, 'I didn't look at you.'

I did look at her, but it was, like, an *unconscious* thing?

'What,' she goes, 'just because I gave Rihanna-Brogan cigarettes, that makes me the number one suspect when Johnny turns up pissed at the dinner table?'

Sorcha's there, 'Of course not, Honor – no one's saying that.'

I'm there, 'Honor, will you stay here and mind these two while we go and get your brother pumped out.'

But that's when Sorcha goes, 'Oh my God, Ross, I don't think he's even drunk,' and – *weirdly*? – that's when she storts to sound really worried.

I'm like, 'Check out his eyes, Sorcha. I recognize that look – it's my old dear in every photograph from my childhood.'

Sorcha sniffs his breath, then goes, 'Ross, it's definitely not alcohol,' her voice quivering. 'Honor, will you babysit while we take Johnny to the Swiftcare Clinic? Fionn will be home soon with Hillary.'

Honor's like, 'Whatever.'

So a few minutes later, we're in the cor with me at the wheel and we're heading for – like she said – Balally. Sorcha is, like, panicking now in a big-time way.

She's going, 'Oh my God, what's wrong with him? Oh my God, Ross, what's wrong with our son?'

I'm there, 'I'm just thinking, if it's not drink, then it might hopefully be that he's storving. Maybe they'll tell us to stop acting the dick and stort eating properly again as a family.'

Eventually, we reach Balally. I throw the cor into a porking space out front, then up the steps we chorge, me carrying little Johnny in my orms and Sorcha behind me, becoming more and *more* frantic?

She's going, 'Oh my God, Ross, what if it's, like, meningitis?'

And I'm there, 'Let's just hope it's the drink, Sorcha. Or – like I said – malnutrition.'

Which admittedly sounds possibly weird to the woman sitting behind the reception desk. We give her our details and we end up being seen pretty quickly, first by a nurse and then by some doctor dude, who checks him over fully, then asks us if Johnny has a history of fainting.

I'm there, 'Yeah, no, he collapsed at a porty in Finglas a few weeks back. And then, a couple of weeks ago, the exact same thing happened at another porty in – I'm not sure if it's relevant – but *Booterstown*? I probably should mention that we've recently become vegans. Is that something you'd recommend or do you think it's utterly focking ridiculous?'

He decides to just ignore this question. He goes, 'Your son has a build-up of fluid in the middle ear.'

Sorcha just nods, so it's down to me to ask the obvious question. I'm like, 'How can he have a *middle* ear when he's only got two of the focking things?'

He goes, 'What I mean is the *inner* ear.'

'Maybe you should try saying that, then.'

Jesus, I'm wondering is this dude even qualified? And why is he so quick to rule out the giving-up-meat-and-dairy angle? Unless he's a vegan himself.

'That's what's affecting his balance,' he goes. 'Have you noticed any evidence of hearing impairment?'

I'm there, 'He does fock-all that we tell him to do. But it's the same with his brothers. We just put that down to them being, I don't know, little shits.'

'Doctor,' Sorcha goes, 'are you saying that our son is, like, deaf?'

The dude's like, 'Not deaf. But I would be surprised if his hearing isn't compromised in some way. He's got quite a lot of fluid in there.'

'Oh! My God!'

'Look, it's nothing to get upset about. It's a relatively simple problem to fix.'

Sorcha's like, 'Thank God! Thank God!' and she kisses him on the top of the head – Johnny, I mean, not the doctor. That'd be weird.

'I'm sure it's a huge relief to you,' the doctor goes. 'I'm going to give you a prescription for something that will help him in the short term. But you do need to get something done about it because it *will* keep filling up and becoming infected. I'd recommend that you take him to see a specialist in the Eye and Ear Hospital. It's quite likely that he'll have to have grommets fitted.'

I chuckle to myself.

Sorcha goes, 'Grommets?'

And the doctor's there, 'Yes, they're tiny plastic tubes, small enough to fit on the tip on your finger. Is something funny, Mr O'Carroll-Kelly?'

I'm like, 'Yeah, no, it's just the name. I'm thinking of that dog who reads the newspaper! Anyway, continue.'

'It's a simple enough procedure,' he goes. 'Actually, my son had it done recently and it was hugely successful. It involves cutting a small slit in the eardrums –'

I'm there, 'Okay, I've heard enough! I can't listen to any more. I'll vom.'

Sorcha thanks the doctor dude and we walk out of there.

As we're sitting in the phormacy, waiting for his prescription, Johnny spots a life-sized cordboard cut-out of Garry Ringrose, advertising Gillette's new Fusion5 ProGlide Razor with FlexBall

Technology, with – fair focks – a precision *trimmer* on the back? He takes one look at it and he goes, 'Rugby!'

And me and Sorcha both smile at each other. It's definitely a relief to know that our five-year-old son isn't a drunk. But what I don't realize at that stage is that it's actually worse.

A lot worse.

Someone Someone or Other from the *Bray People* rings – a woman, believe it or not – and she says she's doing a piece about the famous Blackrock College coming to Bray to take on Pres this Friday.

She goes, 'Can I just ask you, what's your hope for the match, like?'

I'm there, 'My *hope* for the match? Let me tell you something – hope is for losers! Hope is for teams who go into a match without a game plan!'

I give the players a big wink. Yeah, no, I should mention that I'm standing in the dressing room and it's, like, after training.

She goes, 'You're not saying you think Pres can win, are you?'

I'm there, 'Yes, I'm saying I think Pres can win.'

I watch Dougie and Lenny and Barry and Nailer and one or two others exchange looks. It's the first time they've heard me say. We can beat Blackrock College. And it's like hearing me say it to someone outside the group makes them suddenly believe that it might *actually* be true?

Ricey goes, 'He definitely thinks we can beat them – otherwise, he wouldn't be telling the papers, like.'

The woman on the phone goes, 'Is this *on* the record?'

I'm there, 'On the record, off the record – any way you want it, Baby.'

'Er, okay.'

'You sound definitely dubious.'

'It's just, it's Blackrock College, like.'

'They're just another rugby team. That's what I've been drilling into the goys here.'

'They call them the Dream Team, like.'

'Well, maybe *we're* going to be their Worst Nightmare!'

The goys all laugh. They're pumped for this match. I wish we could actually play it right now.

'Well, win, lose or draw,' the woman goes, 'it's exciting for the people of Bray to know that these rugby players from Blackrock will be walking our streets, shopping in our shops and eating in our restaurants.'

They certainly won't be eating in your restaurants. The fockers have a sushi chef who travels with them everywhere they go. I don't mention it, though, because I don't want to dampen her enthusiasm.

I'm there, 'Anyway, I have to go. I need a moment with my players,' and I hang up on her.

The goys are suddenly standing a few inches taller for having heard me talk them up like that.

Little Nailer goes, 'Do you really think we can win, like?'

And I'm like, 'I'm not in the habit of lying.'

Which is horse shit, of course. I lie all the time. But not on this occasion.

I'm there, 'I've seen an unbelievable change in you goys over the course of the last few weeks. Stick to the game plan and – trust me – we can win. It's going to involve defending like our lives depend on it and taking the opportunities when they arise. Which they will. Blackrock's main weakness – aport from being a pretty average school – has always been over-confidence. They will cough up chances.'

They all nod.

I'm there, 'Remember what I told you. When you're tackling, get there a split-second before the player in possession is expecting the contact. Their game has always relied on getting a decent rhythm going to their passing. Put them off their stroke and they stort making all sorts of mistakes.'

I'm looking at the – I'm going to use the word – *awe* on their faces and I'm thinking, this is what I was born to do. I honestly wish Joe Schmidt could see me now, given that he was the one who persuaded me to take the job in the first place.

'So what happens tomorrow, Boss Man?' either Dougie or Lenny goes. 'Are we training, like?'

And I'm there, 'No, you've enough hord work banked now. I want you to chill for a couple of days. Maybe hit the gym if you think you need to. But mostly, I want you to rest up and think in terms of the game plan we discussed,' and I wave the Tactics Book at them. 'And I'll see you all on Friday!'

A chorus storts up of 'We are Pres! We are Pres! We are Pres!' and I walk out of there feeling as confident about this match as I've ever felt about anything.

And you can only imagine how confident that is.

A letter has arrived. From the Eye and Ear Hospital.

'They've had a cancellation,' Sorcha goes. 'They can take Johnny on Friday after lunch.'

I'm like, 'Friday after lunch? Er, we're playing *Blackrock* on Friday after lunch?'

'You don't have to actually be there, Ross.'

'I *want* to be there. Our son is going under the knife.'

'It's hordly under the knife. It's a very simple procedure. I told you what the consultant said to me on the phone. He does, like, fifteen to twenty of these things a week.'

I'm there, 'I feel like I'm letting him down by *not* being there? What if something goes wrong?'

She's like, 'Nothing is going to go wrong.'

She makes me that promise. Then she combs Johnny's hair with her hand and goes, 'Are you going to be a brave little boy while your daddy's at his rugby match?'

'Fock off!' he goes.

And his little face when he says it – it'd nearly break your hort.

That's when, suddenly out of nowhere, the house phone rings. I look at Sorcha – only because *she* usually does all the phone-answering in this house.

But she goes, 'Will you get that, Ross?'

I'm like, 'Er, okay,' because I don't want to be accused of being sexist.

I pick it up and I hold it to my ear like it's a new invention and I'm trying it out for the first time.

I'm there, 'Hello?'

'This is Sister Consuelo from Mount Anville,' the voice on the other end of the line goes. Except it's not the happy-clappy Sister Consuelo that we met the last time we were at the school. Her voice sounds all cold and businesslike. 'I'd like to speak with Ross or Sorcha, please.'

I'm like, 'Hey, Sister Consuelo – you've got Ross.'

I see a look of worry cross Sorcha's face. She mouths the words, 'What's happened?' and I end up asking Sister Consuelo the exact same question.

I'm like, 'What's happened? Is there something wrong?'

'Yes,' she goes. 'You need to come to the school immediately.'

I'm there, 'What, again?'

Sorcha's just arrived home from dropping Honor off. I'm wondering what the fock she could have done in that time.

I'm like, 'What's she done? Is it bad?'

Sorcha puts her hand over her mouth. 'Oh! My God!' she goes.

Sister Consuelo's there, 'That all depends on your definition of the word.'

'As in, has she killed someone?' I go.

She's like, 'No, she hasn't killed someone.'

I cover the mouthpiece and I'm like, 'She hasn't killed someone, Sorcha,' sounding surprisingly relieved.

Sorcha goes, 'What's she done, Ross? Find out!'

I'm there, 'We'd really like a bit more information before we drive all the way back to the school, Sister Consuelo. I'm thinking about the environment here.'

And Sister Consuelo goes, 'She's placed a barricade on the school cor pork.'

I pass this information on to my wife in a by-the-by sort of way. I'm there, 'She's apparently placed a barricade on the school cor pork.'

Sorcha goes, 'She's what?'

I'm like, 'That's what the woman said, Sorcha. Word for word.'

Sister Consuelo goes, 'Come to the school! Now!' and she just hangs up.

'Oh! My God!' is all Sorcha can say as we load the boys plus Hillary into the back of the cor and set off for Goatstown again. 'Oh! My! God!'

As we're passing The Galloper, just before Stillorgan, she goes, 'Okay, it makes total sense now why she asked me to drop her to school half an hour early this morning. She said there was some, I don't know, project that she was working on with some of the other girls. This must be some kind of protest against parents driving their children to school in single-occupancy vehicles.'

From the way she says it, it's obvious she hasn't made her mind up yet whether to be happy or angry about this. I suppose she'll need to see it for herself and take the temperature of the crowd.

I'm there, 'I blame Fionn for this.'

She's like, 'Fionn?'

'Er, who was it who gave her that book and filled her head with all that bullshit about unnecessary cor journeys?'

'Ross, just drive, okay?'

So I lean on the accelerator and pretty soon we're turning up Trees Road Lower. About half a mile from the school, the traffic suddenly grinds to a halt and people are, like, leaning on their cor horns in an angry way, or they're getting out of their SUVs and asking what the fock is going on.

'Come on,' Sorcha goes, taking off her seatbelt and opening the door. 'We'll walk the rest of the way.'

So we abandon the cor on the side of the road and we take the kids out of the back. I put the boys on their leash and Sorcha puts Hillary into his stroller and we stort making our way towards the school.

The closer we get, the angrier people seem to be – especially the moms. They're standing beside their cors, with their orms folded, and they're saying that it's a disgrace – an *absolute* disgrace – and I hear one or two go, 'This isn't the kind of thing you associate with a school like Mount Anville!' and 'I blame the parents!'

We push our way through the throngs of people, with Leo going, 'Get the fock out of the way, you ugly focking bitches!' which definitely helps to clear a path.

We eventually reach the school.

Honor and about ten other girls from her class – I recognize Sincerity Matthews, Currer Bell Whelehan and Sally-Anne Morkey – are holding hands and they've formed, like, a human chain across the entrance to the school.

'Oh! My! God!' Sorcha goes – because she's suddenly made up her mind how she feels about it. She just bursts into tears – except they're tears of, like, *pride*?

I'm like, 'What the fock are you doing, Honor?'

And Honor goes, 'What does it look like? We're protesting! Hi, boys!' and she smiles at her brothers.

The goys are like, 'Honor! It's focking Honor, look!'

'Protesting?' I go. 'Protesting against what?'

Honor's there, 'Against parents driving their children to school when they could just as easily get public transport.'

The crowd don't love that. They're going, 'Public transport? Did she just say public transport?'

I'm like, 'Er, you get driven to school every day – in either my A8 or your old dear's Toyota Seqouia.'

'Not any more,' Honor goes. 'From now on, I'm going to be getting the bus.'

'The bus? Honor, you're talking like a crazy person.'

'I'm not. I'm going to get the 59 from Killiney to Dún Laoghaire, then the 75 to Goatstown and walk the rest of the way.'

Jesus Christ.

I'm like, 'Honor, what kind of parents would we be if we allowed our daughter to use public transport?'

She has an answer for everything, of course. She goes, 'The kind of parents who care about the planet they're leaving for the next generation.'

Sincerity – who Honor used to hate, although now they seem to be bezzies – goes, 'There are, like, nine hundred students in this school, Mr O'Carroll-Kelly. Seven hundred of them are dropped off each morning by cor. In the vast majority of cases, they are the only passenger. In terms of corbon emissions, that's like, Oh! My God!'

I hear someone clapping behind me. I turn around and it ends up being Sincerity's old dear, Roz. Who I've ridden. Not that it's relevant to the story. I'm just providing a bit of background colour.

'Well said, Sincerity!' the woman goes. 'Well said!'

Of course, Sorcha isn't going to let Roz or anyone else beat her in terms of being proud of her daughter's efforts on behalf of the environment. She storts clapping even louder, going, 'Good for you, Honor! Standing up for something you genuinely believe in!'

It would be fair to say that we are very much in the minority, though. One of the other mothers – who I think looks like Lucy Mecklenburgh – walks over to the girls and goes, 'Okay, you've made your point – now get out of the focking way!'

Sincerity's there, 'No – this cor pork is closed. And it's going to, like, *remain* closed?'

'I haven't got time for this. I have an appointment in the Merrion Face Clinic in forty minutes' time. My daughter wishes to go to school.'

Honor's there, 'We're not stopping her from going to school. We're stopping you from driving her there.'

She turns on me then, this woman. She goes, 'Is one of these girls yours?'

And I'm there, 'Yeah, no, the mouthy one.'

She goes, 'Well, if you were any type of parent, you'd tell her to step aside and let us into the cor pork.'

I'm actually about to tell Honor that she's made her point and maybe she should think about going to class. But that's when she goes, 'We can't move – we've Superglued our hands together!'

They all lift their orms and – true enough – they do all seem to be stuck together.

'I'm *so* proud of you, Honor!' Sorcha shouts, obviously wanting to get one over on Roz, because she knows about *our* whole history? 'So, so proud, Honor!'

But then Sister Consuelo suddenly appears on the scene. And Sorcha, I notice, definitely quietens down a bit, obviously keen to see how it's going to play out.

The woman who looks like Lucy Mecklenburgh goes, 'Sister Consuelo, are you going to do something about this? We don't pay your fees for our children to have to walk the final hundred yords to school. Do something or I shall be forced to call the Gords – or move my daughter to Alexandra College or Teresians.'

That gets a roar of approval from the crowd, who are becoming seriously, seriously restless now. They must all have botox appointments as well.

Sister Consuelo goes, 'Yes, I'm going to do something,' and there end up being shouts of 'About time!' and 'How dare they inconvenience us like this?'

But you should hear the silence that falls when Sister Consuelo goes, 'I'm going to let the girls have their way. Because they're absolutely right in what they're saying. Your children *should* be using public transport. So, from this day onwards, the Mount Anville cor pork . . . is officially closed.'

This is the moment. That's what I'm telling the goys.

I'm like, 'This is the moment to lay down a morker.'

'A what?' Nailer goes.

I'm there, 'A morker.'

They all just look at each other – our old friend, the language barrier, again.

Nailer goes, 'I'm still not getting it, like.'

'Okay,' I go, 'I'll put it to you another way – this is the moment to send out a message! To the rest of the teams in the Leinster Schools Senior Cup! To the people who think that the Pres Brays of this world are there just to make up the numbers! This is your chance to set tongues wagging! This is your opportunity to let the world know that Pres have got a team this year! This is your chance to make people fear Bray – not for the usual reasons, but for rugby reasons!'

Hey, I'll hold my hands up – it's not the greatest speech ever made. It's not like one of Father Fehily's. But I'm still expecting a bigger response than the one I end up getting. There's, like, no cheers and no even *excitement*? It's like they're, I don't know, flat.

I turn to Barry, who I've made my captain, because I've always believed that outhalves make the best leaders. I'm there, 'Do *you* want to say something, Barry?'

But he just shrugs and goes, 'Not really, like.'

I can't believe what I'm hearing – or rather what I'm *not* hearing?

I'm there, 'There's nothing you want to say to your teammates in terms of, like, motivating them?'

He looks around the dressing room and goes, 'Will we say a prayer, like?'

I go, 'A prayer?'

But before I can say another word, he goes, 'Hail Mary, full of grace . . .' and leads his teammates into – I shit you not – a decade of the Rosary.

At the end of it, they all stand up. Except for Johnny Rice. Because Ricey is asleep. I swear to fock, we're about to go out to face Blackrock College and my hooker is snoring away in the corner. I end up having to shake him awake – he's a very heavy sleeper – while the others slope out of the dressing room.

I'm going, 'Ricey! Ricey! Come on, wake the fock up!'

He opens his eyes, looks around the empty room and goes, 'Is it over?'

And I'm like, 'No, we haven't played the match yet, Ricey. Come on, Dude, stand up.'

He slowly gets to his feet, then I follow him and the rest of the goys outside. There's, like, twenty or thirty people here to watch the match – we're talking mostly locals – and they're all just staring open-mouthed at the Blackrock goys like they're strangers from some exotic land, which, to them, I suppose they are.

Even our players just stand there and watch them do their pre-match drills and stretches like they're looking at some, I don't know, voodoo ceremony. They don't bother warming up themselves, although two or three of them, I notice, have a final, pre-match smoke.

Brother Ciaran sidles up to me on the sideline. He goes, 'It's been a long time since I've seen a crowd like this at one of our matches.'

Seriously, we're talking thirty people – tops.

He goes, 'There's clearly a buzz building about this team!'

Well, if it's true, it doesn't last long. We end up making sure of that.

The referee blows the whistle to stort the match. The Rock out-half kicks the ball high into the air. Our full-back, this unbelievably laidback dude named Conal Crommie, watches it fall from the sky. And that's when I notice – I'm not making this up – the focker still has a fag in his mouth.

He drops the ball – but not his cigarette, funnily enough – and that basically sets the tone for what follows.

It would serve no real purpose to describe the actual events of the match in detail, other than to say that Blackrock end up running in fourteen tries without even breaking a sweat. And pretty much the entire crowd has drifted away by the time they break the magical one-hundred-point mork.

I'm, like, stealing sideways glances at Brother Ciaran, who's watching his team get ripped aport with this look of just, like, *bewilderment* on his face?

I'm on the sideline going, 'Come on, goys, let's try and get *something* on the board – and then we can stort building a score from there,' but I'm pissing into the wind talking to them.

The referee blows his whistle and the teams walk off the field. The dude shakes my hand and goes, 'Bad luck – you just came up against a better team on the day.'

I'm like, 'What the fock do you mean? It's only half-time!'

He actually laughs.

He's there, 'You're not going to play the second half, are you?'

I'm like, 'Why *wouldn't* we play the second half?'

'Why would you put them fellas through another forty minutes of that?'

'We can come back from this. Remember Leinster against Northampton?'

'But it's 110–0.'

'Dude, you are *not* abandoning this match. We're coming out for the second half. End of conversation.'

Unfortunately, the players have other ideas. When I walk into the dressing room, I notice that most of them are already changing back into their school uniforms.

I'm like, 'What the fock are you doing?'

Nailer looks up from tying his shoes and goes, 'We're not playing the second half, like.'

I'm there, 'Goys, I know Blackrock are probably better than any of us expected, but if you get one or two tries on the board –'

'We can't get the ball off them,' Barry Austin goes. 'They're laughing at us, like.'

It's true. They *were* laughing at them. Rock goys are dicks. I've been saying it since forever.

I'm there, 'Goys, let me tell you something about winners – they don't quit.'

And that's when they all end up *turning* on me?

'What do you care anyway?' either Lenny or Dougie says to me. 'You'll still get paid, like.'

I'm there, 'That's not why I'm doing this.'

They all laugh.

The same dude goes, 'There's only one reason you're doing this, Boss – and that's money. You don't care about Bray, like.'

I'm there, 'I do care about Bray,' except I don't manage to make it sound convincing. 'I care about Bray very much.'

He goes, 'You don't care about Bray and you don't about care us.'

I'm like, 'Wrong on both counts.'

'Okay, so you care about us?' he goes. 'What's my name?'

I'm there, 'It's either Dougie or Lenny. I can't tell you aport.'

He goes, 'And what's his name?' and he points at the tighthead. I go to look in my Rugby Tactics Book.

'Without looking at your stupid book,' either Dougie or Lenny goes.

I'm there, 'I don't know. I'm pretty sure it begins with a D. Or an R.'

'It's Lukie McDermott.'

'I was going to say, "Or an L."'

He just shakes his head at me. They *all* do, in fact? Then, one by one, they walk out, leaving me alone.

After five minutes, I walk out of the dressing room to find the place quiet and deserted. Even Brother Ciaran hasn't bothered hanging around. A newspaper blows past. A discorded copy of the

Bray People. There's a photograph of me back in the glory days. I'm pulling up my jersey and flashing the six in front of the Blackrock crowd. The headline says, 'Dream Team? Welcome to Your Biggest Nightmare!'

I'm thinking, could things get any worse? Of course, the answer to that question is always yes.

My phone rings. I whip it out of my pocket and I answer it without even checking who it is. I just presume it's Brother Ciaran, giving me my cords. Putting me out of my misery. And Bray's misery. Except it's not Brother Ciaran. It's Sorcha.

I'm there, 'Not a good time, Babes. We've just had the absolute shit kicked out of us. God, I hate Blackrock.'

'Ross,' she goes, 'I'm ringing from the Eye and Ear Hospital.'

Shit, I forgot that was happening today.

I'm there, 'Er – yeah, no – how did it go?'

Sorcha's like, 'The operation was a complete success! The doctor is very pleased! He's a brave boy, aren't you, Johnny?'

In the background, all I can hear is silence, except for the sound of my son going, 'Fock this shit!' in a really groggy voice. It's obvious that he's still feeling the effects of the anaesthetic and I'm wondering would they maybe give Sorcha some of that shit to go.

I'm there, 'So is that it? He's all fixed?'

She goes, 'Absolutely! He shouldn't have any more issues with his balance. Although –' and she lets it just hang there.

I'm there, 'Although? Although what, Sorcha?'

And that's when she says it – as calmly as you like. She's there, 'The doctor said he should refrain from any kind of rough exercise that might dislodge one or both of the grommets. Meaning he won't be able to play rugby, Ross.'

'Jesus Chirst!' I go. 'Is *that* what you call a successful operation?'

'The doctor said it's only a temporary measure,' she tries to go, 'until his eustachian tubes have storted working naturally.'

'How temporary is temporary, Sorcha?'

'At least a year, the doctor said. Although, more likely, eighteen months.'

'Eighteen months? Do you know how far behind he's going to be in terms of his development as a kicker? I can't believe you let them go ahead with the operation, knowing the risks!'

What I don't realize, of course, is that I haven't even heard the worst of it yet.

'You might as well know,' she goes, 'there's a possibility that Johnny might *always* have a problem with fluid in his inner ear? The doctor said that balance might go on being an issue right into adulthood.'

This is turning out to be the worst day of my life.

I'm there, 'Are you saying – Jesus focking Christ – he might never play rugby again?'

Sorcha – I swear to God – goes, 'There are *other* sports, you know?'

But I don't hear a single word of what gets said after that.

4.

Mother's Friend (With Benefits)

Confession time. I end up struggling with it. I'm talking about my son's – I'm going to have to use the word – *disability*?

Yeah, no, I'm in the kitchen, throwing the ball around with Brian and Leo, while Johnny just sits and watches, with a sad look on his face, from the safety of the Eggersmann free-standing island.

'Rugby,' he goes, his bottom lip quivering. 'Rugby, Daddy.'

And I'm there, 'Not for you, Johnny. Not for you any more.'

I'm ashamed to admit it, but I'm seeing him differently – now that I know he's probably never going to wear the number ten jersey for Ireland. Not even five years old. That's a very early age for a father to be told that the dream is over. My old man got to hold onto it until I was in my mid-thirties. I actually think there's a little bit of him that *still* believes it might happen?

My phone all of a sudden rings. It's Ronan. So I end up answering.

He goes, 'Rosser, how's things?'

I'm like, 'I'm bearing up, Ro. I'm bearing up.'

'Jaysus, yeah, the match was the utter day – how'd you get odden?'

'We got shat on from a height, Ro. I won't go into the details. Suffice to say that I'm going to be resigning first thing Monday morning.'

'That's fuddy. I nebber had you dowun as a quitter, Rosser.'

'Like I said, I won't go into the details. Anyway, I've got bigger things to worry about than teaching people from Bray how to play rugby. We got a bit of bad news yesterday – from the Eye and Ear Hospital.'

'I was talking to Hodor last neet – she said Johnny was arthur getting grobbets fitted in he's eeyores. The pooer little fedda.'

'She obviously didn't tell you the *full* story? Let's just say the operation did not go well.'

'Is he alreet, Rosser?'

'Are you sitting down?'

'Yeah, Ine in the libroddy. Ine stiddle boning up on me grand-da's case.'

'The doctor said he's not allowed to play any contact sports for the next eighteen months. And even beyond that, there's a chance that he's always going to have issues with his balance.'

'He's *badance*?'

'Yeah, his balance.'

'And *that's* yisser bad newuz?'

'He was *going* to be my kicker, Ro.'

'Fook's sake, Rosser, it's oately bleaten rubby – there's mower important things to be woodied about.'

'Such as?'

'Bleaten democracy, Rosser. This Roderdic Grainger sham is godda stitch Cheerlie up – udless I can prove that this inquidy he's caddying out is illegult.'

Sorcha suddenly sticks her head around the kitchen door. She goes, 'Ross, are you ready?'

I'm like, 'Ready? For what?'

'George Lee is on his way.'

'George Lee? Okay, the only George Lee *I* know is the dude on the RTÉ news.'

'Yeah, that's the George Lee I'm *talking* about? He'll be here in, like, five minutes.'

I tell Ro that I'll talk to him later, then I hang up.

I'm there, 'Sorry, am I missing something here? Why the fock is George Lee coming to my house?'

'He rang me the other day,' she goes. 'He wants to do a piece about Honor.'

'Are you telling me that our daughter getting the bus to school has made the actual news?'

'It's not *just* about her getting the bus to school. He heard about the Mount Anville Climate Justice Committee and the cor pork blockade. Ross, I explained all of this to you last night.'

'I was upset about Johnny, Sorcha. You could have been up all night riding Dan Cole and I wouldn't have noticed.'

'Well, he's going to interview Honor – and hopefully me, *as* the person who's been talking to her about environmental issues since the day she was, like, born – and then he's going to get some footage of her getting onto the number 59.'

Jesus.

The buzzer goes.

'Oh my God,' she goes, dialling the number to open the front gate, 'that'll be him! How does my tan look?'

The answer is, obviously fake. It's the middle of winter and she's as black as Beyoncé.

I'm there, 'Yeah, no, it looks real alright.'

She goes, 'Hurry up and get dressed.'

I go upstairs and I throw on my Leinster home jersey and a pair of classic beige chinos.

I meet Honor on the landing. I'm there, 'This must be exciting for you, is it?'

And she goes, 'Yeah, I'm not focking doing it to get on TV, Dad.'

We tip downstairs just as – yeah, no – *actual* George Lee knocks on the front door. Sorcha is out through it like she's woken up in the night with the corbon monoxide alorm going off.

'Oh my God,' she goes, 'it's, like, an honour to meet you!'

Sorcha always treats RTÉ celebs like they're royalty. She once spotted Bryan Dobson topping up his AdBlue in the Applegreen on the Stillorgan Road and she literally *curtsied* to him? Mind you, I'm a bit like that around Conor O'Shea. I once spilled cheesy nachos all over his lap when I found myself sitting next to him during *Fast & Furious 6* in Dundrum a few years ago. I'll never forget how understanding he was about the whole thing.

George is all, 'It's very nice to meet you, Senator Lalor. And you too, Honor.'

Honor's there, 'Hi,' not as easily won over as her old dear. 'So, like, what's going to happen here?'

George goes, 'Well, we just wanted to have a chat with you about, you know, the decision *by* Mount Anville to close the car park as a way to encourage more children to use public transport. And then we're interested in the, I suppose, more personal story of what inspired a little girl to think that she could make a difference?'

'Actually,' Sorcha goes, 'I suppose *I* was a major port of that, given that I've been talking to Honor about the challenges facing the planet since she was – oh my God – five years old. And when you look at some of the speeches I made in the Seanad –'

George cuts her off. He's there, 'It's, em, really Honor we'd like to hear from. I think people are sick of listening to adults talk about what we all *need* to do to save the planet and then doing absolutely nothing about it themselves.'

It's one hell of a slap-down for the woman who used to drive to the recycling centre in Ballyogan with three empty wine bottles in a Lexus LX570.

They mic Honor up while Sorcha reminds her yet again how proud she is of her. Then they stick her in front of the camera and George storts hitting her with questions. He's like, 'What inspired you to want to become involved in environmental advocacy?'

Honor goes, 'It was actually my dad!' which doesn't please Sorcha one little bit. She gives me an absolute filthy and goes, 'You?'

I'm there, 'I think she's talking in terms of me never being afraid to call it.'

Honor goes, 'My dad is always leaving the lights on when he walks out of a room and the taps dripping.'

Sorcha's delighted, of course. She goes, 'It's so true, Ross. You're actually the worst polluter *in* this family?'

Honor's there, 'I just lost it with him one day because I'd just been watching . . .'

She stops talking. Jesus Christ, I think she's about to burst into tears. She *does* burst into tears. She's suddenly crying her eyes out.

George goes, 'Take your time, Honor.'

Honor's there, 'I'd just been watching a video of this, like, polar bear? He was looking for food for his cubs. But because the ice cap had melted, there was nowhere for him to stop for an actual rest. And he drowned.'

Shit, I notice that even George has tears in his eyes.

'So it was the image of this polar bear drowning,' he goes, 'and then your father acting in a reckless way with regard to the Earth's precious resources that persuaded you to do something?'

She's there, 'We have, at most, three years to do something about our greenhouse gas emissions. Otherwise, the damage we're doing to the planet will be, like, *irreversible*? I was sick and tired of listening to grown-ups talking about the problem. I was thinking, it's not *their* future – it's, like, *our* future? So I thought, why are we waiting for *them* to do something about it? Why don't *we* do something ourselves?'

'And that's where the idea of blockading the Mount Anville car park came from?'

'We were doing, like, projects in school where we were learning about ways to reduce our impact on the health of the planet by, like, limiting waste and pollution. And then we were all being driven home in, like, SUVs. It was just, like, oh my God – *hypocrites* much? So a few of us First Years got together and we were like, "Er, there's an actual bus stop opposite the school. Why don't we just, like, Superglue our hands together and stop people using the cor pork?"'

'And how has it gone down with the other students – being forced to use public transport?'

'Not very well. But then I'm not one of the popular girls – people hate me anyway – which kind of makes me the *best* person to do this?'

Sorcha goes, 'People don't hate you, Honor.'

But they do. They really, really do. And they will even more when they hear what she ends up saying next.

'As, like, individuals,' she goes, 'we each have to take responsibility for our own corbon footprint. That means sitting down at the end of each day and asking ourselves, "Okay, did I really *need* to drive the cor today?" It's the same with taking unnecessary flights. Like, for instance, every year my school arranges this, like, skiing trip to, like, *Pinzolo*? Now, I don't want to be telling people what they should and shouldn't do. But I, myself, have decided *not* to go this year – in view of, like, the *climate* emergency?'

'Oh! My God!' Sorcha goes.

And I'm thinking, yeah, she could have focking told me that *before* I paid the three grand balance we owed.

George goes, 'We'd love to get some footage of you, Honor, getting on and off the bus – if that's okay?'

I'm there, 'I actually wouldn't mind seeing that myself,' because there's still a little bit of me that doesn't quite believe it, like when Johnny Sexton played for Racing, or when Cat Deeley married Patrick Kielty.

George goes, 'Before we do that, Honor, I have one last question for you. Your grandfather is, of course, *Charles* O'Carroll-Kelly, who may or may *not* be the next Taoiseach of this country. He is a well-known and unapologetic climate change denier. He's described the whole thing as a hoax. Do you have a message for him?'

Honor doesn't even flinch in the face of pressure. She just looks into the camera and goes, 'Granddad, I love you very much. But you're actually *wrong* about this? Climate change *is* actually happening. That's why us children have to do something about this crisis – because people like you are, like, *literally* killing us with your ignorance?'

Sorcha goes, 'Oh my God, Ross, our daughter is turning into, like, a spokesperson for her generation!'

I'm there, 'Hmmm.'

'I just hope the other Mount Anville moms and dads won't react badly to what she said about the skiing trip to Pinzolo.'

I'm there, 'Yeah, I'm sure they're going to be *very* understanding, Sorcha.'

The footage of Honor crying about the polar bear who drowned went viral within, like, an hour of the news ending. John Lewis are going to have to pull out all the stops if they're going to produce a Christmas ad that's more moving.

By nine o'clock on Saturday night, there was a campaign on

social media calling on Mount Anville to cancel its skiing trip in view of the climate emergency and #NoGoPinzolo has been trending on Twitter for, like, pretty much two days now.

But the old man is not a happy rabbit about being called out on national television by his own granddaughter. I'm listening to one of the nine voice messages he left on my phone after watching the news last night.

He's like, 'How *dare* that man try to come between me and my granddaughter! How *dare* he try to play us off against each other to try to undermine me politically!'

I don't bother my hole listening to any of the others.

I'm porked outside the school. It's, like, half four on a Monday afternoon and the place is totally deserted. Yeah, no, I waited on purpose until the school was closed because I didn't want to face any of the goys, having filled their heads with false hopes.

I find Brother Ciaran. He's, like, hobbling across the lobby on his stick. He looks weirdly pleased to see me.

'Ross!' he goes. 'I was going to call you later! Thought I'd give it a day or two to let the dust settle.'

I'm there, 'Dude, there's no need to sack me. I wouldn't want that on my CV. Which is why I've decided to resign.'

'Sack you?' he goes, like it was the, I don't know, *furtherest* thing from his mind? 'Why on Earth would I sack you?'

'Er, we got the actual shit kicked out of us by Blackrock College on Friday in case you weren't watching.'

'Well, it's like I said to the boys in assembly this morning – we'll be ready for them the next time!'

I reach into the inside pocket of my Helly Hansen and I whip out a folded-up sheet of A4 paper. I'm there, 'This is my letter of resignation. There's probably a few spelling mistakes in it. My daughter usually helps me with that kind of thing, but she's been kind of busy trying to save the planet.'

He takes the letter from me, except he doesn't bother reading it.

He goes, 'Richie Murphy said one thing you definitely *weren't* was a quitter.'

'That's just Richie being nice,' I go. 'Richie lined me up with a trial for Old Belvedere back in the day and I never bothered my hole showing up. Same when he tried to get me into Clontorf. I turned up for training twice – once hungover and once actually pissed.'

He just nods like he respects what I'm saying. He goes, 'The boys will be disappointed.'

I'm there, 'Dude, they don't even like me. They think I'm only coaching them for the money.'

He doesn't say shit. From his silence, I get the impression he thinks they may have a point. He's like, 'How did you get here today, Ross?'

'Audi,' I go. 'A8.'

'No, I mean, which way did you drive?'

'N11. Same as always.'

'You've never driven through the town at all?'

'No, the quickest way here – according to the satnav – is to take the N11, then the 768, then the 761, then whatever the road is called that the actual *school* is on?'

'Satnav?'

'Yeah, no, it comes as standard.'

'The 768 – as you call it – is called the Southern Cross Road.'

I'm like, 'Riiigggghhhttt?' wondering where the fock this is going.

'The 761 is called the Vevay Road.'

'Vevay? Okay, random.'

'And the road that the school is on,' he goes, 'is called the Putland Road.'

I'm there, 'Sorry, what is this, a Geography lesson?'

'Do you not see what I'm saying, Ross? Is it any wonder that the boys think you're only here for the money when you show such little interest in the town?'

'Are you saying I should care about what particular roads are called?'

'I'm saying the boys see you arrive for training in your big car, having taken the motorway to avoid driving through the town. And they see you going home the same way. Have you ever considered spending time in Bray?'

'Are you being serious?'

I must have some look of disgust on my face because he just smiles at me and doesn't bother pushing it. He goes, 'Come on!' and he storts making his way to the door using his stick.

I'm there, 'Where are we going?'

Except he doesn't answer me. He just goes, 'We'll take *your* car – since you seem so fond of it!' and he has a little chuckle to himself.

So I stort her up. Then a few seconds later, we're pulling out onto the – I think he said – *Putland* Road? As we reach the T-junction at the top of it, he goes, 'Head for the Main Street, Ross.'

Of course, I end up, I don't know, *hesitating* – because I literally have no idea whether it's, like, left or right, which seems to amuse him, as well as confirm everything he said.

He's there, 'It's a right turn, Ross.'

So – yeah, no – I turn right, then I follow the road down to Bray actual Main Street. I throw the cor into this, like, porking space on the way into the town. Then – I swear to fock – he goes, 'The church is this way,' and I follow him, thinking, I don't think actual *prayer* is the answer to Pres Bray's problems. Barry said a decade of the Rosary and got no answer.

But it ends up not being that at all. There's a giant Christmas tree in front of the church and it turns out they're about to switch on the lights, even though it's not even the second week in November. The Main Street has been closed off to traffic and there's, like, hundreds and hundreds of people crowding around in front of the thing.

I'm like, 'Jesus, you stort Christmas early out here, don't you?'

We make our way through the throngs of people, except he keeps getting stopped every few feet by past pupils, going, 'How-iya, Brother Ciaran?' and he's all, 'Hello, Patrick!' or he's all, 'Hello, Dave!' or he's all, 'Hello, Frank!' remembering – I shit you not – each and every one of them by name.

Thankfully, no one seems to recognize me and I pull my baseball cap down further, just in case I'm spotted.

'So this is Bray,' Brother Ciaran goes. 'Take a moment to look around you.'

So – yeah, no – I do. The first thing I notice is how – weird as it sounds – *happy* everyone seems? We're talking, like, *properly* happy. Not like in, say, Foxrock, where the only time anyone actually smiles, even at Christmas time, is to show off their new veneers or to express delight at someone else's misfortune.

The Lord Mayor of Bray steps up to the mic then. He's just some random dude wearing chains of office. They're kind of similar to the ones my old dear used to wear everywhere when she was the Lady Captain of Foxrock Golf Club – including in bed, I discovered one night when I walked in on her and the old man going at it like two prison releasees. It's a memory I've never been able to fully erase from my mind.

The dude says a few words about Bray having so much to be proud of, although I notice he avoids going into specifics. You can only shake that Katie Taylor tree so many times, I suppose. He flicks a switch and the tree lights up, as do all the lights on the Main Street. At the same time, everyone cheers.

There's, like, a Gospel choir on the steps of the church and they're singing 'Merry Christmas Everyone' by – I *think*? – Shakin' Stevens. The crowd storts suddenly joining in. And I can't help myself. Being a sucker for Christmas – even six weeks out – I end up joining in as well.

Brother Ciaran gives me a sideways glance and smiles to himself.

'You know, you laughed,' he goes, 'when I told you that I believed the people of Bray were the very finest people on God's Earth. Well, I didn't want you to walk away until you'd seen this. You've been coming to the school for weeks, Ross, but – be honest – you've never *been* to Bray. You can spend your whole life visiting places, but you'll never truly know a place until you get to know the people. Until you understand their hopes, their dreams – and, yes, their problems too, Ross.'

Jesus Christ, he's suddenly sounding like a Wicklow version of Father Fehily.

Some random dude storts handing out paper cups to everyone. He puts one in my hand and then some random woman pours Champagne into it. I knock it straight back, no questions asked.

And I don't know if it's Brother Ciaran's words of wisdom, or if it's the booze going to my head, or if it's seeing all these people being so strangely proud to come from Bray, or if it's simply Shakin' Stevens singing about love and understanding, but I'm suddenly overcome with this, I don't know, *feeling* for the place?

I turn around to Brother Ciaran and I hear myself go, 'That letter I gave you – scrunch it up and fock it in the bin, will you?'

And he just smiles at me and goes, 'I did that before we left the school.'

Oisinn says he heard the news and he's sorry.

I'm there, 'Yeah, no, thanks, Dude. I'm wondering now is Brian going to be my kicker? Or is it going to be Leo? It's a lot of pressure on young shoulders.'

He's like, 'What are you talking about?'

I'm there, 'I'm talking about Johnny's rugby career being over due to his ears being focked.'

'I was talking about Blackrock College beating Pres Bray.'

'Oh, that.'

'There was no need for them to go that hord on you. I mean, what are they looking to prove by scoring fourteen tries in the first half?'

'They're proving that they're dicks. But then we already knew that.'

'It was unnecessary is all I'm saying.'

'I wouldn't mind another crack at them. I would love it if we came up against them in the cup.'

This seems to genuinely surprise him.

He goes, 'So you're *not* resigning?'

I'm like, 'Why did you think I was resigning?'

'It's just that Fionn said you were driving out there the other day and you'd written out a letter of resignation.'

I spot Fionn coming back from the accreditation desk.

Yeah, no, we're at the Deportment of Housing, Planning and Local Government's Big Homelessness Think-In at the K Club, where JP and Christian are about to showcase the Vampire Bed in front of two thousand delegates from the worlds of business, sport and entertainment, as well as the non-profit and vulture-fund sectors.

He hands us our laminate passes and we hang them around our necks.

I'm there, 'Why are you putting the word around that I'm resigning as the coach of Pres Bray?'

He looks at me like *I'm* the one with the problem?

He's like, 'You *said* you were resigning. You said you were sold a pup and the players were all shit. You said you were going to threaten the school with legal action if they ever revealed that you coached them because you were scared that it would damage your chances of ever landing the Leinster job.'

'Well, I've changed my mind. So I'd appreciate it if you stopped spreading unfounded rumours about me.'

'Ross, I really don't care what you do or don't do.'

Oisinn and Magnus end up having to step in between us.

Magnus goes, 'Guysh, come on, we are shupposhed to be here for JP and Christian, remember?'

And Oisnn is like, 'Seriously, you two are going to have to sort your shit out. Come on, shake hands.'

I'm there, 'I'm not shaking his hand.'

And Fionn goes, 'Hey, I'm fine with that.'

'First you get my wife pregnant. Then you accuse my daughter of trying to murder your son and you pack her off to Australia. Then, suddenly, you're lending her books about the environment and trying to be her best mate.'

'I made a mistake, okay?'

'You made more than one.'

'And I'm trying to make amends.'

'Well, don't,' I go. 'Don't focking bother.'

Into the auditorium we go and we find our seats. The place is – like I said – rammers. We end up being bang on time because we're only sitting down for, like, sixty seconds when the dude who's, like, emceeing the event steps up to the mic and goes, 'Now, sometimes the best ideas are the simplest ideas. You hear them and you think,

"Why didn't someone come up with that before?" or even "Why didn't *I* come up with that before?" That's very much the case with our next presentation. *I'm* not going to tell you about it. I'm going to let them do that. Ladies and gentlemen, it's my pleasure to introduce JP Conroy and Christian Forde.'

Out onto the stage they walk, Christian pushing this famous bed of theirs – although it's not standing upright. It's actually lying flat. Everyone claps and we make sure to give them an extra loud cheer as well – just so they know that we're here.

'Thank you very much,' JP goes. He's wearing one of those, like, headset microphones. 'Thank you very much indeed. I'm JP Conroy, the inventor of the Vampire Bed, and this is Christian Forde, my Head of Morkeshing for the EMEA region. And we've come here today to tell you why *we* believe this simple invention can take Ireland's homelessness crisis – and turn it into Ireland's homelessness opportunity.'

He hands over to Christian then.

'Now,' he goes, 'some of you may have seen my colleague discuss this revolutionary idea on *The Late Late Show* earlier this year. Some of you may be aware that it *is* already available in selected retail stores, including Brown Thomas. The reason we've come here today is to talk to you about the role that vertical sleeping can play in changing the paradigm in relation to homelessness – and thus changing the conversation.'

'But first of all,' JP goes, 'what *is* homelessness? Well, as an estate agent by profession, I would define homelessness as the state of having nowhere to live. So what causes it? Well, there are many contributory factors, some of them very, very complex. So what's the solution? Well, that's not simple either, since every homeless person has his or her own reason for being homeless. Unless . . .'

He pauses for dramatic effect. He's actually very good on stage. I sometimes forget that he stole the show as the Mother Abbess in the production of *The Sound of Music* that we did with Muckross Pork College in Transition Year.

'. . . unless,' he goes, 'we stort to see the problem as one of basic human storage! Yes, as every estate agent knows, space in this country is at a premium, especially in urban areas, which is where most of our homeless people happen to be. Sadly, we have nowhere to put them. But this invention can help alleviate that problem. The Vampire Bed is based on a very simple principle that I'm going to demonstrate for you now.'

He lies down on the thing.

'When we sleep in a standing position,' he goes, then he nods at Christian, who presses the spring lever on the side of the bed, suddenly turning it upright, 'we take up exactly half the space as when we sleep lying down!'

It's a real *Hey presto!* moment. The audience claps.

'Now,' Christian goes, 'those of you who are seeing the Vampire Bed for the very first time may be thinking that this looks like an unnatural way to sleep. But this is to ignore the fact that humans – as *flight* rather than *fight* animals – are actually hordwired, genetically speaking, to sleep standing up. Believe it or not, horizontal sleeping is a relatively recent development in the timeline of human evolution. But is it comfortable? JP, I'll let you answer that question!'

Except JP has his eyes closed and he's pretending to be asleep. We all laugh. They're like a focking double act.

'Oh, look at that,' Christian goes, 'he's out for the count! So it looks like *I'm* going to have to explain it instead! Well, as you can see, the word "vertical" is a bit of a misnomer, since it stands at a slight angle. The footboard at the bottom there will ensure that the bed will bear your weight and you won't fall out! The mattress is made of memory foam and it has a pillow that's attached to the bed by Velcro and a duvet that buttons to the side. So the answer to my question is, yes, it's *very* comfortable. There are also a lorge number of health benefits – some of them scientifically proven – that come from sleeping in a standing position. These include improved vascular function, metabolic action and mental health.'

JP suddenly storts snoring. It's genuinely hilarious.

Christian's there, 'As my colleague here likes to say, one day we will look back at the time when we all slept on our backs and we'll think, "Oh my God – what a waste of space! What were we thinking?" Which brings us back to the subject of how the Vampire Bed can be used in the fight against homelessness.'

Christian gives the bed a shake and JP suddenly stops snoring and sort of, like, wakes with a jolt. The audience are all cracking their holes laughing.

Christian's there, 'Wake up, JP, it's time to talk to the nice people about homelessness!'

'Okay,' JP goes, throwing back the sheets, yawning and stepping off the bottom board, like it's all a major effort, 'although I wish you'd woken me sooner!'

They're like – what are they called – the Morx Brothers?

'As a society,' JP goes, suddenly changing his tone to serious, 'we may never solve the problems that *lead* to people becoming homeless. But, by storing the, let's just say, hord-of-housing in a more spatially efficient way, we *can* ensure that they take up a lot less space than they currently do. Right now, in Ireland, we have somewhere in the region of 10,000 homeless people – or, as we'll call them for the purposes of this presentation, *units*. A Vampire Bed, taking up no more than two-point-five square metres of floor space, would allow us to accommodate all 10,000 units in a space no lorger than an average-sized aircraft hangar. So there you have it. A revolution in the way we sleep, ladies and gentlemen – which might just make the world a happier place for those people not fortunate enough to have a home.'

It goes down like you wouldn't believe. The goys end up getting a standing ovation, which is fully deserved. They're actually still buzzing off it when we meet them afterwards.

Yeah, no, we're in the break-out room, enjoying the refreshments, when the two goys walk in, all focking smiles.

JP's like, 'What did you think?'

Oisinn goes, 'What did we think? Goys, you absolutely owned it up there!'

I'm there, 'Can I just check – you were just *pretending* to be asleep, weren't you?'

'Yeah,' JP goes.

'Because I really loved that bit – especially when you storted snoring!'

I chest-bump both of them. There are times when nothing but a chest-bump will do.

Magnus goes, 'Hey, guysh, ash Rosh alwaysh shays, fair focksh to you.'

While we're all laughing at that – the accent is comical – this random dude tips over to us and goes, 'Sorry to interrupt.'

He looks vaguely familiar and there ends up being a reason for that. He tells us that his name is Éadbhard – spelt the Irish way – Ó Cuinneagáin and that he played for Wesley College back in the day.

Quick as a flash, I go, 'We won't hold that against you!' and we all crack our holes laughing – even him.

Oh, rugby.

He goes, 'I certainly remember this guy,' flicking his thumb at me. 'I mean, what a focking player!'

I'm there, 'I'm not sure I was *that* good,' subtly fishing for more.

'Are you shitting me? I remember seeing you for the first time and thinking, "There's the future Ireland number ten right there!"'

It's a lovely thing for me to hear. A pity he was focking wrong, of course.

'Anyway,' he goes, 'I just came over to say hi and tell you goys that I really enjoyed your presentation. I'm on the stage myself after lunch. I own a company – well, my dad owns it, although he's been taking more of a back-seat role ever since the whole Panama Papers thing – called Manila Capital. We're a property investment company – obviously, solutions-focused – and we work to identify, then fill infrastructural deficits in Ireland, post-crash.'

I love that kind of talk – even though I've no idea what the fock he's on about.

JP does, though. He has his Certificate in Morkeshing, bear in mind. He goes, 'I know who you are. I'm a big admirer of your business model.'

'Look, don't get me wrong,' this dude goes. 'Like I said, I loved what you did up there. And the homelessness thing – kudos, definite kudos. There's nothing wrong with coming across as caring. We used to do the sleep-out for homelessness every Christmas, even though I never lasted a full night. My point is that I think you need to be a bit more ambitious.'

'What do you mean?'

'Okay, you sell ten thousand beds to the Deportment of Housing, Planning and Local Government and that's homelessness solved. Where are your next ten thousand sales coming from?'

'Er . . .'

'Look, goys, forget the homeless for a minute. We have an accommodation crisis in this country – we're talking tens of thousands of people in their thirties, and even forties, still living at home with their mommies and daddies. Fine Gael have said they trust the morket to solve the problem. Well, congratulations, goys – vertical sleeping *is* that solution.'

Christian and JP just look at each other.

'Challenging centuries-old prejudices in favour of horizontal sleeping,' the dude goes, 'will allow us to redefine what actually constitutes a livable space. This bed of yours will allow developers to build smaller, and thus more affordable, accommodations. And that's why I wanted to talk to you goys – because we're trying to get something off the ground that I think would dovetail perfectly with what you goys are doing.'

JP's like, 'What is it?'

'Okay, I'll give you the pitch. The way we live our lives is changing dramatically. Agreed? Young people, in particular, are embracing more global, transient lifestyles. They're more focused on enjoying experiences. They want to be flexible. In other words, they certainly don't want to be enslaved by thirty years of mortgage debt. So we're trying to respond to this changing paradigm around home-ownership in Ireland – this, frankly, nineteenth-century idea that we all should aspire to own our own house, with our own sitting room and our own kitchen and X number of bedrooms. I mean, yawn! That's why we've come up with a brand-new concept in living. It's called the Homedrobe.'

Christian's there, 'The Homedrobe? Is that what it sounds like?'

'It's exactly what it sounds like,' the dude goes. 'It's a living space, but it's compact, ergonomic *and* functional. And if we can persuade the government to change the law relating to minimum aportment sizes, we believe that it's how young Irish people will choose to live in the future.'

'So it's basically a wardrobe?' Fionn goes, trying to piss on his parade.

The dude's like, 'Essentially, yes. But then you would also have access to communal living areas – kitchen, living room, utilities.'

'But you'd be sharing that space with strangers?' Fionn goes.

He's being rude and it's not appreciated.

'Hey, we all stort out as strangers,' Éadbhard – spelt the Irish way – goes. 'You've all seen *Friends*, right? Joey and Rachel and Chandler and Ross?'

We all nod. Sorcha has every episode on DVD.

Fionn's like, 'They didn't live in wardrobes, though.'

'Maybe they would have,' the dude goes, 'if they'd had vertical beds!'

It's a great comeback line, in fairness to him. He's a seriously, seriously impressive goy, and I'm not just saying that because he thinks I could have played rugby for Ireland if there was any justice in the world.

I'm there, 'The thing I always found unbelievable about *Friends* is that three dudes could live that close to Courtney Cox and, for five years, not one of them tried to ride her. Although one of them *was* her brother.'

No one says anything for ages. It's a real thinker, that one.

'Anyway,' the dude goes, handing JP and Christian his cord, 'it'd be great to hook up and chat some more.'

He gives us the guns and off he focks.

I'm eating a bowl of muesli that looks like it's been swept from the floor of a Dingle pub, minus the cigarette butts and the bookies' pencils. Although, in fairness, cigarette butts and bookies' pencils might actually improve the focking taste.

I look at Honor across the table. I'm like, 'This is a focking penance of a breakfast. I keep thinking, I wish that polar bear was still alive – just to see the trouble he's caused.'

'Well,' Sorcha goes, 'to quote George Lee, it's refreshing in this day and age to find young people who are so passionate about the future of the planet.'

I'm there, 'What about your vlog, Honor? You used to be passionate about that. We haven't done one of our famous unboxings in, like, months.'

'If you must know,' Honor goes, as coolly as you like, 'I've given it up.'

Sorcha goes, 'You've given up vlogging about fashion?' and now *she's* the one who sounds suddenly worried? 'Oh my God, Honor, you had, like, a massive, massive following.'

'The fashion industry is one of the biggest polluters on the planet, Mom.'

I laugh. I'm like, 'How do you like them apples, Sorcha? Now that she's turned on something that *you* actually love?'

Sorcha's there, 'Unlike you, Ross, I'm prepared to listen. Honor, is that true about the fashion industry being major polluters?'

'Er, *obvs*?' Honor goes. 'It's the fashion industry that encourages the idea that clothes have, like, a limited lifespan – and that trousers, shirts, coats, dresses and shoes should become waste items before they're actually worn out. I read this orticle online that said we all buy, like, fifteen times more clothes than we did fifty years ago.'

I laugh. I'm like, 'What's your answer to that, Sorcha?'

'My answer to that,' Sorcha goes, 'is that we should give our – what I like to call – *previously loved* clothes to charity shops or, like, vintage *clothing* stores?'

'But, Mom,' Honor goes, 'think of all the pollution that's caused by actually *making* all these clothes that we don't actually need. I'm talking factories – oh my God – belching hormful gasses into the air.'

I'm like, 'You should see your face, Sorcha.'

Honor goes, 'Here's the orticle here,' calling it up on her phone. 'It says that the fashion industry consumes more energy than the aviation and shipping industries *combined*? And – oh my God – wait till you hear what it says about water wastage. Okay, listen to this. The average water footprint of a kilo of cotton is between ten and twenty thousand litres. That's to make, like, one shirt and one pair of jeans.'

'Oh! My God!' Sorcha goes.

Honor's there, 'And most of the companies involved are massive overproducers. It says here that approximately seventy per cent of what they make is incinerated.'

'Contributing to corbon dioxide emissions,' Sorcha goes, shaking her head. 'Oh! My God, Honor!'

'And don't even get me started on online shopping,' Honor goes. 'There's another orticle I read about the environmental cost of, like, two-day *shipping*? It's like, Oh! My God!'

'Well, you have me convinced. I'm going to definitely cut back on the number of clothes I buy – especially online. I'm actually going to stort, like, *re-wearing* a lot more?'

Her phone suddenly beeps and she looks at it.

'Oh my God!' she goes.

I'm like, 'What now?'

'It's a message on the Mount Anville Moms WhatsApp group! Sister Consuelo has cancelled the skiing trip to Pinzolo!'

I look at Honor. She just shrugs her shoulders.

Sorcha goes, 'She says that, in light of the reaction on social media to the piece on the RTÉ news – and following a period of prayer and reflection – the school has decided that it can't afford to be tone-deaf to the public's concerns about greenhouse gas emissions. Accordingly, they've decided to cancel the trip.'

I'm there, 'Meaning, presumably, we'll get a full refund. Happy focking days.'

Sorcha gives Honor a sad smile. She goes, 'I know I shouldn't be, but in a way I'm kind of sad.'

Honor's like, 'Er, *why*?'

'The annual skiing trip to Pinzolo was always, like, a rite of passage for Mount Anville girls, Honor.'

'Mom, how can I lecture people about making unnecessary

cor journeys and then take a flight to Italy – er, *why*? To learn how to ski?'

'It's important to know how to ski, Honor. You don't want to become an adult and discover that you're the only one in your social circle who doesn't know how to ski. Ross, will you go and wake the boys?'

I'm there, 'Yeah, no problem.'

So I tip upstairs. I'm passing by Fionn's room and I decide to tell him that I thought he acted like a dick at the Homelessness Think-In yesterday, trying to run down that dude's Homedrobe idea and ruin things for JP and Christian. So I push the door and I stick my head around it. But I am not ready for the sight that greets me.

Fionn is lying on the bed with his trousers around his knees and he's – I'm trying to think of a nice way of saying it – pulling the *stomach* out of himself?

I actually scream. We're talking, like, a proper Hollywood scream – like Sorcha when she gets a fright at a horror movie, or sees my Google search history.

I'm like, 'Aaarrrggghhh!!!' and I back out of there, pulling the door behind me.

He tries to go, 'Ross!'

But I'm like, 'For fock's sake, Dude. Could you not lock the door?'

'There's no lock *on* the door.'

'I can't believe I've just walked in on you having a wank.'

'I wasn't . . . *doing* that.'

'Dude, I know what someone having a wank looks like. I boarded in Castlerock for a year, remember?'

'Ross, can you come in here for a minute?'

'No way! No *focking* way!'

'Ross, I wasn't having a wank! I was checking my testicles!'

I'm dubious. That was the excuse I always used whenever my old pair walked in on me when I was – I'm going to use the phrase – making mayo.

He goes, 'Ross, please. I want you to look at this and tell me what you think.'

I'm there, 'Could you not, I don't know, take a picture with your phone, then I'll look at it later with a few drinks on me?'

'Ross, I'm focking worried, okay?'

From his voice, it's obvious that he's more than worried – he's actually *scared*? And that ends up being the main reason – the only reason – I go back in there.

'Okay,' I go, walking slowly back into the room, 'I'm going to have a look at it for you.'

He's like, 'Not with your eyes closed, you're not.'

'Jesus, just give me a moment, will you? I'm going to have to build up to it.'

After about thirty seconds, I slowly open my eyes. Fionn is, like I said, lying on his bed with his trousers down and – there's no sugar-coating it – his dick in his hand.

I stort singing to myself – 'Get Lucky' by Daft Punk – just to try to, I don't know, *normalize* the situation?

'Could you just tell me,' he goes, 'is one of my testicles bigger than the other?'

So I'm suddenly staring at my friend's – I can't think of the right medical term, so I'll just say *ball* bag?

'The one on the left,' he goes, 'I think it's swollen.'

I'm there, 'Your left or my left.'

He goes, 'My left.'

I'm like, 'Okay, I'm bending down to get a better look at it now,' for some reason speaking my actions, like a man in a movie disorming a bomb. 'I'm looking at it now. I have taken note of its size. Okay, now I'm about to look at the other one.'

He moves the other one into my line of vision. It's actually hord to tell whether it's bigger than the other one or the same size, although I can't help but notice that the dude is pretty well-endowed. Not that I'm consciously looking at it and comparing it to mine. It's just something that it's impossible *not* to notice? Of course, there had to be some reason why Sorcha kept going there.

'Ross,' he goes, reminding me that there's a reason he's showing me his penis.

I'm there, 'Sorry, Dude. I was lost in thought there. To be honest, I can't actually say. If it *is* swollen, it's not that noticeable.'

He goes, 'Maybe if you felt them?'

I'm like, 'No way! Above and beyond, Dude! Above *and* beyond!'

He pulls up his trousers and goes, 'I suppose I should go to the hospital – to get it properly checked.'

I'm like, 'Definitely do that, Dude,' practically tearing the door off its hinges to get out of there.

'You embarrassed yourselves,' I go, 'and you also embarrassed me.'

The players are all standing around. I haven't even given them balls yet. Balls are for rugby players. That's what I said to them at the stort of the session. And I'm not even sure if they *are* that?

The mind games are definitely working because they can't even look me in the eye. They're all just staring at their feet.

I'm there, 'You didn't embarrass me by the way you played,' even though that's not strictly true – they really were shit. 'You embarrassed me by refusing to come out and play the second half.'

Ricey goes, 'We were getting beaten by a hundred points, like. It would have ended up being 200–0 or something.'

Jesus Christ, he's got a cigarette behind his ear.

I'm there, 'It doesn't matter if it ended up being 500–0. You never, *ever* throw in the towel.'

I decide to turn the heat up a further notch.

I'm there, 'Do you know what *we* used to say about Pres Bray – back in the day when I played for Castlerock?'

There's some serious shrugging of shoulders going on.

I'm there, 'We used to say, "Pres Bray? They're soft. At the very most, you'll get twenty minutes of passion out of them and then they'll collapse like a focked deckchair."'

I notice one or two of them exchange looks.

I'm there, 'As a matter of fact, I don't even remember training especially hord before we played Pres Bray. The attitude was always, hey, it's only Pres.'

They don't like what I'm saying to them. They don't like it one bit. Ricey takes the cigarette from behind his ear. I'm expecting him to ask anyone if they have a light. But he doesn't. He throws the cigarette away.

He goes, 'I hate that people are saying shit like that about us, like.'

I'm there, 'Well, why don't we try to change it? Look, I honestly don't know if you goys are capable of winning a Leinster Schools Senior Cup. I have my doubts. But here's what I do want. This is my ambition for this team – that after this year's competition, no one will ever say again that drawing Pres Bray is basically a bye into the next round. St Michael's might end up beating us next month – hey, they probably will. But they will know they were in a focking match.'

I love *me* when I'm like this.

I'm there, 'Goys, I know you have certain doubts about me. From one or two things that were said in the dressing room the last day, it's pretty obvious that you think the only reason I'm even here is for the money.'

Lukie McDermott, my tighthead, goes, 'Why else would you be doing it, like?'

'It's a fair enough question. But what if I told you that I don't want the money?'

Oh my God, you'd want to see their reaction. I haven't seen this many shocked faces since Christmas last year, when Leo walked into the live animal crib in front of the Mansion House, pulled down his trousers and took a shit in the hay.

I'm there, 'I'm being serious. I'll tell Brother Ciaran. Not a focking cent do I want. So what do you think, goys? I'm backing you. All my chips are on the table and I'm staking them on you. I'm all in. And what I'm asking is, are you prepared to back me?'

It's vintage Ross. I notice one or two nods.

I'm there, 'Because if you're not, I'll happily get back on that N11 and you'll never have to struggle to understand a single word of what I'm saying ever again. But if you *are* prepared to back me – and by backing me, I mean playing rugby the way I want you to play it, which includes all of you giving up smoking, especially on the pitch – then we can stort again. Day one. I'll go back to my cor, grab my Rugby Tactics Book and the journey can begin. So what's it to be?'

'We'll back you, like,' Barry, my captain, goes – no hesitation.

Then the others stort to follow. They're all saying the same thing:

'I'll back you – a hundred per cent, like.'

I empty a bag of balls onto the ground and I go, 'Okay, let's play some basic rugby.'

The goys are, like, warming up, when all of a sudden I hear my phone beep in my pocket, telling me that I've got, like, a text message. I whip it out and it ends being from Fionn. It's like, 'Can you talk?'

It's obviously not a good time for me, but I'm suddenly wondering is everything okay, and did he get to the bottom of the mystery of whether one of his nuts was bigger than the other?

I ring him back and I'm there, 'What's up?'

He's like, 'Hey,' and he sounds, I don't know, definitely worried.

I'm there, 'Dude, what's wrong?'

He goes, 'The doctor wants me to go for a biopsy.'

I'm like, 'Seriously? When?'

'Next week.'

'So you were right?'

'He said one of my testicles was definitely swollen. Jesus, why am I telling *you* this?'

'Because I'm your mate. Because we played rugby together.'

'I didn't know who else to tell.'

'So it's definitely, you know –'

'He said it could be nothing. That's why they need to biopsy it. They get a needle and they stick it in –'

I'm like, 'Jesus!' at the same time crossing my legs while standing up. 'Too much information, Dude.'

He's there, 'Sorry, Dude. It sounds sore, but it's a simple enough procedure. Do me a favour, will you? Don't say anything to Sorcha about it – for now anyway. I don't want to worry her.'

Ronan says this brings back a few memodies.

I'm like, 'A few what?'

He goes, 'Memodies, Rosser. Memodies.'

Ah, memories! Yeah, no, it certainly does. We're in the Lucky Dip Amusement Orcade on the seafront in Bray. Brian, Johnny and Leo are running amok, just like Ronan used to do in Dr Quirkey's Good Time Emporium on all those unsupervised access days we spent together. And poor Rihanna-Brogan is haring around after them, telling them to stop kicking the coin cascades to try to make the money drop – just like I did to her old man all those years ago.

'Hee-or,' he goes, 'did you hear me newuz?'

I'm like, 'Er, no – what news?'

'Thee caddent do it, Rosser!'

'What are you talking about?'

'Thee habn't the authoditty to do what they're arthur doing.'

While this conversation is taking place, by the way, the two of us are feeding cupfuls of coins into two slot machines that are standing back to back. When in Rome – blah, blah, blah.

I'm there, 'Who hasn't? What are you banging on about?'

He goes, 'Ine arthur reading evoddy Electoddle Act that was ebber passed in this countroddy, Rosser – and there's fook-all in addy of them about addy wooden habbon the power to investigate electshiddens. Accorton to the Electoddle Acts of 1992 and 1997, the retoordening officers are allowut to chaddenge specific electoddle offences in the High Cowurt. But there's fook-all in addy legislashidden gibbon them – or eeben the cleerk of Doddle Éirdeann – the power to chaddenge the integrity of the oaberall resudult. It's all boddicks, so it is.'

I'm there, 'Have you told my old man all of this?'

'Yeah,' he goes, 'him and Heddessy are going to the High Cowurt tomoddow to ast for a Judishiddle Review of wedder or not this bleaten Grainger sham has the authoditty to investigate the resudult of the edection. Cheerlie's godda be the Teashocked befower Christmas, Rosser.'

It sounds like *someone* is looking for a fair focks.

I'm there, 'And it's all down to you, Ro. It wouldn't have happened without you reading all that shit you read in the library.'

He's like, 'Thanks, Rosser. Hee-or, why did you waddant to meet out hee-or in addyhow?'

'It's just that Brother Ciaran reckons if I'm going to coach Pres, then I need to get to know Bray a little bit better.'

'Jaysus,' he goes – and *he's* from Finglas?

Poor Johnny arrives over to me. He's like, 'Bomper cors!'

I'm there, 'The bompers are closed during the winter, Johnny. And anyway you're not allowed to do anything that might dislodge those focking things from your ears.'

He goes, 'Me want focking bomper cors!' except even *louder* this time?

I'm there, 'We can't always have what we want, Johnny,' and I am *so* tempted to remind him that I wanted him to play outhalf for Leinster and Ireland one day – and look how *that* turned out.

'Fock you,' he goes, 'you focking fockwaffle!' and off he stomps.

Me and Ronan have a little chuckle to ourselves, then I hear *his* machine make the Ryanair bugle noise and stort spitting out one-yoyo coins – again. He always knows which machine is about to pay out – it's like he has a supernatural instinct for it. He scoops up his winnings and drops them into his cup.

He always knows when to walk away as well.

'Hee-or,' he goes, leaning against my machine, 'I saw Hodor on the Six Wooden news and she was getting on the bus.'

I'm there, 'You must think we're terrible parents.'

'No, you'd have to admoyer her, Rosser.'

'Would you?'

'Yeah, it's veddy brayuv of her, standing up and saying to the grown-ups, "Yisser arthur boddixing up the bleaten pladdit – now it's up to young woodens like meself to fix yisser bleaten mess."'

I don't think she put it *quite* like that. We don't pay six Ks a term for her to end up talking like Imelda focking May. But I take his point.

Rihanna-Brogan arrives over to us then. She goes, 'Rosser,' because I don't like her calling me Granddad, 'you probably should come and see what Johnny's after doing.'

I'm there, 'I've no real interest, Rihanna-Brogan. I've put about fifty focking snots into this machine and I'm not leaving it until it pays out.'

She goes, 'He's arthur switching on the bumpers cars, so he is.'

Of course, when I hear that, I end up having no choice but to leave my machine to go off to investigate. The second I walk away – I swear to fock – Ronan sticks a coin in the slot, presses a button and the thing storts machine-gunning out money. I wouldn't be surprised if the two of them planned it between them.

But no. Rihanna-Brogan leads me over to the bomper cors and – oh, holy fock – it turns out that she's telling the truth. Brian and Leo are sitting in two bomper cors and they're, like, flying around in them – as in, seriously, seriously flooring it. I look over to the little booth and Johnny is sitting inside. He's obviously found the button that switches the power on and now he's barricaded himself in.

Some tall, red-headed dude, who presumably works there, is trying to kick down the door, but Johnny has obviously wedged something against it. And there's another tall, red-headed dude who's chasing around after the cors, except he can't catch them. And then *they* end up chasing *him*. Brian tries to actually run him over and misses him by, like, inches.

And then, all of a sudden, I realize that I know the two dudes. It's, like, Dougie and Lenny.

Ronan appears beside me and he's watching the same scene. 'Moy Jaysus,' he goes. 'They're a bleaten hadden fuddle, ardent thee, Rosser?'

I'm there, 'They're that alright.'

Either Lenny or Dougie manages to finally kick down the door and switch off the power. Then he emerges from the booth, carrying Johnny by the straps of his little dungarees. Then, again, either Lenny or Dougie plucks the other two out of their cors by the straps of *their* dungarees and he carries them over towards us.

Brian is going, 'Put me down, you lanky, ginger prick!'

The two goys are about to ask me if these are my kids when they instantly recognize me. I can see that they're in, like, *shock*?

The one on the left goes, 'Howiya, Boss! What are *you* doing in Bray, like?'

I'm there, 'I told you I was going to be spending a lot more time out here, didn't I?'

Whoa! That rocks their world.

Leo's going, 'Let go of me! Let go of me, you prick with ears!'

I'm there, 'Ronan, this is Lenny and Dougie slash Dougie and Lenny – my two second rows. Goys, this is my son, Ronan, and that's my granddaughter, Rihanna-Brogan.'

Ronan goes, 'Alreet, feddas?'

And they're like, 'Er, howiya, Boss?' still thrown by this sudden turn of events.

I'm there, 'So, like, do you goys work here?'

The one on the right goes, 'Just weekends and Wednesday afternoons. Our dad *owns* the place, like.'

Funfair people. Nail. On. Head.

I'm there, 'Cool. Anyway, I'll see you after school on Tuesday. We've got a hell of a lot of work to do,' and I go to walk away.

The one on the right sort of, like, clears his throat, then goes, 'Er, are these your kids, like?' because they're still holding them like three bales of briquettes.

I'm there, 'Honestly, I have never seen those children before in my life.'

'You focking wanker,' Leo goes.

And I'm like, 'You're the focking wanker, Leo. Yes, they're my kids.'

Either Dougie or Lenny goes, 'You have to keep them under control, like,' and they let go of them.

I tell the two goys I'll see them next week at training and they fock off.

Keep them under control, I think to myself, yeah, no, that's easier said than –' and I suddenly stop. Because that's when I notice Leo's eyes. One of them looks a little bit turned in.

I'm like, 'Leo, are you doing that on purpose?' except he doesn't seem to know what I'm talking about.

He's just going, 'Me want focking bompers!'

I've noticed it once or twice before. It's something that seems to come and go, especially when he's tired.

I hold up my index finger and I go, 'Leo, look at my finger, will you? And keep looking at it!' and I move it from left to right and then back to left again.

Ronan goes, 'What's wrong, Rosser?'

And I'm like, 'Er, nothing,' not wanting to acknowledge it. The kid has wompy focking eyes – as in, one is going into the shop and the other is coming out with the change. 'It's just my imagination playing tricks on me.'

I'm sitting in front of the TV, scribbling down some of my inner-most thoughts into my Rugby Tactics Book while watching *Home and Away*.

All of a sudden, Sorcha appears in the living room, interrupting my train of thought and blocking my view of Ada Nicodemou.

She goes, 'Do you recognize this dress?'

I'm like, 'Er, should I?'

'It's the cream Gucci wool silk Web dress that I wore to the Mount Anville Networking Brunch last year. I'm taking on board what Honor said about the damage that the fashion industry is doing to the planet and I'm re-wearing a lot of pieces from my wardrobe. I wore this to the big opening this morning.'

'What big opening?'

'Wheat Bray Love!' she goes. 'It's Claire's first day in business, Ross! Oh my God, the place is ah-mazing! She got this local ortist – who's, like, Bray's answer to Banksy – to decorate the interior! And, by the way, there are *so* many options on the menu for vegans!'

'Is this the bit where I'm supposed to say, "Yay"?'

'But – oh my God – I have *the* biggest goss! Garret was there!'

'Garret? I didn't even know he was back in the country. The knob.'

'Claire didn't either. He surprised her by showing up – to support her! Isn't that so lovely, Ross? Wheat Bray Love was *their* dream, remember?'

'I'm welling up with tears here. So, what, that's them back together again, is it?'

'They've decided to be friends for now and take things slowly.'

'Friends. That's hilarious.'

'Lauren was there as well and she looks *so* amazing!'

'That's, er, good information for me to have.'

'I was telling her that it's time for self-care now. I was like, "You be you, Lauren!"'

'Fun times ahead, so.'

'You owe her three grand, by the way.'

'Excuse me?'

'For the damage you did to her cor.'

'She wouldn't have known that it was me only I told her. I'm sorry I opened my mouth now.'

'You also owe her four grand for Oliver's medical expenses.'

'Four grand?'

'He had to get his nose reset, Ross. In the Beacon.'

'I'm not paying for that. The kid pushed his luck once too often and he got the decking that was coming to him. It's a focking lesson learned. If anything, *I* should be billing *her*?'

'Seven grand, Ross. She wants it.'

It's at that exact moment that my phone all of a sudden rings. I look at the screen. I'm there, 'I have to take this, Sorcha. It's my old man.'

It *is* my old man. I'm not lying about that.

I'm there, 'It could be important.'

Sorcha takes the hint and leaves the room while I answer.

I'm like, 'What the fock do you want?'

'Ross!' he goes. 'Have you been following my Twitter feed this morning?'

'No, I've got better things to do. My question still stands – what do you want?'

'Hennessy has, this very morning, gone to the High Court to challenge the right of the State to withhold recognition of the election result! Furthermore, he has obtained an injunction, preventing your esteemed friend and mine, Mr Roderic Grainger SC, from continuing with his investigation until the court rules on the matter! *Extra territorium jus dicenti impune non paretur!* Full point, new paragraph! And none of it would have been possible without young Ronan!'

'I need seven grand.'

'Yes, of course! Pop by the house! I think there's something north of that figure in the safe!'

'I'll take whatever's there, then. I'm hanging up now.'

'Wait a moment, Kicker! I just wanted to ask you something!'

'As in?'

'Well, Hennessy and I are here in the famous Chancery Inn, having one or two drinks to celebrate the result! And, well, we got to wondering has Ronan given you any indication yet as to his career intentions when he completes his Law degree?'

'No – er, *why*?'

'It's just that advice he gave us *vis-à-vis* the Electoral Acts – he has a real flair for the law, Ross! Hennessy would be very interested in taking him on as his apprentice!'

I'm suddenly having a flashback to the month I spent on work experience in Hennessy's office when I was in, like, *transition* year? I remember one day leaning against the door for forty minutes while a member of the Criminal Assets Bureau tried to kick it down and Hennessy fed documents into the shredder, screaming, 'Stop focking blubbing and put your weight into it! One more bag! One more bag!'

I'm like, 'No!'

'No?' the old man goes.

'Yeah – as in, no focking way! Hennessy is a crook. I honestly can't think of a worse role model for my son.'

'Well, he *is* offering to put him through Blackhall Place, Ross! We can but ask him, I suppose!'

I'm there, 'You won't ask him!'

'But it's not really your decision to make, Ross!'

'Tell Hennessy to stay the fock away from him.'

'I'll, em, pass that on – although I'll probably paraphrase it!'

'Just make sure he knows. I don't want my son following in his footsteps.'

'I'll let him know your views on the matter!'

'Tell him to stay the fock away from him. Promise me.'

'I will! You have my word, Kicker!'

He hangs up on me.

So I end up – yeah, no – driving to Foxrock, just to grab the money from the safe while it's still fresh in my mind.

When I arrive at the gaff, it ends up being full of people. And when I say people, I mean all the old dear's mates from her various campaigns to stop things coming to Foxrock and put them instead in Ballybrack, Shankill or Sallynoggin.

They're all swilling Veuve Clicquot and there's enough Chanel No 5 in the air to get an entire country high.

Her mate Delma meets me in the hallway – although *intercepts* is probably *more* the word?

'Ross,' she goes, '*you* shouldn't be here.'

Here being the house I grew up in, by the way.

I'm there, 'Why the fock *shouldn't* I be here?'

She goes, 'We've thrown a surprise baby shower for Fionnuala,' and she actually tries to bor my way.

Delma used to be sort of, like, semi-attractive, in a short-haired, hot stepmom sort of way – JP had a major thing for her back in the day.

I'm like, 'A baby shower? The woman is focking seventy years old!'

'She still deserves a day of pampering,' she goes. 'And I don't want you upsetting her – not in her condition.'

Semi-attractive or not, I just brush past her, going, 'Yeah, get the fock out of the way, Delma.'

I head for the study. I take the old Jack B. Yeats down off the wall and I key the number into the safe. 2, 5, 0, 5. I open it, reach inside and stort grabbing bundles of fifties and stuffing them into my jacket.

And that's when I hear a voice behind me go, 'It is you!'

I end up nearly shitting my chinos. I turn around and it's Szidonia.

I'm there, 'You scared me.'

She goes, 'You say you do not know code.'

She's just, like, staring – not at me, but at the open safe behind me.

I'm there, 'I, er, guessed the number – just got lucky, I suppose.'

She goes, 'Give me passports.'

I look over my shoulder. I can see a little bundle of purple passports – looks about six – on the bottom shelf. Suddenly, Szidonia storts moving across the study towards me. She's quick on her feet for a woman who's very visibly pregnant now. But she's not quick enough. I manage to slam the safe shut just in time.

'Open safe!' she goes.

I'm there, 'Szidonia, I can't let you have your passports.'

'Give me passports.'

'Szidonia, no. You're carrying my old pair's babies. I can't let you run away. It would kill them.'

'Go!' she shouts, flicking her thumb in the direction of the door. 'Look at Fionnuala and tell me she is woman who is fit to have six babies! Go and see her now! This crazy lady!'

So I tip back out to the hallway. I can hear Michael Bublé singing 'I Just Haven't Met You Yet' and I follow the sound to the kitchen. Hord as it is, I'll do my best to describe the scene beyond the door.

The old dear is sitting on some kind of throne, while the very heavily pregnant Roxana is rubbing the soles of her feet with a pumice stone and the equally heavily pregnant Lidia II is dropping deep-fried oysters into her mouth like a bird feeding its chicks.

I feel like nearly throwing up.

'Hello, Ross!' the woman goes, trying to smile through a mouthful of mashed-up shellfish. 'Delma and the girls have thrown me a baby shower!'

She's got at least six fingers of gin inside her as well, judging by her eyes.

I'm there, 'Baby showers are for *pregnant* women. You're not even pregnant.'

I notice a humungous pile of presents, unopened, in the corner. I also notice that Lidia I is painting the old dear's fingernails blood-red.

'I am about to become a mother,' the old dear tries to go. 'If that's not something worth celebrating, Ross, then I don't know what is.'

Taffeta Tierney, one of the old dear's knob mates from the Move Funderland to the Northside Pressure Group, goes, 'Yes, we *were* in the middle of playing a game when *you* rudely interrupted,' talking to me, the focking dog.

The old dear goes, 'Oh, yes, let's get back to it, Taffeta! It's a wonderful game, Ross! Taffeta reads out a list of traits and I have to say whether I want the babies to inherit each one from me or from Chorles!'

Taffeta's like, 'Eyes, Fionnuala?'

'Oh,' the old dear goes, 'I definitely want them to have Chorles' dreamy, blue eyes – like pools you can just sink into. Ross got *my* eyes, unfortunately – dork and sneaky.'

Taffeta's there, 'Okay, what about IQ?'

The old dear laughs. She goes, 'Well, obviously I want them all to have Chorles' mind. I always said that if I had any more children, I'd want them to be intelligent this time around.'

I'm there, 'What the fock is that supposed to mean?'

'Oh, Ross,' she tries to go, 'stop being so sensitive.'

'I'm standing here while you're sitting there on your flabby orse listing all the things you hope these babies are going to be – and they just so happen to be all the things I'm *not*?'

Szidonia catches my eye across the the kitchen. She's got a real 'See what I'm talking about?' look on her face.

The old dear goes, 'It's a fun game, Ross – nothing more. I'll love these children however they turn out, just like I, em, loved you.'

'What was that pause for?'

'What pause? I didn't pause.'

'You did. You said you, *em*, loved me.'

'Look, I don't think I'm telling you anything new by admitting that I didn't enjoy motherhood the first time around. That's one of the reasons why I'm so determined to get it right this time.'

'Swallow those focking oysters, will you? I'm nearly getting sick here looking at you.'

'Ross, I don't understand where all this hostility is coming from!'

Of course, it *all* ends up spilling out then? I'm there, 'I'll tell you where it's coming from. Growing up, I would have – oh my God – *loved* a brother or sister? Just like Honor and Ronan and the triplets have each other. I had no one.'

Everyone is glued to this conversation, by the way.

She goes, 'You had your rugby friends.'

I'm there 'That was later on. I'm talking about when I was an actual kid. Jesus, I used to dress the gorden rake up in your clothes and pretend I had a little sister called Brenda.'

'You were a very strange boy, I won't deny it. You were forever poking around in my wardrobe.'

'I was lonely. Jesus Christ, I just wanted someone to love me – I wanted *you* to love me, you focking drunken sow.'

There's a moment of silence then. It's like she's got something to say but she doesn't know whether she *should*? Because saying it will change absolutely everything. But then she obviously thinks, fock it, because she goes, 'Do you want to know *why* I didn't have any more children after you?'

I'm like, 'Yeah, I would actually.'

And she goes, 'Because you burst my cervix, Ross – with your big, fat head!'

As one-liners go, it's a definite conversation-stopper. All over the kitchen, you can see people putting down their tuna rillettes and their wasabi prawns on miniature rice crackers – their appetites obviously ruined.

I'm there, 'Say that again?'

But Taffeta goes, 'Please don't say it again, Fionnuala,' which, on balance, is probably good advice, especially with six heavily pregnant women in the room, all facing the possibility that the babies they're carrying may take after me in terms of head size.

I just glower at the old dear and I go, 'I can't believe you would say something to me like that, you mentally deranged hag,' and I storm out of the kitchen.

Szidonia follows me halfway up the hallway, going, 'I say to you! She is crazy lady! Give us passports and let us go!'

But I just keep on walking. I let myself out and I slam the door behind me.

I'm walking back to the cor when I suddenly hear the sound of sobbing coming from the side of the house. At first, I decide to just ignore it. Why would I give a fock that somebody else is sad? But curiosity ends up getting the better of me. Being too nice for my own good, I decide to go and investigate. I'm expecting to find Roxana or Loredana or one of the other surrogates upset at something my old dear possibly said. But it's not.

Yeah, no, it ends up being Delma.

I'm like, 'What's the story?'

She's bawling her eyes out.

'Nothing,' she goes, wiping away her tears with the palm of her hand. 'Oh, it's just me being silly.'

I'm there, 'Okay, fair enough,' and I turn to walk away.

But that's when she goes, 'I'm jealous, Ross!'

I'm like, 'Jealous? Jealous of what?'

'Of Fionnuala! Of her happiness!'

I laugh.

I'm there, 'She's not happy. She's a focking soak. Plus, she's raddled.'

Delma doesn't even defend her – her supposed best friend. She takes a puff on her e-cigarette and goes, 'Breffni's about to become a father as well. Can you believe that?'

Breffni is her ex-husband. He left her for a young one who worked in the bor of either Delgany or Greystones Golf Club. I know he's a member of both.

'His little tramp is pregnant!' she goes. 'And I find out when I see them coming out of Cavistons – hand in hand!'

She bursts into tears again. I go to comfort her – being a people person. I give her a hug and she sort of, like, sinks her face into my chest and – yeah, no – has a good old bawl. I'm just, like, petting her hair, telling her I'm sorry I was rude to her earlier.

Eventually, when she's all out of tears, she pulls away and sees the mess she's made of my shirt. Yeah, no, it's covered in foundation.

'I'm so sorry,' she goes, rubbing it with her hand. And then something very unexpected happens. She goes from trying to rub the mascara off my shirt to just tracing the outline of my pecs with the tips of her fingers. Our eyes suddenly meet. I notice that her hand is trembling. And I've suddenly got a horn on me like a wok handle.

I lean in and I kiss her on the mouth. She kisses me back. Her lips taste of gin and vape juice, popcorn-flavoured.

She whispers, 'Oh, Jesus, Ross, what are we doing?'

I'm there, 'I don't know. I'm just going to go with it, though,' and I stort kissing her neck, which is actually a lot softer than it looks and smells of *Estée* by Estée Lauder.

She goes, 'We can't do this, Ross. I'm Fionnuala's friend,' but at the same time she's not exactly pushing me away.

I'm there, 'That makes it even hotter.'

I stort kissing her face then and I can tell she's getting seriously turned on. I hear her e-cigarette fall to the ground.

She goes, 'Ross, I've got children who are practically your age,' but she's nearly saying it in a braggy way.

I'm there, 'I've always had a thing for you.'

I can feel her hot breath in my ear.

'Ross, don't,' she goes. 'I was your mother's tennis portner for seven years,'

I'm there, 'I always said you were the hottest of all her friends – aport from a woman who owned a soft furnishings shop next-door to her florist's, although I think she's dead now.'

I kiss her on the mouth again and she responds in kind, one hand on the back of my neck, the other on the small of my back. She's a terrible kisser, it has to be said, her lips moving like she's trying to stop a boiled sweet from slipping out of her mouth.

She's wearing a blue woollen dress with a zip up the front. I pull the zip down and the thing falls open like a shirt. She doesn't even seem to mind the cold. That's how suddenly horny she is. I put my hands on her orse and I lift her up onto the black anthracite jumbo storage box that the old dear uses to keep all her *gordening* gear together?

And there I'm going to finish the story – out of respect for Delma's reputation as an older lady and mine as a, hopefully, feminist.

But, if you absolutely *have* to picture the scene, then imagine me standing there with my chinos and my boxer shorts around my ankles and Delma with her back against the vertical gutter, her short, muscly legs wrapped around my waist and the heels of her

Chanel ballet flats dug into my orse for purchase, her face all flushed and bloated and her sunnies bouncing up and down on her head, me out of breath, with my face buried in her chest, paying her little compliments – 'You could actually pass for mid-fifties' – and her holding on to my ears as she rides herself to a climax so violent that she somehow manages to disconnect the rainwater butt from the overhead gutter.

We disengage without a word and fix ourselves up – again, silently. She gets down off the storage box and zips up her dress while I pull up my chinos. I find her e-cigarette and one of her shoes that managed to slip off in the heat of battle and I hand them to her.

All she says is, 'I better get back – before I'm missed,' and then she puts her shoe on and she focks off back into the gaff.

And I walk back to the cor, thinking, 'What the fock was that?'

5.

Worst. Christmas. Ever.

It's always been one of my, like, *favourite* nights of the year? I'm talking about the night of *The Late Late Toy Show*. It's when me and Sorcha usually sit down with the kids to write their Santa Lists, which basically involves them just pointing at the TV and shouting, 'Me want that! Me want that!' while Sorcha scribbles everything down in her A4 pad until we've reached a ceiling of sixty presents each.

Honor usually writes *her* list during the course of the year and emails it to us two weeks before Christmas.

So anyway, the big night arrives, and we're sitting down with the tin of Quality Street, all ready to go.

'Me want that!' Leo shouts.

And we end up having to laugh because he's pointing at the owl on the opening credits.

I'm there, 'Leo, you have to wait until you see actual toys, okay?'

And it's at that exact moment that Fionn walks into the room.

Sorcha goes, 'Fionn, do you want to join us? You can write down anything you see that you think Hillary might like.'

But as soon as I see his face, I know that he has something to tell us, so much so that I end up pressing Live Pause. Sorcha looks at me, then looks at him. She picks up on the atmosphere immediately.

She's like, 'Oh my God, what's wrong?'

'Put the focking *Toy Show* on!' Brian goes. 'Stop acting the prick!'

I'm there, 'Hang on a second, Brian.'

Fionn takes a deep breath.

'A couple of weeks ago,' he goes, 'I noticed a swelling in one of my, em –'

'His testicles,' I go. 'He showed it to me.'

'Thank you, Ross. I didn't mention it to you, Sorcha, because I didn't want to worry you unduly. At that stage, I thought it might be nothing. But I had a biopsy done and I got the results back this afternoon.'

'Oh my God!' Sorcha goes.

Fionn straightens his glasses on his face.

'And,' he goes, so coolly and so matter-of-factly, 'it seems that I have cancer.'

Sorcha bursts into tears. She gets to her feet and just, like, throws her orms around him. 'Oh my God, Fionn!' she goes. 'Oh my God!'

He's there, 'I told my family tonight – and now I'm telling you.'

I end up getting angry for some reason. I'm there, 'How the fock did this happen? I mean, did the doctor give you *any* indication as to what might have caused it?'

Fionn goes, 'Abnormalities in my germ cells caused it.'

'Are you sure it wasn't reading?'

'Reading?'

'I'm trying to think of all the things *you* do that I *never* do?'

'It wasn't caused by reading, Ross. Look, some people just develop cancer in their lives. Right now, it's my turn. But, luckily, it's one of the more treatable cancers – the doctor said my chances of beating it are actually good.'

'What does "actually good" mean? Are we talking, like, 70/30? Are we talking, like, 60/40? Are we talking, like, 50/50? Jesus Christ, who *trains* these so-called doctors?'

Sorcha goes, 'What are they going to do, Fionn?'

She's still got her orms around him but, for once, it doesn't make me jealous.

'First thing Monday morning,' he goes, 'I've got to go into Vincent's Hospital –'

I'm like, 'Private?'

He's there, 'Private. And they're going to perform a radical inguinal orchiectomy.'

Sorcha goes, 'What is that?'

'It means they're going to remove the mass.'

I'm like, 'The mass?'

He's there, 'My left testicle, Ross. They're going to remove my left testicle.'

'Is that the big one?'

'Yes, it's the big one. I've got what's known as a Stage IIB seminoma.'

Sorcha storts crying again.

'There's a chance that it's in my lymph nodes as well, so I may have to do some chemotherapy – maybe after Christmas.'

Sorcha's like, 'Oh my God, Fionn! Oh! My God!'

I suddenly feel terrible. I've been such a prick to him and now he might . . . I don't want to even think about it.

'Put the focking *Toy Show* on!' Leo goes.

And I end up roaring at him. I'm like, 'I told you to wait, Leo!'

But Fionn goes, 'No, put it on, Ross. I know they've been looking forward to it all week. I don't want to ruin their night.'

I'm there, 'Dude, we're going to be here for you – every step of the way. However long and hord the road might be. Because –'

Shit, I end up suddenly bursting into tears then.

'Because,' I go, 'we're your family and we love you.'

I notice that the boys are all staring at me.

'The fock is he crying about?' Johnny goes.

And Leo's there, 'Don't know. He's *some* focking dope.'

Ronan rings me and he says he heard about Fiodden. Yeah, no, that's what he calls Fionn.

'Ine arthur been thalken to Hodor,' he goes. 'She said the fedda has caddencer.'

I'm there, 'Yeah, no, he has to have one of his you-know-what's removed on Monday. His balls.'

'The pooer fedda. Is he godda be alreet, Rosser?'

'I'm hoping so. Where *are* you, by the way?'

'Ine on the bus.'

That's him *and* Honor using public transport. I really feel like I've failed as a parent.

I'm there, 'Where are you going? Big Saturday night out, is it?'

And he's like, 'Me and Shadden are going out for didder.'

'For what?'

'For didder.'

'Again?'

'Didder.'

'One more time should do it.'

'Didder, Rosser. Foowut.'

'Oh, dinner! Hey, that's great. So which, er, Romayo's is getting your business tonight?'

Shadden's a big fan of the one in Clongriffin. I've heard her refer to it as her Happy Place, possibly because Ronan beat up an ex of hers in the queue one night when he said her family were scumbags – even though her family *are* scumbags.

'No,' he goes, 'we're going out for proper didder. Cheerlie's arthur inviring us out to that place he lubs. Shadahadden's, is it?'

I'm like, 'Are you talking about Shanahan's.'

'The wood on Steeben's Greeyunt. We're meeting him and Heddessy – he said the steak in theer is unbeliebable.'

I'm there, 'Hennessy? The focker! He promised me!'

He goes, 'What did he probise you?'

I grab my Henri Lloyd off the hook in the hallway and I'm like, 'Ro, don't say yes to anything until I get there, okay?'

He's there, 'Are you invirit as weddle, Rosser?'

'No,' I go, 'but I'm coming anyway,' then I hang up and shout up the stairs to Sorcha that I'm heading out.

The four of them are already sitting at the table when I arrive. The old man is actually giving his order. The waiter's there, 'And how would you like your steak cooked?'

The old man's like, 'As the lion said when asked the same question – roar!'

The waiter laughs politely, pretending it's the first time he's ever heard my old man say it.

I'm there, 'This looks very cosy.'

The old man and Hennessy look up. They both look surprised to see me – although shocked is possibly *more* the word? They haven't had a chance to get inside Ronan's head yet.

The old man goes, 'Kicker! What an unexpected surprise!'

Jesus, the smell of food, by the way. I can feel the saliva dribbling down my chin.

I turn around to the waiter and I go, 'Can we get another chair put at this table. I'll have the Bone-In Rib Eye – we're talking medium-rare.'

'You woatunt,' Ronan goes. 'You're not allowut hab addy meat.'

I'm like, 'Fock's sake!'

'Of course!' the old man goes. 'Young Honor has somehow convinced herself – as well as Sorcha – that eating meat is somehow bad for the planet! Have you ever heard the like of it, Hennessy?'

Hennessy's there, 'You can't take a shit nowadays without feeling guilty for flushing.'

I've used the toilet after Hennessy many times over the years and I've never known him to flush.

'It's all port of the same conspiracy!' the old man goes. 'They're using children to spread this kind of propaganda to undermine our wonderful beef industry – so that we remain forever a debtor state!'

Ronan looks at the waiter and goes, 'Rosser will hab the risotho.'

Risotto. The Italian word for wallpaper paste. The waiter focks off with the order, then returns with a chair and sets a place for me. I sit down and wait to hear the old man's pitch. I don't have to wait long.

'So, Ronan,' he goes, 'I expect you're wondering why Hennessy and I have asked you and Shadden here tonight!'

Ronan's there, 'I was a bit curdious alreet, Cheerlie.'

I'm like, 'Hennessy's going to offer you a job, Ro. And I'm advising you to say no.'

Hennessy gives me a look that could stop a clock.

'Well,' the old man goes, 'like Ross said, we *have* been wondering recently what direction you intended to take once you've finished your Law degree! Were you thinking of going down the King's Inns route and becoming a barrister, like our Learned Friend, the idiot Roderic Grainger? Or were you thinking of becoming a solicitor – like the great Hennessy Coghlan-O'Hara here?'

'I habn't gibbon it a lorra thought,' he goes, 'hab I, Shadden?'

Shadden's there, 'The last few munts have been so busy, so thee hab.'

The girl hasn't worked a day in her focking life.

'You're in your final year!' the old man reminds him. 'You'll have to make your mind up soon, I'm sure!'

'What would you say,' Hennessy goes, 'if I were to offer you a full apprenticeship? I'll put you through Blackhall Place and I'll pay for everything. And while you're studying, I'll put you on a salary – a good salary.'

Ronan smiles. He's obviously flattered.

'Look,' he goes, 'Ine veddy grateful to yous for taking an intordest. I hodestly am. Me and Shadden were thinking of mebbe going away for a yee-or, but.'

Which is news to me.

He's like, 'Ine arthur been looking arowunt diffordent peerts of the wurdled for a law feerm that speciadizes in civil reets woork.'

'Civil rights?' the old man goes – like he's just said, I don't know, homoeopathy.

He goes, 'Ine hoping to foyunt mebbe an intoordenship.'

I'm like, 'Fair focks, Ro. Fair focks.'

He's there, 'We were thinking of mebbe somewhere in Amedica – we boat lubbed Amedica – eeben woorking on a *pro bodo* basis.'

'*Pro bono?*' Hennessy goes – like he's just said, I don't know, bestiality.

Ronan's there, 'It'll be a good expeerdience – and it'll gib me anutter yee-or to decide what airdea of the Law Ine wanthon to go into and wheer Ine godda go for me professioniddle quadification.'

I've been proud of Ronan many, many times – but possibly never prouder of him than this.

The old man goes, 'That all sounds rather wonderful, doesn't it, Hennessy?'

Hennessy's just there, 'Er, yeah,' looking at Ronan with his head tilted to the side, like a dog when he hears a weird noise.

Our dinners arrive. Rib-eyes for the old man and Hennessy. Turkey and ham for Ronan and Shadden. And focking risotto for me. I take one look at it and I push it away. The old man puts his fork into his steak and I watch the thing bleed out all over his plate.

The conversation moves on to other matters. The old man says he thinks it'll be the New Year before the High Court decides whether anyone has the right to challenge the legitimacy of the election result. Shadden says you can't appreciate how good Mariah Carey's voice is until you hear her perform live. Hennessy says he never got to thank me for teaching Ross Junior how to stand up for himself and break his little brother's nose.

When everyone's finished eating and our plates have been cleared away, the old man decides to have another crack at Ronan, this time adjusting the angle of attack.

He goes, 'By the way, how was Italy, Old Scout?' talking to Hennessy. 'Hennessy has a holiday home on Lake Como, don't you know!'

'Reedy?' Ronan goes. 'Ah, feer fooks, Heddessy.'

'Of course, he *calls* it a holiday home! But that's just Hennessy being modest! It's nearly the size of the bloody well Shelbourne! Has its own private pier and everything! Show him the photographs, Hennessy!'

Straight away I know what's going on, except I'm pretty much powerless to stop it. Hennessy whips out his phone and hands it across the table to Ro, who storts flicking through the photographs, his mouth opening wider with every swipe.

'Moy Jaysus!' he goes.

I'm there, 'Bear in mind, Ro, that there are probably loads of civil rights lawyers living on Lake Como in *equally* nice houses?'

'There's one,' Hennessy goes.

I'm like, 'There you go, Ro.'

'But *she's* married to George Clooney.'

'Amaddle?' it's Shadden who goes. 'Are you thalken about Amaddle bleaten Cloodey?'

'That's right. They live fifty yords up the road. Our gardeners are brothers.'

Ronan shows the phone to Shadden, who storts flicking through

Hennessy's holiday snaps and now it's *her* eyes that are suddenly out on stalks.

She's there, 'The bleaten soyuz of it, Ro-Ro.'

'Look at he's gayums room!' Ronan goes. 'Fuddle-sized snooker tabult and evoddything, look.'

'Yes,' the old man goes, 'the law's been good to you, hasn't it, Hennessy?'

I decide that I have to say something to break the spell.

I'm there, 'Can I just point out, Ro, that the old man is basically looking for a new bag man to replace Hennessy when he becomes the Attorney General. That gaff he's showing you – everything Hennessy owns, in fact – was built with dirty money.'

'Hold on,' the old man pretends to go, 'I've just had an idea! Why don't you two lovebirds spend New Year's in Italy? Hennessy, you'd give them the place, wouldn't you?'

Hennessy's there, 'It'd be a pleasure.'

Ronan lights up. Shadden lights up. The waiter comes over and reminds them that smoking has been prohibited in restaurants and bars since 2004. They both put them out.

Ronan goes, 'Jaysus, we'd luvven that, Heddessy. We ditn't hab a proper huddymoowunt.'

I'm there, 'Er, you got married in focking Vegas.'

The old man's there, 'I'll pay for the flights! It'll be our Christmas gift to you both – isn't that right, Hennessy?'

Shadden stands up. She walks around the table and she kisses Hennessy on the cheek. Then she does the same to my old man.

She goes, 'That's lubbly – idn't it, Ro-Ro?'

And that's when I know I'm going to have a serious job on my hands stopping them from tempting my son to the dork side.

My phone beeps and I whip it out of my pocket. I've got, like, three missed calls and then a text message from an 085 number that I don't recognize.

I make the mistake of reading it.

It's like, 'Ross, this is Delma, we need to talk.'

And I'm thinking, no, we don't. No, we *definitely* don't.

And certainly not today.

I'm in St Vincent's – obviously – Private Hospital, where Fionn is, at this moment in time, under the knife. I've popped out to the vending machine to grab myself a coffee while we wait for him to come back from the, I want to say, *operating* theatre?

I think about texting the woman back. Then I think, fock it. She's just had, I'm presuming, the best sex she's had in a long, long time – she was yapping like a handbag dog by the end – and if she can't handle the guilt that comes with that, there's nothing I can say to help her.

I tip back to the ward, where Fionn's old pair and his sister, Eleanor, and her husband – forget name – not to mention JP, Christian, Oisinn and the famous Magnus are sitting around, waiting for Fionn to arrive back.

I'm like, 'There you are, Mrs de Barra. I didn't take no for an answer and I got you a crappycino, which is what I call all machine coffee!'

She goes, 'I said I didn't want anything.'

She used to be a fan of mine, but she's not any more. That all goes back to me shitting in her laptop.

I'm there, 'It was no trouble. I was getting one for myself anyway. And there's something for you as well, Eleanor. A Double Decker – because I remember how much you like them!'

The husband gives her a serious filthy. He knows we had a bit of a scene a few years ago while they were on a break and I made that Double Decker thing sound possibly filthier than I intended.

Eleanor used to look like Carolyn Lilipaly, in fairness to the girl, but unfortunately doesn't any more.

He looks at me and goes, 'She said she didn't want anything either.'

I think his name might be Trev or something along *those* lines?

And instead of giving me 'tude, he *should* be actually *thanking* me. It was being with a selfish prick like me that convinced Eleanor that she was better off staying married to a drip like him. But I don't get the chance to point out that basic fact because that's when Fionn is suddenly wheeled into the ward.

We all jump to our feet.

'Now,' one of the nurses goes, 'he's still groggy from the anaesthetic, so don't crowd him.'

He's like, 'Hey, everyone,' slurring his words and struggling to keep his eyes open.

'Hello, Fionn!' his old dear goes. 'We're all here. Me and your dad. And your sister. Plus, we've got a big surprise for you –'

I'm there, 'Me, Christian, JP, Oisinn and Magnus are here as well, Dude. In other words, your rugby family.'

It turns out she was going to say Hillary. Yeah, no, Fionn's old man is holding him. He shows him to Fionn and goes, 'And your son is here as well!'

When he hears this, Fionn tries to sit up in the bed, but he ends up hurting himself with the effort. Hillary is delighted to see him. He's going, 'Dadda! Dadda!'

Fionn's there, *Comment ça va, Hillary?* because he wants the kid to grow up – and I'm quoting him here – *conversant* in as many languages as possible.

I say fock-all. Today is not the day.

Fionn looks at his old dear. He's struggling to stay awake. He's like, 'Were you talking to the doctor?'

'Yes – and he said the operation was a success,' she goes – that's if you consider losing a testicle a good thing. 'He'll be around later and he's going to talk to you about next steps.'

Fionn looks suddenly worried and I decide that my role here today is to stop him getting too down. So I hit him with a line I've been sitting on all day. I'm there, 'You're one ball down, Fionn, which makes you fifty per cent less likely to impregnate my wife again!'

No one laughs. In fairness, it didn't sound as good as it did when I ran it past the goys in the lift earlier and Oisinn told me that, on balance, it was something I probably shouldn't say.

Oh, well. I'm possibly not in my right mind today. I didn't get more than a couple of hours of sleep again last night, worrying about the dude.

'Do you *have* to be here?' Fionn's old dear goes, fixing me with a look.

She's really holding on to that anger. Jesus Christ, I offered to buy her a new laptop when one came up on DoneDeal. She didn't want to know.

Fionn goes, 'It's fine, Mum,' and then – nice touch this – he goes, 'Thanks for coming, goys. I really appreciate it.'

JP's there, 'Fionn, we're going to be here for you – we're talking me, Christian, Ross, Oisinn and Magnus. Because thick and thin is what we said – and thick and thin is what we meant.'

He has a definite way with words – a bit like me when I'm on form.

Magnus goes, 'We should poshibly leave now to let Fionn have shome time alone with hish mum and dad and hish shishter and hish shon.'

Poor Trev – if that's even his name – must feel like a spare knob with no one even mentioning him.

Oisinn goes, 'Yeah, good idea, Magnus,' and he throws on his jacket.

We all give him a hug and say our goodbyes.

I'm there, 'Looking forward to having you home, Dude,' and, probably recognizing how worried I am about him, he gives me a definitely stronger hug than he does the rest of the goys – although he ends up howling in pain when I try to steady myself and I accidentally put my hand between his legs.

Then me and the goys all leave. On the way out the door, I look at Eleanor and I make sure to give her a wink and go, 'Enjoy the Double Decker!' and I hear *him* ask her, through gritted teeth, 'Is that supposed to be code for something you did for him that you won't do for me?'

As my daughter would say: hill-air!

Sorcha says there's been a backlash.

I'm like, 'A backlash? A backlash against who?'

She goes, 'A backlash against Honor. A lot of parents are furious that the skiing trip to Pinzolo has been cancelled. Oh my God, Ross, the things that people are saying about our daughter on WhatsApp! And not only on WhatsApp, Ross, but on Facebook as well!'

'What kind of things are we talking?'

'The word bitch is being used a lot.'

'Jesus, Sorcha, you *went* to Mount Anville. You can't tell me you're shocked by that.'

'Not only that, Ross, they're saying that *I'm* the one who's actually *behind* this? That I'm basically manipulating Honor and putting words in her actual mouth for my own, like, *political* ends?'

'Who's saying that?'

'Oh my God – *everyone*! Also, Ross, they've arranged a meeting – for tonight.'

I'm there, 'A meeting?' because I know what South Dublin moms are like in lorge groups. 'Fock.'

'They're saying, first it was the cor pork,' she goes, 'now it's the school trip. They're saying they're not going to take any more. Ross, they're all threatening to take their daughters out of Mount Anville.'

All of a sudden, Honor walks into the kitchen, wearing her coat.

Sorcha's like, 'Honor, where are you going?'

Honor's there, 'Where do you think I'm going? There's a meeting on.'

'Honor, you can't go to the meeting.'

'Why the fock not?'

'Because it's *about* you.'

'All the more reason for me to be there.'

Sorcha gets this look of, like, defiance on her face then. 'You know what,' she goes, 'you're absolutely right. You actually have a legal right to be heard in your own defence. I'm coming with you.'

Fionn walks into the room then, walking very gingerly. When I think about what he had done to him the other day, it makes my teeth itch.

I'm there, 'Are you alright, Dude?'

He's like, 'Yeah, fine.'

Sorcha goes, 'We're going out, Fionn. We've decided to go to the meeting.'

Fionn's there, 'Sorcha was showing me some of the things that the other parents have been saying. What a way to talk about a young girl.'

I'm like, 'Mount Anville.'

'Are you going to the meeting, Ross?'

'Er, I wasn't planning on it. Someone has to obviously stay home and mind the kids.'

'I'm happy to babysit,' he focking has to go.

Sorcha's there, 'You wouldn't mind?'

He's like, 'Not at all. They're in bed, aren't they?'

'Yes,' she goes. 'And if they play up, Fionn, just tell them that Santa won't come to them if they're bold. Come on, Ross, get your coat. It'll look better if people see that Honor has support from both parents.'

So we end up going to Mount Anville – yeah, no, by bus. Because Honor doesn't want to be accused of being a hypocrite.

We get to the school just as the meeting is about to stort. The assembly hall ends up being rammers and the air is filled with the screechy sound of South Dublin people being outraged about something. Honor walks in a few feet ahead of us and this, like, shocked hush falls over the place.

There's, like, no empty seats, so we end up having to stand at the side with our backs against the wall.

Up on the stage, Sister Consuelo looks tense. She could end up losing a lot of students here. That's how seriously these people take their skiing.

She steps up to the mic and she goes, 'Ladies and gentlemen, thank you all for coming this evening. I thought it would be helpful to convene a meeting just to explain the reasons why we decided –'

A woman at the front, Treasa Mitchell's old dear – not great in terms of looks – suddenly stands up. She goes, '*You* didn't call this meeting, Sister Consuelo – *we* did. And before we stort this discussion, can I just say that this is supposed to be a meeting for parents. And yet there is one student – and we all know which student I'm talking about – who has come here, uninvited, with her parents tonight.'

Sorcha is straight on the defensive. She's there, 'Her name is

Honor, Vanessa. She has a right to be present – and that right is enshrined in the Constitution.'

Sister Consuelo goes, 'I think it's very early in the evening to start quoting the Constitution.'

Yeah, no, that usually storts happening about an hour in.

Mallorie Kennedy – as in, Courage Kennedy's old dear – stands up then. She's been totally overdoing it with the filler, by the way. She looks like someone melted down Simon Cowell and fed him to Sharon Osborne through a funnel.

'Well,' she goes, 'I myself personally am *delighted* she's here. I think it's important for her to hear first-hand how she's ruined absolutely everything. Courage and Phenella have been looking forward to going skiing for months. Now that the trip has been cancelled, my husband and I are going to have to take the two girls with us to the Maldives, even though we were going there to celebrate our twentieth wedding anniversary.'

A lot of people shake their heads in sympathy and thank her for sharing.

'That took a lot,' I hear someone shout.

Then Rachel Lynch – Eponine Lynch's old dear – decides that she's got something to get off her chest. She has *no* chest, by the way. I'm only mentioning it to give the story a bit of context.

'This is exactly what the girl *wants* to hear,' she goes. 'She gets a kick out of upsetting people. I mean, look at the girl – she clearly finds the whole thing funny.'

And it's true, in fairness. Honor does have a big smile on her face.

'I hesitate to use the word,' Rachel Lynch goes, 'but she's a little bitch.'

Sorcha's like, 'How *dare* you speak about my daughter in those terms!'

And Sister Consuelo attempts to restore some order. She's there, 'I will not tolerate any student of this school being referred to by that name.'

She'd definitely want to stay off WhatsApp, then.

But then Roz Matthews gets to her feet.

'Firstly,' she goes, 'I have to declare an interest here. My daughter, Sincerity, is also a member of the Mount Anville Climate Justice Committee and she too is in favour of cancelling the trip to Pinzolo. I just wanted to ask the other parents here, am I the only one who's actually *proud* of the stand that these girls have taken?'

That goes down like Gemma O'Doherty in a halal butchers.

People are going, 'Proud? How can you say that?'

She goes, 'I mean, I can't be the only one who listened to Honor's interview with George Lee and thought, "What an amazingly positive role model she is for young people!"'

There ends up being absolute uproar in the hall.

'Look,' Roz goes, 'I know Honor came to this school with a reputation. But what she is doing is having a *hugely* positive effect on a lot of students, and that includes my daughter.'

Some dad sitting behind her – a randomer – goes, 'And, what, you're happy to see your daughter getting the bus to school every day, are you?'

'I'm not saying it's ideal,' Roz goes. 'The point is that she's happy knowing that she's doing her bit to reduce her corbon footprint.'

Sorcha decides it's time to have her say. She stands up and clears her throat.

She goes, 'Thank you, Roz. That line about Honor being a role model is a lovely, lovely thing for Ross and I to hear as her parents. Sister Consuelo, teachers, ladies and gentlemen, fellow parents, I'm glad to have the opportunity to speak here tonight in defence of my daughter, Honor, and her efforts on behalf of the planet.

'I know, from some of the conversations that I just so happened to see on WhatsApp, and also Facebook, that many of you are questioning the seriousness of my daughter's concern with the issue facing the planet. I know some of you believe that her real intention in engaging with environmental issues is to cause chaos – to force your children to take public transport and to stop them from skiing.

'I know many of you also believe that I'm the one who's feeding my daughter all this information, that I'm somehow manipulating her, just because of my own history of activism in the same area, both inside and outside the Oireachtas. But I can assure you, nothing could be further from the truth.

'We all see so many awful things in our daily lives now that we've become sadly immune to them. But my daughter was moved – yes, *moved*, ladies and gentlemen – by the sight of a polar bear drowning because of what *we've* done to cause rapid glacial ice melt in the Orctic.'

Mallorie Kennedy goes, 'I did *not* cause rapid glacial ice melt in the Orctic!'

'We all did, Mallorie. And that includes you, Vanessa, and you, Rachel. We should actually be celebrating her, not putting her on trial like this. Look outside the bubble of your own WhatsApp groups and listen to what's being said out there. All over social media, people are talking about Honor and they're talking about Mount Anville – and, for once, it's not in a negative way. They're looking at all these initiatives and they're saying, "Oh my God, this is what we *all* need to be doing?" Other schools are taking their actual lead from us. Loreto Foxrock and Loreto Dalkey have both closed their cor porks and Muckross Pork College have cancelled their skiing trip to Borovets in Bulgaria.'

She lets that hang there. And for a moment we are all united in our general disapproval of Muckross Pork College and their affordable winter breaks.

She goes, 'My daughter is encouraging other young people to stand up and say to people in power: "You have failed us – er, now *we're* taking chorge?" And another thing I want to say is –'

Sorcha ends up getting interrupted then – but not by one of the other parents. It's actually Honor who cuts her off mid-sentence.

She goes, 'Sorry, can I just say something here? Fascinating as this conversation is, I don't have the time to be sitting here for the next two hours, listening to this shit. I came here tonight because I want to say this. I don't give a fock what you say about me on WhatsApp or Facebook or at your private get-togethers like this one. I'm not doing what I'm doing for, like, praise and I'm not doing it for, like, popularity. I don't care what people think of me, but I do care about the world that I'm going to hopefully bring my own children into one day.

'So fock off, Vanessa Mitchell – your daughter's a bigger bitch than I'll ever be, by the way. And as for Mallorie Kennedy, having to bring Courage and Phenella to the Maldives with her – boo-focking-hoo. Your generation has destroyed the planet and my generation has a *slight* chance of fixing it? And, however much it inconveniences you, that is what I intend to focking do.'

Honor finishes her little speech, raises two middle fingers to the room, then walks out of there, leaving the audience stunned.

We follow her outside, then we walk behind her – at a safe distance – to the bus stop.

Sorcha links my orm and goes, 'I'm so proud of her for standing up for herself, Ross. And for the Earth. She's turning into the daughter I've – oh my God – *always* wanted!'

Sorcha tells me not to come into the living room. She practically roars it as well. She's there, 'Don't come in here!'

And then I hear Fionn go, 'Yeah, just give us a minute to finish up, Ross.'

The obvious question is, finish up what exactly? I know the dude is a ball down and everything, but, let's be honest, he has form.

But then, to my great relief, I hear Honor go, 'We're just finishing decorating the tree, Dad. We want it to be a surprise for the boys.'

Leo is kicking the door, going, 'Me want see! Me want see!' but I manage to calm him down by telling him that Santa Claus doesn't come to kids who act the prick.

A minute or two later, Sorcha opens the door with a massive smile on her face, clapping her two hands together. I haven't seen her look this excited since the time Lena Dunham liked a meme she posted on Instagram that said 'Fake Happiness is the Worst Sadness', even though she very quickly unliked it and Sorcha couldn't figure out whether the liking it or the unliking it was the actual mistake.

'Okay,' she goes, 'close your eyes!'

I'm there, 'Sorcha, is this really necessary?'

'Come on, Ross, close them! You too, boys! That's it – close them!'

We do what she says – it's generally easier all round – and we sort of, like, shuffle blindly into the room.

She goes, 'Okay, you can open them now!'

We do.

She's like, 'Are you surprised?'

Oh, I'm surprised alright. We *all* are?

'The fock is that?' Johnny goes.

I'll answer that question for him. It's a giant, wooden cable reel, laid on its side, with a sheaf of bamboo canes, tied together, standing upright in the hole in the middle and then the old venetian blinds from the study – which I've been promising to bring to the recycling centre for four years – wound around the canes.

'It's an ethical Christmas tree,' Sorcha goes.

It's not, though. It's exactly what I just described.

Brian takes a run at it, obviously intending to kick it down. I decide not to stop him – I actually shout, 'Do your worst, son!' – but Honor catches hold of him just as he's swinging a kick at it and she manages to sweep him up into her orms.

She goes, 'We made this, Brian! Me and Mom and your uncle Fionn!'

I'm like, 'No focking shit! And it looks *just* like one you'd buy in the shops!'

'Well, unlike the ones you buy in the shops,' Sorcha goes, 'this one isn't made from plastic and it didn't result in a precious tree being cut down – right, Fionn?'

Fionn's like, 'Exactly.'

I'm there, 'It looks genuinely, genuinely shit – and I mean every word of that.'

'We're *going* to decorate it,' Sorcha goes. 'We're going to walk up Killiney Hill tomorrow to forage for fallen acorns and pine cones.'

Honor goes, 'I want to take a picture of it for my Instagram,' which is what she ends up doing – getting the boys to pose in front of it – while Sorcha tells me that this is only the stort of what's going to be a zero waste Christmas for the O'Carroll-Kelly-Lalor family.

I'm like, 'Zero waste? Okay, what exactly does that involve?' already regretting asking.

Sorcha lowers her voice to a whisper. She goes, 'I've been looking again at the Santa Lists we drew up for the boys, Ross. There's an awful lot on them – way too much generally and also way too much P, L, A, S, T, I, C?'

I don't know why the fock she's spelling it out for me. The boys have more chance of cracking the code than I do.

I'm there, 'Can you just say the word, Sorcha, rather than getting me to guess?'

She goes, 'Plastic, Ross. There are too many things on their lists made from plastic. So I'm saying they might not get all the toys they asked for this year.'

'You can't be serious.'

'I'm also saying that the toys they *do* receive might end up being previously loved.'

'You mean second-hand?'

'Santa is just as concerned about the future of the planet as we are, Ross. That's why he sometimes shops in C, H, A, R, I, T, Y, S, H, O, P, S.'

'Jesus Christ. If that spells what I think it spells, God focking help us all. What about you, Honor? Would you be happy with a load of second-hand shit?'

And Honor goes, 'I actually don't *want* anything for Christmas this year?'

Sorcha's like, 'Nothing? Nothing at all?'

'I have everything I need. I don't want presents just for the sake of getting presents.'

I'm there, 'But that's what Christmas is about, Honor. Come on, you have to have something.'

She goes, 'Okay, there's something, but you'll probably think it's stupid.'

Sorcha goes, 'We won't think it's stupid.'

And I'm there, 'Let's hear what she has to say first before we give that guarantee, Sorcha.'

Honor is silent for a few seconds, then she goes, 'Okay, instead of presents, I was going to ask would you maybe make donations on my behalf to one or two, like, environmental charities I've been reading about?'

I actually laugh in her face.

I'm there, 'You're right, Honor. We do think it's stupid.'

Fionn lets me down in a big-time way then. He goes, 'That's a lovely, selfless gesture, Honor. I'm very impressed.'

My phone all of a sudden rings. I check the screen. Shit, it's Delma again. The third time today. I decide to finally answer it because she's just going to keep ringing otherwise.

The woman is nothing if not dogged. She's been picketing Funderland for thirty-five consecutive Christmases.

I'm there, 'I, er, might just take this outside. It's one of the goys from the team asking me about a particular setpiece that I'm trying to teach them.'

No one seems to give a fock. There's no reason why they should.

I tip down to the kitchen and I answer the phone. I'm there, 'Delma, how are you getting on?' deciding to play it easy-breezy.

She goes, 'I've been ringing you all week. Sometimes three times a day.'

I'm thinking, Jesus, if she's thinking of getting back into the dating game on a permanent basis, she needs to chill the fock out.

I'm there, 'Yeah, no, I've had a lot on my plate, Delma. What's up?'

She's like, 'I texted you and I said we needed to talk.'

I'm there, 'I'm presuming you're not pregnant!'

It doesn't get the laugh it possibly deserves.

She goes, 'I was ringing to say I don't think it would serve any purpose telling Fionnuala about what happened that day.'

I'm there, '*That's* what you're ringing me to tell me? What, did you think I was going to drop it into my next conversation with the woman? "By the way, I lashed your mate Delma out of it in the gorden during your baby shower last week! Small world, huh?"'

'As long as we both understand that. I wanted to say as well that it was a big mistake and I wish it had never happened.'

'Yeah, you keep telling yourself that.'

'I *beg* your pordon?'

'I'm just saying you didn't seem sorry at the time. You know you disconnected the rainwater butt from the overhead guttering with your bucking and your writhing?'

'I don't wish to be reminded of every sordid detail, thank you.'

'That'll be dripping now for the entire winter.'

'I said I wanted to forget the whole disgusting experience.'

'Disgusting? Was I doing something with my face?'

Yeah, no, I sometimes pull weird expressions when I'm turned on. I once caught sight of my own reflection in the window of House of Ireland on Nassau Street while I was trying to chat up Maïa Dunphy and I genuinely thought it was a man inside the shop having a stroke.

'It wasn't your face,' she goes. 'It was what you called me.'

'Called you? Er, what are you talking about?'

'You called me a name.'

'Oh, er, you don't want to take that too seriously. Yeah, no, sometimes random shit just pops out of my mouth when I'm on the job.'

'I couldn't believe what I was hearing.'

I'm like, 'What was the name – just out of curiosity?'

But she doesn't answer me because she's already hung up.

They're all looking at me like I'm basically off my meds.

Yeah, no, they all got a call from me at, like, eight o'clock this morning to say that we were training today. It's something they definitely weren't expecting.

'It's Christmas Eve, like,' Nailer goes.

And I'm just like, 'What do you want me to say? Merry Christmas?'

Either Dougie or Lenny goes, 'What he means is, we're supposed to be on our holidays, Boss. Why are we training today, like?'

And I'm there, 'Because St Michael's definitely *won't* be? And that'll give us a psychiatric edge.'

It's an old trick of Father Fehily's. We *always* trained on Christmas Eve – even if half of us were still half mashed from the night before.

I'm there, 'And do you know why they *won't* be training today?'

It's just, like, blank faces all round. I can nearly smell last night's booze coming out of their pores.

I'm there, 'Because they've only got Pres focking Bray in the first round of the Leinster Schools Senior Cup.'

Hearing that sobers them up a bit.

I'm there, 'Yeah, no, the Michael's boys won't be letting the thought of playing you goys ruin their Christmas. They'll be enjoying their usual traditional Christmas Eve.'

Lukie McDermott goes, 'What do the likes of them do for Christmas, like?'

They're genuinely fascinated by my little insights into South Dublin life.

I'm there, 'Christmas Eve? They'll be going on a hunt. Yeah, no, they'll all be up on horseback since about seven o'clock this morning, dressed in red coats, surrounded by hounds, chasing some poor, unfortunate fox through a field.'

'Dirty, West Brit fooks, like,' Ricey goes.

I'm just making this shit up, of course. I mean, these goys are unlikely to ever meet a Michael's boy in later life and I'm tempted to say, lucky them.

Barry Austin's there, 'Is that what they're like, like?'

And I'm like, 'That's exactly what they're like, like.'

Ricey goes, 'They actually hunt foxes, like?' and it seems to upset him.

I'm there, 'They used to hunt humans. It was usually bursary students from working-class areas who were accepted into the school as port of the Social Diversity Programme. They'd take them to Herbert Pork, give them a sixty-second headstort, then go after them with the dogs. I think they had to knock it on the head when they lost one or two and the Gords got involved.'

They actually believe me.

'They sound like a bunch of bad bastards, like,' either Dougie or Lenny goes. And I love the way this conversation is suddenly going.

I'm there, 'Look, we've got, like, four weeks to prepare for this match – and we've got a hell of a lot to do in that time. I want to do some work on the lineout calls today – and, goys, I want you thinking about them between now and the time you come back to school in January. Barry Austin, I want to spend a bit of time today watching you kick – mainly with a view to identifying glitches in your technique. And, Nailer, I want to do a bit of work with you passing off your left hand. How does that all sound?'

They're all like, 'Ah, yeah, fair enough, like?' but for some reason I'm not seeing the enthusiasm that I want to see from them.

I'm like, 'Goys, we can win this match!' but no one says shit.

All except Barry, supposedly my captain, who goes, 'Sure, we'll give it a go, like.'

I watch them warm up with – yeah, no – heavy horts. I'm suddenly seeing what Brother Ciaran meant when he said that the only thing that Bray lacked – aport from a decent Nando's, which he didn't mention – is confidence. As someone with an abundance of it himself, it's something I find very hord to relate to.

Speak of the devil, I suddenly spot him standing on the opposite sideline. I tip over to him and I go, 'Brother Ciaran. Season's greetings.'

I really am a brilliant goy. That doesn't get said enough.

He's like, 'What are the boys doing here? They're supposed to be on their holidays.'

I'm there, 'We'll take holidays when we win the Leinster Schools Senior Cup. I want to talk to you about something.'

'I want to talk to you about something too. Your money. Your wages for coaching. It bounced back. It's back in our account.'

'I don't want it.'

'What?'

'Oh, you heard right. The goys thought I was doing this for the money. I'm showing them that I'm not.'

'But sure, you're entitled to it.'

'I don't want it. Now I want to ask you something. Can you get two hundred Pres Bray jerseys?'

'Two hundred?' he goes, looking at me like it's *the* most random thing he's ever been asked. 'I don't think we have anything like that number. I'd have to order them from the wholesalers after Christmas.'

'You do that. You can use the money I sent back to you to pay for them.'

'What do you want two hundred Pres Bray jerseys for, Ross?'

'It's a surprise for the goys. Now, if you don't mind, I've got a team to train.'

Cranberry and lentil bake. Red cabbage with coriander seeds. Shredded sprouts with pistachios and pomegranates.

You honestly haven't known misery until you've been served up a vegan Christmas dinner. The only upside, it has to be said, is that it's pissing Sorcha's old pair off even more than it's pissing me off.

'Christmas without turkey,' Sorcha's old dear goes. 'I'm just going to come out and say it – it's unnatural.'

I haven't seen her look so disgusted since Sorcha showed her our photographs from a holiday in Dubai before I'd managed to filter out the one of me setting fire to my pubic hair the night I crashed the Leinster Rugby Awards Ball.

Sorcha goes, 'Give it a chance, Mom – you haven't even tried the porsnip gnocchi with walnut crumbs and kale pesto.'

Sorcha's old man looks at Fionn. He goes, 'Do *you* approve of this?' and – father-in-law or no father-in-law – I get this sudden urge to slap the paper crown off the focker's head.

In fairness to him, Fionn goes, 'I'm a guest in Ross and Sorcha's home, Mr Lalor. It's not up to me to approve or disapprove. What I will say is that I really admire what Honor is doing.'

Sorcha's old man is there, 'You haven't eaten a thing, I see.'

And Fionn goes, 'I haven't really had much of an appetite since the, em, you know.'

He looks like shit, by the way. I'm just putting that out there.

'Focking presents!' Leo goes – because he's keen to see what Santa brought him. Sorcha insists that we open our gifts *after* dinner – another Lalor family tradition.

Honor's there, 'Eat your winter slaw, Leo,' and he does what his sister tells him. 'Then we'll do presents.'

Sorcha's old man goes, 'Well, I can't believe you're all still buying into this. It's as clear as day that the girl has embraced this *thing* because she gets a perverse thrill out of upsetting people. I mean, what the hell am I even *eating* here?'

'They're harissa and mormalade roasted roots,' Sorcha goes. 'And you're wrong, by the way. Honor has found something that she's actually genuinely *passionate* about? I haven't even told you yet that the *Irish Times* is doing a feature in the Saturday magazine next week about 18 People Under the Age of 18 Who are Predicted to Shape 2018 – and Honor's going to be number seven.'

I'd love to know who's number one to focking six. See, that's the competitor in me.

Sorcha's there, 'This is a girl who didn't want a single thing for Christmas, Dad. She asked us to donate all the money to non-profit organizations working to try to reverse climate change.'

'Presents!' Brian shouts.

I'm like, 'When we've finished dinner, Brian.'

Sorcha's old dear goes, 'Well, I still say that Christmas without turkey is unnatural.'

'I'll tell you what's unnatural,' Honor goes. 'The fact that sea levels are going to rise by one point five metres before the end of the century.'

Sorcha's old dear makes the mistake of going, 'One point five metres? That doesn't sound like very much.'

Honor absolutely rips into her then. She's like, 'Why don't you Google what the map of the world will look like in the event of a one-point-five-metre rise in sea levels?'

'Honor and I were looking at it the other night,' Sorcha goes, 'weren't we, Honor? There are huge ports of Ireland that would be totally wiped off the map.'

'Do we know *which* ports?' Sorcha's old man goes.

'Oh my God, Dad, does it actually matter?'

'Of course it matters! I mean, are these places even *worth* saving?'

Fionn – in fairness to him – goes, 'Ireland is only a tiny part of the story, Mr Lalor. Because of flooding, there are entire countries that could cease to exist in a hundred years. People will have to move. I mean, if you think the current refugee crisis is bad, this will be a thousand times worse. We're talking about entire nations – fifty or sixty million people – on the move.'

'What, all because we had turkey for Christmas?' *he* goes – the dickhead. He turns to Sorcha then. He's like, 'And no Christmas cord from you this year. That was Honor's idea as well, was it?'

Sorcha's there, 'I sent you an e-cord. Oh my God, Dad, I can't believe that you're being like this. You were always so supportive of *my* environmental activism?'

'That's because I thought it was leading towards something.'

'It was – saving the planet.'

'I was thinking about a career. In politics. And now you *have* one – except you don't seem to want it. Whether you like it or not, you're still a member of Seanad Éireann, Sorcha, until this business with *his* father is resolved. And yet you're wasting your time with this girl, who's pulling the wool over *all* of your eyes.'

Honor goes, 'I'm not pulling the wool over anyone's eyes. Look up that map. Because that's the Ireland that *my* children will grow up in – just so your fat focking wife can feed her already bloated face with the flesh of dead animals.'

'How dare you!' Sorcha's old dear goes – even though she *could* do with losing a few pounds. She's a serious biscuit barrel botherer.

'On a related point,' I go, 'you left your exercise bike here when you moved out. Would you have room for it in the cor when you're going?'

They're driving a SEAT Ibiza – two-door. Focking good enough for them.

Sorcha's old man rips off his porty crown and throws it down on the table. He goes, 'Are you going to let them speak to me and your mother like that?'

Sorcha's there, 'While – yes – I do have *some* reservations about the way Honor sometimes expresses herself, I actually think it's *time* for strong language?'

'Focking presents!' Johnny goes. 'Me want focking presents!'

And Sorcha decides that the time for waiting is over.

She gets up from the table, tips over to our ridiculous excuse for a tree and returns carrying a handful of presents, wrapped not in wrapping paper – because it's not recyclable, apparently – but in pillow cases and old newspaper.

I stand up and I go, 'I, er, might give Ronan a ring – see how *he's* getting on,' because I can already sense that this is going to be ugly.

Sorcha goes, 'Ross, sit down – the boys have been looking forward to this moment for weeks.'

Leo has this look of, like, confusion on his face. He reaches into the pillow case that Sorcha hands him.

She's there, 'It's exciting, Leo, isn't it? It's like a lucky dip!'

It's the focking opposite of a lucky dip, of course.

A few seconds later, Leo whips out a remote control cor that's, like, clearly second-hand because the door is broken off the thing.

Leo just stares at it for a good ten seconds without saying shit. Then he looks at me and he goes, 'The fock is this?'

I'm just like, 'Don't look at me, kid. Definitely do *not* look at me.'

Johnny has the same puzzled look on *his* face when he rips open a little newspaper envelope containing – I shit you not – vouchers for hugs. I actually can't wait to hear Sorcha's explanation for these.

'The fock?' he goes, just staring at them.

Sorcha's like, 'They're vouchers, Johnny,' and then she looks around the table, trying to drag the rest of us into it. 'I actually got the idea from reading an interview with, like, Michelle Obama, where she said they give each other, like, thought-presents. Fun things – like vouchers for hugs or a five-minute massage.'

Poor Johnny is still staring at these ridiculous things that Sorcha printed off on the computer last night – a woman who's just been banging on about the unnecessary use of paper, by the way.

'Read what it says on them,' Honor goes. '*This voucher entitles the bearer to a hug!* There's twenty of them altogether. The good news is that you can redeem them from me *or* your daddy *or* your mommy!'

And that's when Brian says what's on the minds of the other two.

He's like, 'Where's our focking presents?'

Yeah, no, he's opened *his* pillow case to find the Tyrannosaurus Rex from *Toy Story* inside – with his two focking orms missing.

He says it again, except *louder* this time? He's like, 'Where's our focking presents?' and he focks the thing across the table, knocking over a bottle of good red wine.

Honor goes, 'That *is* your present, Brian! Look, you got a little envelope as well – see did Santa give you vouchers for hugs like he did your brothers!'

Johnny, having got over his initial shock, goes, 'Santa's a focking prick!' and, I have to say, I would find it very hord to disagree with that analysis. 'He's a fat focking prick!'

I'm thinking, God focking help the dude when he comes back to Dundrum Town Centre next year. He'll have to hire The Viper for security.

Leo storts bawling his eyes out then. It breaks my focking hort because Brian gets up from the table and storts looking around the back of our ridiculous excuse for a tree, then behind the curtains, then behind the sofa, convinced there must be more presents somewhere else.

When he discovers that a broken Tyrannosaurus Rex and a little wad of vouchers for hugs is all that Santa has brought him, he decides to take it out on Sorcha's tree. He makes a run at it and he hits it – I'm proud to say – like Ma'a focking Nonu. The thing snaps in two, then Leo suddenly stops crying and races over to it, all business, like he's cleaning out a ruck. He storts stomping on the sheaf of bamboos and the venetian blinds, at the same time going, 'You're focking dead, Santa! You're focking dead!'

Fionn picks Hillary up out of his chair and covers his little eyes, presumably to protect him from splinters.

Johnny, meanwhile, is just crying his little hort out. Sorcha holds out her two orms and asks him if he'd like to use one of his vouchers. He just focks them across the table at her and goes, 'Fock you, you focking bitch!'

Sorcha goes, 'I know it's upsetting, Johnny, but Santa says we all have to make sacrifices if there's still to be a planet for him to travel around in a hundred years. And Santa actually lives in the North Pole – he'd be one of the first to be directly affected if the polar ice cap totally disappears.'

'Santa's a bastard!' he goes. 'Santa's a fat focking bastard!'

Sorcha's old pair have heard enough. Her old man stands up from the table first and goes, 'I can't listen to any more of this. Come on, Dorling, we're leaving.'

Sorcha's old dear stands up then as well.

I'm there, 'So are you taking the exercise bike with you or not?'

6.

Video Killed the Rodeo Stor

I'm a sucker for the old South Dublin traditions. And Stephen Zuzz Day is the day when the O'Carroll-Kelly men, plus Hennessy, like to put on sheepskin coats and spend the day at Leopardstown, pretending to know something about horses while getting ridiculously shit-faced and generally sending it. Although it won't be the same this year without Ronan.

'I thropped them off at the eerp . . . p . . . p . . . p . . . owurt this morden,' Kennet goes. 'Two loveboords, wha? Off to Itoddy – it's w . . . w . . . w . . . w . . . w . . . weddle for some!'

Yeah, no, Kennet collected me from the gaff. We have a rule that when we go to the races, we always leave the cors behind – especially since the old man lost his licence for two years and Hennessy was disqualified from driving for life.

I'm there, 'Kennet, don't feel like we have to talk to each other just because my son is married to your daughter, okay?'

But he goes, 'I habn't seen Sh . . . Sh . . . Sh . . . Sh . . . Sh . . . Shadden so excirit since the last toyum I got ourra prison. She caddent wait to see this house of Heddessy's – she's been all thalk abourrit, ebber since she seen the p . . . p . . . p . . . p . . . p . . . pitchers.'

I'm there, 'Yeah, no, I bet she has.'

'Heddessy steerted out from v . . . v . . . v . . . veddy humboddle begiddings.'

'Yeah, insurance fraud, wasn't it? I know what him and the old man are trying to do, by the way. They think if they give Shadden a glimpse of what crooked money can buy, she'll talk Ronan into taking his apprenticeship offer.'

'All's Ine saying is it's godda be veddy heerd for her, l . . . l . . . l . . . l . . . libbon wirra husband who's woorken for n . . . n . . . n . . .

n . . . nutten. How's he godda k . . . k . . . k . . . k . . . keep her in the st . . . st . . . st . . . st . . . st . . . st . . . style to which she's accustomed?'

'The style to which she's accustomed? When she was five years old you had her stealing the lead off the neighbours' roofs.'

'Must be where she got her t . . . t . . . t . . . taste for the high life, wha'?'

He laughs like this is the funniest thing that anyone has ever said. It's a relief when we finally pull up outside the old pair's gaff.

He goes, 'I'll t . . . t . . . t . . . toorden the keer arowunt – you go in and tell Cheerlie Ine h . . . h . . . h . . . h . . . h . . . hee-or, will you?'

I let myself into the gaff. There's, like, a smell of paint coming down the stairs. I head for the study. I push the door and the smell of paint gives way to the smell of cigor smoke.

The old man is sitting in his ormchair, smoking a Cohiba that looks like something from a porno movie, the same with Hennessy and – I'm surprised to see – Fyodor, who's sitting behind the old man's desk.

'Ross!' the old man goes. 'Greetings of the season and so forth!'

I'm like, 'Why is there a smell of paint in the gaff?'

'Oh,' the old man goes, 'the girls are decorating the nursery for our impending progeny!'

'Decorating? They're, like, heavily pregnant.'

'Oh, I wouldn't worry about that, Kicker! They're not using lead paint – and Fionnuala is making sure they hold the ladder for each other!'

He hands me a cigor.

I'm there, 'Your stuttering fock of a driver is outside.'

He's like, 'Right you are! I've invited Fyodor to take Ronan's place for the day, Ross! As it happens, he has a favour he'd like to ask you!'

I'm there, 'What?' suddenly thrown by this. 'As in?'

Fyodor goes, 'My son, Sergei, wishes to improve his English. So after Christmas he and my wife will come to Ireland to live for one year. So now I look for school for him. He would like very much to play rugby. Your father tells me that you are the coach of school.'

'That's right!' the old man goes. 'Pres Bray! Leinster Schools Senior Cup champions 2018 – eh, Kicker?'

'Your father also tells me that you have a brain made of rugby.'

'A rugby brain!' the old man goes. 'It's a phrase often used to describe him – by Gerry Thornley *and* others!'

'Your father tells me that if anyone can turn Sergei into a great player, then it is you. So, in January, he will start school in this Pres Bray.'

I'm like, 'Er, yeah, no, whatever. Are we going to the races or not?'

Ten seconds later, we're heading for the door. I stop in the hall-way to light my cigor and that's when I hear a whisper coming from the toilet under the stairs.

It's, like, a woman's voice, going, 'Ross . . . Ross . . .'

I walk over to the door. It opens. A hand appears and pulls me inside. And suddenly I'm back in the old pair's downstairs toilet with Szidonia. She switches on the taps.

I'm like, 'Jesus Christ, this is becoming a bit of a habit.'

She goes, 'Give me code,' and she says it in a really, like, *cold* voice? 'Give me code for safe.'

She's wearing, like, dungarees, which make her belly huge. And she's covered in paint.

I'm there, 'I told you I'm not giving you your passports. What makes you think I've changed my mind?'

She goes, 'Because this.'

She holds up her phone. There's, like, a video playing on it. It's a video of –

Oh, holy living fock!

It's a video of me and Delma, doing the old pants-off dance-off up against the gable wall of the house. It's shot from up above – from presumably Szidonia's bedroom.

'That could be anyone,' I try to go.

It's weak and she knows it.

She goes, 'Perhaps I will send to your lovely wife and she will decide if it is you who is having the sex with this friend of Fionnuala.'

I'm there, 'No, please don't. Just hand me the phone there and let me have a closer look.'

'You think I am stupid? Give me the number or I send to her now.'

'Szidonia, they're not your actual babies.'

'The number.'

'Why don't you let me have a think about it between now and New Year's? Leave it with me, okay?'

'I am not pretend here. I have phone number for your wife. I send to her right now if you do not give me this code.'

Fock.

'Okay, okay,' I hear myself go. 'It's Seán FitzPatrick's birthday. The twenty-fifth of May. We're talking two, five, oh, five.'

She repeats the numbers, memorizing them.

'Is wrong,' she goes, 'and I will send video.'

I'm there, 'It's not wrong. That's the actual number.'

Out in the hallway, I can hear the old man going, 'Where the hell has Kicker got to? Fionnuala? Fionnuala, is Ross upstairs with you?'

The old dear's there, 'No, Dorling, he hasn't come to say hello at all.'

I can't tell you how shit I suddenly feel.

Szidonia's like, 'Go to your races.'

I'm there, 'So when are you going to do it – as in, the actual runner?'

Except she doesn't answer my question directly. She just smiles at me and goes, 'It is funny video.'

I'm like, 'What are you talking about?'

'Loredana almost chokes when she hears what you call this woman when you are making sex to her.'

I'm there, 'Okay, just as a matter of curiosity, what name did I actually call her?'

And Szidonia smiles at me in a cruel way and goes, 'You call her Mommy!'

I end up, like, shitting myself for the next few days.

I honestly haven't felt so scared since the time in the Aviva Stadium when I refused to hold the lift for Peter Clohessy – I actually

laughed in his face as he came running towards the closing doors –
then looked down to see one of his big size-twelves stuck between
them.

I'm expecting a call at any moment to say that Szidonia and the
others have pegged it.

And, while I actually agree with the girl that my old pair aren't
fit to be parents – they're not even fit to parent me – I keep waking
up in the middle of the night, thinking the exact same words that I
muttered to myself throughout that long elevator ride up to
Corporate – Level Four in the company of The Claw: 'What the
fock have you done, Ross? What in the name of God have you focking done?'

Sorcha and Honor are sitting at the island, with an A4 pad in
front of them, writing down their New Year's resolutions. It's, like,
an annual ritual that Sorcha insists on putting us through.

Usually, Honor's are things like 'Take less shit from people' or
'Be an even bigger bitch' and I can honestly say she's one of the few
people I know who manages to stick to her promises for the full
twelve months of the year.

Except this year the atmosphere is, I don't know, a lot more
serious.

Sorcha goes, 'I know I say this every year, but one of *my* resolutions is going to be to tell Chastity and Borislava that I only want
them to use natural and non-toxic products when they're cleaning
our house in future.'

Honor's like, 'Oh my God, Mom, there's this woman in the States
who blogs about the environment and she says the only cleaning
products that you *actually* need in your home are apple cider vin-
egar and, like, *baking* soda?'

It bothers me, for some reason, seeing Honor and Sorcha all
thick as, suddenly, thieves. And – yeah, no – it possibly *is* just jeal-
ousy? Me and Honor used to be close, but these days I'm not even
getting a look-in.

I'm there, 'Hey, Honor, do you want to see a video of a woman
in Cavan shitting her dress on her wedding day?'

She goes, 'Er, we're kind of *busy* here, Dad?'

'Yeah, you're missing the point, Honor – it's very funny.'

Leo goes, 'Me see!' and I call up the video and hand him my phone.

Fock. His eye looks bad today. Thankfully, Sorcha hasn't noticed it yet – and hopefully, she never will.

She picks up the *Irish Times* magazine and opens it to the feature on 18 Under the Age of 18 Who are Predicted to Shape 2018. She stares at it for, like, the millionth time and goes, 'I'm so proud of you, Honor. I actually think your father has a point, though. I'm just looking at some of the people who are ahead of you. Number three is, like, a singer-songwriter who's *already being compared to Ed Sheeran*. Oh my God, *how* does that compare with a young girl who's trying to safegord the future of the planet?'

Leo laughs and goes, 'She shit in her dress!' and he looks at me with his boggledy eyes.

Brian's like, 'Me see!'

But I'm there, 'I'll show it to you later, Brian. Let's hit Scrumdiddly's and get some ice cream, will we?'

The boys cheer.

'Make sure it's vegan ice cream,' Sorcha goes.

Johnny's like, 'Fock you and your vegan shit!' because he – like the others – will probably never get over what happened on Christmas Day.

Anyway, I put their coats on them and then we head outside. And that's when that famous fifth sense of mine tells me that something is wrong. Something is seriously wrong. And then I cop it.

Jesus Christ, the Audi is gone.

'Where's the focking cor?' Johnny goes.

I'm there, 'It's obviously been stolen.'

With my free hand, I whip out my phone and I ring 999. At the same time, I also shout for Sorcha.

I'm like, 'Sorcha! Sorcha!'

Some dude answers on the seventh ring. He's there, 'Which service do you require?'

And I'm like, 'Is that supposed to be a joke? The focking Feds! My cor's been stolen!'

Again, I shout for Sorcha.

I'm like, 'Sorcha!'

The dude's there, 'I'm sorry, Sir, that's not actually an emergency.'

'What,' I go, 'even if it's an Audi A8?'

'You'll need to ring your local Garda station to report it stolen. This isn't a 999 matter,' and he hangs up on me.

Sorcha finally gets up off her orse and steps outside. Honor as well.

I'm there, 'Do either of you know, off-hand, the number for the Feds in Dalkey?'

Sorcha goes, 'Why are you ringing the Gords, Ross?'

I point to the empty space on the gravel where my cor used to be.

I'm there, 'Er, my *cor* has been stolen?'

She looks at me like I've lost it.

She goes, 'We sold the cor, Ross – yesterday?'

I'm like, 'Excuse me?'

'We sold it. Well, we traded it in.'

'Sorry, is this a focking nightmare I'm suddenly having? What the fock are you talking about?'

Honor pipes up then. She goes, 'Dad, we had this conversation on, like, Stephen Zuzz Day.'

I'm there, 'Stephen Zuzz Day? Okay, can we all just stop having important conversations with me when I've been drinking. Jesus, I don't even remember how I got home from Leopardstown.'

'Well, we talked about it before you fell asleep at the kitchen table.'

'Okay, was that not a clue, Honor, as to how shit-faced I possibly was?'

Sorcha actually defends her. She goes, 'Ross, our daughter has just been described by the *Irish Times* magazine as *the* emerging voice of the environmentally woke generation. What if it then comes out that her dad is driving around in a big, gas-guzzling German cor. *Not* a good look, Ross! *Not* a good look.'

I'm there, 'So how the fock am I supposed to get around?'

'*This* is our new cor,' Honor goes and she points to this – I shit you not – tiny, red, boxy thing.

I'm like, 'What the fock?'

'It's a Mitsubishi i-MiEV,' Sorcha goes, like she's hurting no one.

'It actually reminds me of the cor my granny used to drive back and forth to the Active Retirement Centre.'

I'm there, 'Yeah, that's *not* a selling point, Sorcha?'

I'm just, like, walking around it, wondering how the fock we're all going to fit in there.

I'm there, 'How do you even stort the thing? Do you pull it backwards or something?'

And that's when I see the – quite literally – *flex* leading from the cor, through the living-room window, and into the house – they don't put charging ports for electric cars into garages.

I'm there, 'You have *got* to be kidding me!'

Sorcha's like, 'There's nothing wrong with an electric cor, Ross! Gwyneth Paltrow drives an electric cor!'

'Gwyneth Paltrow talks to clouds and uses her own shit for compost! Jesus Christ, I can't believe you traded in my beautiful A8 for *this* heap of junk.'

'There was some money left over. But we gave it away.'

'You did what?'

'We donated it to the Global Footprint Network – an amazing, amazing non-profit that helps individuals, companies and even governments to make wiser, more sustainable ecological decisions by offering actionable insights into natural resource management, consumption and capacity.'

My phone suddenly rings. I look at the screen.

Oh, fock.

'Who's that?' Sorcha goes.

I'm there, 'It's, er, my old man,' and I can actually hear the wobble in my voice.

'Oh my God, Ross – answer it!'

So I do.

I'm like, 'Er, hello?'

Straight away, I can hear the upset in his voice. He's there, 'Ross! Ross, it's Szidonia! She's gone –' except he can't get the actual words out.

I'm there, 'She's gone?' acting the innocent. 'She's gone where? You're not making any sense.'

He's like, 'She's gone –'

'So she's gone. For what it's worth, I don't blame her. The whole thing was ridiculous from the stort. You're both too old to be parents.'

Sorcha's there, 'Oh my God!'

But then he manages to get his shit together and he goes, 'She's gone into labour early, Ross! She's just this minute given birth!'

I'm like, 'Oh,' at the same time thinking, Thank fock! Thank fock for that!

'On the final day of the Year of Our Lord, two thousand and seventeen – six weeks prematurely! – a baby was born unto your mother and I! And here I am, the man who would be Taoiseach, crying like a damn fool!'

'Six weeks?' I go, knowing that's, like, *very* premature? 'Is the, I don't know, baby okay?'

Sorcha's like, 'Oh my God! One of the babies was born!'

The old man goes, 'He's receiving the best care that our country's wonderful private health service can offer!'

I'm like, 'He?'

'That's right,' the old man goes. 'Congratulations, Kicker! You have a little brother!'

I don't know what the fock is wrong with me, but my hort is beating like I don't know what. I'm on the way into Holles Street to meet my little – I still can't believe I'm even saying this – *brother* for the first time. And a man who never had an attack of nerves on the rugby pitch, even when he was taking vital kicks, late in the game, with the entire crowd booing him, is suddenly having a meltdown.

I end up telling Sorcha and Honor to go on up to the ward with the boys.

Sorcha's like, 'Is everything okay, Ross?'

And I'm there, 'Yeah, no, I just, em, need a moment. I'll follow you up.'

So I end up standing there for, like, fifteen with my hand against the wall of the building and I feel like I'm going to have a *literally* hort attack? That's when Ronan and Shadden arrive on the scene.

Ro's like, 'Alreet, Rosser?'

I'm there, 'Hey, Ro, how was Italy?'

'Itoddy was moostard,' he goes. 'Wadn't it, Shadden?'

She's like, 'It was lubbly. And the house was out of this wurdled, so it was.'

I notice she's still dressed like she's *on* her holidays, even though they got back last night and it's minus focking one outside.

Ronan's there, 'Nice to see how the utter half libs, wha'?'

Shadden's there, 'You heerd what Heddessy said to you – *we* could lib like that if you gev up this civoddle reets bullshit. There's no muddy in it, Ro-Ro.'

It's obvious that the girl has been turned.

I'm there, 'Don't listen to them, Ro.'

And, thankfully, he doesn't. He goes, 'I hab to foddy me heert, Shadden – and human reets is the airdea Ine wanthon to go into, so it is. Have you seen the babby yet, Rosser?'

I'm like, 'Er, not yet.'

'So what are doing out hee-or? Why ardent you insoyut seeing yisser little brutter?'

And that's when he picks up on the fact that I'm having a pretty much anxiety attack.

He suddenly has his orm around my shoulder and he's going, 'Breed, Rosser! Breed!'

I'm there, 'I'm *trying* to breathe! Jesus Christ, look at me, Ro! The greatest kicker in the history of the schools game and I'm shaking like a focking leaf, look! Imagine if the likes of Joey Corbery walked around that corner and saw me like this. It'd kill him stone dead.'

'What's wrong, Rosser?'

'I don't know. It's just so random. When I was a kid, Ro, all I ever wanted was a little brother to play with. And now I finally have and I'm closing in on forty.'

'Rosser,' he goes, 'this babby – this little brutter of yoo-ers – he's godda grow up woorshipping you.'

'Do you think?'

'The sayum as I woorship you. The sayum as alls yisser kids woorship you. Now get the fook up to that ward.'

It ends up being all I need to hear.

Into the hospital and up in the lift we go, then down one corridor, turn right, then down another corridor. I see them all gathered in this, like, waiting area – we're talking my old man and my old dear, we're talking Sorcha and Hillary, we're talking Honor, Brian, Johnny and Leo.

I walk up to them and – I swear to fock – I stort shaking everyone's hand, going, 'Hi, I'm Ross O'Carroll-Kelly,' which obviously everyone finds a *bit* weird?

'The fock is his problem?' Leo goes.

Ronan's like, 'Your fadder's habbon a birrof a padic attack, Leo. It's alreet, Rosser – keep breeding.'

I've honestly never seen the old dear look so happy. She goes, 'I'm sorry you all had to wait a few days to meet him. He's still in the ICU, but he's doing much better now.'

'Well,' the old man goes, 'I hope the thing is bloody well sound-proof! Otherwise, the chap would have heard the debate that your daughter and I were just having, Kicker, on the subject of the – inverted commas – environment! What were those things you mentioned, Honor?'

'Er, *greenhouse* gases?' Honor goes.

'Greenhouse gases! Have you ever heard the like of it, Ross? Well, it all got rather heated – reminded me of us having one of our famous political debates, Kicker!'

Honor's there, 'Greenhouse gases *are* an actual thing, Granddad. They're what's causing all these, like, extreme weather events.'

The old man just chuckles. 'It's all a hoax!' he goes. 'Designed to prevent countries like Ireland, with a vast wealth in untapped natural resources, from extracting them from the Earth – thus keeping us weak and dependent!'

The old dear goes, 'Do you want to meet your brother, Ross?'

And all I can do is just, like, nod dumbly.

She leads me – leads all of us, in fact – down the corridor to this, like, door, then through the door into this dorkened room. And there, in the centre of the room, is what looks like a lorge fish tank, except inside this lorge fish tank is this teeny, tiny baby. His skin is pink and his eyes are firmly shut. He's got, like, an oxygen tube fixed to his nose and a wire connecting his hort to a monitor. I see the little hospital wristband with 'O'Carroll-Kelly' on it and then I notice his tiny little fingers.

Yeah, no, my little brother.

And that's when I end up just losing it. 'Jesus Christ,' I go, my forehead leaning against the glass, tears spilling down my face. 'Jesus focking Christ.'

'Oh my God,' Sorcha goes. 'He's beautiful, Fionnuala.'

Honor's there, 'Brian, Johnny, Leo – see that little baby in there? That's your uncle!'

Ronan goes, 'He's the bleaten spits of you, Rosser.'

The old dear puts her orm around my shoulder to comfort me.

'His name is Hugo,' she goes. 'Do you like it, Ross?'

I just nod. I'm there, 'It's a great focking name. Is he going to be okay, Mom?'

'He's doing well!' the old man goes. 'He's like his father – a little fighter who doesn't know the *meaning* of the word surrender!'

We end up standing there and staring at him for a good, like, ten minutes, oooh-ing and awww-ing every time his facial expression changes, even *slightly*?

'The cranky face on him,' Ronan goes. 'That's you, Rosser, all oaber.'

Everyone laughs, including me.

Sorcha hugs the old dear and goes, 'Oh, Fionnuala, I'm so happy for you – for you too, Chorles!'

And the old dear's there, 'With Ross, I did everything wrong. I'd be the first to admit it. With Hugo, I'm going to do everything right.'

Eventually, we step out of the room and into the corridor, then we walk back towards the waiting area. The old man is telling Ronan that he thinks Hugo is going to be an inside-centre – based on fock knows what.

We pass this, like, ward on our right and I just so happen to look in. And there, in a Juicy tracksuit, packing her dressing-gown into a bag, is Szidonia. No one's even acknowledging her now that she's done her job of delivering my old pair's baby into the world.

I let the others walk on down the corridor. I hear the old dear go, 'There's no doubt I blamed Ross for my post-portum weight retention. That won't be an issue with Hugo – as you can see, Sorcha, I've kept my wonderful figure!' and she laughs like the wagon she can't help being.

I turn into the ward.

I'm like, 'Hey, Szidonia – are you being discharged?'

The girl looks wrecked. She doesn't say shit. She just, like, stares at me.

I'm there, 'You obviously didn't get the chance to do that runner you were planning.'

'We make plans to leave,' she goes, 'then my waters break.'

I'm like, 'That's a bummer,' because I'm thinking that's obviously the end of that. As in, fleeing the country while pregnant is one thing – but stealing an actual baby and then pegging it is another.

But that's when she goes, 'You meet Novac?'

I'm like, 'Novac? Who the fock is Novac?'

'My baby is Novac.'

'Except his name is *Hugo*, Szidonia? And he's not your actual baby.'

'He will be. When I take back to Moldova.'

'I can't let you take him, Szidonia. It'd kill my old pair.'

'Your mother and father are too old and too crazy to have these babies. So we take. That is all.'

'He's literally my brother. I'm going to tell my old pair what you're planning.'

'You will not tell. If you do, your pretty wife will get video. Two minutes of her husband having the sex with this Delma person –'

'It was longer than two minutes.'

'–going, "Mommy! Mommy!" like sick bastard.'

'It was definitely longer than two minutes.'

'So now we make new plan. We wait until all babies are born and then we go.'

'I can't let you do it.'

'You *will* let. And also, when times comes, you will help us.'

*

I drive to Bray in the Mitsubishi i-MiEV. The least said about the journey, the better. All I will say is that, at one point, I end up being overtaken by a GoCor.

I pork the cor – so-called – in front of Brother Ciaran's gaff. I knock on the door and he answers. He wishes me a happy New Year and goes, 'I hope it'll be one to remember for Pres Bray.'

And I'm there, 'We'll see,' not making him any promises this time.

He invites me into the house, then he points out four lorge, torton-covered laundry bags under the hallway stairs.

'The jerseys are there,' he goes. 'Two hundred of them. You haven't told me why you want them yet.'

I'm there, 'It's a surprise – for the goys.'

He goes, 'I'm sure I'll find out about it in good time.'

I pop the boot of the cor and I throw the bags in. Then I drive off, turning right at the top of the Putland Road and heading for the town. I throw the piece of shit in a space next to McDonald's, then I grab one of the bags out of the boot and I stort hitting the shops.

The first one I walk into ends up being a borber's called Shears to You at the top of the Main Street. There's an elderly dude in the chair and a younger dude – the borber – standing behind him, cutting his hair. Without looking at me, the borber dude goes, 'Take a seat. I'll be with you when I finish with this gentleman, like.'

I'm there, 'I'm not here for a haircut, Dude.'

He turns his head, then he looks at me over the top of his glasses.

I'm like, 'I wanted to ask would you mind putting something in the window for me?'

I unzip the bag and I whip out one of the jerseys. I open it out and show it to him.

He goes, 'What is it, like?'

It's the old dude in the chair who actually recognizes it. He goes, 'It's Pres Bray – rugby, like.'

I'm there, 'You know it?' a note of surprise in my voice.

He's there, 'Of course I know it – didn't I play for them, like?'

I'm like, 'You? Seriously?'

The dude laughs. He goes, 'I wasn't *always* eighty years of age, like.'

'So, like, when was this?'

'It was in 1954, like. Are you going to put the jersey in the window for him, Eric?'

The borber goes, 'I'd be delighted to, like.'

I walk out of there and I swing into the next shop, which ends up being a florist's called Austin Flowers. The woman – who's called Hetty Austin – says her nephew is actually on the team and it turns out that she's Barry Austin's aunt.

After a bit of flirting between us – her husband is dead ten years, she makes sure to mention – she agrees to let me put a jersey in the window. She stares hord at my orse and licks her lips as I use masking tape to stick it to the glass.

I'm actually relieved to get out of there.

I swing into the next shop, which happens to be Ron's Butchers. The smell of meat. Suddenly, I'm the one licking my lips. It turns out that Ron is a past pupil of Pres Bray and he had Brother Ciaran for Civics in First Year and for Irish in Second and Third.

He goes, 'I saw the *Bray People*. You got hammered by Blackrock, like. You didn't even bother playing the second half, like.'

I'm there, 'You're going to see a totally different team against Michael's. Dude, it'd be great if you could maybe hang the jersey up. I know it'd mean a lot to the goys.'

He walks over to window. There's, like, a steel rail with lumps of – Jesus – delicious-looking meat hanging from it. He pushes them to one side, creating some space in the middle, then he hangs the jersey on it from two hooks.

And that's how it goes for the next, like, hour. I swing into every shop, pub and business on the Main Street and ask them to put a jersey in the window. We're talking Holland's pub. We're talking Dubray Books. We're talking Anvil Home. We're talking Lifestyle Sports. We're talking Ink, Inc, the tattoo studio. We're talking Spar. We're talking Bannon Jewellers. We're talking Hallmork cords. We're talking Mount Everest of Kathmandu restaurant. We're talking the Bray Head Shop, a dodgy-looking place specializing in bongs and 'legal highs', where the long-haired dude behind the counter keeps laughing in my face and saying, 'Radical!' while I try to explain the laws of rugby to him. But he still puts a jersey in the window.

Not one shop turns me away. And it's not long before I end up having to go back to the cor to grab the second bag.

I'm walking up the Main Street when I end up getting a beep from this, like, bus driver. I'm actually about to give him the finger. It's, like, an automatic thing where I come from when you hear a cor horn beep. But then the dude pulls over, opens his door and shouts, 'You're – what's this your name is? – Ross O'Kennedy-Something, like.'

'Ross O'Carroll-Kelly,' I go. 'Yeah, no, it's Ross O'Carroll-Kelly.'

He's there, 'You know my son, like.'

'Your son? As in?'

'Steven Nagle. He's your scrum-half, like.'

'Ah, Nailer!' I go. 'Yeah, no, he's doing great. He couldn't throw the ball a few weeks ago, but I'm seeing definite improvements.'

He goes, 'He says you're a gas man altogether, like.'

'Does he?'

'Although he finds it mad hard to understand you sometimes.'

'And me, him, my friend. And me, him.'

'Anyway, good to meet you, Ross.'

And with that, he drives away.

Then I hit the Quinsborough Road. Again, I go into every single shop and business. We're talking Oxfam. We're talking Molloys Coffee Shop. We're talking Goldsmith's pub. We're talking the post office. We're talking The Gem newsagents. We're talking O'Brien's off-licence. We're talking the Zip Yord, where the owner of the place says she'll adjust the jersey to make it look fitted and she'll put it on a mannequin in the window.

It ends up being yes after yes after yes.

And then suddenly, just as I'm running out of shops, I find myself standing outside Wheat Bray Love. I notice the sandwich board outside on the path with today's lunchtime special written on it in chalk – a cardamom-rubbed chicken sandwich on Old Testament bread with fortified tomatoes and mortified chives.

I pop in with the intention of obviously ripping the *piss*? I suppose you could say that I end up being surprised by what I see. I'm expecting the place to be empty. Except it's the exact opposite. It's rammers. And it's not just people drinking – as Sorcha mentioned – the free afternoon teas and coffees and using the wi-fi. It's full of, like, actual customers genuinely ordering shit, or rather asking questions about the menu.

You couldn't introduce hipster food to a place like Bray and not expect there to be questions.

'What's a salted caramel lobster melt, like?' I hear one old woman go.

And Claire's there, 'It's exactly as it sounds, Mrs Deegan. It's ethically sourced Crookhaven lobster on a toasted artisanal brioche bun, with smoked ricotta, seasonal Gouda and white cheddar curds melted, topped with a salted caramel drizzle.'

The woman – none the focking wiser, by the way – goes, 'I'll have one of those, like. And a side of sprouts in season.'

Claire scribbles it down and returns to the counter. And that's when she spots me. She goes, 'Hi, Ross! Oh my God, congrats!'

I'm like, 'Congrats? On what?'

'I was talking to Sorcha,' she goes. 'She said your mom and dad had a little baby boy.'

I'm there, 'Er, yeah. This place seems to be flying,' and I can hear the disappointment in my voice.

She goes, 'Oh my God, I've been *literally* rushed off my feet?'

I'm there, 'Don't take this the wrong way, but I walked in here hoping the place would be empty and you'd fallen flat on your face.'

'Do you want something to eat, Ross? I'd recommend the foraged grasshopper taco with massaged plums and unselfconscious mushrooms.'

I'm there, 'No offence, Claire, I'd rather eat a yord of my own shit in a hot-dog bun. The only reason I swung in was to ask you if you'd put one of these in the window?'

I flash the jersey at her. She goes, 'Oh my God, Sorcha said you were coaching Pres Bray!'

I'm there, 'Yeah, no, I'm just trying to create a bit of a buzz about them in the town.'

She says, 'I'll definitely put it in the window.'

She takes it from me. And then, with fock-all else to say to each other – we've had sex about twice as many times as we've had a conversation – I pick up my bag of jerseys and out the door I fock.

So – yeah, no – I'm standing outside the place, getting ready to cross the road to the Boulevord Centre, when all of a sudden I become aware of some dude who looks vaguely familiar, walking towards me.

He's got, like, a full Gordon D'Arcy Grand Slam beard and one of those ridiculous, long moustaches with the *ends* curled up? He's wearing low-slung jeans and a tweed waistcoat with a shirt underneath, open to about three inches above his belly button, even though it's the first week in January. He's got his hair cut like Conor McGregor, long on top, swept back, and shaved at the sides. He's also got his eyebrow pierced, a bull-ring in his nose and a small tattoo of a half-moon on his right temple.

He suddenly cops me grinning at him – like a dog eating its own sick.

I'm like, 'Hey, Garret – I heard you were home. You still look like a knob, in case you were wondering.'

The best he can do is, 'What the fock are *you* doing in Bray?' because he doesn't follow rugby and is unlikely to have heard the news.

I don't even mention the fact that I'm coaching Pres. It'd be lost on him anyway.

Instead, I go, 'I just popped in to see your wife. Oh, sorry, she tells me you two are just friends now.'

'She wouldn't tell you shit,' he tries to go. 'She hates your guts.'

I have this sudden flash of memory. The dude at one of our summer borbecues. He whipped out his guitor and he shushed me – in my own gorden, by the way – so that he could sing some bullshit *Crowded House* song – focking 'Weather With You' – even though it wasn't that kind of porty.

I'm suddenly filled with this, I don't know, irrational hatred for the dude. I think that's probably the reason I end up going, 'Is that what she told you, yeah?'

He's like, 'What's that supposed to mean?' and he's suddenly uncomfortable because he's obviously still in two minds about whether he can trust Claire or not.

'I know you don't want to hear it,' I go, 'but there's always been something between me and your wife.'

He's like, 'Yeah, you wish. She told me that you two never slept together.'

'Dude,' I go, 'she's lying to you. Are you seriously that slow on the uptake?'

He stares at me, tears forming in his eyes, then he turns on his heel and – hilarious – walks off in the direction of Bray Bowl Entertainment.

The goys are all just staring at me, totally mesmerized. It's, like, our first training session since Christmas and we've got a hell of a lot of work to do between now and the day of the match.

It's big Lukie McDermott who finally says it. He goes, 'There's Pres Bray jerseys in the window of every shop in Bray, like.'

I'm like, 'Is that so?' acting the innocent.

Barry Austin's there, 'My auntie said this mad posh fella came into the florist's and asked her to put a rugby jersey in the window. She said he was flirting with her – asking her where she tended to do her socializing, like.'

There's no point in denying it. It's a chat-up line I pretty much invented. So I laugh along with everyone else.

'She told him she does line-dancing two nights a week in Little Bray and then she helps out with the Meals on Wheels for the Bray Old Folks Association on the Killarney Road. She said his face nearly dropped, like.'

Jesus, I was just giving the woman's confidence a little bump while trying to sweet-talk her into putting the thing in the window. Talk about taking the ball and running with it.

Little Nailer goes, 'I heard you met me auld fella. He's the fella drives the bus, like.'

I laugh. I'm there, 'I did, yeah.'

Either Lenny or Dougie looks at me and goes, 'So it *was* you?'

and I can feel a definite softening in their attitude towards me. It's the first time I feel like they actually respect me. 'You went around with the jerseys from shop to shop, like?'

I'm there, 'Yes, I did. Because, goys, I want Bray to be proud of you. I want this town to know that it has only one team in the Leinster Schools Senior Cup –'

Conal Crommie, my full-back, goes, 'There's also Gerard's, like.'

And I stare him down and roar, 'Fock Gerard's! Seriously – fock them to Hell and back!'

It's possibly a bit over-the-top, but it gets the message across and I can sense the excitement growing.

Ricey goes, 'Seven grand a term. Pack of pricks, like.'

He has the right attitude for a hooker.

I'm there, 'Come on, let's go out there and do some work. Like I said, we don't have a lot of time.'

Out onto the field we go.

As I'm standing there, watching them flinging balls around, I suddenly become aware of this, like, thin, weedy-looking kid, who's standing a few feet away from me, trying to catch my eye.

I'm there, 'The fock are you looking at?' because I have literally no idea who he even is.

He goes, 'Hello, I am Sergei,' and he says it like the name is supposed to *mean* something to me?

I'm there, 'Yeah? The fock do you want?'

He goes, 'I am come to school in Bray to learn my English. My father is speaking to you.'

I'm suddenly remembering my conversation with Fyodor on Stephen Zuzz Day.

I'm like, 'For fock's sake,' because this kid does *not* look like a rugby player. 'Dude, what position do you supposedly play?'

'In Russia,' he goes, 'I am number ten.'

I laugh in his face. No choice in the matter, because the dude is, like, not even five feet tall and he looks like he weighs not much more than Honor – the vegan version.

I'm like, 'Yeah, no, thanks, but I've already got a ten,' trying to let him down gently. 'Barry Austin over there. Maybe come back to me when you hit puberty.'

He looks crushed. But if I'm going to be a world-class rugby coach, I have to get used to looking people in the eye and telling them to hit the focking bricks. God knows, Declan Kidney had no qualms about saying it to me when he left me off the Ireland Schools team.

'I am fast,' he tries to go. 'Also, I have big skills.'

'I'm trying to give you the polite brush-off here. Dude, look at these goys. They're, like, twice your size. And they'd be considered small compared to the goys from the likes of Rock and Belvo and Michael's.'

'My father says you will say this to me. So he tells me that I must give to you this letter.'

He hands me a sheet of A4 paper that's, like, folded over twice.

'The fock is this?' I go.

He's there, 'He says you must read.'

So that's what I end *up* doing? In just, like, disbelief.

'Ross,' the letter says, '*I am very proud of my son, Sergei, just like your father is very proud of you. He is good rugby player. He is small but he is very fast and he has learned good skills. If you are reading this letter, it means you already say to him no, you have no place for him on Pres Bray team. I wish to tell you that this would be a terrible mistake for you. I warn you that if you do not put him in team, you will regret and there will be big consequences for you. Best wishes, Fyodor.*'

My blood turns literally cold.

I go, 'Dude, you wait there,' and I walk away from him to find a quiet spot to ring my old man.

He answers on the fifth ring. He goes, 'Kicker! I'm at the hospital! Just to let you know, little Hugo is doing wonderfully well! They might even let us take him home in a week or so!'

I'm straight on the attack. I'm there, 'I can't believe what I've just focking read!'

'Was it Pat Leahy's column in this morning's *Times* saying a Charles O'Carroll-Kelly government would be the worst thing to happen to Ireland since potato blight?'

'I'm talking about the letter that your mate Fyodor told his son to give to me.'

'Oh, yes, the famous Sergei! You met him, did you? I said to Fyodor this morning, "No better man to bring out the best in him than the future Ireland rugby coach!"'

'Fyodor threatened me.'

'Threatened you? That doesn't sound like the Fyodor I know, Ross!'

'Er, he cut the brakes in my cor and burned down Erika's gallery. He fixed an election and got fake Gordaí to fire tear gas into a crowd of people. And – yeah, no – now he's threatened me. In a focking letter.'

'It's probably just a language barrier issue! I'm sure that whatever he said has been lost in translation – inverted commas!'

'If you are reading this letter, it means you already say to him no, you have no place for him on Pres Bray team. I wish to tell you that this would be a terrible mistake for you.'

'There's absolutely nothing sinister in that, Ross! It's no different from the letters I wrote to Warren Gatland back in the day!'

'Okay, what about this line, then? *I warn you that if you do not put him in team, you will regret and there will be big consequences for you.'*

'To me, he seems to be saying that, without Sergei in the team, you'll have less of a chance to beat St Michael's! I can't see how you could put any other construction on what he's saying, Ross!'

'I'm not putting his son in the team.'

'And I'm sure that Fyodor will be totally understanding when he hears that! You might find some role for him, though – eh, Ross?'

'Oh, I'll find a role for him alright.'

I hang up, then I call the dude over. His face is all hopeful – he obviously thinks his old man has succeeded in, like, *intimidating* me?

I'm there, 'Okay, you know the outhalf role inside-out, I'm presuming?'

'Yes,' he goes. 'In Russia, this is my job in team.'

'Right, so you see Barry Austin over there, practising kicking by putting the ball between the posts from a variety of different angles and distances?'

'Yes, I see this.'

'Right, well, I want you to retrieve the balls for him.'

He just nods – although I can tell he's disappointed.

I'm there, 'And do it quickly! I never want to see him without a ball in front of him! Let's see how supposedly fast you are!'

Sorcha is standing over the cooker, stirring a pot of something.

'Sit down at the table. Honor will be home from school soon. I've made vegan chilli non corne from a recipe I found online!'

I'm like, '*Non* corne?' because, while I'm open to contradiction on this point, nothing in the history of the world has ever been improved by the addition of the word 'non'.

Non-fat. Non-contact. Non-alcoholic. Non-sexual.

This is what we're reduced to now.

I'm like, 'Fock's sake.'

The kitchen door opens – except it's not Honor.

It ends up being Fionn. He's like, 'Hey,' and he walks over to Hillary and lifts him out of his high-chair. '*Comment ça va,* Hillary?'

Something is up. I pick up on it immediately. It's his tone of voice. There are no secrets between people who played rugby together.

I'm like, 'What's wrong?'

And Sorcha turns around and looks at Fionn. She's like, 'Oh my God, what is it?'

He's there, 'Oh, I, em, got a bit of news. From the hospital.'

I'm like, 'Dude, tell me.'

He's there, 'So it turns out that it's in my lymph nodes.'

Sorcha stops stirring the pot and puts her two hands over her mouth. She's like, 'Oh my God, Fionn!'

But he's there, 'It's fine, Sorcha. I always knew there was a chance I was going to have to have chemo.'

She walks across the kitchen and she, I don't know, *encloses* him and little Hillary in a big hug.

Then she goes, 'For how long?'

He's like, 'They're saying six to eight weeks. They're putting in the chemo port this week. Then I stort Monday.'

I'm like, 'I'm going to be there. So will all the goys.'

'Ross, you don't have to do that.'

'Rugby, Fionn. I rest my case.'

'You could be sitting there for six or seven hours.'

Six or seven *hours*? Fock it. I've already committed to it now, though.

I'm like, 'Whatever it takes, Dude. Even if we end up doing it in shifts.'

Sorcha remembers her chilli non corne. She races back across the kitchen to whip it off the hob.

'Ross,' Fionn goes, 'can you do something for me?'

I'm like, 'Er, yeah,' wary of making any more promises.

'Will you shave my head?'

'What?'

'My hair is going to fall out. A friend of Eleanor's went through chemo last year. She said that doing proactive things is a good way of wresting back control. So, rather than just letting the chemo take my hair, I've decided to have it all shaved off.'

I'm there, 'I've got a clippers. Will I go and get it?'

He shrugs his shoulders. He's like, 'Why not?'

So I tip upstairs and I grab it from the en suite. By the time I get back to the kitchen, Hillary is back in his high-chair and Sorcha is putting a towel around Fionn's shoulders.

I'm like, 'So what do you want – blade one, blade two?'

But he goes, 'Take it all, Ross.'

'So, like, totally bald?'

'I'm going to lose it all anyway.'

He takes off his famous glasses and he sits down. I flick the switch and the thing storts buzzing in my hand.

I'm like, 'You're definitely, definitely sure you want me to do this?'

He's there, 'Just do it.'

So I put the blade flat to the back of his neck, then I stort pushing it up towards the top of his head. And suddenly I'm watching Fionn's black curls fall at my feet in just, like, giant clumps.

As I'm doing it, I end up getting this flashback to when we were, like, seventeen or eighteen years old. The day before every big game, we'd all get our hair cut together – we're talking me, we're talking Fionn, we're talking Christian, we're talking JP, we're talking Oisinn. We'd hit Bren's next-door to Kielys and we'd all get the exact same haircut, we're talking short on top, we're talking blade one at the back and sides.

It only takes a couple of minutes before Fionn's head is as bald as a grapefruit. I switch off the razor. He runs his hand over his totally hairless head and goes, 'What do you think?'

Sorcha's like, 'Oh my God!'

He stands up, puts his glasses on and walks over to the mirror above the kitchen fireplace. He stares at his reflection for a good, like, ten seconds without saying a word. Fionn is a strange-looking focker at the best of times, but I think even he's taken aback by how weird he looks without hair.

Poor Hillary is just, like, glaring at him like he's a stranger who has suddenly walked into the room. Fionn sits down next to him and goes, 'Do you want to touch it?' and he sort of, like, pushes his suddenly bald head at his son.

Hillary just, like, bursts into tears and turns away. He's terrified of this odd-looking randomer who talks like Daddy but *isn't* his daddy?

Fionn goes, 'It's alright, Hillary! *Je suis ton père. Is mise d'athair. Ich bin dein Vater.*'

I'm staring at the dude and I'm overcome with this feeling of – I'm just going to come out and use the word – *love* for the goy?

I'm sitting in P. Mac's, having a pint of some – yeah, no – random craft beer and scribbling some notes in my Rugby Tactics Book when Christian all of a sudden rings.

He's like, 'Where are you, Dude?'

'I'm in Dundrum,' I go. 'Sorcha's shopping with the kids and I'm just grabbing a quick coffee slash a few pints.'

'I was talking to Fionn. He said he's got to have chemo.'

'Yeah, no, he had this thing fitted yesterday called a port. That's how they give it to you – through that.'

'Jesus.'

'I told him we'd go with him – at least for the first one or two.'

'Of course we'll go with him.'

'Try not to stare at him, by the way. He asked me to shave his head – just to get ahead of the thing. He looks weird. I'm just mentioning it in advance.'

'Right.'

'So what are you up to, Dude? You've been M.I.A. for weeks now.'

'Yeah, no, between moving out of the gaff and then work, I haven't had a minute to even scratch myself.'

'Where are you even living these days?'

'Yeah, no, I've moved into a one-bedroom aportment in, like, Carrickmines.'

Fock. Divorceland.

I'm like, 'That's, er, great – handy for the M50,' the estate agent in me trying to put a positive spin on it.

He's there, 'It's obviously only temporary.'

Yeah, that's what they all say.

'Hey,' he suddenly goes, 'I believe congratulations are in order. I hear you have a little brother.'

I'm like, 'Yeah, no. Hugo. He's still in the hospital, although there's talk of him being allowed home soon.'

'So what's he like?'

'You know what I'm like around babies. And even though I'm obviously biased, he's just the most, I don't know, perfect little –'

He instantly picks up something in my voice. He's there, 'What's wrong?'

I'm like, 'Nothing.'

'Ross, you sighed.'

What I said about rugby and secrets is true.

So I end up just telling him the whole story. About how Szidonia and the others have decided that my old pair are too old slash insane to parent six babies. And how they're planning to snatch them and bring them back to, whatever it's called, Monvania? And how Szidonia wants me to actually help them escape.

Christian, who's always been a rock of sense, goes, 'You know what you've got to do, Ross – you've got to tell your old pair.'

I'm there, 'It's, er, not as easy as that.'

'What do you mean?'

'Szidonia has a – let's just say – incriminating video of me. The only reason I'm telling you, Christian, is because I know you won't judge me.'

'You focking idiot!'

'Okay, I take that back.'

'You had sex with a woman who's carrying your mother and father's baby?'

'Jesus Christ, no, I didn't! What do you take me for, Christian?'

'Who did you have sex with, then?'

'Delma.'

'The only Delma I know is your old dear's mate from the Funderland –'

'Yeah, it was *that* Delma. It was during the old dear's baby shower. It was a quick knee trembler up against the gable wall of the house.'

'Jesus Christ.'

'I can't believe you thought I'd have sex with one of the surrogates.'

'And, what, this girl was filming it?'

'Yeah, no, from the window above. I may have blurted out one or two embarrassing lines that I wouldn't want anyone knowing about.'

'Delma, though? Jesus, Ross, what were you thinking?'

'Hey, she made a move on me. I just thought, why not? The body on her, by the way. You'd never know she was sixty. I think she still plays veterans tennis in Rathgor.'

'So presumably, what, this girl is threatening to send the video to Sorcha?'

'Exactly. So you can see my dilemma. If I say nothing, they're going to do a runner with the babies. But if I tell my old pair, then that's my marriage gone. I know I'm on my last life with Sorcha. I won't even get to see my own –'

Shit.

I end up having to suddenly hang up on him because I spot Sorcha walking through the door of the pub with Hillary and the boys.

She looks upset about something. I might have told her I was going to Storbucks, but I presumed she knew what that meant.

I'm there, 'I'll just knock this back in one.'

But *she* just goes, 'Ross, have you noticed anything wrong with Leo's eyes?'

Leo's there, 'The fock are you saying about me?'

She goes, 'Leo, look at your father for a second!'

He looks at me. The poor kid. Yeah, no, they're well and truly focked.

I'm there, 'I can't see anything wrong with them, Sorcha – and that's me being one hundred per cent honest with you.'

She goes, 'Can you not see a turn in his left eye?'

'Not really. Not at all, in fact.'

'My mom said it to me a couple of weeks ago. She said she thought he was developing a lazy eye – like my dad sometimes gets when he's *tired*?'

The Lalors and their shit genes. I might have focking known it.

Then she utters the words that every rugby father must secretly dread.

She goes, 'I think our son needs G, L, A, S, S, E, S.'

I'm there, 'The answer is no.'

'Ross, one of his eyes is clearly weaker than the other. That's why it keeps turning inwards – to *compensate*?'

'Well, it can *keep* turning inwards. I'd rather a son with a turn in his eye than a son who wears those things. Fionn wears glasses. And everyone made his life a misery at school.'

'*You* made his life a misery at school.'

'Birds don't make passes – at boys who wear glasses. That's what they used to say to him. And by *they* – yes, I do mean me.'

Sorcha goes, 'Come on, we're going to the optometrist's,' and from the way she says it, she makes it clear that I have no actual choice in the matter.

Three minutes later, having downed the last of my beer, we're walking through the shopping centre. Poor little Leo is muttering the word 'rugby' under his breath, not a clue where we're taking him, no idea of how his life is about to change forever.

Sorcha thinks I'm overreacting.

'Oh my God,' she goes, 'who are you ringing?' because I've got my phone to my ear.

I'm like, 'Ryle Nugent.'

'Why are you ringing Ryle Nugent?'

'He's Leo's godfather, Sorcha – he's entitled to know.'

'Ross,' she goes, 'hang up that phone right now!' and she ends up just snatching it out of my hand.

We walk into the optometrist's – it's what middle-class people call the optician – and we're told to wait. I'm still trying to persuade Sorcha that this is a bad idea.

'Okay,' I go, 'I'll put it to you another way. When I was, like, five years old, one of my teachers in Constance Markievicz National School in Sallynoggin sent me home with a note saying she thought I needed glasses. My old man took me outside to the gorden and he said, "Can you see the sun up there in the sky, Kicker?" I said, yeah, no, I could. And he said, "That thing is one hundred and fifty million kilometres away. There's clearly nothing wrong with your bloody well eyesight!" '

She's there, 'Sorry, what exactly is that story proving? You couldn't read and write until you were fourteen years old.'

'It saved my – very nearly – rugby career.'

She just shakes her head and goes, 'So this is about rugby, is it?'

I'm there, 'Everything is about rugby, Sorcha.'

She goes 'What's more important to you – your son's eyesight or his rugby career?'

I let my silence answer the question for me.

Eventually, the receptionist says that the optometrist will see us now. So in we go. It ends up being a woman in her – I'm tempted to say – fifties? She's, like, totally calm about the whole thing.

She goes, 'Look at you! What's your name?'

Leo's like, 'Fock you!'

And the woman is professional enough to totally ignore it. It's Dundrum. It probably happens a hundred times a day.

Sorcha goes, 'His name is Leo. My husband and I think he might have a lazy eye.'

The woman goes, 'Oh, yes, I *can* see a slight turn. Okay, come with me,' and she leads us all into this, like, dorkened room with a big, leather chair in it that looks like a dentist's chair.

'Now,' she goes, 'sit up there, little man, and we'll get you checked out.'

She moves this thing in front of his face that's like a periscope, with eyeholes in it and handles on the side.

I'm there, 'Remember, Leo, just do your best. We won't be angry with you if you fail – as long as you try your hordest *not* to?'

'Okay,' the optometrist goes, 'I'm going to ask you to rest your chin here, Leo, and look in through the two little holes.'

On the wall opposite him, there's a chort with, like, *letters* on it?

The woman goes, 'Now, can you see the letters, Leo?'

I'm there, 'Of course he can see the letters. The first one is an A. Then the second line is a T and a U – you can see that, can't you, Leo? The third line is obviously an F, a G, an M and an L. There's fock-all wrong with *his* eyesight. Thank God is all I can say. Thank God.'

The optometrist goes, 'Perhaps it might be best if you waited outside while I tested your son's eyes.'

And Sorcha's there, 'She's right, Ross. Wait outside.'

So I end up having no choice in the matter. I go, 'The Lalors and their shit genes,' and then I trot out to the reception area.

I sit there just staring into space. It'll tell you how upset I am that I don't even bother flirting with the receptionist, even though she's a ringer for Cobie Smulders except with eczema.

I'm staring at all these photographs on the walls of, like, models wearing glasses, which they clearly don't need, and even *they* look shit in them?

Fifteen minutes later, the door opens and out they walk. I notice straight away that – oh, Jesus Christ – Leo is wearing a humungous pair of glasses with lenses as thick as the bottle from which my old dear probably drank her breakfast this morning. And, over his left, he's wearing – I shit you not – a massive, pink patch.

And in that moment, my hort *literally* breaks?

I go, 'Don't worry, Leo. Mommy and Daddy aren't going to love you any less just because you have to wear those ridiculous focking things.'

And, while I hate lying to him, as a parent that's my job.

I'm driving Fionn to Vincent's. Which sounds like the opening line to a Chris Rea song, but it's also a fact. He's got his first chemo session this morning.

'Ross,' he goes, 'can you actually hear yourself?'

I'm like, 'What do you mean?'

'Your son has to wear glasses – and you're comparing it to cancer.'

'I'm saying that cancer isn't necessarily a death sentence, Fionn. What Leo's got *is* a death sentence – socially, I mean. Johnny and Brian were calling him Gogglebox Ireland all morning.'

'Er, *you* came up with that name, Ross.'

'Yeah, behind his back. I didn't know the other two would latch onto it. I'm going to be totally honest with you, Fionn. I can't even bring myself to look at the kid. With the focking pink patch over his eye and his Coca-Cola lenses. No offence.'

'Ross, you're being ridiculous.'

'Am I, though? Because I've already lost one son to rugby – with his focking grommets in his ears. Now I've lost another one.'

'I played rugby – and *I* wore glasses.'

'I wanted him to play for Ireland, though. How many cross-eyed internationals have you ever seen?'

He has no answer to that.

I'm there, 'Why us, Fionn? That's the question I keep coming back to – why us?'

He has no answer to that either.

We're in the focking Mitsubishi i-MiEV, by the way. Fionn keeps telling me that I don't have to do this, but I tell him I'm doing it anyway and that's all there is to it.

He goes, 'It's just–' and he goes suddenly quiet.

And I'm like, 'What?' but *he* just stares out the window at, I suppose, Booterstown. 'What's wrong, Dude?'

'Why are you doing this?'

'Er, because I *want* to do it?'

And that's when he ends up just blurting out what's on his mind.

He goes, 'Ross, I got your wife pregnant.'

And I'm there, 'Did I not say I'd forgiven you for that?'

'Er, no, you told me you would never forgive me, even if we lived to be a thousand years old.'

'I changed my mind. You're forgiven. How's that?'

'I just don't understand how you could – forgive me, I mean.'

'Hey, I rode your sister, Fionn. Don't ever forget that. Not that I'd ever let you.'

'It's not the same thing.'

'I rode loads of girlfriends of yours as well. That one you were with in Trinity who wasn't great. And the other one with the massive forehead who lived on Roebuck Road. She had a funny name.'

'Delphine?'

I laugh. I'm there, 'Delphine! Where do they come up with them?'

He's quiet then for about ten seconds. I take the left turn into hospital.

He goes, 'I didn't know you were with Delphine.'

I'm like, 'Loads of times. It was going on right under your nose.'

'Really?'

'What a prick, huh? So *now* do you still feel guilty?'

'Yeah, because that's also different, Ross.'

'How is it also different?'

'Because Sorcha is your wife.'

'Who I was on a break from at the actual time.'

'I'm just saying, I don't think I'd be so quick to forgive you if the roles were reversed.'

'You would.'

'How can you be so sure?'

'Because rugby.'

'Rugby isn't the answer to everything.'

'I'm going to let that go and just put it down to nerves.'

I pork the cor, then into the hospital we go. We're directed upstairs to the day care oncology ward, where a nurse – six out of ten – storts hooking a tube up to Fionn's chemo port. Then she says she'll be back in a minute and she focks off.

I check the time on my phone. I'm there, 'I wonder what's keeping the goys – they should *be* here by now.'

Fionn goes, 'I texted them and told them not to come.'

I'm there, 'What? Why would you do that?'

'Because they've all got jobs, Ross. I don't expect anyone to spend their day watching me have bags of chemicals emptied into my bloodstream.'

I'm like, 'Jesus, is that what chemotherapy is?' because I hadn't actually *thought* about it?

'Yes,' he goes, 'that's what chemotherapy is.'

And I'm there, 'Well, I still say they'll *be* here – because loyalty still means something to –'

I suddenly stop. Because I've just come up with an idea.

'Dude,' I go, 'can I ask you a favour? And I want you to say yes.'

'Well, that all depends on what you're going to ask me.'

'Will you help me coach Pres – as, like, my Assistant?'

He laughs. He's there, 'No.'

I'm like, 'What do you mean, no?'

'Ross, you don't need anyone to help you coach – least of all me.'

'Then why would I ask you?'

'Because you feel sorry for me. And because I heard Sorcha tell you this morning that depression was a side-effect of chemotherapy and you want to give me something to do to distract me.'

'Dude, I need that big brain of yours. Plus, there's too much work and too little time for me to do it all by myself. We've got Michael's in, like, a week's time and there's some issues with the scrum that I need to iron out. I need someone to work with the backs while I'm doing that. Dude, just come out with me once and have a look at the set-up.'

He sighs and says he will.

'As long as you do a favour for me,' he goes.

I'm like, 'Absolutely – name it, Dude.'

He doesn't say shit for ages, then he goes, 'Ross, if I don't make it –'

And I'm like, 'Whoa, whoa, whoa – stop that now.'

'Ross, I'm being pragmatic here.'

'I'm not interested in you being pragmatic. You *are* going to make it. You're going to fight this thing and you're going to win. And you might as well be warned – every time you try to finish that sentence, I'm just going to shout, "Rugby!" over you. Go ahead, Dude. Go ahead and watch me do it."

'Ross, if I don't –'

'Rugby!'

'Ross –'

'Rugby!'

'Ross –'

'Rugby!'

'Ross, I want you to –'

'Rugby!'

'Ross, please –'

'Rugby!'

'Ross –'

'Rugby!'

'Ross!'

'Rugby! Rugby! Rugby! Rugby! Rugby! Rugby! Rugby!'

And at that exact moment, the room is suddenly filled with voices. They *are* here. We're talking JP. We're talking Christian. We're talking Oisinn. We're talking Magnus.

Fionn's face just lights up when he sees them.

Oisinn goes, 'Why is Ross shouting rugby?'

I'm there, 'I was just thinking out loud,' and I give Fionn a big wink.

JP's like, 'Have we missed anything?' and he rubs his hand over Fionn's totally bald head. 'Whoa, that is one serious scalping that Ross gave you.'

Fionn laughs. He's there, 'No, you haven't missed anything. Goys, I can't believe you all came.'

Magnus goes, 'Ash Rosh likesh to shay – rugby!'

The nurse returns holding a plastic bag containing this, like, see-through liquid. She hooks the bag up to the drip and goes, 'Are you ready?'

And Fionn looks at each of us in turn, then looks back at the nurse and goes, 'Yes, I'm ready.'

The goys are walking out of the dressing room when we arrive. They all end up doing a double-take when they see me standing there with this total randomer with glasses and a big bald head on him.

I'm there, 'Goys, I want to introduce you to someone.'

Fionn gives them all a nod and a smile.

I'm there, 'This is Fionn de Barra. Another Leinster Schools Senior Cup winner. And, I don't think it would be an exaggeration to say, one of the best passers of the ball in the history of the schools game. I've asked Fionn to be my Assistant Coach.'

The goys are like, 'Howiya, Boss?' but they're looking at him a bit, I don't know, *unsurely*?

He's there, 'Hello, everyone. Okay, I should explain the hair thing – just to get it out there. I'm having chemotherapy at the moment and I just had my head shaved because I didn't want to go through the whole thing of watching my hair fall out.'

Either Lenny or Dougie goes, 'Fair fooks to you, like. Our ma did the same thing, like.'

I'm there, 'I've asked Fionn to work with the backs today – especially in terms of your passing and handling. I'm going to work with the forwards, okay?'

They all seem happy with this.

It's, like, Friday lunchtime and the match against Michael's is on Monday. So we set to work. I'm standing on the scrummaging machine, bawling instructions at my front eight as they put their shoulders to it and stort pushing it down the field.

I'm going, 'That's it! Come on, goys, if your thighs aren't burning, then you're not doing it properly! That's it! Mush! Mush! Mush!'

While this is going on, I'm watching Fionn from a distance. He's getting the goys to run from one side of the pitch to the other while passing the Gilbert to each other and he's studying each player really closely to try to identify glitches that are possibly slowing the ball down.

When they've done it, like, ten or eleven times, he gets them all in a huddle and storts giving each of them his analysis of where they're going wrong individually and collectively. I can see them all nodding – *actually* interested – and then I remember that Fionn has always been a teacher at hort, even though I've never really paid attention to him because I've always found teachers boring to listen to.

After ninety minutes of, like, serious, serious work, I tell the goys that we're going to call it a day. They're not happy rabbits at all – they're, like, keen to keep going – but I tell them that rest and recovery is important at this level, then I throw in the fact that the Michael's goys will probably be spending the weekend in a spa hotel.

I definitely know what buttons to press with them.

'Posh bastards, like,' Ricey goes.

And I'm there, 'Are you off the cigarettes, by the way?' because I noticed him coughing and wheezing quite a bit out there today.

He goes, 'I'm down to ten a day, like.'

And I'm there, 'I want you off them altogether, Ricey. Seriously – all of you, in fact, okay?'

They all just, like, nod their heads.

I give them one last little pep talk before the weekend.

I'm there, 'Goys, remember, rest up tomorrow and Sunday. We've got a lot of seriously, seriously good work banked. People are expecting you to just roll over against Michael's, like you did against Blackrock. I think we've all learned enough in the last few weeks to know that's not going to hopefully happen.'

I can see the goys are pumped.

I'm there, 'You've got Saturday, then Sunday, then Kick Orse Day – let's do this thing!'

The goys all clap their hands together. There are high-fives and – I might as well say it – there are chest-bumps too.

I tell them all I'll see them on Monday, then fifteen minutes later, me and Fionn are walking back down the Putland Road – I didn't pork in the school for fear that seeing the Mitsubishi i-MiEV would mean the players respected me less – and I'm telling him that he was obviously a major, major hit with the goys.

I'm there, 'I could see the likes of Nailer and Barry Austin hanging on your every word. It was great to see.'

'Ross,' he goes, 'who was that goy running around behind the posts?'

I'm like, 'Which goy?'

'The sort of, like, thin goy – he was retrieving the balls for Barry.'

'Oh, him? Hilariously, that's Sergei – his old man is that dodgy Russian focker who fixed the election for *my* old man. Why are you asking about him?'

'Have you been watching him at all?'

'Not really. You know he turned up with a note from his old man threatening me if I didn't put him in the team?'

'I was watching him today. Every time he kicked the ball back, Barry didn't even need to move to get it.'

'That's how it should be. A kicker's time is valuable.'

'And he was throwing the ball to him, twenty, thirty metres, right on torget.'

'Again, same point.'

'Ross, I have a feeling that he might be good.'

'I wouldn't give his old man the pleasure of picking him, Dude. But I'll stick him on the bench. That'll piss him off even more.'

We reach the cor – so-called.

Fionn goes, 'Are you hungry, by the way?'

I'm there, 'I'm a vegan, Fionn. I'm permanently hungry.'

'I was thinking of checking out Claire's new place. Sorcha was raving about the cauliflower and fennel mash with activated almonds and deactivated hazelnuts.'

'Sounds disgusting. Let's do it.'

So we drive to Wheat Bray Love.

'Ross,' Fionn goes, once we're nearly there, 'I was trying to ask you something the other day in the hospital. I've been thinking about it a lot ever since I was diagnosed.'

I'm like, 'Dude, what?'

'I don't want you to keep shouting "Rugby!" over me, okay?'

'I can't promise anything, but I'll certainly give it a go.'

'Ross, if I die –'

'Rugby!'

'Ross, please listen to me. This is really important to me, alright? *If* I die . . . I want you to be Hillary's father.'

'Dude, I don't want to hear that kind of talk.'

'If I don't make it – and, let's be honest, there's a chance I won't – I want you to legally adopt him.'

I pork on the street outside the place.

I'm like, '*Me*, though? Jesus Christ, Fionn, I can't teach him languages or any of the shit you know about the world. I'm a complete focking idiot. Ronan knew more than me when he was seven. Honor passed me out when she was, like, five.'

'Ross,' he goes, 'I can't think of anyone I'd rather have bringing up my son than you.'

It's a moment. It's a definite moment. There on the Quinsborough Road.

I'm there, 'Okay, I'll do it. But you're not going to die, Fionn – because I'm not going to let that happen.'

He goes, 'Even you can't make that promise, Ross.'

I get out of the cor. I leave the door unlocked in the hope that some focker will steal it. But they won't. Even joyriders have standards.

The special today, according to the board outside, is an open, pulled bison sandwich with folk broccoli and reawakened seaweed croquettes.

I'm actually chuckling to myself as I push the door and we walk in. Claire is standing behind the counter. She doesn't say shit to Fionn – doesn't even comment on the fact that he's totally bald. She just looks at me and goes, 'What the fock did you say to Garret?'

I'm there, 'Er, are we talking Garret, as in your ex? I thought he was still travelling around Arasia?'

'You told him we had sex. On a regular basis.'

Poor Fionn doesn't know where to put himself.

I'm there, 'Yeah, no, I'm just racking my brains here, Claire.'

She goes, 'We were back together, Ross! He'd agreed to give our marriage another go! And you focking ruined it!'

7.

The Beast from the East

'Chorles,' the old dear goes, 'will you *please* take that thing out of the bassinet?'

I thought a bassinet was a musical instrument. It turns out it's, like, a wicker basket that you put a baby in. I'm staring into the thing, grinning like an idiot. Somewhere underneath that rugby ball is my little brother, Hugo, who's just arrived home – happy and healthy – from the hospital.

The old man goes, 'It's important, Fionnuala, to familiarize the little chap with the shape of the ball! We did it for Ross and look how he turned out!'

The old dear takes the ball out of the – again – bassinet and hands it to the old man. And there he is underneath, fast asleep. God, he's beautiful.

The old dear smiles at me like she's trying to squeeze out a silent fart at a funeral. She goes, 'Would you like a little hold, Ross?'

I'm like, 'Er, yeah, no, I would.'

She picks him up and slowly hands him to me. His little eyes are still closed but he looks all cranky at being taken out of his warm bed. She puts him into my orms. He weighs, like, nothing.

I stare into his little face, still struggling to get my head around the fact that he's my – I have to keep reminding myself – *brother*?

'He's got your nose,' the old dear goes.

A focking humungous thing. The poor kid.

The old man's there 'I can see a lot of you in him, Ross!'

'Me want hold!' Brian shouts. 'Me want hold!'

We all laugh at the idea of handing a baby to Brian. He'd probably box-kick it across the kitchen.

I'm there, 'Goys, this is my little brother, Hugo,' and I crouch down to their height so they can get a better look at him. 'He's actually your uncle – wrong as that sounds.'

They're all suddenly struck dumb. You'd never know they were three little psychopaths. Leo pats the baby gently with his hand.

'Hugo!' he goes, looking at me through his stupid glasses and his patch.

As if reading my mind, the old man goes, 'Why on Earth have you got him wearing those things, Ross? And that bloody well patch over his eye!'

I'm there, 'Sorcha seems to think he needs them – just because he's cross-eyed.'

And the old man is like, 'Nonsense! There's nothing wrong with his eyesight! It reminds me of the time – do you remember this, Fionnuala? – when a teacher told us that Kicker might need glasses! I took you outside to the gorden, Ross, and I pointed at the sun –'

I'm there, 'Yeah, no, I've heard the story about a hundred times before.'

The old man nods. He goes, 'I'm sure you were listening to the lunchtime news, Ross?'

I'm there, 'Why do you ask me stupid questions like that?'

'The High Court has ruled that Roderic Grainger's investigation *is* lawful and can proceed!'

'Bummer.'

'I said to Hennessy, "If I am *never* to be Taoiseach, then I shall learn to accept it! Unfortunately, I can't vouchsafe the same for Ross! I'm sure it's only a matter of time before he snaps! You know as well as I do, Old Scout, that if there's one thing that Kicker hates, it's seeing the Constitution of Ireland traduced!" Is that what you're thinking, Ross?'

No, I'm actually thinking that, for the past two years, I've been giving Honor fifty snots a week for bassinet lessons.

I stand up again because my knees are getting suddenly sore. I hand Hugo back to my old dear. She takes him and holds him close to her chest and kisses him on the top of the head with a tenderness you wouldn't know she possessed if you ever saw her trying to parallel pork, eat snails from their shells or remove a broken cork from the neck of a wine bottle.

I'm sort of, like, mesmerized by it. She really does love him – in a way, I fully realize, that she never loved me.

And that's when the doorbell rings.

'Oh,' she goes, 'that'll be Delma!'

I end up nearly soiling my chinos there in the kitchen.

I'm like, 'Delma? The fock does *she* want?'

The old dear's there, 'She's come to meet Hugo, of course!'

The old man goes outside to let her in and I'm suddenly eyeing the back door. I'm there, 'We, er, might make tracks – are you ready, goys?'

I'm too slow, though. The kitchen door opens and in walks the old man, followed by – yeah, no – the famous Delma.

To say she's surprised to see me would be the understatement of the – *probably?* – century.

'Ross,' she goes, her face reddening. 'I didn't . . . see your cor outside.'

The old man goes, 'That's *his* Mitsubishi whatever-it-is out there, Delma. Young Honor is convinced that the world will suddenly end if we all keep driving German!'

It's the first time I've seen the woman since the day I – not to put too fine a point on it – rode her at the old dear's baby shower.

The old dear plonks the baby into Delma's orms and goes, 'Say hello to Hugo, Delma! Hugo, this is your auntie Delma!'

The poor woman is like a jelly. For a second, I think she might even drop him on his focking head.

The old dear goes, 'Delma, what's wrong? Delma, you're shaking!'

She's there, 'I'm just feeling a bit –'

'Emotional,' the old dear goes, taking the baby out of her hands again – probably wisely. 'I think you need something hot inside you, Delma. Ross, would you do the honours?'

I'm like, 'What?'

'Would you make some tea for Delma?' she goes.

The old man's there, 'Unless you fancy a stiff one, Delma?'

Jesus Christ, the woman looks like she's about to pass out.

'Yes,' the old dear goes, 'we could make bellinis. I've got a bottle of Veuve Clicquot in the fridge.'

I watch the poor woman's knees suddenly buckle and I end up having to catch her.

'Good Lord!' the old man goes. 'I think she's fainted!'

Brian's like, 'Stupid focking bitch!'

The old dear's there, 'I'll get you some water, Delma!'

I sort of, like, slow-walk her over to the table and I sit her down.

'Ross,' the old dear goes, 'loosen some of her clothing, will you?'

I'm like, 'What? Me?'

'What's wrong with you? It's Delma!'

'I know it's Delma.'

'She's practically your godmother.'

'I don't know what you mean by loosen her clothing, though?'

'Unzip the back of her dress, for God's sake. Unhook her bra.'

Delma – thankfully – goes, 'No, it's fine, Fionnuala . . . Really, I'm okay . . . It's just seeing the baby . . . It's just stirred up a lot of things . . . Breffni and that whore . . . I'm absolutely delighted for you, Fionnuala.'

The old dear offers her a sip of water. Delma puts her lips to the glass. 'Open your mouth wider,' the old dear goes. 'Take the whole thing.'

I'm standing there, thinking, I have to get out of here.

And that's when the kitchen door opens again. And – shit the bed and kick it out – in walks Szidonia.

She's unbuttoning her shirt, going, 'Is time for baby's feed,' when she suddenly cops *me* standing there. Then she cops Delma, sitting at the table, all upset – and immediately jumps to the wrong conclusion.

'You tell them you make fucky-fucky in garden?' she goes.

I'm straight away like, 'Nooo!' at the same time shaking my head. 'Delma's just overcome with the emotion of seeing the baby. Her ex just had a kid with a bormaid from a golf club.'

'She's not a bormaid,' the old dear goes. 'She's a Hospitality Co-Ordinator.'

'Make *fuggy-fuggy* in the gorden?' the old man goes. 'What on Earth are you talking about, Szidonia?'

But Szidonia goes, 'Is nothing,' then she walks over to the old dear and takes Hugo out of her hands. 'I feed Novac.'

'His name is Hugo,' the old dear goes. 'I don't know why you keep calling him Novac.'

'I forget.'

Szidonia carries the little dude to the door. She looks back at me, smiles cruelly, then goes, 'Mommy! Mommy!'

The atmosphere on the bus is tense. As a matter of fact, no one says shit between Bray and pretty much Cornelscourt. The goys are all just staring out the windows, lost in their own thoughts.

Ricey, I notice, is listening to music on his Beats. I walk down the aisle to him, whip the things off his head and I go, 'Dude, I said no headphones.'

He's there, 'Music relaxes me, like.'

'You're about to play St Michael's College at Donnybrook Stadium. It's the Leinster Schools Senior Cup. What the fock is there to be relaxed about?'

And that's when Fionn – in fairness to him – stands up.

'Ross is right,' he goes. 'Be present in the moment. Otherwise, life will just pass you by,' and I suddenly realize that he's talking about more than just this match. 'Whatever happens today, you will always be able to say that you played for Pres Bray in the Leinster Schools Senior Cup. Just make sure you remember how it felt.'

That gets an actual round of applause from the players and one or two shouts of 'Come on, Pres Bray!' and 'Let's bate these snobby bastards – no offence to you two fellas, like!'

We eventually reach Donnybrook. The road leading to the ground is, like, thronged with people – mostly Michael's fans, who bang the side of our bus and shout abuse as we turn right into the ground.

'Fock off back to Bray!' they go, as the stewards open the big gates and we drive through.

The goys are in an absolute rage by the time they reach the dressing room. Ricey goes, 'Fox-hunting bastards, like,' and I end up having a little chuckle because I forgot I even told them that.

He kicks the wall. It's exactly what I want to see from him.

I'm there, 'You see what they think of us?' getting into the mind games with them. 'They think we're a joke. They think we're here to be beaten.'

They're all practically tearing off their civvies, gagging to get out there onto the pitch.

'Sergei,' I go, 'hand me that bag, will you?'

Yeah, no, I made the little focker carry the kit from the bus – and he could barely even do that, the little weed.

I reach into the bag. All the jerseys are in there, neatly folded – not the red and black of Castlerock College, but the pure, brilliant white of Presentation College Bray. One by one, I hand them out and I make sure to say each player's name and number as I do – as in 'Steven Nagle – number nine!' – just to let them know what an honour it is to get to wear their school's colours, Pres Bray or not.

I'm there, 'Goys, I'm not going to fill your heads with more instructions than I already have. Just let them know they're in a match.'

Barry Austin goes, 'Come on, Pres!' sounding like a true captain for once, then he leads his teammates out onto the pitch.

I turn around to Fionn and I go, 'That was great – what you said on the bus.'

He's like, 'Thanks, Ross.'

Then out we go.

The first person I end up running into is my old man. He's actually waiting for me outside the dressing room, a humungous Montecristo burning between his fingers.

'Kicker!' he goes, 'I've just seen the players run out! No room in the storting fifteen for young Sergei, eh?'

Behind him, I notice the famous Fyodor. He looks seriously pissed off as well. He's going, 'Why is my son not play?'

I'm there, 'Because *I* pick the team, Dude.'

The old man goes, 'I said to Fyodor, it'll be a tactical decision!

You see if it isn't! He'll spring him from the bench in the second half – like a secret weapon!'

I end up just laughing in his face.

He goes, 'You see what I mean, Fyodor? The chap knows precisely what he's doing!'

We end up getting off to *the* worst possible stort. There's, like, not even sixty seconds on the clock when Nailer throws a long, lazy pass to Barry and it ends up being intercepted by the Michael's inside-centre – a kid called James Fitzpatrick, who's already being talked about as a future Ireland number thirteen – and he runs, like, fifty yords, unchallenged, to put the ball down underneath the posts.

The goys are still in shock when, five minutes later, the same James Fitzpatrick basically waltzes through our defence to score a second, this time finishing the move with a swan dive that I'm tempted to say is typically Michael's.

The two tries end up being converted. And not only are we fourteen points down but our players are fighting among themselves, arguing over who was at fault for the two tries.

I'm going, 'Goys, it doesn't matter! Just play the focking match!'

The Michael's crowd are totally drowning out our supporters with chants of 'Fock off back to Wicklah! Fock off back to Wicklah!' and 'Are you Gerard's in disguise?' which hurts the goys – I can see it.

Two things prevent it from being an *actual* rout? Firstly, Ricey, Dougie and Lenny end up taking the whole thing personally and they put in one hell of a shift in the scrum. Secondly, the Michael's boys take their foot off the pedal and instead of closing out the match they decide to turn on the style for the benefit of the girls who are watching.

I end up spending the entire first half roaring at Barry to make something happen – he's supposed to be a focking ten – but the dude is, like, hopelessly out of his depth. We end up going into half-time fourteen points down and I'm suddenly remembering the nickname we used to have for Pres Bray back in the day – as in, Pres Bray Nil.

There's no disgrace in that, though. Michael's are a seriously good outfit and on the way back to the dressing room I overhear Gavin Cummiskey from the *Irish Times* say that three or four of their players will walk into the Ireland senior squad in a year's time. That puts the scoreline in context. Although I still make sure to give him a genuinely hord shoulder nudge when I'm walking past him.

The dressing room is a scene of *literally* cornage? Either Dougie or Lenny has a dead leg. Paul Preece – our number eight – has two black eyes and a possible broken nose. And Ricey has a four-inch cut above his right eyebrow that's, like, pumping blood and that – Jesus Christ – he's attempting to stitch himself.

I'm like, 'Goys, this match isn't over,' which is obviously horse shit. It was over after five minutes.

Out of the coner of his mouth, Fionn says I need to change something.

I'm there, 'I'm open to ideas here, Dude.'

He doesn't even hesitate. He goes, 'Ultan is being bullied out of it in the centre. Take him off and move Barry there.'

I'm there, 'So who's going to be my outhalf, then?'

He goes, 'Sergei.'

I look at him just sitting there – a little wimp of a kid.

I'm like, 'No way.'

Fionn goes, 'Ross, trust me – I really think he's got something.'

I just think, okay, I owe it to these goys at least to *try* something different in the second half?

So I go, 'Ultan, you're off. Barry, you're moving to inside-centre. Sergei, throw a jersey on. You say you're a ten – let's see how true that statement is.'

Ultan isn't happy. But Barry doesn't object to being moved. He's done fock-all and he knows he's lucky to still be on the pitch.

I tell the goys to keep plugging away and opportunities are sure to come – although I'm bullshitting, to be completely honest.

As we're walking out for the second half, Brother Ciaran sidles up to me on his stick and he tells me he's been – I shit you not – praying!

I'm like, 'Yeah, no, that'll help, Ciaran – thanks.'

As the match kicks off again, I hear the old man go, 'He's made the switch! What did I tell you, Fyodor? Your chap's playing out-half, look!'

It doesn't take long for Michael's to settle back into their rhythm and they're suddenly pinging passes around for the sheer fun of it. You can tell they're already thinking about the quarter-final against Clongowes.

But ten minutes into the second half, something un-focking-believable happens and I'm saying that as someone who thought he'd seen – and done – pretty much *everything* on a rugby field?

Nailer somehow pulls the ball out of a ruck and feeds it to Sergei, who catches it standing completely still and exposed. Two Michael's players close on him with the intention of absolutely creaming him and I'm already looking around to see are the Saint John's Ambulance goys ready with the neck brace and the spinal board.

But, suddenly, with a flick of his hips, Sergei feints one way, then the other way, and leaves the two dudes grabbing for air as he sets off on – I swear to God – a seventy-metre run. He goes inside one player, then outside another, leaving the two of them on their orses, before planting the ball underneath the posts.

It's one of the greatest tries I've ever seen. But our players are too in shock to even celebrate.

I turn around to Fionn and I'm like, 'What the fock was that?'

And he laughs and goes, 'I hate to say I told you so!'

Barry adds the cheese and crackers and it changes the entire complexion of the match. We're still losing 14–7, but you can suddenly see the doubts creeping into the minds of the Michael's players. No one does that to them. For the first time, I can actually hear our supporters on the opposite side of the pitch, singing, 'We are Pres! We are Pres! We are Pres!'

Suddenly, all the tactics we discussed go out the window. There is now only one tactic – get the ball to Sergei. And that's what the goys end up doing at every opportunity.

The kid has it all. We're talking skill. We're talking courage. We're talking acceleration from a standing stort. He reminds me of – I'm going to have to be honest here – me in my *heyday*?

While they know fock-all about rugby, Mount Anville girls have an uncanny ability to sense when the balance of power is shifting. It ensures they marry well and maintain the purity of the South Dublin bloodline. And you can suddenly hear them going, 'That little goy playing for Bray – oh my God – *actually* looks like Chris Hemsworth!'

Midway through the second half, Sergei proves that the first try was no fluke by repeating the trick, this time leaving five Michael's players on their orses before grounding the ball as near to the posts as matters.

And this time the goys do actually celebrate, because – once Barry adds the extras – we're suddenly level.

And the Michael's boys are shitting themselves. You can see it in their eyes. The fear. They can't string three or four passes together because all they can think about is how to stop Sergei getting his hands on the ball.

On the sideline, the old man is going bananas. He's there, 'It was all a tactical ruse! Didn't I tell you, Fyodor? Kicker knows what he's doing!'

The Michael's boys are asking the referee how long is left. They're not thinking about winning the match – they're thinking about not *losing* it?

'If it's a draw, is it a replay?' one of them wants to know.

The referee's like, 'No, it's extra time,' and you can see from their faces that they're, like, dreading the prospect.

But little do they know that Sergei is about to put them out of their misery. There's, like, nothing left on the clock – as in, the eighty minutes will be over the next time the ball goes dead. Sergei has the ball in his hands. He's on the halfway line. He launches a Garryowen to try to put the Michael's full-back under pressure.

Which is exactly what ends *up* happening?

The poor dude is shaking like a focking jelly watching the ball fall out of the sky. Sergei keeps running. The full-back is, like, six-foot-four and Sergei is, like, five-foot-three. And yet, when Sergei jumps, I have no doubt in mind who is going to win the ball.

Sergei catches it cleanly and manages to flatten the full-back in the process. The whole of Donnybrook Stadium falls silent as Sergei stumbles forward a few steps, almost losing his balance. For a second, I think he's going to snot himself, but he somehow manages to keep his feet and hang onto the ball.

And then everything seems to go into slow motion.

He staggers towards the line. A Michael's player appears out of nowhere and tackles him hord around the waist. Sergei hits the deck. But, as he does so, he stretches out his orm, the ball looking like it's stuck to his hand with glue.

He manages to place it right on the line.

And our little corner of the stadium explodes. Two orms surround me and I'm suddenly enclosed in a bear hug. It's Fionn. He's screaming in my ear, 'You did it! Ross, you did it!'

Which isn't true. I only wish it was.

A couple of hundred people – Bray people – run onto the pitch. There's no chance that Barry is going to get to even take the conversion. He's being carried around the pitch on the shoulders of our supporters, who are chanting, 'We are Pres! We are Pres! We are Pres!'

Dougie and Lenny are hugging each other. Nailer and Ricey are both lying face-down on the ground, openly weeping, while Sergei has disappeared under a mountain of bodies.

The old man is shouting, 'The mighty Michael's – humbled! Remember, all of you who saw it today! The stort of the career of a future Ireland coach! Exclamation mork! Exclamation mork! Exclamation mork!'

I walk out onto the pitch. Fionn tries to hang back, except I go, 'No focking way – this is as much about you as it is about me.'

So we walk out there together. One by one, the players throw their orms around us. They're all going, 'We beat Michael's! I can't believe it, like!'

We wander over to where Sergei is lying underneath about thirty delirious Bray teenagers. I grab his orm and I free him from the pile of human rubble.

'Ross, Fionn, thank you,' he goes. 'You have faith in me. I hope I repay today.'

I can suddenly feel Mount Anville girls closing in around him from all sides. They're going, 'Oh my God, his accent is *so* cute!' and 'I wonder is he, like, *seeing* anyone?'

I smile. Let's just say that it brings back one or two memories.

Barry – who has tears streaming down his face – introduces me and Fionn to his girlfriend, a Loreto Bray girl named Breena, who's, like, six feet tall with red hair. She has her big orms wrapped around his shoulders, clinging on to him like she's riding a stortled horse.

She goes, 'I've heard so much about you, like,' and I give her a sympathetic smile. I suspect Barry is going to be trading up soon. It's the law of the jungle – it's certainly the law of the Leinster Schools Senior Cup.

I spot Brother Ciaran. He has his two hands joined in prayer and he's looking up at the sky, tears streaming down his face. And then he spots me and he hobbles over to me on his stick.

'I was just thanking the Lord for answering my prayers,' he goes. 'He answered my prayers by sending you our way.'

Delma rings me. The following night – when I'm still on a high. For fock's sake. Talk about being brought back down to Earth with a bomp.

I stare at my phone, considering not answering it. But then I get this sudden fear that she might be about to do something stupid – namely, come clean about us.

So – yeah, no – I *do* answer?

I'm there, 'Delma – this is beginning to feel like stalking.'

I was totally right, by the way.

She goes, 'I'm going to tell Fionnuala what happened.'

She's, like, bawling her eyes out.

I'm there, 'You're not going to tell her shit, Delma.'

She goes, 'I can't carry this guilt around any more. That day in the house was awful.'

'You're being hysterical, Delma.'

'That girl! How does she know about us?'

'Are you talking about Szidonia?'

'Of course I'm talking about Szidonia!'

'Okay, if you must know, she witnessed the entire incident.'

'What?'

'Plus – and I don't know if I should tell you this, given how already worked up you are – but she has a video of it.'

'A video of what?'

'Me ploughing into you and you blaspheming at the sky.'

'Jesus Christ!'

'Just like that. And now she's blackmailing me.'

'Blackmailing you? What the hell does she want?'

'Something. I can't tell you what it is. But it's all in hand.'

'I have to tell Fionnuala. I can't stand it any more. One minute she's thanking me for a lifetime of friendship, the next your father is saying that the rainwater butt had become disconnected from the downward gutter.'

'That was you. I'm not pointing fingers.'

'I didn't know where to look.'

'Delma, just trust me, okay? I'll eventually sort it. Just keep your trap shut for now.'

I hang up on her.

I'm in Monkstown, by the way, standing outside one of those humungous gaffs on Longford Terrace. I check the number again. Yeah, no, this is the place.

I walk up the steps and I press the bell. Thirty seconds later, the door opens and he's standing there.

It's Fyodor.

He goes, 'What is matter?'

I'm there, 'Sergei. What the fock?'

'I tell you he is good, yes? I say to you in letter – is mistake if you not pick.'

'You never told me *how* good, though. What happened yesterday – I've never seen anything like that before.'

He opens the door and invites me in. It's some gaff. I think the old man said he's, like, renting the place – presumably until his work is done undermining Ireland's democracy.

He leads me down to this, like, massive kitchen, where Sergei is sitting at the table, doing – and I mean this quite literally – his homework. He sees me and he greets me like a long-lost friend. He goes, 'Coach!' standing up from the table and embracing me. 'It is pleasant that I see you!'

I actually feel kind of bad about being such a wanker to him now.

I'm there, 'Hey, it's cool, Sergei. What are you doing – homework?' just letting him know, subtly, that I don't approve.

'Yes,' Fyodor goes. 'I say to Sergei, yes, rugby is important, but not as important as school lessons.'

Fyodor might be a criminal mastermind who can rig elections and arrange a riot at the drop of a hat – but he has a hell of a lot to learn about rugby at this level.

Sergei goes, 'Is very hard for me to understand what is happening. Is very exciting but also confusing.'

I'm like, 'Confusing? As in?'

'After match, there are many girls. They are smiling at me. They say to me I am hot and I have sexy voice and they ask me if I have girlfriend.'

'That's Mounties for you. If you're good at rugby, they'll be on you like ants on a focking slug.'

'This is difficult for me to understand. In my country, I play rugby and no one care. They say, "What is this rugby? Why you not play ice hockey?"'

Fyodor interrupts us then. He goes, 'Sergei, will you tell your mother we have guest?'

Sergei goes, 'She is not my mother,' and there's suddenly this – I don't know – frosty atmosphere in the room.

Calmly, Fyodor goes, 'Sergei, will you tell Raisa that we have guest?'

Sergei leaves the room. Fyodor obviously feels the need to fill me in because he's there, 'I divorce Sergei's mother when he is ten years old. Sadly for her, she is very ugly lady. Second wife is pretty! But boys not always like second wife.'

'To be honest,' I go, 'I much preferred my old man's second wife. Even though his first was my old dear. The focking scrotum with eyes.'

Fyodor smiles, even though I'm not a hundred per cent sure he knows what I'm talking about. He goes, 'Your father is brilliant man. He will make great leader for Ireland.'

'There's a good chance that might never happen, though.'

'I say to him, do not rule out, Charles. Much things can happen in politics. Is like rugby, yes? Is full of surprises.'

'Yeah, no, I suppose it is.'

'You and your father are same. You are clever.'

'Me? I wouldn't have said that.'

'You look at Sergei and you know he is special talent. But you wait until after half-time to put him on pitch because you know it will catch opposition by surprise.'

I'm like, 'Er, yeah, no, that was the plan alright,' even though it's S, H, One, T. 'Straight out of the Rugby Tactics Book.'

'Your father tells me this! "Is plan, Fyodor! Is plan!" '

That's when the kitchen door suddenly opens and in walks a woman wearing nothing but a bathrobe and I am suddenly stunned into silence. Because I am looking at – no exaggeration – *the* most beautiful woman I have ever seen in my life.

'How is your sauna?' Fyodor goes.

The woman's like, 'Is good – but now I am so hot!' and she sort of, like, fans herself with her hand. 'Who is this person?'

She's talking about me.

I'm there, 'I, er, em, I, er, er, em, I . . .' but I can't finish my sentence. I can't even think straight.

I have bedded many, many beautiful women in my life, but I have never found myself struck literally speechless by a member of the opposite species.

She looks like a young Melania Trump, except less frightened.

'This is Ross,' Fyodor goes. 'He is coach for Sergei. Also, he is the son of the future leader of Ireland. Ross, this is my wife, Raisa.'

I'm like, 'Hey, Raisa,' offering her my hand.

She shakes it, but then holds on longer than seems normal, and I watch her eyes move up and down my body like she's drawing up a mental snag list for a kitchen she's just had fitted.

Fyodor says something to her in presumably Russian, which sounds kind of shorp, and she lets go.

As Honor might say – *awks* much?

I'm there, 'I, er, better hit the road. I've been asked to talk to Declan Meehan from East Coast Radio tomorrow morning – in Bray, that's, like, bigger than the *Late Late*. I want to figure out what I'm going to say. Will you tell Sergei I'll see him at training tomorrow?'

'Of course,' Fyodor goes, as he shows me to the door. Then – out of nowhere – he goes, 'Raisa likes you very much. I can see.'

Which is obviously – yeah, no – a random thing to hear from the woman's husband.

I'm like, 'Er, thanks.'

He opens the front door for me. And, as I'm stepping outside, in a cheery voice, he goes, 'Because your father is good friend, I think is fair I warn you. If anything happen with you and her, I kill her – and also I kill you.'

'Now,' the famous Declan Meehan goes, 'unless you've just returned to Earth from outer space this morning, you will be aware that Presentation College Bray pulled off one of the greatest shocks in the history of the Leinster Schools Senior Cup on Monday when they came from fourteen points behind to beat the mighty St Michael's College. And I'm delighted to say that the man who masterminded that victory, Ross O'Carroll-Kelly, joins me on the line. Good morning, Ross! How are you?'

I'm like, 'I'm in cracking form, Declan.'

The players are all sitting around the dressing room while this conversation is taking place, hanging on my every word.

He goes, 'Now, I was talking to someone this morning who compared this victory to Katie Taylor winning an Olympic gold medal in terms of what it's done for Bray. Is that overstating it?'

I'm there, 'That's for other people to say,' because I decide not to be a dick about it. 'All I would say, without wishing to take anything away from Katie Taylor, is that the Olympics is the Olympics. But the Leinster Schools Senior Cup is the Leinster Schools Senior Cup – and always will be. World without end. Amen.'

I watch all their faces light up. Ricey. Nailer. Barry. Dougie and Lenny. Not Sergei, though – he never seems to smile.

'Er, right,' Declan goes. 'And this St Michael's team that you defeated – they were no slouches, I'm told.'

I'm there, 'I don't know if you read Gavin Cummiskey's report in the *Times* on Tuesday morning? He's a writer I'd have a hell of a lot of time for and he reckoned three or four of those Michael's players will walk into the Ireland squad in a year's time. So I'll leave it to others to say how good that makes us.'

All the goys are, like, laughing and punching the air with excitement. You could say I've grown on them.

'And what about the performance by Sergei Shengelia?' Declan goes. 'This young Russian who scored a hat-trick of tries after coming on at half-time.'

I'm there, 'Sergei? Yeah, no, he's a very special talent.'

He looks down at his feet – all modesty. We'll have to knock that out of him.

'But I don't want to stort singling out individual players,' I go. 'This victory was a real team effort – as in, *everybody* played a port?'

It's important that the goys hear it, even if it's horse shit.

'Well,' Declan goes, 'it's Clongowes Wood next, in the quarter-final. How far do you think this Pres Bray team can go? Maybe all the way?'

I'm there, 'Dude, I know what it takes to win a Leinster Schools Senior Cup, having done it as a player back in 1999,' and I make sure to give Fionn a big wink. 'Even though the medals were subsequently taken off us for reasons I don't want to go into. I'm saying it's hord. That's why we're not getting ahead of ourselves. We're taking it one game at a time. We're not looking beyond our next match against – like you said – Clongowes,' and then I can't resist adding, 'a school for focking dicks.'

I'm playing to the crowd, I fully realize.

Declan – a total pro – goes, 'Er, okay, we'll, em, leave it there. And I'd like to apologize to our listeners for some of the offensive language in that interview – obviously, it's a result that has ignited a lot of passion in Bray. Coming up after the break, I'll be talking to the eighty-two-year-old former post mistress from Ballinaclash who's hoping to break the world record for saying the most consecutive Hail Marys.'

I hang up and the goys give me a humungous cheer. I wait until it dies down, then I go, 'I meant every word of what I just said, by the way. We take each match as it comes. That means don't go thinking about the semi-final or the final. It also means forgetting about what happened against Michael's on Monday.'

'Be hard to forget about it,' little Nailer goes. 'There was quare ones throwing themselves at us after the match, like. My girlfriend's paranoid now. She keeps going through me text messages, like.'

Ricey shows me his neck. It's, like, full of hickies. 'Look at this,' he goes. 'Fat bastard like me – I expected to be a virgin into me twenties, like.'

All the goys laugh. I catch Fionn's eye and we exchange a smile. It brings me back – as I'm sure it brings him back as well.

Fionn *was* a virgin until his twenties, by the way.

Either Dougie or Lenny goes, 'A gang of quare ones came into the amusements last night. They were mad posh, like. Started talking to us. One of them asked me if I wanted to go for a drive up to the Glen of the Downs, like.'

I'm like, 'What's the Glen of the Downs?'

'It's a forest,' his brother goes, 'on the N11, just before Kilpedder. There does be fierce riding going on in there at night, like.'

It's obviously *their* Dalkey Hill.

I'm there, 'Goys, look, I know it's exciting. There's doors opening up for you everywhere. You're meeting girls from all sorts of backgrounds. Mount Anville. Alexandra College. Holy Child Killiney. Loreto Foxrock. Girls who, a week ago, couldn't have found Bray on a map of the DORT line. But, goys, that will only continue as long as you keep winning.'

Oh, that grabs their attention.

I'm there, 'The second you lose, they'll move on. I've seen it happen. All those schools that won a big match and got carried away with themselves. I could mention CBC Monkstown here. Yes, you beat Michael's. But no one remembers quarter-finalists. We have a match against Clongowes to win. So let's get changed and let's go focking train.'

They all stort clapping. I'm pretty good when it comes to speaking in front of a crowd.

Even Fionn goes, 'That was great,' and – like I said – he's a born teacher.

I'm there, 'Are you feeling okay?' because he looks – being honest? – absolutely focked.

He's like, 'I'm just tired, that's all. From the, you know –'

The chemo.

Barry claps his two hands together like a true captain and goes, 'Come on, Pres Bray, let's train!'

And Fionn smiles at me and goes, 'It's like looking at ourselves twenty years ago, isn't it?'

Barry throws the dressing-room door open and out they run. I shout after them. I'm like, 'Remember, goys, we've won fock-all! Keep your feet on the ground!'

It's easy for me to say. Because I have no idea yet what's waiting for us beyond that door.

I pull on my Pres Bray jersey and I tip outside with Fionn following closely behind me. And that's when I end up getting one of *the* biggest surprises of my life – and I've seen a few things in my thirty-eight years.

I'm there, 'What the actual fock?'

There must be, like, three hundred people standing around the side of the pitch. Even the players look like they can't actually believe it. They're all, like, frozen to the spot – not knowing what to do.

'Apparently,' Ricey goes, 'they're here to watch us train, like.'

Most of the crowd are, like, total randomers, although some I do actually recognize, including Eric from the borber's and even the long-haired dude from the Bray Head Shop. Barry's randy auntie from Austin Flowers is also there and a few of the other shop and business owners who put jerseys in their windows.

They're singing, 'Allez, Allez, Allez', except they're changing the words to 'We're Bray, we're Bray, we're Bray!'

The only thing I've ever seen that remotely compares to it – in terms of numbers and excitement – is when Jamie Oliver turned up to open his place in Dundrum and thirteen people – including my old dear – were hospitalized in the crush.

I hear a voice behind me. It's Brother Ciaran. He goes, 'You see what you've done?'

Me and Fionn both turn around.

He points his walking stick at the crowd.

'Look!' he goes. 'Bray is dreaming!'

Christian and JP say nothing about us beating Michael's the other day. But then they're excited. The Deportment of Housing, Planning and Local Government was so impressed by their demonstration at the K Club that they've ordered two thousand Vampire Beds for a pilot scheme to accommodate some of the city's homeless in a disused airplane hangar near Weston Airport. Not only that, but they've ordered two thousand Homedrobes as well.

I'm like, 'Fair focks!'

Fionn says it as well, even though he was definitely dubious about it when it was first mentioned.

The nurse walks in and connects the tube to his chemo port. She's not much to look at.

'What one is this?' she goes.

Fionn's like, 'Second.'

'And how many are they giving you?'

'Six.'

The nurse leaves the room and Fionn changes the subject. He goes, 'So how did the meeting with the HSE go?'

Oisinn and Magnus arrive – late, although only a petty man would mention it.

'Nice of you to show your faces,' I go. 'Some of us have been sitting here for the last twenty minutes.'

Yes, I *am* that petty man.

They each pull up a chair. 'I am shorry we are late,' Magnus goes. 'We have jusht come from the airport.'

Yeah, no, I forgot, they were in, like, Finland for the week.

Happily – and not before time – that's when the conversation turns to rugby.

'I heard you beat Michael's!' Oisinn goes. 'That's focking huge!'

I'm like, 'Yeah, no, thanks, Dude.'

'And this Russian kid I'm reading about – where the fock did he come from?'

'He's Fyodor Shengelia's son.'

'Who?'

'My old man's mate – the dude who's supposedly trying to undermine our democracy.'

'I saw his three tries on YouTube! Jesus!'

'Hey, it was Fionn who spotted his talent, in fairness. I had him fetching and carrying balls for our kicker – no idea how good he was.'

JP – finally – goes, 'I hear you goys have created a bit of a stir in Bray.'

I'm there, 'You could say that. We had, like, three hundred people there to watch us train the other morning.'

'Three hundred? Jesus!'

Oisinn's there, 'Is it not, like, weird, though? As in, coaching a team *other* than Castlerock College?'

'It's a bit like cheating on your wife,' I go. 'It's actually fine as long as you don't think about it too much.'

He nods. But then I catch Christian shooting me a look of definite disapproval. Yeah, no, he's obviously worried about me, in fairness to him.

'Anyway,' I go, 'I've never been afraid to be friends with goys from other rugby schools – as long they're second-tier.'

I'm remembering my friendship with the great Shane Jennings, who was like a brother to me back in the day, despite going to St Mary's College. We used to cruise around Sandyford Industrial Estate in his old man's Toyota Camry, elbows out the window, pretending we were Mike Lowrey and Morcus Burnett from *Bad Boys* – 'Put the gun down,' he loved to shout, 'and get me a pack of Tropical Fruit Bubblicious!' – until he made it onto the Leinster panel and he stopped returning my calls.

JP goes, 'We should do something when we're finished here.'

Fionn's like, 'What do you mean by *do* something?'

'The kind of shit we used to pull in the old days,' JP goes, 'before we all got middle aged and boring.'

We all laugh. Then I suddenly have an idea.

'Let's go to Castlerock,' I go, 'and make shit of McGahy's morket gorden. We could do, like, doughnuts and handbrake turns – like we did to the Blackrock College pitch back in the day.'

Fionn's there, 'No way. Seriously. Not a chance.'

But me and the goys just stare at each other, saying fock-all, while a silent plan forms in our heads.

Fionn's like, 'Ross, we are *not* doing that. No way – okay?'

I'm there, 'Yeah, no, whatever you say, Dude,' and I decide to drop the subject – for now. We sit there for the next few hours, shooting the shit about everything and nothing.

It's all good.

Eventually, when it's time, the same nurse arrives – I think I mentioned she wasn't great – and she disconnects the tube from Fionn's chemo port.

Then – yeah, no – we head for the cor pork.

Standing at the pay station, me and Fionn say our goodbyes to JP, Christian, Oisinn and Magnus. It's, like, high-fives and hugs and whatever else is going, then we pay for our porking fee and we head for our separate cors.

Me and Fionn get into the Mitsubishi focking i-MiEV. I stort her up and we get on the road. I try talking to the dude, except he's lost in his own little world.

He doesn't notice me take the turn until it's too late for him to do anything about it. He goes, 'What are you doing?'

He looks over his shoulder and he sees, presumably, Christian, JP and Oisinn following us in their *own* cors?

He goes, 'Ross, no!' except he's laughing. He can't help himself. 'Ross, turn the cor around.'

But I have no intention of it.

Through the famous black gates I drive, with the words 'Castlerock College' written above them, then up the driveway, before taking a shorp left.

The morket gorden comes into view – the once hallowed ground where we performed our magic, which is now filled with vegetables, albeit prizewinning.

Fionn puts his head in his hands. He goes, 'I can't believe we're really going to do this.'

I'm there, 'Buckle up, Dude!' and I suddenly slam my foot down hord on the accelerator. I go over the kerb with a bump, followed by Christian in his silver Toyota Avensis, JP in his blue BMW Five Serious and Oisinn and Magnus in their red Honda Elysion. The next thing Fionn knows we're bouncing over these neat rows of vegetables, our tyres turning up the soil, then I suddenly pull hord on the steering wheel, sending carrots and cabbages and cauliflowers flying.

There's so much dirt in the air that I can barely even see the other goys. But I can hear the squeal of their tyres and their screams of laughter as they churn up the ground, destroying the gorden that was McGahy's pride and joy, while joyfully beeping their horns.

Up ahead, I spot a sign. It says 'Sugar snap peas', and – yeah, no – I end up suddenly seeing red.

I'm there, 'Okay, Fionn, hold on to your handbag!' and I slam my foot to the floor. Straight through the sugar snap peas I rip, breaking the sign into a million splinters, then I give the wheel a seriously hord yank with the intention of turning the cor around and giving them a second going-over.

Unfortunately, the Mitsubishi i-MiEV is a much lighter cor than I'm *used* to? And, instead of turning the cor around, I end up flipping it over.

Fionn actually screams as it rolls onto its roof, then – by some miracle – over onto its wheels again. It cuts out.

'Fock,' I go, 'are you okay?'

Fionn's like, 'Er, I think so, yeah,' doing a quick, mental stock-check to find out if he's in pain anywhere. 'Yeah, I'm fine.'

Christian pulls up a few feet away from us. His cor is totally covered in mud – as is, presumably, *ours*?

He goes, 'We better get out of here. I just saw McGahy running across the cor pork.'

I stort the engine – it catches first time, in fairness to it – and we take off, first Christian, then JP, then Oisinn and Magnus, then me and Fionn, all of us laughing and tooting our horns as we make our escape just as McGahy arrives on the scene.

Christian, JP and Oisinn fly past him down the driveway, JP shouting, 'Fock you and your sustainable morket gorden!' out the window as he disappears in a muddy blur.

But the Mitsubishi i-MiEV's lack of horsepower ends up letting me down in a major way. I'm, like, a good five seconds behind the others. And McGahy decides to be the hero then. He literally steps in front of the cor – that's how much he cares about vegetables. The problem is that I can't actually see him – and presumably he can't see me *either*? – because the windscreen is so caked with mud.

It's Fionn who ends up telling me. He goes, 'McGahy's right in front of you, Ross! He's waving his orms!'

I'm there, 'He'll hopefully jump out of the way!' deciding that this is basically a game of chicken.

Fionn goes, 'I don't think he's getting out of the way, Ross.'

I'm like, 'Trust me, Dude!' keeping my foot hord against the accelerator.

'Ross,' he goes, 'you're going to kill him!'

Fionn closes his eyes and braces himself for the impact. But there *isn't* one?

A second or two later, I see McGahy in the rear-view mirror, waving his fist, but shrinking quickly into the distance.

Fionn ends up roaring at me. He's there, 'You could have focking killed him, Ross!'

But, as he says it, I can't help but notice that he's laughing. And exhausted and worried as he is about the future, I know that deep down he's not ready to say goodbye to any of us just yet.

Ricey tells me I look like shit. This is after an evening weights session in the school gym. Fionn gave it a swerve because he's wrecked today – although it's me who apparently looks like death warmed up.

I check myself out in the mirror and the dude isn't wrong. I look pale and – I want to say – *drawn*?

I decide to tell him the truth.

'Yeah, no,' I go, 'it's because I'm a vegan.'

He laughs. They all laugh.

'A vegan?' it's either Dougie or Lenny who goes. 'Are you mad, like?'

I'm there, 'Believe me, goys, it's not out of choice. My daughter has got it into her head that eating meat and drinking milk is the reason the weather is all focked up.'

'Here, Barry,' Ricey goes, 'do you know what he needs? A Henry & Rose, like.'

I'm there, 'What's a Henry & Rose?'

'It's a chipper,' Barry goes, 'where my girlfriend works. They do the best burger in the world, like.'

I'm like, 'That's, er, quite a claim,' but I'm already salivating.

Barry goes, 'It's just next to the DART station, behind the Bowler, like.'

Which is handy, because that's where I threw the focking Mitsubishi i-MiEV.

Barry's there, 'Why don't we all go, like? As a team? I don't know about you lot but I'm starving, like?'

'Yes, also I am hungry,' Sergei goes. 'I would like to eat this beef burger.'

So – yeah, no – we all end up going? We walk the fifteen minutes to this place, which is right next to the DORT station.

It's the smell that hits me first. I catch it from the far end of Albert Walk – we're talking the length of a rugby pitch away. Beef and fried onions. I suddenly quicken my pace and the goys all laugh.

Ricey goes, 'You must be starving, like!'

I'm there, 'Dude, you've no idea. I haven't eaten meat in months. I had cranberry and lentil bake for Christmas dinner.'

'That's not normal, like.'

'You're telling me.'

There ends up being no queue. Which means I'm the first to order. It's Breena – as in the ginger giant who Barry's going out with – who actually serves me.

Barry goes, 'Give him a double-double, Bree.'

I'm there, 'What's that?'

'It's two quarter-pounders,' he goes. 'One on top of the other, like.'

'Do you want anything on it?' Breena goes. 'Onions, tomato, mushrooms . . .'

I'm like, 'Cheese. Lash it on. And do you do milkshakes? As in, non-vegan ones?'

'We've got chocolate, vanilla or strawberry.'

'Make it a chocolate one – and make it a lorge.'

We grab our orders – I end up paying for everyone – and we sit on the wall of the cor pork opposite the place, about twenty-five of us. I tear open the wrapper and then I'm just staring at this humungous burger, the smell of cooked meat making my entire body tingle.

My hands are literally shaking and my hort – I swear to fock – is beating like a jack hammer.

I throw my mouth on it like I'm in prison and I've just got a conjugal visit from Lais Ribeiro. It tastes like nothing I've ever tasted before. I can feel my sinuses clear as grease dribbles down my neck.

'He's got his eyes closed, look,' Paul Preece, our number eight goes.

Everyone laughs. But I don't care. All the better to savour it.

I horse the entire thing in about six bites and Barry goes, 'The colour's coming back into your face already, like,' and the funny thing is that I *can* actually feel it happening. My cheeks are suddenly hot and my forehead is damp with sweat.

We end up spending a great hour together. I find out loads of shit about the goys that I didn't actually know. Like, for instance, Ricey is a first cousin of Dougie and Lenny on his old man's side and a second cousin of Paul Preece on his old dear's side. Dougie and Lenny are also 'step-cousins' of Barry through their old man's second marriage and Barry is also a cousin of Nailer, owing to the fact that their mothers are sisters.

But we don't spend the entire time talking about the ways in which everyone in Bray is related to one another. I find out other shit as well. Like, for instance, Nailer's old dear focked off on him when he was, like, six years old and his old man – the bus driver – has been raising him on his own ever since. Like, for instance,

Dougie and Lenny work as lifegords on the seafront in the summer months and last summer they saved two kids from drowning. Like, for instance, Barry wants to be a Civil Engineer, like his old man, after he finishes his Leaving Cert.

We end up having *the* best chat. And, while it's fair to say that we didn't exactly get off on the right foot, I'm storting to genuinely warm to them just like they've obviously warmed to me.

Eventually, one by one, the goys all stort to drift away. I shoot the shit with Barry for a bit longer. He tells me that him and Breena have been going out with each other since they were, like, thirteen years old. I'm staring at her through the window, trying to figure out who she *reminds* me of? And then I cop it. The red hair. The height. She looks like Dougie and Lenny. And there's a very good reason for that.

It turns out they're cousins as well.

'Does that not make you and *her* cousins?' I go. 'And I'm not saying that in a judgy way.'

I am saying it in a judgy way.

Barry's like, 'No, my mother married Dougie and Lenny's father, so we're not actually blood relatives, like.'

Jesus Christ, it's like trying to figure out who's who in focking Westeros. I'm going to have to get Fionn to draw me a family tree like he did when I watched *Game of Thrones*.

Barry decides to, like, *confide* something in me then? He goes, 'I really love her. It kills me that I have to say goodbye to her, like.'

I can't say I'm surprised by this news. He's a good-looking dude and the kicker on the Pres Bray team that dumped Michael's out of the Leinster Schools Senior Cup. It'd take a strong man not to have his head turned by all the female attention he's no doubt suddenly getting.

I'm there, 'You can definitely do better, Dude – certainly from a looks point of view. With the greatest will in the world, she's no beauty.'

This seems to come as news to him. He actually looks a bit upset by it.

He goes, 'I'm not breaking up with her, like.'

I'm there, 'I thought you said you were saying goodbye to her?'

'She's going to America on a basketball scholarship in the summer. But we're going to keep the relationship going – long-distance, like.'

I don't know when to stop digging, of course.

I'm there, 'Dude, take my advice. You're punching way below your weight there. You should be with as many girls as you possibly can – while you're hot.'

Then *he* says something that surprises *me*?

'That's not the way to honour the Lord,' he goes. '*Many a man claims to have unfailing love – but a faithful man, who can find?* That's from the Book of Proverbs, like.'

Yeah, no, he's obviously one of them.

I'm there, 'So, you're, er, into that whole Bible thing, are you?'

He goes, 'I live my life by the Bible. So does Breena, like.'

I give him a nod as if to say, you know, whatever bloats your goat, then I tell him that I have to make tracks.

I hop down off the wall and I stort walking towards the DORT station cor pork, where – like I said – I threw the Mitsu-focking-bishi i-MiEV earlier.

At the entrance to the cor pork, I become aware of a serious borney happening between a man and a woman. They're, like, really going at each other in a language I don't understand. I decide to stay the fock out of it. I remember once trying to pull aport two women who came to blows over the last box of stollen bites in Avoca Handweavers on Suffolk Street four or five Christmas Eves ago and getting a crack across the head with a Louboutin heel for my trouble.

I can still feel the half-inch dent in my skull.

So I keep on walking. But, as I'm passing them, I have a quick look and I realize – to my great shock – that I actually know them.

Yeah, no, it's Sergei and Raisa.

They don't actually see me – that's how, like, *engrossed* they are in it? She's, like, roaring at him and he's, like, roaring back at her. All of a sudden, she slaps him hord across the face, then he turns and storms off in the direction of the DORT station.

Raisa watches him go, then she bursts into tears. Of course, I end up *having* to say something? I just hate seeing a woman in distress.

I'm there, 'Raisa?'

It takes a second or two for her to recognize me. Once she does, she comes running towards me and throws her orms around me.

I'm like, 'What's wrong?'

She goes, 'I try to be his friend. I come to Bray to see does he want lift. He calls me slut.'

I'm there, 'You're not a slut,' even though she might well be a slut. I don't know her from a hole in the road. 'You're definitely not a slut.'

She pulls away from me and stares into my eyes, her head tilted and her lips slightly ported, the way women do when they're inviting you to kiss them.

So I throw the lips on her. She suddenly pulls away from me, back far enough to slap me across the face – even horder than she slapped Sergei.

I'm still reeling from the shock of it – my face stinging, my eyes watering – when she grabs me by the back of the neck with two hands, pulls me towards her and storts kissing me hungrily.

Adultery – as I would have told Ronan in my Father of the Groom speech – is like getting a dent in a brand-new cor. Once you've done it once, it makes easier to do it again and again and again.

'Your mouth tastes like beef,' Raisa goes.

I'm there, 'Thanks,' even though I'm not sure it was intended as a compliment.

She's like, 'Do you know is there somewhere we can go?' meaning, presumably, to do the deed.

I end up having to think for a few seconds. Let's just say I haven't forgotten the fact that her husband threatened to kill us both if anything happened.

'Yeah,' I hear myself go, 'I know just the place.'

Twenty minutes later, we're driving through the Glen of the Downs in the focking Mitsubishi. Raisa has her hand down the front of my chinos and she's squeezing my nuts like a focking stress ball.

She goes, 'I like you. I like you very much.'

And I'm there, 'Yeah, no, you're making that pretty obvious, Raisa.'

With her other hand, she's unzipping her knee-high boots.

'And you like me,' she goes, slipping them off with her feet.

I'm there, 'I said it the first time I saw you – a young Melania Trump, except less frightened.'

'I see you look at me when I am out of sauna,' she goes, tightening her grip on my knackers. 'And I know you are attracted.'

I'm like, 'Go easy on the old mebs there, Raisa. I've nearly swerved into a focking tree twice.'

'Stop the car,' she goes. 'I must have. I must have now.'

So – yeah, no – I just pull up in the middle of the forest path and Raisa doesn't wait for an invitation. She pulls off her jeans and her knickers together in one movement, then she throws her left leg over me so that she's suddenly – I don't know – straddling me there in the driver's seat.

She helps me out of my sailing jacket, then she pulls my Pres Bray jersey over my head and takes a few seconds out to cast an appreciative eye over my upper body.

I've been doing a hell of a lot sit-ups since Christmas and it doesn't go unnoticed.

I manage to get her leather jacket and her top off as well. She looks uncomfortable with her neck cranked forward – the lack of headroom is an issue with the entire Mitsubishi electric range – but she reaches down and flicks the lever to push my seat back and then she relaxes a bit.

Once I'm horizontal, she tears open my fly, then yanks my chinos and my boxers down to my knees. She takes off her bra, then she moves my bits and her bits into position and suddenly we're going at it like rats in a focking sewer.

And there I'm going to bring the entertainment to a close. I've never been one to kiss and tell – something for which I'm hopefully respected – and I'm not going to make an exception in this case, other than to mention that Raisa clearly likes to be the dominant one and she squeezes my throat so hord that I end up blacking out

twice before she roars in my face to wake me up again and eventually gallops me over the finishing line with one hand pulling hord
on my hair and the other hand slapping my flank like a jockey
who's improvising after losing his whip.

I end up coming with a long, girlie scream, which surprises me,
because it sounds like someone else.

'Is finished?' she goes, still sitting astride me, a note of definite
disappointment in her voice.

I'm like, 'Er, yeah, no, it's Game Over alright. There's some wipes
there in the dashboard – although they're actually leather wipes, so
I wouldn't let them touch your you-know-what. Your bajingo.'

She's there, 'We do again?'

And I'm like, 'Yeah, no, I wouldn't say no. What day would suit
you? Tuesdays and Thursdays work for me if you're thinking in
terms of an evening.'

She goes, 'I am talking about now.'

'Now?'

'Yes, now.'

'Raisa, I'm done. I'm empty. I'm all out of the good stuff. You
heard me there – I wasn't faking that.'

She suddenly – I'm going to use the word – *dismounts* me, then
storts pulling on her clothes and telling me to drive her back to
Bray. I sit up and I bring my seat upright while she calls me a selfish
orsehole and tells me I have a penis like an AA battery – or maybe
it was an AAA – and that I could never satisfy a woman with a
penis like that.

I turn the key in the ignition and nothing happens.

I'm like, 'What the fock?'

I turn it again and still nothing.

'Shit,' I go.

Raisa's like, 'What is shit?'

'The cor won't stort,' I go. 'I must have forgotten to chorge the
focking thing.'

'This is joking.'

'Unfortunately, this isn't joking.'

She loses it with me then. She's like, 'Electric car is shit car.'

And I'm there, 'Yeah, you're preaching to the converted, Raisa.'

'Why you have shit car?'

'Let's forget about the whys and the wherefores and think about how we're going to get out of this. I'm wondering is there a back-up battery or something?'

'I cannot stay here. Fyodor is jealous man. He will kill me and also you.'

'Yeah, he mentioned something to me about that. Okay, I'm going to have to ring Sorcha.'

'Who is Sirryka?'

'She's my wife.'

'You cannot tell your wife. No one can know I am here.'

'Chillax, Raisa. I'm just going to ask her if there's any way of storting an electric cor if you forget to actually chorge the thing. Just stay quiet, okay?'

'You are asshole.'

I dial Sorcha's number. She answers on the fifth ring. She goes, 'Hey, Ross! Is everything okay?'

I'm like, 'Hypothetical question, Sorcha. If you forget to chorge the cor and then it just stops in the middle of nowhere, is there any way to get it storted again?'

'No.'

'Right.'

'Where are you?'

'I'm in, em, Bray. Of all places.'

'Bray? Oh my God, so am I!'

Oh, fock.

I'm like, 'Excuse me?'

'Yeah,' she goes. 'I came out with Mom and Dad. They wanted to check out Claire's place. We all had the artisanal falafel burger with incarcerated walnuts and a jealous berry reduction.'

I'm like, 'Er, cool. Who's looking after the boys?' as if that's my *actual* concern.

'Honor offered to babysit,' she goes. 'They're watching *An Inconvenient Truth*.'

'Er, fair focks.'

'Where *exactly* are you, Ross? I think my dad has a tow rope in the boot.'

'Er, it's kind of hord to explain my exact location, Sorcha. As a matter of fact, I'm going to hang up on you now.'

She's like, 'Wait, don't hang up,' and then she goes silent for about thirty seconds. I have no idea what the fock she's doing, but then she comes back on the line and goes, 'Ross, you're in the Glen of the Downs.'

I'm like, 'The Glen of the Downs? I don't know where you're getting your information, Sorcha. I'm definitely *not* in the Glen of the Downs.'

'Ross, I'm using the Find My Phone app. I'm looking at your location on the screen here. Dad, have you still got that tow rope?'

I hear her old man sigh – the focking cheek of him.

I'm there, 'I don't want to be towed by a SEAT Ibiza, Sorcha. Forget I even rang. I'll sleep here tonight and maybe join the AA in the morning.'

'Stop being ridiculous, Ross. We'll be there in, like, fifteen minutes.'

She hangs up on me.

I'm there, 'Fock.'

Raisa's there, 'What happen?'

'What *happen* is that my wife is on her way here – with her old pair, who already hate my guts.'

Raisa looks suddenly worried. She's there, 'What will we do?'

'Okay,' I go, 'I know this is going to be hord for you to hear. But when they get here, you're going to have to hide.'

'Hide? Where I hide?'

'Behind a tree. In the undergrowth. Use your imagination.'

'And then after I hide, what?'

'Wait until we've driven off and then – yeah, no – follow the path back to the N11.'

'You mean walk?'

'Er, yeah.'

'Is pitch dark.'

'It's only about twenty minutes. Quicker if you run. It'll be easy enough to Hailo a cab from the hord shoulder.'

She doesn't *love* the plan?

'You leave me alone in forest at night?' she goes.

I'm there, 'I don't see any other option, Raisa.'

She absolutely rips into me then, calling me this and that – my penis gets another unfavourable mench or two – and then she gets out and storts kicking the side of the cor.

The girl has lost her shit and it takes a good ten minutes for me to get her calm again. I'm there, 'Raisa, we're on the same side here – neither of us wants this to get out.'

She goes, 'You are not leave me in forest alone.'

'What choice do we have?'

'I get in boot.'

'What?'

She walks around to the back of the cor and she pops the trunk.

She goes, 'I get in boot,' and she climbs in.

I'm there, 'No way. What if Sorcha looks in there?'

'I not give shit!' she goes, pulling the boot closed on herself.

Then, all of a sudden, I hear a cor come chugging up the path and I know straight away that it's Sorcha's old man's shitty SEAT. I'm suddenly committed to the plan.

He pulls up just in front of my cor. Sorcha gets out. She's like, 'Oh my God, Ross, what are you even doing here?'

I'm there, 'Excuse me?' trying to buy myself enough time to come up with something.

She goes, 'Ross, what are you doing in the middle of a forest at, like, ten o'clock at night.'

I'm there, 'I was, em, *foraging* – if that's the word?'

'Foraging? What were you foraging for?'

'For, em, berries. Yeah, no, one of the goys on the team told me there were great berries in here.'

I hear her old man laugh. He goes, 'He's up to something. And, judging by the guilty look on his face, you've caught him in the act.'

I'm there, 'Honestly, Sorcha. I'm really getting into the whole vegan thing and I wanted to surprise you and Honor by making something with – again – foraged berries.'

For a good five seconds, it's impossible to tell whether she buys it or not. But then she just smiles. 'That's so sweet,' she goes.

Her old man is focking fuming. He's there, 'That's not even *vaguely* credible, Sorcha! Check the boot!'

'Dad,' Sorcha goes, 'if Ross says he was foraging for berries, then he was foraging for berries, okay? Now, will you please just get the tow rope?'

Her old man just shakes his head like he's given up on her. He gets back into his shitty little cor, turns it around, then reverses it back towards us. He gets out again, attaches one end of the rope to his tow bor and the other to our front bomper. Then he goes back to his cor. He storts it up.

I sit into the i-MiEV to steer and Sorcha sits into the passenger seat beside me. A few minutes later, we're back on the N11, heading north.

We're just passing Whelehans in Loughlinstown when my phone suddenly beeps. It's a text message from my old man to say that Roxana and Lydia II both went into labour today. I tell Sorcha the happy news.

'It turns out I've got two sisters,' I go. 'Lydia II gave birth at, like, six o'clock tonight and Roxana had hers literally fifteen minutes later.'

Sorcha's like, 'Oh my God, that's amazing news!'

'I don't know, does that make them twins?'

'Ross, you don't seem excited.'

Yeah, no, I'm not – because I'm suddenly thinking about Szidonia. I'm thinking three down and three to go. Then she's going to force me to help them flee the country. I'm suddenly so preoccupied by this that I end up totally forgetting about the Russian in the boot.

We pull up at a red light outside St John's School in Ballybrack. And that's when Sorcha suddenly lets out a scream.

I'm like, 'What's wrong?'

She goes, 'What the fock is that, Ross – sticking out of your pocket?'

My entire body freezes. For a second or two, I don't even want to look down. I'm wondering what it could possibly be. A used Johnny? Jesus, did I shove Raisa's bra into my jacket as a screwvenir out of pure habit?

After a silence that seems to go on forever, I finally get my answer.

She goes, 'You had a burger!'

I'm like, 'What?'

'You had a focking burger! I can see the wrapper sticking out of your pocket!'

'Er . . .'

'Don't even *try* to deny it, Ross.'

I look in the rear-view mirror and I notice that the boot is suddenly wide open.

'Yeah, no, cords on the table,' I go, 'it was a moment of weakness.'

Sorcha's like, 'You're focking unbelievable, Ross!'

I don't bother arguing with the girl. Given where I was forty minutes ago, getting caught eating meat is not a bad result, on balance.

I'm there, 'Hang on a second, Sorcha. The boot has somehow popped open.'

I'm thinking, one day, when I get around to it, I'm going to try to simplify my life.

I get out and I walk to the back of the cor. The boot is empty. Raisa has presumably pegged it. But, weirdly, it's not actual relief I feel. I'm thinking about all the messes I've suddenly created for myself. Szidonia. Delma. Raisa. Three time bombs, one of which, I just know, is going to blow up in my face one day soon.

Or maybe it'll be all three of them.

8.

Baby Driver

Honor says that, every year, we cut down an area of the Amazon Rainforest that's equivalent to the size of Belgium – and I ask the question that's on everyone's lips.

I'm there, 'Is Belgium a big place?'

'Thankfully not!' the old man goes. 'As a matter of fact, it's one of the smallest countries in Europe!'

Honor's like, 'Oh my God, Granddad, that's not the point – it's still, like, half the size of Ireland!'

Sorcha's there, 'Well, at least we can do something about it, Honor – by only using paper manufactured by companies with a certified Zero Net Deforestation policy.'

There's suddenly a ping. We've reached the third floor. The lift doors open. Yeah, no, I forgot to mention that we're back in Holles Street – on our way to meet my newborn *sisters*.

'It's not enough,' Honor goes. 'People still aren't focking listening.'

Sorcha's there, 'Don't get frustrated, Honor. Look at all you've achieved in just a few short weeks. We've given up meat and we've switched to a hybrid cor. You stopped the school trip to Pinzolo. There are literally hundreds of Mount Anville girls using public transport for the first time in their lives. You've been on the *Six One* news and the *Irish Times* magazine has described you as an unflinching speaker of truth to power.'

'I need to do something big. Something that makes the entire country sit up and take notice.'

'Or maybe you need to learn what all of the great activists came to understand,' Sorcha goes, 'from Mortin Luther King to even Emma Watson – you can't change the world overnight, Honor.'

The old man goes, 'I just fail to understand how chopping down

266

trees, or burning coal, or dumping our rubbish in the sea has any-thing to do with so-called global warming! It seems a tenuous link at best!'

We're walking down the corridor towards the ward. Honor's face all of a sudden lights up.

'Oh my God!' she goes. 'I've got it! I'm going to arrange a National School Strike!'

Sorcha's there, 'A National School Strike? Is that not a bit extreme, Honor? I'm thinking about all the parents who'd have to arrange childcare at short notice.'

'Oh my God, I'm going to do it. I'm going to choose a date – maybe Valentine's Day – and I'm going to tell everyone in the country not to go to school that day. And, oh my God, instead go to a Climate Justice Rally – in, like, College Green!'

'Oh my God,' Sorcha goes, 'College Green is where I used to arrange, like, Amnesty protests when I was in Mount Anville!'

The old dear – *déjà* focking *vu* – is sitting in the waiting area, along with Lidia I, Brigitta and Loredana, who are all still pregnant, and Szidonia, who's clutching Hugo to her half-exposed breast.

Sorcha goes, 'Congratulations, Fionnuala! We're *so* happy for you!' the crawler.

And I'm like, 'Yeah, no, fair focks. I'm looking forward to meet-ing them – whatever.'

She's supposed to be bringing the babies home today.

'Everything okay, Dorling?' the old man goes.

The old dear's there, 'Yes, the doctor is with them. Lidia has low blood pressure and Roxana has high – or maybe it's the other way around. They asked us to wait outside for a few moments.'

I can feel the weight of Szidonia staring at me. I can't even look at her, even though she's breastfeeding, something I've always found weirdly – I want to say – *erotic*?

Honor goes, 'Have you chosen names yet, Fionnuala?'

The old dear's like, 'Yes, Dorling, they're called Emily and Lou-isa May. After two of my favourite authors.'

Yeah, no, I've never heard of them either.

After a couple of minutes waiting there, Ronan and Shadden

show up. He goes, 'Congratulashiddens, Cheerlie! Congratulashiddens, Fidooda! Two little geerdles, wha'?'

The old man goes, 'I shall love them, Ronan, as if they were boys.'

Szidonia manages to somehow catch my eye. She gives me a look as if to say, 'I told you – they're focking doolally, the pair of them.'

I can see a lot of tit.

Ronan goes, 'Hee-or, Cheerlie, I know you're not wanthon to heerd it, but Ine arthur being doing some mower reading arowunt yisser case. I think you've a veddy good chaddence of widding an appeal to the Supreme Cowurt.'

The old man's there, 'No, I've played all my cards, Ronan! It's in the hands of the inestimable Roderic Grainger SC now! I just have to trust that he will deliver the correct verdict for democracy!'

'Accorton to some of the leaks cubbing out of the investigashidden, he's arthur finding out all sorts, Cheerlie! Dead shams voting. Nayums of udder shams removed from the voting registodder for no reason.'

'If his investigation concludes that that was somehow my doing, Ronan, then I shall have no choice but to accept the finding, however much I disagree with it. I remain hopeful, though – as does Hennessy!'

Shadden goes, 'Did you ted your grandda your *udder* newuz, Ro?'

Whatever it is, she doesn't sound in the least bit excited by it.

He's there, 'Ine arthur getting meself an intodderview.'

'An interview?' the old man goes. 'What kind of interview?'

'It's for an intoordenship wirra feerdum in New York. Madison Abenue, Rosser. Thee speciadize in civoddle reets law, this crowut.'

Shadden's there, 'He's godda be woorking pro-bodo, Cheerlie – for no bleaten muddy, in udder woords.'

Shadden's skin is orange, by the way, a sure sign that she's been topping up her holiday tan in the Sunny Days Solarium Express above the vape shop on the Ballygall Road.

Ronan's there, 'There's mower to life than muddy, Shadden,' and suddenly we're caught up in one of their domestics.

She goes, 'You know my feedon on the mathor – I caddent wontherstand why you woatunt joost take Heddessy's job offer.'

'Ine wanton to use me brayuns to heddelp people less fortunate thadden meself – the fook is wrong with that, Shadden?'

'Yeah, *you* woody about helping the rest of the wurdled, Ro – *I'll* woody about providing the best life I can for eer thaughter. Hab you nebber heerd of the phrayuz chadity begins at howum?'

'Ast me boddicks. Alls *you're* woodied about is swadding arowunt Itoddy thinking you're Amaddle bleaten Clooney.'

It's horrible to listen to – the only consolation for me is that I told him it was a mistake, firstly, to get her pupped up, and, secondly, to marry her.

A lady doctor appears and tells us that we can see them now and we all pile into the ward for a look at the two new arrivals. Roxana and Lydia II are lying next to each other in two beds, looking – it has to be said – shocking.

They end up barely getting a look from anyone, though. We all head straight for the two – that word again – *bassinets* in the corner, where Emily and Louisa May are lying, fast asleep.

'Oh my God,' Sorcha goes, 'they're beautiful, Fionnuala!'

And they are – no orguments from me on that score.

Shadden goes, 'They're boat the ibage of you, Fidooda!'

But this time I'm actually standing right back. I don't want to get – being honest – too attached. Because I know, in a week or two, there's a chance they're going to be gone.

The old dear goes, 'Come on, Chorles, let's get them home!'

They each pick up a bassinet and they head for the door.

I'm there, 'While I think of it, Honor, have I been giving you fifty yoyos a week for bassinet lessons for the last two years?'

And Honor goes, 'Er, I can't help it if you were thick enough to believe it was a musical instrument.'

Everyone laughs – even Sorcha – as they disappear out of the ward without even acknowledging Roxana and Lidia II. It feels, I don't know, seriously cold.

I hang back to talk to them.

I'm there, 'So, er, when are you two being dischorged?'

'Perhaps the weekend for me,' Lidia II goes.

And Roxana's there, 'For me, it will be four, maybe five more days.'

They look miserable. You couldn't *but* feel sorry for them?

A second or two later, I watch Szidonia walk into the ward – Hugo still fixed to her left udder. She closes the door behind her. She obviously wants a word.

'So now,' she goes, 'I tell you plan.'

I'm like, 'Szidonia, I'm still not a hundred per cent –'

'You listen. I speak. My eyes are here, Ross.'

Yeah, no, my gaze keeps being drawn to the old drink station.

'Look at me,' she goes, 'not my chest. Brigitta is one week away. Other Lidia is eight days. Loredana is nine days. As soon as all babies are born, you will steal car from stuttering man who drives your father.'

I'm like, 'Kennet? Are you talking about the stretch Merc?'

'Is big enough for all of us, yes?'

'Yeah, no, it's got, like, eight seats.'

'I will put sleeping tablets in Fionnuala's breakfast – enough to send her to sleep for twelve hours. Then we take babies and we get in car.'

'And where are we supposably going?'

'We drive to Rosslare.'

'So the ferry, in other words?'

'Again, you are talking to my chest.'

'It's habit more than anything.'

'You will come with us to France. You will drive us to Paris and then we find way home.'

'*With* the babies, though?'

'We have this conversation. We give them better life.'

'I'm still torn, Szidonia.'

'I will call your wife in here right now and I will show her video of you fucking this Delma woman like sick asshole.'

'No, please, don't. And keep your voice down.'

'Then you do what I say to you.'

It's time for some tough talking. We're playing Clongowes in the quarter-finals in, like, three days and I need to say something to focus their minds.

I'm like, 'Goys, I have a question for you. Who were the beaten quarter-finalists in the Leinster Schools Senior Cup last year?'

The dressing room is full of, like, blank faces.

I reach into my pocket and I whip out a wad of notes. I'm there, 'I've got, what, the best port of a grand here for whoever can name me even one of the beaten quarter-finalists from last year's Leinster Schools Senior Cup.'

They stort just randomly throwing the names of schools at me.

They're going, 'Wesley College, like!' or 'High School Rathgar, like!' or 'Kilkenny College, like!' and I'm just there, 'Wrong! Wrong! Wrong!'

Actually, I think one or two of them might be right, but they're only guessing, which just goes to prove my point.

'No one remembers Leinster Schools Senior Cup quarter-finalists,' I go. 'It's sad, but it's a fact. The world out there is full of goys who went to St Andrew's in Booterstown, or CUS, or Sandford Pork, who'll tell you that they won a match back in the day against the Belvedere Dream Team or the Gonzaga Dream Team or the Blackrock Dream Team. I meet them all the time. Dudes who want to buy me a drink and tell me about the time they reached the quarter-finals of the Leinster Schools Senior Cup. And do you know what I do when I meet those dudes? I just walk away.'

Actually, I usually let them buy me the drink first. I don't mention that, though, because it sort of undermines my story a bit.

I'm there, 'I walk away. Because I'm not interested. No one is interested. What you did against Michael's was incredible. But outside of Bray – trust me – no one is talking about it any more.'

They're all nodding their heads. They don't look happy, but it's something they need to hear.

I'm there, 'You don't want to grow up to be a boring old fart, propping up the bor in Holland's, or Duff's, or Jim Doyle's, or the Horbour Bor, telling tourists about the great giant-killing act you pulled off back in the day. It's up to you goys to decide whether that win over Michael's is an end in itself – or if it's the beginning of something. Enjoy your weekend. Take it easy on beerage. And I'll see you all on Monday.'

Ricey shouts, 'Come on, Pres!' and the goys all stort cheering and punching the air.

On the way out of the dressing room, Fionn pats me on the back.

'That was a great speech,' he goes. 'Father Fehily would have been proud of that.'

I'm there, 'Yeah, no, the whole waving a wad of money in their faces was pure him.'

'You do know a couple of them guessed the right answer, don't you?'

'Yeah, I thought so. Let's just hope they don't Google it over the weekend.'

'Can I suggest something to you, Ross?'

'Dude, you're my Assistant Coach – I actually *want* you to suggest shit?'

'What would you think of the idea of switching Sergei and Barry?'

'You mean move Barry back to ten and stick Sergei in the centre?'

'Exactly.'

'What's the logic?'

God, I love the way my voice sounds when I'm talking about rugby.

He goes, 'Sergei isn't a secret any more. Everyone knows about him. And Clongowes are probably going to torget him.'

I'm like, 'They definitely will. They're dicks.'

'They do their homework, Ross.'

'That's what I mean by dicks.'

'They'll have a plan for hiim, which will probably involve taking him out at every opportunity. But if you move him to the centre –'

'He'll have more time on the ball – and hopefully more protection.'

'It's just something to think about over the weekend.'

As we're leaving the school building, I hear my name all of a sudden being called. Well, not my name. It's just like, 'Coach!'

I turn around and it ends up being Sergei.

He goes, 'I can speak with you?' and he obviously means in private, because he looks at Fionn, then back at me.

Fionn takes the hint. He goes, 'I'll, er, see you back at the cor, Ross.'

I hid the thing down at the bottom of the Putland Road. I hand him the keys and he focks off.

I'm like, 'What's up, Sergei?'

He seems a bit, I don't know, troubled. Jesus Christ, I'm wondering does he know about me riding his stepmother in the Glen of the Downs?

He goes, 'What I have to say to you is hard for me.'

I'm like, 'Er, okay.'

'Attraction between man and woman is sometime difficult to explain, yes?'

'Er, keep going.'

'Sometime when you meet woman and you like her, you cannot help. Is hormones. You have to have it, yes?'

Oh, fock.

'You do not mean for it to happen,' he goes. 'You meet in car park. Is accident. You kiss. You drive to Glen of Down for sexy-sexy in car.'

I'm there, 'Dude, can I just say that *she* came on to *me*? And that's not me being a dick.'

His expression suddenly changes. He's suddenly looking at me like he hasn't a focking clue what I'm on about.

'What are you talking?' he goes.

Shit. I've possibly got the wrong end of the stick here.

I'm like, 'Er, sorry, it must be the language barrier. *Continue* with your story?'

'So,' he goes, 'I am in car park and I meet girl. She tell to me I am good rugby player and have good game against Michael school. Very much I like this girl. She tell me very much she like me. I kiss. She say we go to Glen of Down. Soon we are making the sexy-sexy.'

I'm like, 'Whoa, Dude, I'm not sure you should be telling me this.'

'For me is first time. For her is also first time. Is bit awkward.'

'Jesus Christ, is there not someone else you could talk to about this shit?'

'My father always is working. His wife is slut.'

'What about one of the goys off the team? Ricey or the twins?'

'Is too difficult for me to talk to them about.'

'Dude, look, you're an unbelievable rugby player. All I'm going to say to you is that you're going to get a lot of offers from randomers like that. Just enjoy it, okay?'

'She want to meet tonight. She say we go back to Glen of Down for making more of the sexy-sexy.'

What a focking weirdo.

'Dude,' I go, 'I'm cutting this conversation short, okay?'

'So you say I should go for – yes?'

'Dude, do what feels right. I'll see you on Monday.'

'Should we not maybe accept this as a sign?' I go.

Sorcha's there, 'A sign? What are you talking about?'

Yeah, no, Brian punched Leo in the face at breakfast this morning and smashed his glasses.

Every cloud – that would be my feeling on the matter.

'I'm saying maybe there's an actual reason they got broken,' I go. 'And that reason is that he doesn't actually need them. As a matter of fact, I had a sneaky look under his patch before we left the house and his eye seems to be fine again. It was pointing in pretty much the same direction as the other one.'

'Ross,' she goes, 'we are getting new glasses for Leo and that is the end of the matter.'

Which is why we're back in Dundrum Town Centre – we're talking me, Sorcha and the three boys.

I shouldn't even be out this morning. The quarter-final against Clongowes is, like, forty-eight hours away and I have far more important things to be thinking about than my son's eyesight.

Like, for instance, Fionn's suggestion that I move Barry back to outhalf and play Sergei in the centre.

I follow Sorcha onto the escalator. I check my phone. I have a text message. It's from my old man.

Sorcha goes, 'Is everything okay?'

I'm there, 'Brigitta had her baby this morning.'

Four down, two to go.

Sorcha's like, 'Oh! My God!'

'Another girl,' I go. 'Mellicent. Where the fock is she getting these names?'

'Do you want to go into the hospital later?'

'Er, do you know what, Sorcha? I'm a little bit over Holles Street at this stage. I might just wait until all six arrive and then see them all in one go. Where are we going anyway?'

'Specsavers.'

'Specsavers? Jesus!'

'It's pointless buying Leo expensive glasses at his age. He's going to end up breaking so many pairs.'

'I might end up breaking a few myself.'

We reach the top of the escalator and there's a familiar figure standing there, right in front of us, on the mezzanine level. Yeah, no, it's Lauren.

Of course, Sorcha's all, 'Oh my God, Lauren!' and it ends up being hugs and air-kisses and the whole drama.

The girl totally blanks me. There's no, 'Fair focks for masterminding one of the greatest shocks in the history of the Leinster Schools Senior Cup!' or 'Good luck against Clongowes on Monday!'

Which I can live with.

I'd rather be someone's shot of tequila than everyone's cup of tea. I heard Simon Zebo say that to a bouncer one night as he was leaving Buck Whaley's with Elvira Fernández on his orm and I was so impressed that I wrote it into my Rugby Tactics Book.

Sorcha goes, 'How have you been, Lauren?'

And Lauren's like, 'I'm coping.'

My eyes are suddenly drawn to little Oliver, who's sitting in his stroller with his nose still strapped up.

A few feet away, there's one of those, like, pianos that are put there by God knows who for passing musical geniuses to sit down and show off. Little Ross Junior is sitting at it, banging out some tune by, I don't know, Mozort or one of *that* crew? The kid has been having piano lessons since he was old enough to support his own head.

'Look at this wanker,' Brian goes, because I've raised my boys to hate kids who have talents that they don't.

I just laugh. I possibly shouldn't, but it's the exact same thing *I* always say whenever I see some kid playing a musical instrument really well on, say, *The Late Late Toy Show.*

I watch Brian, Leo and Johnny walk over to the piano. Little Ross Junior is playing away with his eyes closed and a little smile on his face.

Sorcha goes, 'Oh my God, is that Chopin's Nocturne in E-flat Major?'

Lauren's like, 'Yes, it's his favourite.'

And Sorcha's there, 'Mine too. I had it as my ringtone for, like, two years. Whenever I'm having a massage and I'm offered a choice of music, I *always* ask if they have Chopin's Nocturnes.'

And that's when it happens – from suddenly out of nowhere. Brian goes, 'Focking piano prick!' and – I swear to God – he just slams the cover down on Ross Junior's fingers.

Poor Ross Junior lets out a howl loud enough to be heard by passengers getting off the Luas in Balally.

He's like, 'Aaaaaarrrrrrgggggghhhhhh!!!!!!'

Sorcha goes, 'Oh my God!' as do – let's just say – more than a few passers-by.

Lauren runs over to Ross Junior, going, 'His fingers! His fingers! His poor fingers!'

Brian walks over to me with a big grin on his face, going, 'Focking piano wanker!' and I'm there, 'Brian, you possibly shouldn't have done that,' just to let Lauren know that I'm taking it seriously as a parent. 'I might have to dock you fifty euros out of your pocket money this week.'

I'm so busy disciplining my son that I don't see little Ross Junior coming until it's too late. He comes running towards Brian with a look of rage on his face and his orms stretched out in front of him. Then he shoves him in the back.

And Brian – Jesus Christ – falls head-first down the escalator.

Now it's *my* turn to scream?

I'm like, 'Aaaaaarrrrrrgggggghhhhhh!!!!!!' as I watch my son – my only remaining rugby son, bear in mind – tumble over and over and over again down the escalator steps. He ends up falling for a good sixty seconds, because it's, like, the *up* escalator?

Sorcha's going, 'Brian! Brian!'

He eventually stops falling and the escalator delivers him back to our feet. As he reaches the top, sprawled out on his back, I look down and I notice, to my total and utter horror, that his right leg is sticking out at a sickening angle.

Sorcha obviously cops it too, because she goes, 'Oh my God, his leg is broken!'

And I'm there, 'It's his kicking leg, Sorcha! Jesus Christ, it's his kicking leg!'

I bend down and I carefully scoop him up in my orms. Brian howls with the pain of being moved at all.

Lauren – no sympathy whatsoever – is going, 'I'm sorry, Sorcha, but your husband taught my son that violent streak – and now it's come back to bite him.'

I don't even have time to get into it with her. I head for the Information Desk. From the top of the escalator, I'm shouting, 'My rugby son is hurt! Call an ambulance! My rugby son is hurt!'

We wait for what seems like ages but is probably only five minutes, before I lose patience and go, 'Let's drive – we'll take him to The Beacon!'

Brian is screaming with the pain as we run for the cor pork, me carrying Brian, Sorcha running behind me with Johnny and Leo. We reach the cor. Sorcha drives and I sit in the front passenger seat with Brian on my lap. He roars his hort out while I try to comfort him by telling him that I fractured by posterior malleolus on my Confirmation day when I tripped over my drunken mother in the kitchen and I still came back to play Junior Cup rugby. But it doesn't do any good. I can hear it in my own voice. Deep down, I know that things aren't going to be okay.

We end up being seen pretty quickly. It *is* The Beacon and I make sure to mention to the receptionist that he's a rugby player and hopefully still a future Ireland number ten.

Sorcha snaps at me. She goes, 'Will you stop focking saying that?

How is that even relevant?' but she's upset – we *both* are? – so I don't make an issue out of it.

Two nurses – one good-looking, one less so – appear through the double doors, pushing a trolley. As gently as I can, I lay Brian down onto it, then I go to follow the trolley, except Sorcha tells me to wait in the reception area with the boys.

I'm like, 'Sorcha, I want to go with him. I think what he needs to hear right now are positive words from me.'

But Sorcha goes, 'Lauren was right, Ross. This *is* all *your* doing.'

'Jesus Christ, don't say that. I don't think I could live with the guilt if I thought that was true.'

'You gave her son that vicious streak. The old Ross Junior would never have done something so wicked. You can stay here with Johnny and Leo.'

So Sorcha follows the trolley through the doors and I'm left sitting in the reception area with – like she said – Johnny and Leo, wondering, is she right? *Is* this my fault? Am I a bad father?

Johnny gets his orm stuck inside the soft drink vending machine after reaching up into the chute to try to steal a drink. He storts howling. Everyone in the waiting room is just, like, staring at me, expecting me to do something.

But I'm there, 'Good enough for you, Johnny. Focking good enough for you,' because I've got enough on my mind without having to deal with *his* bullshit?

Leo – in fairness – tries to help his brother free his orm from the machine and *he* ends up with his orm stuck up the chute as well.

He goes, 'Focking orm! My focking orm!'

But I'm like, 'Not interested, Leo. Not interested at all.'

Eventually, after, like, an hour, the double doors open and Sorcha appears, pushing Brian in an – oh, my focking God – wheelchair. His right leg, from his hip to his ankle, is in a plaster cast and it's raised up in front of him.

I burst into tears. I straight away burst into tears. I'm like, 'Noooooo!' drawing all eyes in the waiting room on me. 'Noooooo!'

Sorcha manages to hold it together better than I do. She goes,

'Ross, I've asked the doctor to have a word with you because he's got something to tell you that I think would be better coming from him than me.'

Suddenly, this dude appears through the doors. He's from – and this isn't meant to sound racist – but Pakistan. And, if not Pakistan, then somewhere very near it.

He goes, 'You are the father of this boy?'

I'm like, 'Yeah, no, Brian is my son, yeah.'

He nods as if slowly taking this information on board. Then he delivers the bad news. He goes, 'Your son has oblique fractures to his tibia and his fibula.'

I'm there, 'Why is he in a wheelchair? Could you not have given him crutches?'

He goes, 'Unfortunately, your son does not have the upper-body strength to support himself using crutches.'

Of course, I end up taking this as a criticism of me. I'm there, 'I didn't think there was any point in working on his upper-body strength if he was going to be an outhalf,' and I practically scream the words at him.

'If he rests the leg completely,' he goes, 'it will improve the chances of healing.'

'So it *will* definitely heal?' I go.

'Yes, but there is also bad news, which I explained to your wife.'

I'm like, 'Bad news? As in?'

'Your son is at an age where his bones are growing every day – do you understand?'

'Er, yeah.'

'Breaking bones like this can have consequences for children because, while his right leg is recovering, his left leg will continue to grow.'

'Okay, I'm a bit slow on the uptake in general – what are you actually saying here?'

And that's when he says it. He looks me dead in the eye, then – in a calm voice – he goes, 'It's quite likely that your son will have one leg marginally shorter than the other.'

My entire body just goes cold.

Sorcha goes, 'Oh my God, Ross, the boys have got their hands caught in the Coke machine!'

But I barely even *hear* her?

The dude goes, 'I am sad to tell you that your son will always walk with a limp.'

The noise beyond the dressing-room door is absolutely deafening. It's, like, fifty per cent Pres Bray supporters and fifty per cent Clongowes supporters.

There are no neutrals here today. Not with a place in the semi-final of the Leinster Schools Senior Cup at stake.

I almost don't need to *say* anything? That's how seriously, seriously pumped the goys are.

I read out the team. There's, like, no surprises, except for the positional switch.

'Centre?' Sergei goes. 'In Russia, I am ten.'

I'm there, 'Well, today – in Donnybrook – you're thirteen. Fionn, explain it to him.'

Fionn goes, 'Look, Clongowes will have watched the video of what happened against Michael's.'

I'm there, 'Sneaky fockers. That's what they're like.'

'Their entire game plan will be centred around stopping Sergei from dictating things at ten.'

'They'll try to take him out like the dicks that they are.'

'But if he suddenly appears in the centre, well, it gives us a jump on them. It'll be half-time before they can come up with an alternative plan.'

'And by then the damage will be hopefully done.'

Barry goes, 'But Sergei is –'

And I know what he's about to say. That Sergei is a better player than him. I don't want to hear it. Even if it *is* true?

'Don't even *think* about finishing that sentence,' I go. 'You're a very good rugby player – take that from someone who knows a thing or two about playing at number ten. Now is the time for you to let the world know who Barry Austin is.'

I look around the dressing room.

I'm there, 'That goes for the rest of you as well. You know what the Clongowes coach will be saying to the goys next-door? He'll be telling them that Pres Bray are a one-man team. Yeah, no, cut off the supply of ball to Sergei Shengelia and it's game over. That's why I need every one of you to step up to the plate today. Show them. Show them we're not a one-man team.'

Ricey shouts, 'Why are we still sitting here talking, like? Let's go out there and bate the shite out of these fuckers, like.'

He doesn't wait to be handed a jersey. He grabs the bag and tips them out onto the floor, then he finds the number two jersey, pulls it on over his head and walks out of the dressing room. It's exactly what I want to see. The others do the same and they follow him outside.

I turn around to Fionn and I go, 'This is a gamble, Dude.'

He's there, 'I think it'll bring the best out of everyone.'

I'm struggling to stay focused, by the way. It means having to blank out what happened to Brian in Dundrum Town Centre on Saturday and the fact that none of my own kids is ever going to play rugby at this level.

Fionn goes, 'Are you okay?'

I'm like, 'Yeah, no, let's do this thing.'

We walk out. I end up running into Brother Ciaran outside the dressing room. As a matter of fact, I'm pretty sure he was *waiting* there for me?

'Young Sergei,' he goes, leaning on his stick. 'He's playing centre.'

I'm there, 'Is that a question or a statement?'

'I just wanted to make sure it wasn't a clerical error.'

'I don't make clerical errors.'

I've actually never heard of a clerical error, so it's quite possible I make tonnes of them.

I'm there, 'Enjoy the match.'

I join Fionn in our seats.

You can actually see the confusion of the Clongowes players as Sergei makes his way to the centre. They look totally baffled – like me having Sudoku explained to me by Malcolm O'Kelly the night of Peter Stringer's thirtieth.

It made no sense to me then and I'm proud to say it still makes no sense to me now.

We get off to *the* best possible stort. And, again, it's Sergei who does the actual damage. There's, like, six minutes on the clock when little Nailer whips the ball out of a scrum on the halfway line and passes it back to Barry with a super-fast delivery. Barry doesn't even catch it. He sort of, like, passes it straight through his hands to Sergei, who takes it into his chest and sets off like a runaway train. You can see the Clongowes players desperately scrambling to get to him, but he goes inside one, outside another, then inside another, before putting the ball down under the posts.

The Pres crowd goes absolutely mental. They're singing, 'We're Bray, we're Bray, we're Bray!'

Barry adds the *petits fours* and dancing – and we're, like, seven– nil up before Clongowes have had the chance to even settle.

It has to be said, though, it's our defence who end up stealing the show. Clongowes come back at us – I really hate Clongowes – but the goys end up putting in tackle after tackle after tackle after tackle, three times holding them up when they were porked right on our line.

Three minutes before half-time, we're under the serious cosh. Clongowes have breached our twenty-two and you can sense their confidence growing that they're going to get something on the board before half-time.

Their number eight breaks through our defensive line and makes about ten yords. But then, for no reason at all, he snots himself, spilling the ball. Preecer just boots the thing as hord as he can down the field and Barry chorges after it. It hits the ground, bounces backwards and ends up just lying dead on the turf like a roadkill badger. And suddenly Barry is involved in what looks like a 50–50 race with the Clongowes full-back, coming from the opposite dir- ection, to reach the ball first.

I'm, like, screaming at him, going, 'Be first, Barry! Be first!'

He gets there a fraction of a second before the Clongowes dude. He gives it a massive hoof. The ball goes one side of the Clongowes dude and he goes around the other, taking him out of the game. The ball bounces, end to end, towards the line.

The Pres crowd goes insane.

I'm going, 'Yes! Yes! Yes!'

Barry scoops the ball up in one hand, runs the last five metres to the line and dives over it with the ball. A minute or two later, with the crowd still going bananas, he adds the points and we're fourteen–nil up going into the break.

At half-time, I tell the goys that the second half is going to be all about – I'm chancing my orm that it's even a word – but *consolidation*? I'm there, 'What we have, we hold. That means the second half is going to be defence, defence, defence – do you understand?'

But they're not really listening to me. They're all – and I don't mean this in a *jealous* way? – but queuing up to hug Fionn.

'It was *his* idea,' Ricey goes, 'to switch Barry and Sergei! Genius, like.'

I'm there, 'I'm agreeing with you that, yes, it was a good idea. But, goys, you're going to have to listen to me.'

'They're bricking it, Fionn,' Nailer goes. 'Should we go out hard in the second half and finish them off, like?'

And Fionn, in fairness to him, goes, 'Goys, I'm not your coach. Listen to Ross, okay? He's trying to tell you something.'

I'm there, 'Thanks, Fionn. Goys, I'm telling you to do the exact opposite of what Nailer just said. If we go at them now, we're going to leave gaps. Let's just keep defending. See can we keep them scoreless for five minutes, then another five, then another five. The longer we stop them scoring, the more desperate they're going to become – and they're the ones who'll leave openings for us to exploit.'

The goys are, like, gagging to get back out there.

It's as we're walking back out onto the field that I notice that Fionn looks suddenly pale.

I'm there, 'Dude, are you okay?'

He goes, 'I'm just feeling a bit, I don't know, weak.'

He had, like, his fourth chemo session the other day and it's really kicking the shit out of him.

I'm there, 'Are you going to be alright?'

And he goes, 'I'm sure I'll be fine.'

We return to our seats. In the crowd I spot Fyodor. Next to him is the lovely Raisa – her face as hord to read as ever. It's actually the same with him. He's wearing this sort of, like, dead expression. It's impossible to tell whether he's unhappy with how Sergei is playing or whether he suspects me of riding his wife.

Some people would say it serves me right for riding his wife.

The match kicks off again and my prediction is proven right. Clongowes come at us in a big-time way, we're talking wave after wave of attack. We manage to hold them out for fifteen minutes, but they eventually get over in the corner after – get this – twenty-nine phases of play, then their kicker nails the conversion and it's suddenly a one-score game.

I'm telling the goys to keep their concentration. I'm going, 'Let's keep doing the basics right, goys! Let's keep doing the basics right!'

We manage to stop them scoring for the next twenty or so minutes, then we even manage to break out of our own half.

There's, like, five minutes left when Fionn grabs a tight hold of my wrist and goes, 'I think I'm going to faint.'

I'm there, 'What?' trying not to sound annoyed – but probably failing.

He goes, 'I just feel suddenly dizzy.'

I'm there, 'Could it not wait until the final whistle?'

He's like, 'Jesus, my vision has gone fuzzy.'

'Okay, you just faint away there. I'll get help when the final whistle goes.'

He looks at me – made-up word – but *incredulously*?

He goes, 'I can't believe you just –'

But he doesn't get to finish his sentence. He actually passes out. I catch him as he's falling forward. I look around me. No one else seems to have noticed, so – this is maybe going to sound bad – I sort of, like, prop him up in his seat again.

Yeah, no, it's all very *Weekend at Bernie's*.

I just presume he'll understand. Especially because we've only got, like, five minutes more to hold out.

The goys continue to put in the big tackles. Then Barry gets the ball and he storts running a diagonal line at the Clongowes defence. But then *the* most amazing thing happens. He suddenly throws the ball over his shoulder blindly to Sergei, who's running a diagonal line in the *opposite* direction?

The entire Clongowes defence is wrong-footed and Sergei runs, pretty much unopposed, to the line to score the try that puts us into the semi-finals of the Leinster Schools Senior Cup.

The final whistle blows and all hell breaks loose. I run onto the pitch and I'm throwing my orms around the players, going, 'We did it! We did it!'

Nailer is in tears. Barry has his hands joined in prayer and is mouthing something up at the sky. I think they're genuinely storting to believe now.

In all of the excitement, I end up totally forgetting about Fionn.

It's only when Ricey spots him over my shoulder and goes, 'Jesus, what's wrong with Fionn, like?' that I remember him passing out.

I look around. The dude is slumped back in his seat with his mouth open. I feel suddenly terrible.

'I, er, don't know,' I go. 'It looks like he might have fainted.'

Suddenly, everyone has forgotten about the result. All the goys are running towards him, going, 'Fionn? Fionn?' their voices full of concern.

I notice Nailer sort of, like, shaking him, then shouting, 'Can someone phone an ambulance, like?'

Christian calls to the door on Tuesday night. He says he heard about what happened.

I'm there, 'Apology accepted,' even though I don't one hundred per cent mean it. 'It's not your fault that your son made my son a cripple.'

'Your son isn't a cripple,' he tries to go. 'He has a broken leg. And anyway, I'm not talking about that. I'm talking about Fionn collapsing. Is he okay?'

I'm like, 'Yeah, no, he just fainted,' and I open the door to let him in. 'He hasn't been eating enough calories apparently. The doctor told him – get this – he needs to get off the vegan diet. A human body needs meat and it needs dairy. Which is something I've been saying for months.'

The door of the kitchen flies open and Leo comes running up the hallway, pushing Brian in his wheelchair, at high speed. Brian is shouting, 'Fock off, you focking Gogglebox fock!' and Leo is going, 'Focking wheelchair wanker!'

I'm like, 'Go easy, goys.'

Leo gives the chair a seriously hord push and then he lets go of it. Me and Christian end up having to jump out of the way as Brian flies past us, hits the back of the door and is deposited in a heap on the floor.

I'm like, 'Leo, pick your brother up and stop being a prick – you focking four-eyed freak of nature. Come on, let's go and see Fionn.'

He follows me up the stairs. We pass Honor's room and Sorcha calls me.

'Ross,' she goes, 'who was that at the door?'

Christian's there, 'It's me, Sorcha.'

She steps out onto the landing.

'Oh my God, Christian!' she goes – because she hasn't seen the dude since he broke up with Lauren downstairs in our hallway. 'How are you?'

I'm there, 'I've been telling him not to blame himself for what happened to Brian.'

He goes, 'I'm not blaming myself.'

'That's the spirit. It's not Ross Junior's fault that he comes from a broken home. If anything, it proves that he needs a strong male role model more than ever.'

Sorcha goes, 'Christian, I'm sorry about the way things ended between you and Lauren. It's like, Oh! My God!'

'It is,' he goes.

'I'm going to say to you the exact same thing that I said to Lauren, Christian. Remember to be kind to yourself.'

'Er, thanks.'

The dude decides to change the subject then. He goes, 'What have you got there, Sorcha?'

Yeah, no, she's holding a placord that says 'Learn to Change – Or Learn to Swim!'

She goes, 'It's for the Climate Justice Rally tomorrow. Honor, come and show Christian the sign *you* made.'

Honor steps out of her room, holding a placord that says 'No, I Won't Clean My Bedroom – I Have to Save the Planet!'

Christian's there, 'What's all this about?'

Sorcha's like, 'Honor's arranged a national school strike for tomorrow.'

'We're having a meeting in, like, College Green,' Honor goes, 'to demand action from grown-ups on climate change.'

Christian's there, 'Er, cool,' because he doesn't know what else to say.

And I'm like, 'Come on, Dude, let's go see Fionn.'

I knock on the door and Fionn – in a pissed-off voice – goes, 'What?' which I take as an invitation to come in.

I push open the door.

I'm there, 'Christian's here to see you, Dude.'

Fionn's lying on the bed with Hillary next to him and he's reading him a story.

Christian goes, 'Hey, you gave us all a fright, Fionn.'

I notice the steak sandwich that his old pair dropped off earlier is still lying untouched on his laptop bed tray. I pick it up and take three quick bites out of it. Through a mouthful of mashed-up meat, I go, 'Don't mention this to Sorcha or Honor.'

Yeah, no, we had crispy polenta balls for dinner.

Christian's there, 'What happened, Fionn? Ross said the doctor told you that you weren't eating enough calories.'

Fionn goes, 'Did Ross tell you what *he* did?'

Christian's like, 'Er, no.'

'I told him I was feeling faint and he asked me could it wait until the match was over.'

I'm there, 'I'm not sure if those were my exact words.'

'I told him my vision had gone fuzzy and he said, "You just faint away there. I'll get help when the final whistle goes." Then, when I actually *did* faint, he sat me up in my seat for the last five minutes.'

Christian goes, 'I can't believe you'd do something like that, Ross.'

'Dude, the match was still there to be lost,' I go, grabbing the toothpaste from Fionn's *en suite* bathroom. 'I didn't want the players to lose their focus. I'll tell you something, though, Christian – we wouldn't have beaten Clongowes without him. It was *his* big idea to move Sergei to the centre, where he did all the damage.'

I squirt some toothpaste into my mouth. Yeah, no, since she found out about me eating that sneaky burger, Sorcha has storted smelling my breath at pretty much hourly intervals. The girl has definite trust issues.

'Even when the match was over,' Fionn goes, despite the compliment I've just paid him, 'he didn't do anything to help. He ran on the pitch to celebrate.'

I'm there, 'I forgot – in all the excitement, that's understandable.'

'It's a good job the players noticed. Otherwise, I could be still sitting there, unconscious.'

'That's a ridiculous statement. I would have eventually remembered.'

'Still,' Christian goes, 'a semi-final against Mary's. That's something to look forward to, Fionn, isn't it?'

Fionn's like, 'Not for me, no.'

I'm there, 'I don't want to hear that kind of talk, Fionn. I need you beside me on the sideline. Conscious or not.'

But Fionn goes, 'Yeah? Well, I don't want to *be* your Assistant any more, Ross. As a matter of fact – yeah – I focking quit!'

Sorcha says that of all the things she hoped that she and Honor might hopefully one day bond over, she never in her wildest dreams imagined that it would be their shared concern for the future of the planet.

She's grinning like a giraffe who's just discovered he can lick his own hole. She links my orm.

'That's our daughter over there,' she says proudly.

The Climate Justice Rally has turned out to be a massive, massive success – certainly if the turnout is anything to go by. According to the lunchtime news, the Gords are putting the crowd at some-where between three and four thousand. Apparently, there isn't a school in the country open today.

You'd have to say fair focks to the girl.

I'm looking around at the crowd. It's nearly all kids and they're holding up signs and banners and placords that say 'Climate Justice is a Human Right!' and 'One Earth, One Chance!' and 'Be Port of the Solution, Not the Pollution!' and 'I Stand for What I Stand On!' and 'There is No Plan(et) B!'

I'm looking at Honor, standing in front of Trinity College gates in her yellow rain mac, and I'm – yeah, no – the proud dad. She's chat-ting to Sincerity Matthews and one or two other members of the Mount Anville Climate Justice Committee. She's obviously going to be speaking soon because I notice she's got the megaphone in her hand. Sorcha's very proud of the fact that it's the same megaphone she used to use to shout, 'Murderer! Murderer!' at rich old ladies popping into the furriers on South Anne Street back in the day.

My phone beeps. It's, like, a text from my old man. Loredana and Lidia I had their babies in the early hours of this morning – born six minutes aport. Two more girls. They're calling them Diana and Cassiopeia.

That's it, I think. That's the full set. And they're going to be gone very soon.

Roz Matthews – as in, Sincerity's old dear – tips over to us then. She goes, 'Hi, Ross! Hi, Sorcha! Look at our girls! Look what they've done!'

And Sorcha – who isn't keen on sharing the credit – bitch-smiles her and goes, 'Oh, yes, I see Sincerity over there! It's great that she came!'

I don't think Sorcha will ever get over me knocking the orse off Roz when we were on a break.

'Well, of course she came,' Roz goes, rising to the challenge. 'Just because she's not advertising her concern for the planet on the *Six One* news doesn't mean she cares any less than Honor.'

Whoa!

I'm there, 'You'd want to swing by Boots to get some aloe vera for that burn, Sorcha,' just trying to keep the conversation light, while at the same time not wanting to look like I'm coming down on any particular side.

Thankfully, Sister Consuelo shows up then and the two of them are suddenly on their best behaviour.

She goes, 'You must be so proud of your daughters!'

And Sorcha's like, 'We were just saying exactly that, Sister Consuelo! The megaphone that Honor's going to use to address the crowd is the same megaphone I used to use to try to educate people about the realities of the fur trade on Saturday mornings outside Sydney Vord!'

I remember her shouting, 'You've got blood on your hands!' at a woman who turned out to be my old dear. Then she tried to go, 'I obviously don't mean that literally, Fionnuala!'

Sister Consuelo goes, 'Look at all these young people! So full of hope and optimism and confidence that they can save the planet! And to think – it was girls from our own, dear Mount Anville who made it happen!'

Sorcha spots George Lee near the front of the crowd and she makes a complete show of herself trying to catch his attention. She's like, 'George! George! George!' until he eventually has no choice but to turn around.

He's like, 'Oh, hello! You're, em, Honor's mum!'

'That's right,' she goes. 'Senator – well, *outgoing* Senator – Lalor. I was the one who tried to introduce a bill to ban single-use coffee cups in both houses of the Oireachtas by the year 2056. I'm so glad you're here to see this moment!'

'Yeah, I'm trying to cover this *and* the farmers' protest.'

'Formers' protest?'

'Yeah, they're complaining about beef prices. There's about five hundred tractors blocking Kildare Street and every surrounding street as well.'

'Oh my God!'

'I'm actually surprised that the Gardaí let both of these protests go ahead on the same day. A lot of these farmers see environmentalists as their enemies.'

'Oh my God, is there any chance these formers might cause trouble?'

'No, the Guards have got Nassau Street totally blocked off. They won't get their tractors anywhere near College Green.'

'Thank God, George! Thank God!'

Honor steps forward then. It's time for her big speech. She holds the megaphone to her mouth and goes, 'Boys and girls, thank you all for coming today. It means – oh my God – *so* much to know that so many of you share our concerns about the climate emergency and the threat that is facing our planet.'

That gets a humungous cheer – *and* a round of applause.

'Our planet is dying,' she goes. 'And our civilization is, like, dying *with* it? The condition of the Earth is deteriorating so fast that I *actually* can't sleep at night worrying about the kind of world that my children and my children's children are going to be, like, *born* into? It's making me – oh my God – really anxious and depressed and I know a lot of you are anxious and depressed about it as well.'

'Oh my God,' Sorcha goes. '*Goosebumps!*'

Honor's like, 'That's why I want today to mork a new stort. We created climate change and global warming by our way of living. But we still have time to reverse it – provided we do the right things. And that means taking control away from the so-called grown-ups who caused the problem in the first place. It means taking the issue out of the hands of politicians with their focking empty words and promises. We need to understand that our lives are not in *their* hands. Our lives are in *our* hands. We can, like, *do* something about this. So let's focking do it!'

There's, like, roars from the crowd.

Sorcha goes, 'Oh my God, Ross, they love her!'

I'm there, 'Yeah, I just hope she stops effing and blinding so George Lee can use even five seconds of her on the news.'

'We have the power!' Honor goes. 'We have! The focking! Power! Let's show them that power today!'

Sorcha shouts, 'I'm so proud of you, Honor!' and she ends up getting shushed by a group of teenagers behind us, who go, 'Who asked you, Boomer?'

I slowly become aware of a – let's just say – change of atmos in the crowd.

Honor goes, 'Right now, a couple of hundred yords away from where we're all standing, there are focking formers in – literally? – tractors!'

All the kids stort booing. It's, like, South Dublin – represent!

Honor goes, 'They are trying to put pressure on the government to protect an industry – the animal exploitation industry – that is the greatest contributor to greenhouse gas emissions in the world today! What do we say to the formers?'

'Fock off, formers!' the crowd all shout as one.

'WHAT DO WE SAY TO THE FORMERS?'

Even Sorcha is like, 'FOCK OFF, FORMERS!'

Honor goes, 'WELL, COME ON, THEN – LET'S SAY IT TO THEIR FOCKING FACES!'

Sorcha's like, 'Oh my God, I don't think *that's* a good idea,' but there's fock-all she can do about it.

Honor, Sincerity and the rest of the Mount Anville Climate Justice Committee stort moving in the direction of Nassau Street, with the crowds following them.

Sorcha shouts, 'REMEMBER, HONOR, TO KEEP IT PEACE-FUL!' but suddenly we're being swept along in a river of young people, who are shouting, 'Fock the formers! Fock the formers! Fock the formers!' their anger growing with every step.

The Gorda cordon at the bottom of Nassau Street proves useless. They go through it like an ormy of ants on the morch.

We're running to keep up with Honor, who is using the mega-phone to point out all the ways in which intensive forming causes land degradation, biodiversity loss, acid rain, deforestation and coral reef degeneration. I mean, it's pretty interesting – if that's your bag – but it's only getting the crowd even *more* worked up?

We eventually arrive at the bottom of Kildare Street. We can see the tractors halfway up the street – like a tank division waiting to attack us. Honor hands the megaphone to a girl behind her – her job of riling up the crowd seemingly done.

Out of nowhere, Sincerity produces a tin of red paint. She pops the lid, then I watch her offer it to Honor and the other members of the Mount Anville Climate Justice Committee. They all dip their hands in it, up to their wrists.

'Oh my God,' Sorcha goes, 'it's a bloodied hand protest!'

Poor Roz is like, 'Sincerity Matthews! That paint was supposed to be for the vestibule!'

Suddenly, Honor shouts, 'Let's get them!' and the crowd chorges up the street.

You'd nearly feel sorry for the poor formers, sitting outside the Dáil in their tractors, when they see these thousands of schoolkids running towards them with red paint on their hands and murder on their faces.

I watch my daughter leave red handprints all over a brand new Massey Ferguson while two other girls climb up the ladder on the side to try to get at the former. The poor dude looks terrified and pulls the door shut. But they manage to get it open – shouting, 'Kill-er! Kill-er!' – and they drag him out of the cab and onto the road.

There are scenes like this happening up and down Kildare Street. I watch one former lying in the foetal position on the road while a gang of girls – no older than eight years old – whip him with his own flat cap. I spot another former, covered in red handprints, cowering in the doorway of Buswells, begging a group of children not to hurt him because he has four hundred acres of land and a thousand head of Hereford and Shorthorn cattle to think of – no idea, of course, that he's only making things worse for himself.

Sincerity discovers a formyord trailer that's got, like, fifty or sixty sheep crammed into the back of it, which the formers were apparently planning to release into the lobby of Leinster House.

She shouts, 'Forming is exploitation! Free the sheep! Free the sheep!'

Which is exactly what she then does. She slides the bolt at the back of the trailer and opens the door. The sheep spill out onto the road. Panicked by the mayhem going on around them, they stampede down Molesworth Street in the direction of the Royal Hibernian Way, with boys and girls chasing after them, shouting, 'Be free!' and 'Live your best lives!'

I watch a group of teenage boys stort rocking a massive John Deere with humungous wheels. You wouldn't believe their strength. They build up a bit of momentum and suddenly the thing is really moving from side to side. The former sitting at the wheel of the thing tries to stort it, then changes his mind and dives out – just as they manage to turn it over onto its side.

All over Kildare Street, the scene is being repeated. Formers are begging to be spared and tractors – actual tractors! – are being tipped over by essentially children.

It's not long before the formers – their faces smeared with red paint – decide to make a strategic retreat, abandoning their form machinery and seeking the sanctuary of Stephen's Green, where emergency aid workers are distributing vegetable soup and trauma blankets.

The final image I have of the day, which will be burned into my memory forever more, is my daughter, standing on an overturned tractor, red hands resting on her hips, watching this scene of terrible violence with a big, fock-you smile playing on her lips.

'Oh! My God!' Sorcha goes, watching this scene of absolute cornage unfold. 'Oh! My literally? God!'

And – hand on hort – I have to say that I agree with her.

'I'm not going to apologize for our daughter,' Sorcha goes, when she's had a night to sleep on it. 'There's nothing to even apologize *for*.'

I'm like, 'Er, she caused a *riot*?'

'It was hordly a riot, Ross. Yes, some tractors were overturned, but it's like Honor said, the time for making speeches is over. If formers keep going the way they're going – exploiting the Earth's precious resources, including animals, for short-term profitability – the damage to the planet will be irreversible. It's time for action – and, yes, that includes *drastic* action?'

She's changed her tune, by the way. Her first response to what happened was one of shame and embarrassment. The Irish Formers' Association demanded to know why the children involved weren't in school and one of the Healy-Raes said he hoped the parents of the ringleaders would face the wrath of the Tuatha Dé Danann in the Otherworld.

But the tide of public opinion turned within hours. On social media, the general view was fair focks to young people for actually doing something about the climate crisis instead of just talking, and that formers are a pack of whinging, tax-avoiding bastards who got what was coming to them anyway.

Sorcha goes, 'There was an Op Ed in this morning's *Irish Times* that said Mount Anville girls have a reputation for being spoiled princesses who care only about their hair and their make-up and what cor their daddies are buying them for their Sweet Sixteenth – but now there's a new, selfless generation, whose activism has turned the spotlight on adults, including formers, who have failed in their duty of care to the planet.'

'Talking about me again?' Honor goes.

Jesus, I didn't even hear her come in from school.

Sorcha goes, 'We were only saying good things about you,' because, after what she witnessed yesterday, Sorcha is as terrified of her as anyone. 'How was school? Sister Consuelo wasn't angry with you, was she?'

'She was,' Honor goes, laughing. 'She was – oh my God – *so* pissed off!'

Sorcha's there, 'Do you know did she read the Op Ed piece in the *Irish Times*?'

'But she calmed down in the afternoon,' Honor goes, 'after Mary Robinson rang.' She throws it out there as casually as that, then she goes over to say hello to Brian in his little focking wheelchair. She's like, 'How's my brave little man doing today?'

Sorcha is just staring at me with her mouth unhinged.

'Mary Robinson?' she eventually goes. 'Are you talking about *the* Mary Robinson?'

Honor goes, 'Yes, I'm talking about *the* Mary Robinson.'

'Why did she ring the school, Honor?'

'She wanted to know if I'd be interested in going to New York to address the United Nations General Assembly on the issue of climate change.'

Talk about a conversation stopper. It's a good, like, thirty seconds before Sorcha can get her shit together to say anything. And even then, all she can manage is, 'Mary Robinson? Wants you to address the United Nations?'

'I told her to shove it up her orse,' Honor goes.

Sorcha's like, 'Excuse me?'

'Well, I think Sister Consuelo reworded what I said – she told her I wasn't interested.'

'Not interested? How could you not be interested in addressing the United Nations on an issue that we're both, like, passionate about?'

'Er, because it's in New York,' she goes.

I'm like, 'The City of Love!'

Sorcha's there, 'Shut the fock up, Ross! So what if it's in New York, Honor?'

'Er, it would mean having to *fly* there,' Honor goes. 'What about my corbon footprint?'

'But think of the greater good you could do, Honor. You could end up sporking a global youth movement for action on climate change.'

'I can't fly to New York – not after getting the skiing trip to Pinzolo cancelled. Er, *hypocrite* much?'

Sorcha looks at me then. She goes, 'Ross, will you please talk to your daughter?'

But I'm there, 'I have to go out, Sorcha.'

Yeah, no, I'm supposed to be going to Bray this afternoon. Barry has called – yeah, no – a team meeting after school in Molloys Coffee Shop on the Quinsborough Road.

What the fock it's about, I have absolutely no idea.

I tip upstairs and I walk into Fionn's room without even bothering to knock. He's having a – believe it or not – nap. I tear open the curtains, then I stort focking his clothes across the room at him. I'm there, 'Come on, get up!'

He's like, 'What are you doing?'

'Barry's called a team meeting. He wouldn't say what it was about on the phone.'

'Ross, I told you, I don't want to *be* your Assistant Coach any more.'

'Well, you're going to have to tell *them* that.'

'Who?'

'Dude, I'm not doing your dirty work for you. You can tell the players to their faces that you're quitting, okay?'

'Fine,' he goes, throwing back the covers. 'I will.'

Twenty minutes later, we're in the Mitsubishi i-MiEV heading for Bray. Fionn doesn't say shit during the journey. I try to talk to him once or twice, but he's obviously still pissed off with me. And then, just as we're taking the turn for Bray, I end up getting a text message from Szidonia to tell me that Saturday is going to be the day, obviously meaning the day I help her kidnap and then traffic my brother and five sisters to, whatever it's called, Munrania. She tells me to be at the old dear's gaff at midday. Which means that I have exactly forty-eight hours to come up with a plan or I'll never see my brother and sisters again.

I throw the cor in the cor pork behind the church, then we head for – yeah, no – Molloys.

'I know what you're thinking,' Fionn goes as we walk along.

He doesn't, though. He couldn't.

I'm there, 'What am I thinking?'

'You're thinking I'm going to change my mind,' he goes. 'You're thinking that when I see the goys, I won't be able to go through with it. But I'm not going to change my mind, Ross. I can't believe you left me sitting there, unconscious, for a full five minutes.'

'Dude, we still had a match to win. I thought you of all people would understand that. I saw you play an entire second half once when you were unconscious.'

'I was concussed.'

'Same deal. Seriously, you can't quit now. We're a double act, Dude. The goys think the focking world of you.'

'What happened has made me realize something.'

'As in?'

'Ross, if the chemo doesn't work –'

'Don't say that.'

'If the chemo doesn't work, I don't want to look back and realize I wasted whatever time I had left doing something meaningless, like helping to coach a rugby team.'

Of course, neither of us has any idea yet why we're even in Bray this afternoon. But we're about to find out. I push open the door and I walk into the coffee shop.

'What the fock?' I hear a voice go.

It turns out that it's my voice.

I'm like, 'What the actual fock?'

All of the goys are sitting around. We're talking Barry, Lenny, Dougie, Ricey, Sergei, Nailer – the entire team. And, looking at them, one thing is immediately obvious.

They're all bald.

Now it's, like, *Fionn's* turn to say it?

He's like, 'What the fock?'

'They've all had their heads shaved,' I go. 'Blade zero, by the looks of things.'

When they see us standing there, they all stand up as a team and they stort clapping.

I just burst into tears. So does Fionn.

Jesus, I've said some shit about Bray in my time, but in that moment I want to take every focking word of it back. Because Brother Ciaran was right. These are the greatest people in the world – and anyone who makes the mistake of slagging Bray off again within earshot of me will be the subject of a decking. An instant one.

'I can't believe this,' Fionn goes, suddenly sobbing his hort out and wiping away tears with his hand. 'I can't focking believe it.'

I walk over to the goys and I stand with them. I'm looking at Fionn across the floor of the coffee shop, tears fogging up his ridiculous glasses, and – yeah, no – I join in the applause.

And I know from just looking at him that he's not going anywhere.

Szidonia opens the door with a scowl on her face.

She goes, 'You are late.'

I'm there, 'Three hours is plenty of time to make it to Rosslare.'

'You should hope so,' she goes, 'for your sake.'

I notice the old dear passed out on the hallway floor behind her. Memories of Confirmation day come flooding back.

I step past Szidonia into the gaff. I pick the old dear up. It's like lifting a sack of bowling balls.

'Jesus Christ,' I go, 'how much did you give her?'

She's like, 'Enough to sleep for perhaps twelve hours.'

I carry her upstairs to her bedroom and I lie slash drop her down onto the bed. I take off her slippers and I roll her onto her side so that she doesn't choke on her own vomit. Yes, I've done this before. Then I pull the duvet over her.

I'm just glad that she's out of the game. Because it would kill her if she knew what I was doing right now.

I pull the curtains closed, then I tip back downstairs again.

They're all waiting in the hallway. We're talking Loredana. We're talking Brigitta. We're talking Roxana. We're talking Szidonia. We're talking Lidias I and II. They're all holding their babies – well, not *their* babies – but my old pair's babies. Some of them I haven't even laid eyes on yet. The way things look, I possibly never will.

'You have car?' it's Brigitta who goes.

Yes, I have cor. That bit was easy. The old man and Hennessy were playing golf in Elm Pork this morning. Kennet was caddying for them. Hennessy left his locker open with Kennet's uniform hanging up inside and the keys to the limo in his trouser pocket.

'I have passports,' Szidonia goes. 'We go.'

So we all pile into the limo. There are no, like, child seats in the cor. But then they're basically stealing six babies. It's not the biggest law that's being broken today.

We're passing by Loughlinstown Hospital when little Hugo suddenly storts crying. This is going to sound random, but it's like he *knows* that we're heading for a foreign land – and, for once, I'm not talking about Wicklow.

That storts – I'm trying to remember who's who – but I'm pretty sure it's Cassiopeia bawling as well. Szidonia and Roxana are trying to comfort them. But suddenly I feel *myself* filling up?

'Why are you cry?' Szidonia goes, actually angry with me.

I'm there, 'It kills me that I'm not going to see them grow up.'

'I cannot talk to you about this again! Drive!'

At least Brigitta speaks softly to me. She goes, 'You make right decision, Ross. You save marriage and you give babies better life.'

'But they're my brother and sisters.'

'Your parents are crazy, but also they are very old. Perhaps they not live long. Who will look after children if Charles and Fionnuala die?'

'Me.'

Szidonia ends up losing it with me. She goes, 'You fuck your mother's friends and this is what happen. Is tough shit for you. Drive faster. You are trying to miss boat.'

'I'm not trying to miss the boat. The speed limit is, like, sixty when you hit Kilmacanogue.'

'I not give shit about speed limit. I see number drop below one hundred kilometres, I send video to your wife. Now stop talking.'

She turns around to the others and says something in, I don't know, but not English, which I take to be her telling them to basically stop engaging with me. Which is exactly what ends up happening. I drive on in silence, heading south on the N11, passing the turn-off for Brittas Bay, then Orklow, then Inch, then Clonattin, then Gorey, then Camolin, then Ferns. The only sound in the cor is the sound of babies bawling and Szidonia and the others saying occasional things to each other in hushed, tense voices in a language that – like Gaelic – is a total focking mystery to me.

Jesus Christ, there's some whiff in the cor all of a sudden. I'm wondering is it me or is it – where even *are* we? – Ballycarrigeen?

'Novac needs nappy changed,' Szidonia goes.

Okay, that would explain it.

'Also,' Brigitta goes, 'Valeria needs change.'

Valeria. That's obviously what she's calling Mellicent.

I'm there, 'We're just coming up to Enniscorthy. They're bound to have a petrol station with toilets.'

So I take the turn for Enniscorthy and we find a humungous Apple Green. Szidonia takes the cor keys from me, then she and Brigitta go inside to change Hugo and Mellicent.

I'm there, 'There's actually a Burger King in there. Would anyone object if I grabbed myself a Whopper?'

'Stay!' Lidia II roars at me, like I'm a focking King Chorles Cavalier. 'Szidonia says you do not leave car!'

Five minutes later, the two girls are back and we're suddenly back on the road, again watching the names of towns go by. We're talking Oilgate. We're talking Wexford. We're talking Rathaspeck. We're talking Tagoat. We're talking Kilrane.

I'm a long, long way from home.

I see the sign for Rosslare Europort. The women are suddenly chattering in excited voices.

I'm there, 'Szidonia, will you make me a promise?'

She goes, 'What promise?'

'Will you make sure that Novac plays rugby?'

'No, I will not. Is shit game. And also I will not tell him about idiot brother he has in Ireland.'

Then she says something to the others and Loredana and Lidia II stort doing this, like, heavy breathing thing, which I know is an impression of me riding Delma.

'Mommy! Mommy!' Szidonia goes, then they all laugh their heads off. We're, like, minutes away from boarding the ferry and they're getting giddy with excitement.

And that's when I suddenly hear the sound of a siren.

I look in the rear-view mirror. There's, like, a Gorda cor behind us with its roof light flashing.

The laughter in the cor suddenly stops.

'What is this?' Szidonia goes.

I'm there, 'It's the Feds.'

'What do they want?'

'It's, er, kind of hord to tell at this stage. But I'm guessing it has something to do with the fact that I'm doing a hundred-and-fifty Ks per hour.'

I indicate to pull in to the hord shoulder.

Szidonia goes, 'What are you doing?'

I'm there, 'We're being pulled over, Szidonia.'

'Do not stop!'

'I have to stop. It's the Feds.'

'Put foot down.'

'I'm hordly going to outrun them. I'm in a focking limo.'

'If you stop, I will send video to your wife.'

She whips out her phone. I know she'd do it, so I slam my foot on the accelerator. Everyone is suddenly bouncing around in the back of the cor and the Feds are quickly disappearing in my rear-view mirror.

'Faster!' Szidonia goes. 'Faster! Faster! Faster!'

I shout over my shoulder. I'm like, 'Just please hold on tight to my brother and sisters, will you?'

But she just goes, 'Never mind babies! Drive! Drive! Drive!'

Suddenly, I can see the ferry terminal in the distance.

Roxana goes, 'We are here!' and I can hear the excitement in her voice.

I'm thinking it's weird that the Gorda didn't respond when I put my foot down. And, as we round a bend in the road, I discover why. Up ahead, there's a Gorda checkpoint.

'Drive through!' Szidonia shouts.

I'm there, 'You want me to crash through a Gorda cordon?'

'Yes! Fucking drive!'

Lidia I goes, 'No! You will hurt babies!'

Szidonia screams something at her in Foreign and Lidia I screams something back. I press down hord on the accelerator again, getting ready to drive straight through the checkpoint. But at the very last second, Szidonia goes, 'No, don't do! Don't do!'

So I lean on the brake and I swing the limo into the shoulder. It comes to a halt with the screech of rubber. A few seconds later, the Gorda cor that *was* chasing us pulls in behind us. In the rear-view mirror, I watch the doors open and two Gords get out.

Then, suddenly, there's a figure standing in front of the cor. He's wearing a humungous grin on his face.

It's Hennessy.

Brigitta also sees him because she goes, 'Shit! Is crooked lawyer of Charles! Drive! Drive!'

Szidonia's like, 'You hear her! Drive! Drive!'

But it's too late.

Hennessy walks around to my window and I open it. He's there, 'Going on a little holiday, are we?'

Suddenly, the back doors of the cor are opened. I look over both shoulders. We're, like, surrounded by Gords. They order the women out. And they do as they're told, clutching the babies tightly to their chests, there in the hord shoulder.

I get out as well.

Hennessy goes, 'It's rare I get the opportunity to say this to you, Ross – but you did good.'

Szidonia looks at me and the penny suddenly drops.

She goes, 'You tell him?'

'Yes,' Hennessy goes, 'he tell me. He rang me last night and laid out the whole sordid story. A rare instance of him using the brains that God gave him.'

I just smile. I'm a sucker for a compliment.

Szidonia whips out her phone. She goes, 'I send video to your wife.'

'Szidonia,' Hennessy goes, 'I would suggest that you think very carefully about your next move – and that goes for all of you.'

'You are asshole.'

'I've heard it said. But you are a child abductor – all of you are. You've been caught in the act of attempting to traffic six tiny babies outside the country. And not just any tiny babies. The children of the man who might one day soon be the leader of this country. What do you think they're looking at, chaps – five years in prison?'

'Ten years each,' one of the Gordaí goes. 'Maybe even more.'

The women all look at each other. I'd nearly feel sorry for them if Szidonia hadn't said what she'd said about rugby.

Brigitta and Lidia II stort crying. Oh, they're suddenly not mocking me about my sex noises any more.

'But,' Hennessy goes, lighting a cigor long enough to inseminate an elephant, 'I can offer you a way out of this.'

'Way out?' Lidia II goes. 'What is way out?'

'The ferry leaves in fifteen minutes. I've got six tickets in my pocket – all in your names. You get on the boat and you never come back to Ireland again.'

'You are saying we leave without babies?' it's Szidonia who goes.

Hennessy just laughs. He's there, 'Do you really need me to answer that question?'

There's, like, two Gorda cors porked up ahead at the checkpoint. I notice two lady Gords taking child seats out of the boots of the two cors – six in all.

The women stort orguing among themselves in – again – whatever language it happens to be. Then, slowly, one by one, they stort handing the babies over to the Gords.

Hennessy helps me put the child seats into the back of the limo, then we put my brother and sisters – we're talking Hugo, we're talking Cassiopeia, we're talking Diana, we're talking Mellicent, we're talking Emily, we're talking Louisa May – into the seats.

Hennessy clicks his fingers at Szidonia.

'Phone,' he goes.

She looks at me, then back at Hennessy, then she hands it over.

'And just in case you made a copy of this,' Hennessy goes, 'you can see that I have friends in very high places. You ever take a notion and decide to send this to Ross's lovely wife and you will be extradited back here to face trial. Do you understand?'

Szidonia doesn't answer him.

He goes, 'Now, these members of our wonderful police force are going to give you a lift to the boat.'

The women are shown into the back of the two Gorda cors. Szidonia stares at me, then she spits in my face. Hennessy hands one of the Gords the tickets. Szidonia gets into one of the cors. Then, ten seconds later, she and the others are gone from my life forever.

'I take it they weren't real Gords?' I go.

He's there, 'The less you know, the better.'

'More of Fyodor's people, I'm presuming?'

'Let's get the fuck out of here. God, I hate Wexford.'

A short time later, we're back on the road, except heading north this time, my brother and five sisters sleeping soundly in their child seats and Hennessy watching the video of me riding Delma up against the gable wall of my old dear's house.

'You are one sick fuck,' he goes.

I'm like, 'Yeah, how many times are you planning to watch it? I mean, that must be, like, your fifteenth time.'

'I mean, Delma! Jesus Christ! Hey, is that how the rainwater butt got broken?'

'Yes, it's how the rainwater butt got broken. Can you maybe stop watching it for a second?'

'I'll try. I mean, it's painful to watch – you calling for your mother – but it's strangely addictive.'

'What's going to happen now?'

'Nothing. I told Charlie I had to cry off after two holes and I needed to borrow the limo. He knows not to ask. Your mother will wake up in a few hours and think she just overdid it with the bellinis at breakfast. Then she'll find the house empty. Maybe she'll spend the rest of her days trying to figure out why they all just fucked off. Maybe she'll hire a new bunch of nannies and never think about it again. But at least her six little kiddies will be sleeping soundly in their rooms.'

We drive on in silence. He watches the video again.

'So is that it?' he goes. 'You haven't fucked anyone else I should know about, have you?'

I consider telling him about Fyodor's wife. But in the end, I decide not to bother.

I'm there, 'Er, no.'

He goes, 'Like, for instance, Fyodor's wife. The lovely Raisa.'

'Did anyone say I was with her? Is someone claiming that something happened?'

'Jesus, calm down, will you? You're just her type, from what Fyodor says. And you can't keep it in your fucking trousers.'

'True.'

'I'm just saying, make sure nothing does happen. Because that is one mess I will *not* be able to extricate you from. Now, I'm going to try and get some shut-eye.'

He reclines his seat a bit and puts his hat over his face like a cowboy. A few seconds after that, I hear him snoring softly.

I drive on in silence. From time to time, one of my – yeah, no – siblings, either Hugo or Cassiopeia or Diana or Mellicent or Emily or Louisa May, storts crying, but I leave them to self-soothe and it soon stops.

We're passing the turn-off for Redcross when my phone suddenly rings. I check the screen and it ends up being – randomly – Claire.

I'm like, 'Claire? What's the Jack?'

She goes, 'You and your big focking mouth. Garret wants a divorce.'

I'm there, 'I don't know what you want me to say, Claire. I've always said you were too good for him – and I've never thought you were great in terms of looks.'

'He's divorcing me on the grounds of my adultery with you. Do you know what that means, Ross?'

'Er – *explain* it to me?'

'It means it's all going to come out – what happened between us.'

'Can you not just keep on denying that we ever had sex?'

'In a sworn legal testimony, Ross? No, I focking can't keep denying that we had sex.'

'I don't want Sorcha finding out, Claire.'

'She's *going* to find out. Because of you, we have no focking choice.'

She hangs up on me. I drive on for a good sixty seconds, wondering what fresh hell is this I'm facing into and how the fock I'm going to get out of it.

From under his hat, I hear Hennessy go, 'You stupid, stupid fuck.'

9.

Je ne Greta Rien

'Gone?' Sorcha goes.

And the old man's like, 'Gone! Like a thief in the night! Or rather six of them! In the daytime!'

Sorcha won't let it go. 'And there was, like, no indication that they were even unhappy?' she goes.

The old dear's like, 'None whatsoever. I went upstairs for my afternoon nap –'

I make sure to laugh at that one. 'Yeah,' I go, 'afternoon nap, my sweaty hole.'

'And when I woke up,' she goes, 'they'd disappeared! Bags packed and gone!'

The old man's there, 'I must have left the bloody well safe open because they took their passports with them! I still don't understand it! They weren't prisoners here! If they didn't want to nanny the children, they just had to tell us and we'd have let them go with our thanks and a very generous severance package! But to just walk out like that while Fionnuala was having one of her famous naps . . .'

'But the babies were all still here?' Sorcha goes.

'Sleeping soundly, Sorcha! Sleeping soundly!'

'That's, like, Oh! My God!'

'You said it! It's a mystery on a par with that of the *Marie Celeste*!'

The old pair have thrown a big porty – fully catered – to celebrate the arrival of my brother and sisters. The gaff is full of their friends, who are all standing around, knocking back the free Veuve and the pink negronis, also known as Foxrock Facelifts, by the way, on account of the way they suck your lips back over your teeth. They're all talking about this wonderful thing – 'a miracle, even' – that has happened to Chorles and Fionnuala.

309

I'm holding little Hugo, Sorcha has Cassiopeia, the old man has Diana, the old dear has got Mellicent and Emily, while Honor is holding Louisa May.

Sorcha goes, 'So, like, what are you going do, Fionnuala? Are you going to advertise for new nannies?'

'Actually, no,' the old dear goes. 'I've decided that I don't need any help. I'm going to do it myself.'

I'm like, 'Yourself?' and she can obviously hear from my voice that I'm Scooby Dubious.

'Ross, if I can successfully combine my roles as an international best-selling author, as well as a patron for – at the last count – twenty-seven different charities, then I'm sure I can take on the challenge of bringing up five babies.'

'Six,' the old man reminds her.

'Six babies,' she goes.

Sorcha suddenly spots – oh, shit! – Delma across the room. She storts going, 'Delma!' at the same time waving at the woman. 'Delma! Oh my God, hi!'

And poor Delma, who's definitely aged in the past few weeks, has no choice but to tip over to us, going, 'Hi, Sorcha. It's, em, lovely to see you.'

I rang Delma a week ago to tell her that Szidonia was gone and our secret was safe forever. But her nerves are still all over the shop. And Sorcha isn't making matters any easier by complimenting her on her figure and then inviting me to do the same.

'Oh my God, you look fabulous,' she goes, 'doesn't she, Ross? Are you still playing veterans tennis?'

Delma's like, 'I'm, em, hoping to go back to it when the weather gets better, Sorcha.'

'Oh my God, look at your legs in that dress! Ross, look at Delma's legs!'

I'm there, 'Yeah, I'm looking at her legs, Sorcha! I've had a *good* look?'

'Are you still doing reformer Pilates?' Sorcha goes.

Delma's like, 'Er, yes, three days a week.'

The old dear decides to stick her ample hooter in then. She goes,

'You're like a stranger today, Delma? I've seen virtually nothing of you since you arrived.'

'I was, em, mingling,' the woman tries to go, her face all flushed with embarrassment. 'It's, em, lovely to see how happy everyone is for you – for both of you.'

Sorcha goes, 'Oh my God, your hips! You have a figure to die for! Doesn't she have a figure to die for, Ross?'

I'm thinking, shut the fock up, Sorcha, will you?

'Well,' the old dear goes, 'you're here now. Hold one of these, will you? Which ones have I got here, Chorles?'

I'm the one who ends up answering. I'm there, 'That one's Mellicent and that one's Emily.'

The old dear hands Mellicent to her.

'Here,' she goes, 'hold this one for me. I have something I want to ask you and Ross. It's something I've been building up to for a long time.'

Delma immediately tenses up. I can hear the woman suddenly creaking like a rusty hinge in a high wind.

I'm like, 'What do you want to ask us, you stupid focking, I don't know?'

I have to admit, I'm pretty nervous myself.

The old dear smiles – a horrible sight at the best of times. She goes, 'I wondered if you and Delma would be interested in being godparents?'

'Godparents?' Delma goes.

I'm like, 'To which one?'

The old dear's there, 'To *all* of them, Ross.'

'Oh! My God!' Sorcha goes.

I'm like, 'Er, yeah, whatever,' even though I'm secretly delighted. I'm more than delighted. My stomach does an actual somersault.

'I know you two have always been close,' she goes. 'When Ross was younger, Sorcha, he actually had a bit of a crush on Delma! He used to ask her to marry him! Do you remember that, Delma?'

I pretend to laugh along. Jesus focking Christ.

'Oh my God,' Sorcha goes. 'That's so cute!'

Delma's there, 'I'd be, em, delighted, Fionnuala. Thank you. I, em, have to go.'

'Go?' the old man goes. 'The porty is only getting storted, Delma!'

'I've just remembered I had a call from Phonewatch to say the house alorm was going off. It might be just the cat, but I should check it.'

Like I said, she's all over the focking place.

The old dear goes, 'Er, can I have my baby back, please?'

And Delma, who's forgotten she's even holding the thing, goes, 'I'm so sorry,' and hands it over. Then off she focks with one final compliment from Sorcha ringing in her ears.

She goes, 'She'd actually pass for fifty – wouldn't she, Ross?'

I decide to change the subject. I'm there, 'Did you hear we're playing Mary's in the semi-final?'

The old man goes, 'Oh, you'll relish beating *them*, eh, Kicker? I know you're no fan of the place, notwithstanding your friendships with Messrs Jennings, Hickie and Sexton!'

'Yeah, no, they've apparently got a good team this year. They beat Gonzaga in the last round.'

'Oh, I'm sure you've got a plan cooked up for them, Kicker! And with young Sergei in the team, I don't think there's anyone you should fear! He reminds me – if I may make so bold – of a certain Ross O'Carroll-Kelly in his prime!'

Suddenly, behind me, there's a loud crash. Leo has pushed Brian in his wheelchair straight at Johnny, who just manages to jump out of the way in time. Brian ends up crashing into a table full of drinks. I'm like, 'Fock's sake, Leo, mind Brian's leg, will you? And Johnny's grommets?'

But Johnny doesn't need me to fight his battles for him. He morches straight up to Leo and punches him full in the face. It looks like Specsavers are going to be seeing quite a bit of us over the next few years.

Sorcha goes, 'Chorles, did you hear that Honor has a fan in a certain Mary Robinson?'

'Mary Robinson?' the old man goes. 'Is this true, Honor?'

Honor just shrugs modestly. She didn't get that from me.

Sorcha's there, 'She rang the school – as a former past pupil of Mount Anville – and asked if Honor would be interested in going to New York to address the General Assembly of the United Nations.'

'Good Lord!' the old man goes. 'That's wonderful!'

'Yes, she and The Elders are doing a forty-eight-hour workshop on what world leaders need to do to reverse climate change. She wanted Honor to discuss her generation's concern for the future of the planet. Unfortunately, though, she's decided to turn down the offer.'

Honor's like, 'Mom, don't stort this again.'

'I'm not going to try to change your mind, Honor. I totally respect your reasons for not wishing to go, even though I think you're giving up a once-in-a-lifetime opportunity that I would have – oh my God – killed for when *I* was your age?'

The old man's there, 'Why would you turn down a trip to New York, Honor?'

'Er, because it would mean *flying* there?' Honor goes. 'And I happen to *care* about the fact that sea levels are rising?'

Sorcha's like, 'We looked at the possibility of maybe crossing the Atlantic by boat, but Honor would have ended up missing too much school.'

'Er, there was also the fact that cruise ships emit three times more corbon emissions than aircraft,' Honor goes.

The old man's there, 'Here's what I fail to understand, Honor! What the hell has getting on a bloody well airplane got to do with the sea – allegedly – rising?'

Honor's like, 'Allegedly? There's nothing *alleged* about it, Granddad – it's actually *happening*?'

'And yet nobody can explain how or why!'

'Er, yes, they focking can. Airplanes emit corbon dioxide, water vapour, hydrocorbons, corbon monoxide, nitrogen oxide, sulphur oxide, lead and black corbon, all of which contribute to the warming of the Earth, which causes the polar ice cap to melt, which causes sea levels to rise.'

'Allegedly!'

'Will you please stop saying allegedly? Oh my God, you've just

313

brought six children into the focking world! Do you not care about the planet you're going to leave for them?'

Sorcha goes, 'Honor, remember to keep your cool.'

I feel like nearly saying, You used to be hilarious, Honor. Now you're zero focking craic.

The old dear decides to throw her drunken thoughts into the mix then. She goes, 'But these rising seas aren't going to be an issue for People Like Us, are they, Honor?'

Honor's there, 'Er, Antortica and Greenland hold enough frozen water to raise global sea levels by sixty-five metres if they melted.'

'I'm sorry,' the old dear goes, 'I still can't see it affecting places like Dalkey and Monkstown?'

'They're right on the coast – of course it's going to affect them! They'll be *under* the focking sea!'

'I really don't think so, Honor.'

I can see that Honor is on the point of actually *losing* it? She turns around to Sorcha and she goes, 'Okay, that's it, I'm going.'

Sorcha's like, 'Excuse me?'

'I'm going to New York,' Honor goes. 'Book the focking flights. Someone has to wake the adult world up to what's happening before it's too late.'

Claire has a face on her. And here I am only trying to help.

'I got a letter from his solicitor,' she goes, 'saying he wants to make the separation formal. I'm going to have to tell her the truth.'

I'm like, 'No, you're not. Because you're not getting separated.'

'Excuse me?'

'You and Garret are going to get back together.'

'*That's* your plan?'

'Think about it, Claire. You two are made for each other.'

'Er, you always say he's a pretentious wanker with a face that's just crying out to be slapped.'

'Exactly. You never should have broken up.'

It's, like, half five in the evening and Wheat Bray Love has emptied out. She turns the sign on the door to Closed.

She's there, 'And how am I supposed to get him back?'

'Jesus,' I go, 'you must have one or two shots left in your locker.'

'Shots in my locker?'

'Seduce him, Claire. Call out to his gaff in focking – whatever – Greystones. Pretend you're returning, I don't know, a CD or a baseball cap. Wear a perfume that you know he likes. Or a top that shows off your beep-a-gunk-a-choochas.'

'Ross, you're forgetting something. He hates my guts.'

'Claire, love and hate are just two sides of the same menu.'

Speaking of which, I check the board. The special today is shredded native ostrich with a grapefruit rub, beer-braised parsnips, subjugated hazelnuts and late-summer fennel. Jesus Christ.

'Garret made it quite clear,' she goes, 'that there's no way back for us. And that's all because of you and your big focking mouth.'

I suddenly have an idea.

I'm like, 'Claire, give me your phone.'

She goes, 'My phone? Why?'

'Because I'm going to text him, pretending to be you.'

'Er, no, you're not.'

'Claire, this is, like, my speciality. How many times have I sweet-talked Sorcha into taking *me* back?'

'This is different. You have no idea how much he *actually* despises me right now.'

'So what have you got to lose? Seriously, Claire, give me your phone. Maybe fix me up a plate of today's special – which sounds focking revolting, by the way – and leave the rest to me.'

She just shakes her head. She goes, 'I can't believe I'm agreeing to this,' and she puts her phone in my hand. 'Although I know you're a vegan now, so you'll have to have it without the shredded native ostrich.'

I sit there for a good five minutes trying to come up with an opening line. That's the tactician in me – always agonizing over the best point of attack.

In the end, I write, 'Hey, I was just listening to the radio and "Weather With You" by *Crowded House* came on. It brought back memories of you and your focking guitar –'

Then I realize that – yeah, no – that's too *me*? I'm supposed to be playing a port here. So I delete the bit about the guitor and just leave it at 'memories'.

I hit Send.

A minute or two later, Claire's phone beeps. It's him. He's like, 'That's a weird text to send me considering our last conversation.'

What a focking orsehole.

I let it go. I'm just there, 'Garret, we can get separated WITH-OUT ending up hating each other?'

He's like, 'We can't be friends, Claire.'

And I'm there, 'But we're allowed to keep our happy memories, aren't we?'

He goes, 'You can do whatever you want.'

Claire arrives over and puts a plate of food in front of me. It looks like the kind of thing you'd scrape into the compost bin.

She's there, 'How's it going?'

I'm like, 'Yeah, no, he's being a bit of a dick. The next time I see him, I'm just going to walk up to him and punch him in the face. He won't even know why.'

She's there, 'Ross, this is a bad idea. Give me back my phone.'

'Claire, trust me,' I go. 'Is there, like, a pet name he has for you?'

'He used to call me his cuddly wombat?'

'Jesus focking Christ.'

'We met when we were both doing the whole Australia thing, remember?'

'You two focking deserve each other. Okay, give me some space here, will you?'

She focks off back behind the counter again and I text the dude straight back. I'm there, 'Am I still your cuddly wombat?'

That obviously touches a nerve with him because he spends a good five minutes composing his next text, presumably writing and deleting numerous drafts. Then he goes, 'I can't forgive you, Claire. Not after you were with that asshole.'

I'm there, 'I wasn't with him, Garret. He wouldn't touch some-one like me with a focking pole vault.'

Then I think better of the pole vault line and I delete it before sending it.

He goes, 'Why would he say that he had sex with you in your mum's house, then?'

I'm there, 'Because he's jealous of what we had – of what we could STILL have.'

There's, like, no activity on his side for a good five minutes. He's obviously thinking. So I try to help the conversation along by going, 'What are you wearing?'

For about sixty seconds, I think I might have gone too early and frightened him off, but the slow-on-the-uptake focker comes back with, 'Black skinny jeans, my black Chucks, my Marley Beach Organic Food Market t-shirt and my houndstooth waistcoat.'

Seriously, he's getting punched in the face.

I'm there, 'Do you want to know what I'M wearing?'

He's like, 'What?'

'Just a bra and panties.'

'Are you not in work?'

'I don't mean literally, Garret. I'm just trying to have some fun here. As in, like, fantasy shit.'

A good five minutes passes. I think I've maybe blown it, but suddenly he comes back with, 'What colour are they?'

I'm like, 'Black.'

He goes, 'Do you remember I wore your black lace thong under my jeans the first time we ever had dinner with your parents? That was hot.'

I laugh.

Claire shouts over to me. She's like, 'How's it going, Ross?'

'Yeah, no,' I go, 'I think we've definitely turned a corner here, Claire.'

I text back. I'm like, 'That WAS hot!'

He goes, 'We were in the Hungry Monk.'

I'm there, 'I'd love to see you in my thong right now.'

And he's like, 'Are we really going to do this?'

I'm thinking exactly the same thing. I've never actually sexted a man before.

I'm there, 'Are you touching yourself?'

He goes, 'Yes.'

'So am I.'

'What are you imagining me doing to you?'

'Kissing my breasts.'

'Which one am I kissing – Dumpy or Dozy?'

Jesus Christ.

I'm like, 'You're kissing Dumpy AND Dozy. But you're possibly focusing more on Dozy.'

He goes, 'God, I love Dozy.'

'I know you do. And Dozy loves you. Hey, do you know what else I'm imagining?'

'What?'

'You tickling my thighs with your ridiculous focking beard.'

'With my what?'

'Sorry, I just meant your beard. It's tickling the inside of my thighs as you, I don't know, go down on me.'

I've just realized I'm suddenly sweating and my hort is beating like I don't know what.

He goes, 'I can taste you, Claire.'

I'm like, 'Can you?'

'Oh, yes.'

'What do I taste of?'

'Anchovies.'

'Do you like anchovies?'

'I love anchovies.'

Of course he does. Focking hipster.

He goes, 'Oh, look what's happened now!'

I'm there, 'What's happened?'

'I've taken out Mr Peters.'

I laugh out loud. Okay, way too much information.

Claire goes, 'Is he interested in at least having a conversation with me, Ross?'

I'm there, 'He's, em, definitely warming to the idea, Claire.'

I text him, going, 'And what naughty things is Mr Peters doing, Garret?'

He's like, 'It's what YOU'RE doing with him that's turning me on.'

'And what am I doing with him?'

'You're pulling him – REALLY slowly,' he goes. 'While playing with my balls.'

I'm there, 'I want to make you come, Garret.'

'You're GOING to make me come. You're definitely going to make me come.'

'I want you to come all over my breasts.'

'What about your allergy?'

'What allergy?'

'You've got seminal plasma hypersensitivity – do you remember you had that rash in Warrawong?'

'It doesn't matter.'

'Or was it Indooroopilly?'

'Garret, I'll get some focking cream for it, okay? I just want you to come all over me.'

'I'm GOING to come all over you.'

'Hurry up, then, will you? I have to lock up the shop here.'

'Okay, I've got to put the phone down. I need both my hands.'

Jesus focking Christ.

Claire goes, 'Well, Ross, what's he saying? Do you think he'd agree to marriage counselling? A girl I used to go sea swimming with went to Accord and she swore by it. Even though she's separated again now.'

I'm like, 'Hang on a second, Claire. This is a big moment coming up.'

I text Garret. I'm like, 'Jesus Christ, are you nearly finished?' but I don't get anything back for a good, like, five minutes.

He's obviously a selfish lover.

I'm like, 'Garret, what the fock are you doing there?'

Eventually, he replies. He's like, 'Sorry, made a bit of a mess. Had to use kitchen roll. That was lovely.'

I'm there, 'Yeah, no, I really enjoyed it as well.'

He goes, 'Did you come?'

I'm like, 'Yeah, no, all over my belly.'

'What?'

Shit, I forgot I'm supposed to be a woman.

I'm there, 'I mean, yes, I definitely did.'

After about a minute, he goes, 'So what happens now?'

I'm there, 'I don't want to get separated, Garret.'

'Are you saying you definitely, definitely didn't sleep with him?'

'Ross wouldn't be interested in the likes of me. Have you seen some of the women he's capable of getting, in fairness to him?'

The focker doesn't even contradict her.

He just goes, 'We could meet up and talk.'

And I'm like, 'Yeah, no, fair enough. Why don't you come to the shop now?'

He's there, 'I'll be there in half an hour.'

I stand up and I hand Claire back her phone.

'I don't think you're going to need that marriage counselling,' I go.

She's like, 'What happened?'

'He's on his way here. He wants to give it another go.'

'Oh my God! Can I read your texts?'

'Er, maybe wait until I'm gone. And don't expect any action from him tonight, Claire.'

'Excuse me?'

'Yeah, no, I think I've just milked him dry.'

We sing it at the sky – all of us together. And our voices echo out over the sea.

We're like, 'We're Bray, we're Bray, we're Bray! We're Bray, we're Bray, we're Bray! We're Bray, we're Bray, we're Bray! We're Bray, we're Bray, we're Bray!'

Yeah, no, we've just hiked to the top of Bray Head together. It's, like, the day before we play Mary's in the semi-final and Barry thought it'd be good to maybe do something together as a team – just for, like, *morale* and shit?

It's focking freezing, by the way. We're all, like, tucked up in jackets, scorves and gloves and the goys are all wearing beanies to cover their bald heads.

I'm literally looking down on the town. Everything seems obviously tiny from way up here. Dougie, Ricey and Preecer are pointing out their houses – Herbert Road, Oldcourt Avenue, Corke

Abbey – and various other landmorks to me. The Dorgle. The Carlisle Grounds. The big McDonald's at the top of the town.

Lenny, Ultan and Nailer are throwing stones into the sea and having a deep meaningful conversation on the subject of girls – ones they've been with and ones they're trying to get with.

All I can do is just smile.

I notice Barry standing beside me, lost in his own little world.

I'm there, 'Are you okay, Dude?'

He goes, 'Yeah, I'm grand, like.'

'Not nervous about tomorrow, are you?'

'No, I'm just a bit –'

'What?'

'I'm after having a terrible row – with Breena, like.'

'She didn't catch you doing the dirty, did she?'

'No, like I says to you, I'm not interested in anyone else, like. It's just she's been a bit distant, like.'

'Distant?'

'It used to be that there wouldn't be an hour would go by during the day when we didn't either talk to each other or text each other. Now, there's whole days go by and I don't hear from her, like.'

'Maybe she's just preparing herself for going away.'

'Do you think?'

'Look, take my advice, Dude. Use this opportunity to get off with other girls behind her back.'

'Why would I do that, like?'

'Because you are never going to be in this kind of demand again. Do you like any of her mates?'

'Yeah – but I've never thought about them in *that* way.'

'Maybe it's time you storted.'

'I don't think I could. I love Breena, like.'

'All I'm saying is don't be a sucker for her, okay? You don't want to look back on your life and think, "I played for Pres Bray the year we got to the semi-finals and the only girl I got off with was the one I was going out with at the time." That's a hell of a burden to have to carry around with you.'

He just nods and thanks me for the advice. I think I've become a bit of a guru to these kids.

I tip over to Fionn and I ask him if he's okay. He's sitting with his back to the famous cross, trying to catch his breath. It's a brutal enough climb even for those who *aren't* going through chemo?

He's there, 'I'm good, Ross. It'll hopefully be easier going down.'

He looks at the goys then and he smiles. He goes, 'I still can't believe they did that, by the way – shaved their heads, I mean.'

I'm there, 'There's something about this bunch, Fionn. I mean, they're like a family. I suppose they *are* a family, given that three quarters of them are focking related to each other. But as a team, I genuinely believe they're better than they even realize.'

'I think you're right.'

'Look, Dude, I'm sorry again about, you know, leaving you sitting there unconscious for the last five minutes of the last match.'

'It's fine. Look, I possibly overreacted.'

'For what it's worth, I agree.'

'The match was still in the balance. What did I want to happen – for it to be abandoned so that everyone could stand around and watch me being carried to an ambulance with low blood pressure?'

'Yeah, no, that was kind of *my* thinking at the time?'

'I shouldn't have taken it so personally. The thing is, Ross, I haven't even properly thanked you.'

'Thanked me? For what?'

'For this. For sharing this experience with me.'

'You don't have to thank me. You've been a pretty good number two, in fairness.'

'I'm serious, though. You've given me something else to think about – other than what my body is going through.'

Suddenly, the goys all laugh at some, I don't know, private joke. We look at them from a distance and we smile. I know we're both thinking exactly the same thing. That was us twenty years ago.

I'm there, 'I wonder will they be like me and you in twenty years' time? Can't shake each other, no matter how hord we try.'

Fionn smiles.

'You know,' he goes, 'since that day in Molloys, I can honestly say that I've never wanted anything more in my life than for Pres Bray to win the Leinster Schools Senior Cup.'

I'm like, 'Seriously?'

'I actually want them to win it more than I wanted us to win it back in the day. Does that sound focked-up?'

'It does a bit, yeah.'

It's storting to get dork, so we all decide to stort making the trek back down again. When we reach the bottom, we tell the goys to rest easy tonight and we'll see them tomorrow. Then we walk back to the – yeah, no – Mitsu-focking-bishi.

'This town,' Fionn goes, as we're walking through the Albert Walk, 'it gets into your bones, doesn't it, without you even realizing it?'

It's true. It genuinely does.

I'm there, 'I'll tell you something, Fionn, I'd love to actually live here. Obviously, I don't mean that literally. But in some ways, you know, I wish I'd been born here.'

Fionn suddenly stops.

'I'm going to be sick,' he goes.

I'm like, 'Was it something I said?'

We're standing outside a tattoo studio called Tatt's Entertainment. Fionn puts his hand against the shutter to steady himself and he storts spewing his ring up.

He's like, 'BLEEEUUUGGGHHH!!! BLEEEUUUGGGHHH!!!'

I'm there, 'Are you okay, Dude?'

He looks up – his glasses all foggy – and goes, 'I think I just overdid it. You go on, Ross,' because – yeah, no – it's not a spectator sport. 'I'll catch you up.'

Then – again – he's like, 'BLEEEUUUGGGHHH!!! BLEEE-UUUGGGHHH!!!'

So I walk on ahead. Just as I'm reaching the end of the Albert Walk, my phone rings. It ends up being Sorcha.

I'm like, 'Hey, Babes, what's happening?'

She goes, 'I'm just ringing to let you know that I booked our flights to New York.'

'Okay, when you say *our* flights, you obviously mean yours and Honor's.'

'No, Ross, I booked yours as well.'

'Sorcha, I'm not going to New York.'

'Ross, your daughter is about to address the General Assembly of the United Nations.'

'And I've got a Leinster Schools Senior Cup campaign to think about.'

'You could be knocked out of that by this time tomorrow.'

'Yeah, thanks for the vote of confidence, Sorcha.'

I'm looking at Fionn. He's wiping his mouth with the back of his hand. Then he storts walking towards me.

Sorcha goes, 'The final is, like, three weeks away, Ross. I'm talking about a forty-eight-hour trip.'

I'm there, 'Hey, I'm only thinking about the environment. Honor seems to think flying is bad for the planet.'

'Yeah, nice try, Ross. If you must know, Honor wants you there.'

'Does she?'

'Ross, this could be the biggest thing that ever happens in her life. She wants you to be there. And her brothers.'

'We're not bringing them as well, are we?'

'Yes, Ross, we are. And . . . I've another surprise for you as well.'

'What is it?'

'I was talking to Ronan. Him and Shadden are going to New York the exact same day – so I booked us onto the same flight.'

Fionn is suddenly standing where I'm standing. I notice that he's staring at me with just, like, shock written all over his face.

And then I see what he's looking shocked about.

I'm like, 'Sorcha, I have to go,' and I hang up on her.

'Oh, fock,' Fionn goes.

I hadn't even noticed that Sergei wasn't with us on the hike. And this is obviously where he was instead. He's sitting on the wall opposite Henry & Rose, with his hands on the orse – and his tongue in the mouth – of Barry's girlfriend, Breena.

★

Fionn's there, 'Are you going to say something?'

It's, like, the following day and we're sitting on the bus on the way to Donnybrook Stadium.

I'm there, 'I don't know – should I?'

We both look over our shoulders, down the bus. The players look so happy and so up for this. Barry and Sergei are sitting next to each other, having what looks like a chat about tactics.

'I wonder would it best if we just pretended we didn't see shit?' I go. 'He's the one player we can't afford to lose.'

Fionn's there, 'But what if the others find out what he's up to? They were being pretty open about it – you know how quickly rumours spread in a town like Bray.'

The phrase 'like shit through a goose' comes to mind.

I'm there, 'Maybe I'll just tell him to act more discreetly.'

'Or,' he goes, 'you could tell him that he shouldn't be carrying on with the girlfriend of one of his teammates.'

I suppose Fionn was in Barry's position many times over the years. It's no surprise that he'd see it from *his* point of view?

I'm there, 'Okay, I'll talk to him.'

The bus pulls into the ground and the players all stand up.

I shout, 'Sergei, stay where you are. I want to have a quick word with you about, like, tactics and shit.'

Fionn leads the players off the bus and into the dressing room and I walk down the back to where the dude is sitting.

He goes – word for word – 'You have nothing to teach me about tactics and shit. I know how to play rugby.'

It so focking weird – he seems like a totally different person.

I'm there, 'Actually, Dude, it's not tactics I want to talk to you about. It's your, er, off-field activities, if you know what I mean?'

He's just like, 'No, I do not know,' and he stares me down.

'Sergei, I saw you outside Henry & Rose last night, getting off with Barry's girlfriend. Is she the one you rode in the Glen of the Downs?'

'Is not your business.'

'Dude, you can't go around sleeping with the girlfriends of your teammates. It's not good for morale – take it from someone who did it himself – many, many times.'

'You have something to say to me about rugby, you say it. Perhaps I listen. Perhaps I not listen. This girl is not your business, asshole.'

He stands up and he walks past me, giving me a serious shoulder nudge as he does. I'm in, like, shock. I'm thinking, did he just call me an asshole?

I follow him off the bus and into the dressing room, still a bit – I'm going to use the word – *dumbfounded*?

I name the team – unchanged from the XV who beat Clongowes – and while the players change into their gear, I try to give them one of the Rossmeister's famous pep talks.

'Okay,' I go, opening my Rugby Tactics Book, 'I watched this Mary's team beat Gonzaga in the last round on TV. They've got a very strong pack and they keep the scoreboard ticking over by forcing errors in the scrum and taking their kicks.'

The goys are all looking at me – genuinely interested – but Sergei suddenly makes this *blah, blah, blah* hand gesture and goes, 'Talk, talk, talk, talk, talk.'

Suddenly, everyone is looking at him, then looking at me, and they can't believe that I'm being disrespected like this.

He goes, 'Is only one tactic. Give the ball to best player. In case you are in doubt, I am best player. So is easy.'

I can see all the goys – Barry and Nailer and Lenny and Dougie – exchanging looks, obviously wondering what the fock happened to the Sergei they knew from two weeks ago.

Unbelievably, the dude then walks over to the door, throws it open and goes, 'Okay, let's beat these assholes.'

It's always the captain who leads the team out onto the field, but Sergei takes it upon himself to do it, which is a serious, serious liberty. I can see Barry looking at the others in shock, then he runs out after him.

Fionn is like, 'What's going on?'

I'm there, 'I've no idea. It's like his body has been taken over by someone else.'

Out we go.

The Mary's fans are baiting us in a major way. They're singing, 'Non-fee St Gerard's, You're just a non-fee St Gerard's . . .'

And the Mary's players are looking at ours like they find it ridiculous that they have to even play us.

Sixty seconds into the match, their game plan becomes clear, when Barry feeds the ball back to Sergei and two of their players absolutely cream him – one of them hitting him low, the other one hitting him high. We don't even get awarded a penalty.

'What in the name of Hades are you watching, Referee?' I hear the old man shout.

I look around and I spot him in the stand, along with Fyodor and – yeah, no – the lovely Raisa, who's just, like, glowering at me.

But Sergei doesn't complain. He just gets to his feet. And the second time he gets the ball in his hands, he exacts his revenge. He takes a pass right on the halfway line, performs a little skip to stort the engine, goes inside one player, outside another and then straight through three more – as in, he literally walks over them – before scoring underneath the posts.

He runs straight over to the Mary's supporters, pointing at his chest, going, 'You see what I do? You see what I do to your shit team?'

The referee isn't happy with him. He calls Barry over and tells him to have a word with him over his unsportsmanlike conduct. Barry tries to say something to him, except Sergei gives him a shove in the chest.

Beside me, Fionn just shakes his head. He goes, 'He's like you at that age, except – and I can't believe I'm even saying this – an even bigger wanker.'

All I can do is agree with him.

I'm there, 'What the fock has happened to him? Was he just, I don't know, pretending to be a nice goy?'

He's as mystified as I am?

The match restarts. Mary's end up winning a couple of penalties by putting pressure on our scrum – just as I predicted – and they kick them to stay in touch.

But in the five minutes either side of half-time, Sergei scores two more individual tries that anyone who saw them will be talking about for, like, years to come. For the first, it's the acceleration that burns everyone off. No one even attempts a tackle. He throws the

327

ball to Barry to take the conversion, going, 'Now you do your fucking job, asshole.'

For the second, he beats six players – two of them twice – before pushing his hand into the face of the last attempted tackler and grounding the ball in the corner. Again, he runs to the Mary's fans. This time, he removes his jersey to show off his physique. Except he hasn't got one. He's got biceps like Sorcha's Adam's apple and you could play his ribs like a focking xylophone.

The Mary's fans don't like it one bit. I'm kind of laughing because – yeah, no – it's a taste of their own medicine. But he's roaring at them, 'You see what I do again? You are shit school! You are shit school!'

And, while I fully agree with the sentiment, I know the referee is losing patience with him. Midway through the second half – with us 19–9 to the good – he again storts shouting abuse at the Mary's supporters, going, 'Your team is pack of losers! Big losers – you hear? Boo-hoo for Mary's assholes!'

Our fans, I should mention, are loving it. But ten minutes from the end, Brother Ciaran – who always stays well out of team matters – hobbles over to where me and Fionn are sitting and goes, 'What's happened to the boy?'

I'm there, 'I've no idea.'

'This kind of gloating and bad sportsmanship,' he goes, 'is not consistent with the values of our school or our religious order.'

And you wonder why you haven't won a Leinster Schools Senior Cup since 1932, I'm tempted to tell him.

But I don't. Instead, I'm there, 'He's definitely not himself. I'm wondering did he hit his head in training and get a concussion?'

Fionn goes, 'You should maybe consider taking him off?'

I'm there, 'As in, substituting him?'

'Ross, he's going to get sent off if he keeps going the way he's going.'

I tell Girvan Blake, another cousin of Dougie and Lenny's – a second cousin, whose old man owns a chain of fish shops in Bray and North Wicklow – to warm up.

But when I shout to Sergei that he's coming off, he goes, 'Fuck off, no!'

I'm like, 'Sergei, you've done the damage. I just want to throw on a fresh pair of legs.'

'There is no fresher legs than mine! I not come off! Fuck you, asshole!'

All the players are looking at me, wondering how I'm going to respond. He's undermined me in a major way. But I can't walk onto the pitch and drag him off.

Fionn just goes, 'I've never seen a player refuse to come off before. Something's gone wrong in his head.'

And, of course, sixty seconds later, Sergei scores a fourth try, just to spite me, intercepting a desperate, Hail Mary of a Mary's pass to score under the posts and put us out of sight.

When the final whistle blows, I put my orms in the air and go, 'Yeeeeeessssss!!!!!!' but the atmosphere ends up being a bit – being honest? – subdued. Yes, the goys are ecstatic at having reached their first Leinster Schools Senior Cup final since 1971, but they're all genuinely worried about Sergei.

Ricey points at his temple and goes, 'There's something not right, like.'

Instead of, like, celebrating with us, the dude is walking around the pitch, seeking out each and every individual Mary's player and going, 'You have shit game today – that is why you lose!' and then getting involved in pushing and shoving matches.

I notice Fyodor and Raisa walk onto the pitch. Fyodor has a humungous grin on his face. Sergei smiles when he sees him coming. They embrace. Fyodor says something to him in Russian, then goes, 'You do good, my son!'

Raisa goes to say something as well, but Sergei goes, 'I do not need praise from my father's whore!' and he stalks off in the direction of the dressing room.

I tip up to Fyodor and I go, 'What the fock, Dude?'

He's like, 'What is matter?'

'I'll tell you what is matter – that's not the same kid who played for us against St Michael's and Clongowes.'

He just smiles at me. And the penny suddenly drops. I'm sorry, but a man who'd try to rig a General Election, who'd stage-manage a riot, who'd burn down my sister's ort gallery and cut the brakes on my cor is a man who's not to be trusted.

I'm there, 'Did you give him something?'

He's like, 'What are you imply?'

'Did you give him drugs?'

'Not drugs.'

'What, then?'

'Is Russian remedy. Is natural.'

'What is it?'

'Sergei has testosterone deficiency. Is why he has body like a little girl. He take injections and it help him. Look how he plays today.'

I'm watching the dude morching off towards the dressing room with the middle fingers of both hands raised in salute to the Mary's crowd.

I'm thinking, holy fock. This goy is either going to win us the Leinster Schools Senior Cup, or bring everything crashing down around my ears.

'Oh my God,' Sorcha goes, looking at me over the back of her seat. 'You'll never guess who got back together!'

I'm like, 'Who?' and I say it in my cranky voice because I'm trying to watch *Wonder Woman* here.

She goes, 'Claire and Garret!'

I'm like, 'Really? Couldn't happen to two bigger pricks.'

'They're, like, properly, *properly* back together? As in, they're not getting separated any more and Claire says they're having – oh my God – *amazing* sex!'

Jesus, I should offer it as a service to couples having marriage difficulties. I could make a fortune.

An air-hostess arrives down to us, bringing a very guilty-looking Johnny and Leo with her. She goes, 'Your boys were trying to open the emergency door again.'

I'm their, 'Errr, riiiiiight?' waiting to find out how that's *our* actual fault.

'That's the third time it's happened,' she goes.

I'm there, 'Can you not, I don't know, block it off or something?'

'No, we can't block it off. It's an emergency door.'

'And do they not have child locks on them?'

'Sir, it would really be simpler all round if your children just stayed in their seats. The captain says that if it happens again, we're going to perform an emergency landing in Newfoundland.'

'Newfoundland? That sounds made up.'

'That's your last warning.'

Behind me, I can hear a lot of tut-tutting and more than a few people going, 'It's those focking kids again!' and 'What the fock are their parents doing?'

Yeah, like *they* could do better?

Leo goes, 'You ugly focker,' as the air-hostess walks away.

Although with his glasses and his ridiculous eye patch, she'd be well within her rights to point out that it's a case of the pot racially abusing the kettle.

Sorcha's there, 'Ross, I told you not to let them walk around.'

I'm like, 'Er, they're your kids as *well*, Sorcha?'

She goes, 'Yeah, I'm trying to help Honor with her speech,' because – yeah, no – they've spent the entire flight quoting each other facts and figures to prove that the planet is focked seven ways to Sunday.

I'm there, 'Come on, goys, I'll put a movie on for you,' and I fasten the boys back into their seats, pop their little buds into their ears and – this is probably going to sound bad – but I put on *Don't Breathe* for them, figuring that a good horror movie might at least quieten them down slash scare them straight.

Sorcha doesn't even notice. She's too busy going, 'Oh my God, listen to this. Two thirds of all the extreme weather events that happened in the last twenty years were actually *caused* by humans, Honor. It says here that that's an actual fact.'

'Oh my God,' Honor goes, 'I need to write that down.'

I finish watching *Wonder Woman*, then I nap for a bit, then I spend about twenty minutes thinking about Sergei and what I'm going to do when I get back. The thing is, I still haven't made up my *mind*? Do I tell Brother Ciaran that Fyodor is giving him injections of something? Do I tell Barry that the girl he thinks is saving herself for him is doing the fun stuff in the Glen of the Downs with our best player?

I wouldn't say Joe Schmidt had this amount of shit to deal with in Kawakawa.

One thing is for sure, as Fionn said, I need to figure out what I'm going to do before it all blows up in our faces.

Across the aisle from me, Ronan wakes up. Him and Shadden have been asleep since, like, fifteen minutes after we took off – the lucky fockers.

He goes, 'Did we miss the didder, Ross?'

I'm like, 'Yeah, no, we're, like, half an hour away from landing.'

'Jaysus, Shadden, we're arthur sleeping through the entoyer flight, so we are. What was the didder, Rosser?'

'For us,' I go, 'it was beans and rice and a side of focking aubergine.'

He's like, 'How's the speech cubbing odden, Hodor?'

Honor goes, 'Oh my God, I've just got, like, so much material? At this rate, I'm going to be talking for, like, three hours.'

'No bethor wooban, wha'? So go odden, Hodor, gib us an auld flavour of what you're godda be saying.'

'Okay,' she goes, 'here's a fact – there's more corbon dioxide in our atmosphere right now than at any time in, like, human existence.'

Ronan's there, 'Moy Jaysus!' obviously not wanting to hurt her feelings.

I'm there, 'You'd want to maybe throw in a gag or two, Honor, just so it doesn't become too boring – bit of constructive criticism there.'

Shadden goes, 'Hee-or, Ro, we should go up and ast to hab a look at the foorst-class cabint.'

Ro's there, 'Why?'

'See how the utter half libs. Although it'll be a long toyum befower *we're* ebber floying foorst class – what with you wanton to work for bleaten free.'

'Will you leab it out, Shadden?'

'Ine oatenly saying.'

I'm like, 'Here, what time's your interview tomorrow?'

He's there, 'Ted o'clock in the morden.'

'Hey, I'll come along with you,' I go, because I want to make sure that Shadden doesn't try to talk him out of it. 'I could translate for you.'

'Thranslate?' Ronan goes. 'What are you bleaten odden about, Rosser? Thee speak the sayum language as me, for Jaysus sakes.'

'There's, like, a subtle difference in the accent. I spent a few weeks in New York on my J1, bear in mind.'

'Feerd enough. And what toyum are you making yisser speech, Honor?'

She's like, 'Three o'clock.'

He rubs his two hands together. 'Ah, it's exciting, idn't it, Rosser?' and it's lovely to see him so happy. 'Hee-or, is that a bleaten hodder movie the boys is watching?'

I'm like, 'Yeah, no, don't worry about it, Ro. I don't care once it keeps that annoying air-hostess off our case.'

There's suddenly an announcement. Speak of the devil, it's actually *her*? She goes, 'Ladies and gentlemen, we will shortly be starting our descent into JFK Airport.'

There's a buzz of excitement in the cabin. Ronan leans over Shadden to see out the window. He goes, 'I wonther will we be able to see the Statue of Libber Toddy.'

I'm like, 'The Statue of what?'

'Libber Toddy.'

'You're going to have to learn to talk a lot slower if you're going to make a go of it over here, Ro. Go again.'

This time, it's Shadden who goes, 'Libber . . .'

I'm like, 'Okay.'

'Toddy.'

'I'm still not getting it.'

'Libber . . . Toddy.'

'Still no.'

Ronan's there, 'Libber . . . Toddy.'

'Oh, right,' I finally go. 'Yeah, no, I get you now.'

Although, to be honest, I still haven't a clue what he's trying to say, but it's boring to have to keep asking him to repeat himself.

And, anyway, despite originally not wanting to go, I've suddenly got this feeling of – yeah, no – butterflies in my stomach.

At the top of my voice, I shout, 'New York City!' so the entire plane can hear me. 'Beantown!'

Ronan can't stop looking up.

Yeah, no, I was the same way when I came here for the first time. You literally can't believe that buildings could *be* that tall?

I'm like, 'Careful, Ro, you nearly walked under that taxi!'

He goes, 'The Jaysus soyuz of the place, Rosser.'

'I know, it'd melt your head, wouldn't it?'

Shadden's not impressed – or at least she's *pretending* not to be? Ronan took her up to the top of the Empire State Building last night – she's a fan of *Sleepless in Seattle* – and she apparently just pulled a face.

'I doatunt think much of it,' she goes. 'I actually prefeer howum.'

I'm like, 'Don't listen to her, Ro. You're going to focking love it here. Did I ever tell you any of my Ji stories? There was one time –'

'Is this the wooden where you rode a Rockette?' Ronan goes.

I'm like, 'Er, spoiler alert? Maybe Shadden hasn't heard it yet.'

'I *hab* heerd it,' she goes. 'A few toyums.'

Jesus, she's a nightmare of a girl.

'Did you hear the version where she pulled my feet up around my ears and I ended up with a compression fracture in my spine two weeks before the trials for the Ireland Universities team?'

She's like, 'Yeah, you toawult me when we were checking into the hotel last neet.'

The focking Plaza, by the way. And I'm paying – slash, my old man. Not that she's in any way grateful. There was fock-all that she liked on the breakfast menu this morning. I heard her say to the waitress, 'Shurden that's mower like a bleaten didder medu.'

The focking Plaza!

'This is the place,' Ronan goes, suddenly stopping outside this – I don't know – sixty-storey skyscraper on Madison Avenue.

He looks great in a suit, by the way. I just feel so proud of him as we walk into this humungous, morble lobby. We're directed to a lift – 'elevator' – and told to take the thing to the forty-second floor.

The doors open into this, like, reception area, full of glass and cream sofas. A sign on the wall says 'Shlomo, Bitton and Black – Civil Rights Attorneys'.

Ronan trots over to the receptionist and he says he has a ten o'clock appointment to see a Hazel Rochford. Then we sit down. The view of the city is un-focking-real from up here.

'I bleaten hate heights,' Shadden goes – and I'm thinking, of course she focking does.

A few minutes later, a woman in a black suit arrives out – a total focking ride, let's get that out of the way first.

'I'm Hazel Rochford,' she goes, introducing herself.

If I had to say she looked like anyone, it'd be Marisa Miller, except – and this isn't me being a dick – older.

Ro goes, 'Ine Ronan,' jumping to his feet and shaking her hand.

She's like, 'Hi, Ronan!' and you can see straight away that he's going to be a huge hit over here.

He goes, 'This is me wife, Shadden.'

'Sharon?' Hazel goes.

'No, Shadden.'

'Sharon?'

'Shadden.'

'Sharon?'

'Shadden.'

'Sharon?'

'Shadden.'

'Sharon?'

'Shadden.'

'Well, it's very nice to meet you, er, Sharon.'

'And this is me auld fedda – me fadder, in udder woords. Ross, but I calls him Rosser.'

'Hi, Rossa.'

I'm like, 'Hazel, how the hell are you?' turning on the chorm in a big-time way. 'I tagged along – I hope you don't mind – because I thought you might need someone to translate.'

'Translate?'

'Just in case you've any problem understanding his accent.'

'No, I love his accent. Actually, my – okay, let me get this right – great-, great-, great-grandfather was Irish.'

I'm there, 'Was he a Northsider, though?'

She goes, 'Er, I don't know *exactly* where he was from?'

Yeah, no, I'd probably say the same thing if my ancestors were Northsiders.

'Anyway,' she goes, 'can I just say, we were all blown away by the letter you wrote, Ronan, outlining your reasons for wanting to work here. Come inside, I want to show you around and talk to you about some of the work we do.'

So in we go. The offices are, like, massive. Me and Shadden basically hang back while Hazel gives Ronan the tour and also the lowdown on the place.

She goes, 'We're a seventy-eight-year-old law firm and we specialize in civil rights and civil liberties law. We have – as you probably know – a very high media profile due to our work on a number of landmark cases involving police misconduct and illegal state intrusion. But the main bulk of our work is in the area of discrimination based on sexual orientation, religion, race, national origin, marital status, gender, ethnicity, disability and age.'

Ronan is clearly asking all the right things, because three or four times I hear Hazel go, 'Okay, that's a really good question,' and I think to myself, God, I'd love someone to say that to me and actually mean it.

Anyway, the whole tour takes about an hour, then at the end Hazel asks Ronan when he can stort. Ronan's face just lights up.

He's there, 'So I *hab* the job, do I?'

She goes, 'Of course – we're so excited about you coming here.'

'Well, I've me finoddle exaddems in May,' he goes.

I'm there, 'He's telling you that he has his final exams in May, Hazel,' just so there's no confusion.

'I could steert the foorst week in Jewint,' he goes.

I'm there, 'He's saying he could stort in June. The first week.'

Hazel's like, 'That'd be great!'

That's when Shadden decides that *she* has a question she wants to ask?

She goes, 'And there's no muddy in it, is there?'

The focking Tuites. You literally can't bring them anywhere.

Hazel's there, 'I'm sorry, that last word isn't, like, *registering* with me?'

I'm like, 'Money, Hazel. She's asking about money.'

'Er, unfortunately, it *is* an unpaid internship – but all I can tell you is that we had three thousand applications for this position.'

Shadden goes, 'So what are we apposed to lib odden?'

I'm like, 'She's asking what they're supposed to live on. She has focking notions.'

'How are we apposed to reddent an appertment wit no bleaten muddy?'

I'm just there, 'I'll pay your rent.'

Shadden and Ronan both go, 'What?'

I'm like, 'I'll pay your rent. I'll pay all your living expenses while you're here. I'll put groceries in your fridge. I'll pay Rihanna-Brogan's school fees. Everything.'

Ronan goes, 'Rosser, wheer are you godda get that koyunt of muddy?'

I'm like, 'I'll get it from somewhere.'

I'll get it from my old man.

I'm there, 'Just say yes, Ro.'

Ronan smiles. I honestly haven't seen him this happy since the night Darren shot John Boy in *Love/Hate*.

He goes, 'I'd luvven the job, Hazelt. Me addenser is yes.'

They're waiting for us in the lobby of the United Nations building. We're talking Sorcha, Honor and the three boys.

Sorcha is smiling so hord that she's in danger of genuinely hurting herself.

Honor goes, 'Hey, Ronan, how did the interview go?'

He's like, 'Went moostard, Hodor. Thee offered the job to me theer and thedden – and Ine arthur saying yes to them.'

'Yeah, wirrout eeben discussiden it with me,' Shadden goes.

337

We all just ignore her.

Honor's there, 'Oh my God, Ronan, I'm *so* proud of you.'

He's like, 'And Ine prowut of you as weddle, Hodor. I caddent believe you're about to staddend up and speak in fruddent of the Unirit Nashiddens.'

The boys are weirdly quiet, by the way. They're just, like, staring into space, as they have been since I let them watch *Don't Breathe* on the flight over. And, while I hate being critical of myself as a father, I'm beginning to wonder are the two things possibly linked?

Sorcha goes, 'Oh my God, we've had *the* most amazing morning, haven't we, Honor?'

Yeah, no, Mary Robinson offered to show them around the building.

I'm like, 'Yeah, how was the tour?'

'Ah-mazing!' she goes. 'I mean, I'd obviously done it before when I came to New York at the end of my J1. But we actually got to see a lot more because we were – oh, you know – hanging out with the former United Nations High Commissioner for Human Rights! As you do!'

'Yeah, no, fair focks.'

'And she's, like, a *total* rockstor, isn't she, Honor?'

'Oh my God,' Honor goes, 'totally!'

'And even though she didn't remember meeting me specifically, she did remember coming to the school when she was the President of Ireland, for the Saint Madeleine Sophie Barat Endowment for International Peace, Justice and Co-Operation Awards, sponsored by Goldman Sachs.'

Jesus Christ, she's babbling like a focking mad person, which is down to either excitement or nerves, or more likely both.

'And she reminded us that she wasn't the only former Mount Anville girl who worked out of this building,' she goes. 'Samantha Power was the United States Ambassador to the United Nations under Barack Obama, even though she only went to the junior school and not *actual* Mount Anville? Oh my God, we even took a selfie of us sitting at her old desk, didn't we, Honor?'

Honor goes, 'We did, yeah.'

'Oh my God, Ronan, you should *hear* Honor's speech. Actually, what am I saying? You're *going* to hear it in, like, twenty minutes' time. But she read it to me in the taxi on the way here this morning and it was, like, Oh! My God! *Goosebumps?*'

I'm there, 'And the boys, Sorcha, were they well-behaved on the tour? Or were they, hopefully, focking and blinding at the top of their voices as usual?'

'No,' she goes, 'there hasn't been a word out of them all day. It's like they know how big a day this is for Honor and they're determined to, like, *respect* that?'

I'm there, 'Er, let's hope it's that alright.'

'Although I hope they're okay. I know Leo and Johnny had nightmares last night.'

Shit.

I'm about to say something when Sorcha all of a sudden let's a squeal out of her.

'Oh my God,' she goes, 'there's Michelle Obama!'

I turn around, thinking she's probably mistaken, except it turns out that it is actually *her?*

Sorcha's like, 'Oh my God! Oh my God! Oh my God!' trying to think of something to say.

And then, just as the woman is walking past us, Sorcha shouts, 'Michelle, I'm a huge fan slash admirer! We gave each other Vouchers for Hugs for Christmas as well! Tell your husband that I've read *Dreams from My Father* three times and now I'm reading it in Spanish! *Los Sueños de Mi Padre!*'

Jesus focking Christ.

When she's gone, Sorcha goes, 'Honor, she's heading in the direction of the General Assembly Hall!'

Honor's there, 'Oh! My God! I can't believe Michelle *actual* Obama is going to hear my speech!'

Sorcha's there, 'Come on, let's go! You're going to be on in, like, five minutes.'

So – yeah, no – we make our way to the actual main chamber. In we go – Honor first, then Sorcha following with her two hands resting proudly on her daughter's shoulders, then me pushing

Brian in his wheelchair, then Ronan carrying Leo, then Shadden holding Johnny's hand – into the United Nations General Assembly Hall.

We all wish Honor the best of luck. Then off she focks.

She walks right to the front of the chamber, while we find our seats in the public gallery. It's, like, absolutely rammers and there are people of all nationalities here, although I don't want to name them for fear of being racist.

This, like, tiny little girl has the mic. In broken English, she's telling all the adults in the room that they have destroyed the planet and brought human civilization to the edge of extinction.

'How dare you!' she goes. 'How *dare* you!'

Everyone just looks at each other and goes, 'Awww!!!' although Sorcha looks concerned.

She's like, 'There's quite a bit of overlap between *her* speech and Honor's?'

The little girl says what she has to say, finishing with, 'You have stolen my future – you sicken me!' and then – yeah, no – Mary literally Robinson steps up to the mic and goes, 'Now, our next speaker, I'm delighted to say, comes from my own alma mater of Mount Anville Secondary School in Ireland, a school that's been very much in the vanguard of campaigning on social issues – including that of climate change – for many years. And I know she has some very interesting things to say to us today.'

Sorcha has spotted Michelle Obama sitting about twenty feet to our left. She's trying to catch her eye. She succeeds. She mouths the words, 'This is my daughter!' and Michelle Obama smiles back at her as if to say, What the fock is this woman's issue?

'Chairman, delegates, guests,' Mary Robinson goes, 'it is my pleasure to introduce . . . Honor O'Carroll-Kelly.'

Everyone claps – although no one louder than me and Sorcha. We're like her fan club. I look down at my hands and I realize that I'm shaking. That's how nervous I am for the girl. But Honor steps up to the mic, showing no fear whatsoever. I've said it before. Owen Farrell.

She smiles at the audience. My daughter has the most beautiful smile you've ever seen. Everyone is just, like, sitting there, ready and willing to be chormed by her.

Until she opens her mouth to speak.

'Er, no disrespect to that last girl,' she goes, 'but I wouldn't say *she* gets invited to many sleepovers! What a focking drip!'

There are, like, gasps in the United Nations General Assembly Hall. Which is saying something, because I'd imagine they've heard all sorts in here.

Honor goes, 'Seriously, people, what the fock is going on that you're now asking children to come in here and talk to you about the future of the planet? Jesus focking Christ! Has emotion finally won out over reason?'

Sorcha turns to me with just, like, shock on her face. She goes, 'Ross, this wasn't in the speech she read to me in the taxi.'

I'm there, 'Are you sure?'

'I think I would have focking remembered it, Ross!'

Honor waves what I'm presuming is her speech at the audience. She goes, 'I actually prepared some notes for today – but I've decided that I'm not going to use them.'

She makes a big show of ripping it in half and then in half again.

Sorcha goes, 'Oh my God, Ross, what's she doing? Everything was in that speech. All of the facts we researched together.'

'I'm just going to talk off the cuff,' Honor goes. 'And the first thing I want to say to you is this . . . CLIMATE CHANGE IS A FOCKING HOAX!'

She actually screams the words into the microphone – and, again, the gasps echo around the hall.

Behind me, I hear Ronan go, 'Moy Jaysus!'

And then Honor laughs in this, like, evil *villain* sort of way?

She goes, 'Oh, you weren't expecting to hear *that*, were you? You thought I was going to stand up here – like that last girl – and lecture you all about the damage you've done to the planet. But that would mean having to pretend to care about this shit – just like you're doing now.'

Sorcha has her hand over her mouth. Behind it, I can hear her going, 'Oh! My God! Oh! My God! Oh! My God!' as the penny finally drops that our daughter has been punking us for the last six months.

'Look,' Honor goes, 'I've read a lot about the so-called climate emergency. If you must know, I'm *not* a climate change activist. But I'm not a climate change denier either. My position is that I just don't *give* a fock? And, let's be honest, that's an entirely natural viewpoint for a thirteen-year-old girl to take.'

I notice that Sorcha is trying to shield her face from Michelle Obama.

'You see,' Honor goes, 'I'm committed to a thing called principled inaction. Doing nothing. Because if the planet *is* as focked as ninety-nine per cent of scientists say it is, there is no point in any of us getting upset about it. Human civilization – if you want to call it that – is coming to an end. My question is, why is that considered such a bad thing?'

All around us, we can hear nothing but mutters of disapproval and then – oh, fock – I can see Mary Robinson standing in the aisle, giving us a look of serious disapproval.

'As I see it,' Honor goes, 'the Earth is overpopulated – certainly with human beings. There are, like, twice as many people on the planet as there were in 1960, a rate of reproduction that would not be sustainable in any other species, and definitely not one as wilfully destructive as us. We are, let's be honest, a virus on this planet – a virus that kills everything it touches. And now *we* are the ones who are focked. And the United Nations – the great UN – is doing what about it? You're inviting children in here to tell you what you already know. And why? Because it makes you feel good about yourselves.

'My mother was so excited about me standing up here to talk to you today. You see, she's just like you lot – a total focking phoney. I can actually see her, all the way back there, in the public gallery, trying to look invisible. Sorcha Lalor, everyone! She is, let me just say, the worst kind of moral grandstander. Every action the woman takes, from the tweets she Likes, to the books she reads, to the grocery items she puts in her shopping trolley, is calculated towards one end – satisfying her emotional need to be thought of as a good person. But you're not a good person, Mom – are you?'

People are suddenly turning around in their seats, trying to pick us out in the public gallery.

I'm like, 'Jesus Christ, Sorcha, are we dreaming this?'

But, unfortunately, we're not.

Honor goes, 'Let me tell you something about my mom. Last year, she got it into her head that I was secretly poisoning my little brother Hillary.'

Sorcha puts her head in her hands. 'Oh my God,' she goes, 'she knows the truth, Ross.'

I decide not to mention that I was the one who told her.

'But instead of asking me about it,' Honor goes, 'she decided herself that I was guilty – without even informing me of the chorge. This from the woman who's proud to tell everyone that she was the first girl in her class to join Amnesty International, who'll sign any online petition that's going to demand fair trials for people she's never focking met before, living in faraway countries where she'll never go. Orticle 11 of the United Nations Universal Declaration of Human Rights, a copy of which hangs on the wall of our focking kitchen, says: "Everyone chorged with a penal offence has the right to be presumed innocent until proved guilty according to law in a public trial at which he has had all the guarantees necessary for his defence." And yet she condemned her own daughter without even offering her a hearing. So guess what she did then, ladies and gentlemen? She packed me off to Australia – the way they used to treat convicts in, like, the *olden* days?'

Sorcha looks at me, tears streaming down her face.

'*That's* what this whole thing has been *about*?' she goes. '*Revenge*?'

A woman over to our right shouts, 'Shame on you!' in our general direction.

This might come across as selfish, but I'm just relieved that *I'm* not the one being called out here?

Honor goes, 'You see, my mom – despite her best efforts – doesn't actually like me. She has this image in her head of, like, the perfect daughter. It's basically just *her* as a child. But I'm not like that. I'm a bit of a weirdo and no one really likes me, except for my dad, who just accepts me for what I am.'

Sorcha turns to me and goes, 'I might have focking known you'd come out of it looking like the hero.'

I try my best not to look too smug. But I'm not saying I manage to pull it off.

'For my whole life,' Honor goes, 'my mom has tried to turn me into a sort of, like, mini version of her. So I decided, when I got back from Australia, that that's what I would be – just to fock with her head. I pretended to give a shit about the things that *she* cared about? The polar ice cap melting. The Amazon being chopped down. The oceans full of plastic. And, being a sappy bitch who's more interested in ideas than people, she suddenly thought we had this, like, *connection*? I heard her saying it to my dad – that I had finally become the daughter she dreamt I would be. What a focking fraud!'

People are just, like, shaking their heads. There's no doubt whose side they're on – and it's not Sorcha's.

'So I decided to see how far I could push it. I set up this, like, Climate Justice Committee in Mount Anville, because I knew that *she* tried to set one up when *she* was my age? I embarrassed the school into closing the cor pork and cancelling the annual skiing trip to Italy. A lot of people, *real* people, were pissed off with me for doing it – and, like, *rightly* so? But focking saps like my mom were so desperate to feel good about themselves that they pretended that what I was doing was the right thing.

'You see, a lot of people carry around with them this huge sense of guilt – I don't know, just for being alive. And people like *her* – desperate bitches, in other words – have to assuage that guilt by performing little acts of virtue that make them feel worthy, whether it's bringing bottles to the recycling centre or joining in a social media shaming.

'I made my whole family become vegans – but then I carried on eating meat behind their backs. I pretended to take two buses to and from school every day, but I actually set up a Hailo account and got taxis on my dad's credit cord.'

I'm thinking, I really need to stort reading my Visa statements.

'I arranged a Climate Justice Rally in Dublin,' she goes, 'that turned into a riot. We attacked a bunch of formers who were just, like, protesting for their right to earn a living. We caused, like, thousands of euros' worth of damage to their tractors. And my mom waited to see how it played out on social media and in the next day's newspapers before she decided how she felt about it. That's how focking terrified she is of finding herself on the wrong side of an orgument.'

'There's something wrong with her,' Sorcha goes to me, through her tears. 'And I mean that on a psychiatric level.'

Honor goes, 'And then I was invited here – all my mother's dreams coming true – to address the United Nations General Assembly, as a spokesperson for my generation! I mean, what a focking joke! The only reason I came here was to see the look on the stupid bitch's face when she found out that I *wasn't* the daughter she always dreamt I'd be? And, believe me, it's been worth it.'

Honor storts walking away from the podium. But after a few steps, she changes her mind and doubles back. There's obviously, like, one more thing she wants to get off her chest.

'Oh, as for the planet,' she goes, 'the good news is that – while every living thing on Earth is focking doomed, thanks to us – the planet will be fine. It will take millions and millions of years, but it will figure out a way to fix the damage we've done to it. And that process will begin the day we are all gone. And then, millions and millions of years after that, new life forms will emerge – life forms that will be hopefully *better* than us? And, let's be honest, that wouldn't be focking hord. Thanks for your invitation to speak and for pretending to give a shit what a thirteen-year-old girl thinks about anything.'

Yeah, no, that ends up being her mic drop moment. She walks off the stage to just, like, total silence. I turn around to Sorcha and I try to put a positive spin on it – typical South Dublin dad.

'A lot of interesting points,' I go. 'I like the way she tried to give *both* sides?'

But Sorcha just stares straight ahead at the empty stage with an expression on her face that I've never seen before. It's pretty obvious that she thinks Honor has crossed a serious line this time.

'A girl who could stand up and disrespect an important institution like the United Nations – *and* use the f-word in front of a former First Lady *and* Ireland's first female President – is a girl I don't want to know,' she goes. 'I'm finished with her.'

I'm like, 'Excuse me?'

But she's there, 'I mean it, Ross. She's your daughter now.'

And the worst thing is, I know this time she actually means it.

10.

Viva Las Braygas

We've been training for the best port of an hour when the snow storts to fall. According to Fionn, they're calling it the Beast from the East and it's going to bring the country to a literally standstill.

We're practising a few drills, watched by a crowd of three or four hundred people. Everyone is staring at Sergei. It's actually hord to take your eyes off him. He has his top off, even though it's, like, minus-whatever outside, and he's roaring at poor Barry – his captain and the dude whose girlfriend he's riding – accusing him of deliberately playing shit passes to him.

He's going, 'You throw ball here. At my knees. Make me look bad. Make me look like asshole in front of these people.'

And Barry's there, 'It was an accident, like.'

I turn around to Fionn. I'm there, 'Please tell me I wasn't that much of a prick when I played the game?'

Fionn goes, 'You *were* pretty insufferable, Ross.'

I laugh because it's true.

I'm there, 'I still don't know what to do, by the way.'

He goes, 'You're talking about Sergei and Breena?'

'Yeah, no, I tried to have a word with him on the bus before the Mary's match. He told me to mind my own focking business.'

'If I tell Barry that Sergei is riding his girlfriend, then that's Sergei finished. I mean, half of the team are Barry's cousins – they'll round up a posse and ride him out of town. And we haven't a hope of beating Blackrock without him.'

Yeah, no, I forgot to mention, Blackrock College beat Belvo in the second semi-final yesterday.

I'm there, 'You didn't see what they did to us before Christmas.'

In fairness to him, he doesn't push the point with me.

He goes, 'I just don't understand what happened. The change that's come over him.'

I don't say shit. But my face obviously betrays me because Fionn suddenly goes, 'You know something.'

I'm there, 'I genuinely don't – you have my word.'

'Ross, I'm your Assistant Coach. If something's going on, you need to tell me.'

'Okay, fair enough. His old man has been giving him injections.'

'Of what?'

'Of something. That's all I know.'

'Tell me it's legal.'

'According to him, it is. He says Sergei has some sort of, I don't know, testosterone deficiency – that's why he has a body like a girl. This shit he's giving him obviously makes him more, I don't know, aggressive.'

I look over at Sergei. He's roaring at Nailer this time. He's going, 'Is no room for mistakes! Final is two weeks! Blackrock not make mistakes!'

Fionn's there, 'He's the best schools player I've ever seen – no disrespect to you, Ross. Even if you go on to coach Ireland one day, this might be the most difficult decision you ever have to make.'

The snow is really coming down now and people are storting to drift away. Leo Varadkar was on the news this morning, saying everyone should heed the Status Red weather warning and be safe at home by four o'clock this afternoon.

I walk onto the pitch, clapping my two hands together, going, 'Okay, goys, let's call it a day.'

'A day?' Sergei goes. 'What is this bullshit?'

'Leo Varadkar said we've all to be home by four o'clock.'

'Who the fuck is Leo Varadkar?'

'He's the, technically, still leader of this country. Yeah, no, there's a blizzard on the way. They're calling it the Beast from the East.'

'Fuck to the blizzard,' Sergei goes, as the others stort to drift back to the dressing room. 'I am Beast from East, assholes!'

He drops to the ground – no top on, remember – and he storts performing push-ups in the snow. And at the top of his voice, he's shouting, 'I am Beast from East! I am Beast from East!'

We all decide to just leave him to it. Back to the dressing room we go.

In the cor pork, we end up running into Brother Ciaran.

He goes, 'We're closing the school for the rest of the week.'

Fionn's like, 'Yeah, I hear they're expecting a couple of feet of snow.'

'Home to batten down the hatches, eh? I just thought I should mention to you that I had reason to phone young Sergei's father this morning.'

I'm like, 'Fyodor? What was it in, like, regords to?'

'I've been hearing complaints from a number of his teachers – well, from *all* of his teachers. Homework not handed in –'

'Why the fock are they giving him homework? He's the best player we have.'

'Our students are expected to take their education seriously, Ross, whether they're on the rugby team or not.'

I worry about the future of the game in this country.

I'm there, 'The Blackrock goys won't be doing homework, Ciaran. I'm just making that point to you.'

'Well, in addition to homework not handed in,' he goes, 'there's also the question of his behaviour. Some of his teachers say he's been treating them dismissively and also acting aggressively when he's asked to work.'

'And it's not something that these so-called teachers could try to put up with – even for a couple more weeks?'

'He's undermining them in front of the rest of the –' He suddenly stops. He's staring over my shoulder with a look of just, like, disbelief on his face. He goes, 'Is that Sergei out there?'

Me and Fionn both turn around. He's standing out in the middle of the field – top still off – and he's shadow-boxing and at the same time shouting, 'I am Beast and I come from East! I am Beast and I come from East!'

I'm there, 'It, er, certainly looks like him. Yeah, no, he said he

349

wanted to do a bit of extra training. Fair focks would have to be my attitude.'

And that's when a cor suddenly pulls up a few feet away from us. It's, like, a red Maserati Quattroporte. Fyodor is sitting behind the wheel. Nothing screams midlife crisis louder than a red sports cor – except maybe a girlfriend who's twenty years younger than you. And he's got one of those as well. The lovely Raisa, I notice, is sitting in the front passenger seat.

Fyodor throws open the door and gets out. He shouts something at his son in Russian, then he has the actual balls to look at me. I'm thinking, yeah, no, this one's down to you, Dude.

Raisa gets out as well and then *she* storts screaming at him – again, in Russian. Whatever she says to him, it touches an obvious nerve because he stops shadow-boxing and telling the entire Putland Road that he's the Beast from the East and he morches over to where Sergei and Raisa are standing.

He's in an absolute rage as well and suddenly there's this, like, three-way orgument going on between them, which none of us can follow, but which soon draws the rest of the goys out of the dressing room.

'What's going on, like?' Ricey asks me.

I'm there, 'Brother Ciaran rang Sergei's old man and told him he was being a dick to his teachers. Personally, I'd have told them to deal with it or find somewhere else to work.'

There's a lot of shouting and finger-pointing going on. And then suddenly, out of nowhere, Raisa draws back her hand and slaps Sergei across the face. She doesn't leave it at a slap in the face either. She knees him in the nuts and the poor dude is suddenly doubled over. Then she storts raining slaps down on his head and Sergei is bent in two, trying to protect his face with his hands, while begging for – presumably – mercy.

Fyodor eventually steps in between them. I think he's worried about them scratching the Maserati. But Raisa hasn't calmed down.

She goes, 'You call *me* slut? You call *me* slut?'

Oh, fock, she's suddenly looking at me.

She goes, 'I have secret that perhaps I tell to all your friends. How do you like this, Sergei?'

I'm there, 'Er, Raisa, whatever you're about to say, maybe *don't* say it?' and I look at Fyodor.

But, fock, it ends up not even *being* that? It turns out it's *his* secret she's talking about.

She goes, 'Does your coach and your friends know you are having the sex with this girl who is girlfriend of boy on your team?'

The goys are all suddenly looking at each other, obviously wondering who she's talking about.

I'm there, 'This is all news to me, I have to say. Fionn, you didn't know anything about it either, did you?'

He doesn't answer me.

I'm like, 'Let's maybe leave it there, though. Like Leo Varadkar said, we should all be indoors.'

'Is ginger girl,' Raisa goes, 'smelling of chips.'

It's, like, gasps and shocked faces all round.

Barry's there, 'Are you talking about Breena?'

In fairness, it's not exactly a big field.

'She comes to house,' Raisa goes. 'I hear them whisper. She say Barry cannot know. Sergei say, "You need real man – and real man is Russian man."'

And suddenly, just like that, the most difficult rugby decision I'll ever have to make is taken out of my hands. Dougie and Lenny step forward. And one of them – I still can't tell them aport – opens the back door of the Maserati and the other one manhandles poor, half-naked Sergei towards it.

The dude storts screaming at them. He's like, 'What you do? You cannot beat Blackrock without Sergei! You are shit team!'

It's a pretty good analysis, to be fair. But it'd be a brave man to agree with him – especially given the atmosphere.

'You crossed the line, like,' Ricey tells him.

And Sergei's there, 'Who are you? You are fat boy! You are no one!'

Barry then makes a run at him. It takes five or six of the goys to hold him back.

Sergei laughs at him and goes, 'Breena want real man. Not man who say, "Jesus want us to wait to have the sexy-sexy." That is not real man.'

Dougie and Lenny manage to shove him into the back of the cor and shut the door.

'You ever cross the Dargle again,' Barry shouts at him, 'and you'll be taking your life in your hands, like.'

And that ends up being that.

The old man can't take the smile off his face.

'She said *what*?' he goes.

And I'm like, 'She said that climate change was a hoax.'

'In front of the United Nations General Assembly?'

Sorcha's there, 'Chorles, please don't laugh. I don't see the funny side of it and I never will.'

'You see,' he goes, 'this is what happens when you inhabit a social media bubble, Sorcha! You become intolerant of other people's points of view!'

'It's not her point of view,' Sorcha goes. 'She did it just to humiliate me. Sister Consuelo said Mary Robinson rang her to complain – and she storted hyperventilating on the phone.'

Sorcha looks across the cor pork at Honor, who gives her the middle finger.

On the upside, though, we're all back on the meat again. I ate three cheeseburgers when we got to JFK, one after the other, and I was sweating like my old dear when she went through what I used to call the mentalpause.

The old man goes, 'Perhaps the girl listened to some of my orguments on the subject and simply reconsidered her position! It takes real strength of character to change your mind, Sorcha, especially when it means going against the consensus view!'

We're all standing around outside Foxrock Church, by the way. It's the day of the christening. Hugo, Cassiopeia, Diana, Mellicent, Louisa May and Emily are about to be baptized into the Catholic Church and I'm about to agree to take on a leading role in their spiritual and moral development, along with a friend of my mother's who I recently rode in her gorden.

It's true that you never know what twists and turns life is going to take.

It's a beautiful day for it. The Beast from the East has gone. Both Beasts actually. Sergei went back to Moscow a week ago, leaving me with a sense of dread about the final.

Still, I'll cross that bridge when I come to it.

My old dear's decision to bring up the babies without using nannies is turning out exactly as I *predicted* it would? The woman arrived at the church with only five of them in the cor, having left Louisa May behind in – I shit you not – either the hairdresser's, or the beauty salon, or the petrol station.

Her and Delma took off in the cor to try to find her – 'We might try Thomas' as well, Delma, because I'm nearly sure I was in there as well' – which is the reason we're all waiting around outside, enjoying the early-spring sunshine.

'A happy day,' the old man goes, 'eh, Kicker? And hopefully an even happier one to come! Our friend – Mister Roderic Grainger SC – is due to deliver the result of his so-called investigation next week!'

Sorcha sort of, like, bitch-smiles him. She can't help herself. She goes, 'You don't *still* believe you're going to be the Taoiseach, do you, Chorles?'

He's like, 'Stranger things have happened, Sorcha! Enda Kenny was once the Taoiseach, remember?'

Father Thaddeus tips over to us then. He wants to get on with the show. He's obviously got shit to do today.

'It's, em, almost half eleven now,' he goes.

The old man's like, 'Fionnuala has mislaid one of the children, Father! She shouldn't be much longer!'

She's been gone, like, forty minutes already and I'm actually storting to worry. And that's when Brian suddenly storts pointing at the priest and going, 'The bad man, Daddy! The bad man!'

Father Thaddeus, I probably should mention, has got, like, grey hair and a grey beard and moustache and I suppose – yeah, no – he *does* look a little bit like the blind dude from *Don't Breathe*, especially to a kid who's quite possibly traumatized.

Sorcha's there, 'That's Father Thaddeus, Brian. My gran went to Medjugorje with him for nineteen Easters in a row.'

But Leo and Johnny end up getting upset then as well. They're, like, screaming at him, 'Fock off, bad man! Fock off, bad man!'

And of course it's not the kind of thing that a priest wants to have children shouting at him, especially in the – let's just say – current *climate*?

So Sorcha goes, 'Ross, could you maybe –' meaning, get them the fock out of here.

I grab the handles of Brian's wheelchair and I go, 'Johnny, Leo, let's go talk to the goys,' because I notice Fionn, Christian, JP, Oisinn and Magnus standing on the other side of the cor pork.

So over to them we trot.

Christian has Ross Junior and little Oliver with him. I notice Ross Junior looking at Brian with a guilty look on his face.

I'm there, 'Don't worry about it, Ross Junior, he *will* hopefully walk again one day – even *if* it's with a limp. He'll probably never play rugby for Ireland, but I don't want you blaming yourself.'

JP goes, 'Are the boys alright, Ross?'

I'm like, 'Yeah, no, why do you ask?'

'It's just they don't seem their usual boisterous selves.'

'Maybe they're hopefully maturing.'

'Is that it?'

'Yeah, no, to be honest, just between ourselves, I let them watch a horror movie on the way over to the States. I think they might be a bit, I don't know, *disturbed*?'

JP's eyes suddenly light up. 'Hey,' he goes, 'there's Delma.'

I look over. Yeah, no, she's getting out of my old dear's cor – as is my old dear, holding a baby. They've obviously managed to find Louisa May – although fock knows where.

'Sorcha was saying she's single,' JP goes.

I remember that JP always had a thing for Delma when we were teenagers.

I'm there, 'Yeah, no, her husband got some young one pregnant.'

He's like, 'What an idiot. Look at the legs on her. Do you know is she still playing veterans tennis?'

'She's hoping to go back to it. When the weather gets better.'

At the top of his voice, the old man goes, 'The sixth baby has been successfully located! Shall we proceed?'

And everyone storts moving into the church.

Ronan tips over to me. I haven't actually seen him since he came back from the States. He's with Shadden, Rihanna-Brogan and the famous Kennet. He takes the handles of Brian's wheel-chair from me.

'Hee-or,' he goes, 'we'll look arthur the boyuz. You've woork to be doing.'

I'm like, 'Yeah, no, thanks, Ro. How did the rest of the trip go?'

Ronan and Shadden stayed on in New York, while Sorcha insisted on going straight back to the Plaza from the United Nations Build-ing, packing up our shit and getting the next flight home.

He's like, 'It was moostard, Rosser. Saw all the sights, ditn't we, Shadden? The Flat Oyerdin Building. Gerrant Centre Doddle Stationt.'

I don't even bother asking.

He goes, 'Plus, we're arthur foyunting a lubbly apeertment, Rosser – in Greddich Viddage.'

'It's bleaten tiny,' Shadden – typical – goes. 'You couldn't swing a cat in it.'

Ro's like, 'It's a gowergous peert of towun, Rosser. I'll be able to get the subway to woork evoddy day. I caddent wait, so I caddent.'

I'm there, 'Fair focks, Ro. I'm saying it.'

'And thanks, Rosser – for encoudaging me.'

'W . . . W . . . W . . . W . . . W . . . Woorken for nuttin,' Kennet goes. 'P . . . P . . . P . . . P . . . P . . . People widdle take the p . . . p . . . p . . . p . . . p . . . piss if you let them, so thee widdle.'

I end up having to walk away from him because I'm scared that I might end up decking him, there outside the church, on what's supposed to be a day of, like, *celebration*?

People stort filling the pews. It's some focking turnout, in fair-ness. Practically everyone my old pair are on speaking terms with is there. Hennessy and Fyodor obviously. All my old dear's mates from her various campaigns and causes, and all of my old man's mates from the Law Library, and Doheny & Nesbitt, and the various golf clubs where he's disgraced himself over the years – plus, of course, all of the members of the New Republic porliamentary porty.

I tip up to the altar. I'm holding Hugo and Louisa May, the old dear is holding Mellicent, the old man is holding Cassiopeia and Diana, then Delma is holding Emily.

Father Thaddeus races through the – I suppose – *ceremony*? Ireland are playing Scotland in the Six Nations at quarter past two and it's quite possible that he has a ticket.

We do the whole candle thing, and the rejecting Satan thing, and the pouring water on their heads thing. And I end up getting this overwhelming feeling of, I suppose, *happiness* that everything seems to be finally going my way.

I've got a Leinster Schools Senior Cup final to look forward to. My son has landed an internship with an American law firm that might hopefully lead to a career away from the clutches of Hennessy and my old man. Honor is – okay – a problem, but at least she's given up caring about what happens to the planet and I have a brand-new Audi A8 arriving in a month's time.

And to top it all off, I've got one, two, three, four, five, six beautiful siblings. And they *are* beautiful. Hugo. Cassiopeia. Diana. Mellicent. Emily. And Louisa May, who the old dear left in the phormacy, it turns out, when she popped in to ask if it was safe to drink alcohol with her fecal incontinence medication.

I'm determined to be as good a brother as I am a father. I want to teach them – yeah, no – all of the shit I've learned in life. Which isn't much, I realize, but whatever I've picked up along the way is theirs to do with whatever they want. And here's the thought that gives me literally butterflies in my stomach. I just can't wait to see them grow up and get to know them.

So the – again – *ceremony* eventually ends. Father Thaddeus says he has to get to Ballsbridge by a quarter past two – told you – so he wants to know can we do the photographs quickly?

So we move to the front of the altar. And we're standing there, all smiles, while everyone in the church is either clapping or taking photographs of us with their iPhones.

And that's when the day ends up taking what people who watch box-sets would describe as a turn.

I can hear Johnny and Leo – five or six rows back – shouting, 'The bad man! The bad man!' and I can hear Ronan trying to shush them, going, 'It's alreet, feddas – it was joost a movie is alls.'

Then I hear Sorcha go, 'What movie?' and Ronan go, 'Er, you'll need to ast Rosser, Sudeka.'

And then my old dear leans close to me, so close that I can smell the eight fingers of Grey Goose she had for her breakfast, and she whispers in my ear, 'Delma told me what happened, Ross.'

And my entire body turns instantly cold.

I'm like, 'What?' and I suddenly feel like I'm about to vomit.

'She couldn't bear the guilt any more,' she goes. 'She spilled her guts out to me in the cor. So now we know how the rainwater butt became disconnected from the downward gutter.'

I'm there, 'She came on to me rather than the other way around.'

And Delma obviously overhears this because she ends up suddenly losing it with me. She goes, 'I did *not* come on to you!'

I notice Sorcha's ears suddenly prick up, trying to make out what we're saying.

I'm like, 'Maybe keep your voice down, Delma. House of the Lord and blah, blah, blah.'

Delma goes, '*You* came on to *me*!'

And that's when I hear what I instantly recognize as a gunshot, then the sound of glass smashing. I look behind me and I notice that one of the humungous stained-glass windows has been shattered. Then I hear a second shot, which hits the baptism font, and everyone's shock suddenly turns to panic.

There's, like, screams in the church. I recognize Sorcha's, which is the loudest of all. My old man hits the deck, as do my old dear and Delma, all of them instinctively using their bodies to shield the babies.

I hear someone go, 'It's that little boy! He has a gun!'

And then I hear Leo shout, 'Fock off, bad man! Fock off, bad man!'

I look down at the congregation and I straight away spot him, six rows back, pointing a pistol straight at Father Thaddeus.

'Oh my God!' Sorcha goes. 'Leo, no!'

Ronan, very bravely, jumps on him before he can let loose a third shot. Then I spot Kennet in the row in front of him, putting his hand to the back of his belt and going, 'Jaysus, he st . . . st . . . st . . . st . . . st . . . st . . . st . . . stole me g . . . g . . . g . . . g . . . g . . . gudden.'

I'm there, 'Your gun? Why have you even *got* a gun in a church?'

The old man stands up and tries to take chorge of the situation. He's there, 'Now calm down, everyone – no one has been hurt, as far as I can see! I don't think there's any cause for us to go making a bigger deal of this than it needs to be!'

Ronan has managed to get the gun out of Leo's hands. I'm thinking, thank God his eyes are focked – if he hadn't had the eye patch, he might have actually killed the priest.

People are looking at each other in just, like, shock. I suppose if there's one upside to my five-year-old son trying to shoot a priest, it's that my conversation with Delma over who initiated the whole dog and pony show has been seemingly forgotten.

Kennet goes, 'Ronan, I c . . . c . . . caddent go back to j . . . j . . . jayult.'

Ro's like, 'Who's thalken about jayult?'

'If thee f . . . f . . . f . . . f . . . f . . . f . . . foyunt out I hab a gudden, thee'll thrun away the k . . . k . . . k . . . k . . . key this toyum.'

'Gimme it,' Ronan goes. 'I'll get rid of the Jaysusing thing.'

Kennet hands it to him. Ronan stuffs it into his inside pocket and he pegs it from the church.

And the old dear climbs to her feet, as if nothing just happened, and goes, 'We'll be having drinks and nibbles in the Shelbourne Hotel this afternoon. We'd love you all to be there.'

They look – yeah, no – downcast. It's hord to believe that this is the same group of players that took the mighty Michael's aport six weeks ago. But then it's *not* the same group of players? One of them is missing.

And, of course, that's the point of this morning's meeting.

They're sitting in the Scullery Diner in Little Bray when I arrive.

The sign above the door says they do the best breakfast in Bray, but no one seems to have any appetite today. I feel nearly guilty for ordering the full Irish.

Ricey goes, 'What a prick, like.'

He's talking about Sergei, although I get the impression that one or two of the goys think I'm not taking the whole thing seriously enough when I ask the waitress if it comes with beans.

Barry's there, 'Did you know, like?'

'Know?' I go. 'Know what?'

'Did you know that Sergei was seeing Breena behind my back, like?'

I look at him and I look at the others, with their shaven heads, and I realize that I can't lie to them.

I'm there, 'No, I didn't know.'

Okay, it turns out I *can* lie to them. I notice Fionn look away. He's obviously terrified that they're going to ask him next and he'll find himself having to tell the truth. To lie like me takes real strength of character. Thankfully, they let him off the hook.

'Because when that foxy Russian one said she had a secret,' little Nailer goes, 'you told her not to say anything, like.'

I'm there, 'That was about something totally different.'

They all just stare at me. I can tell they're dubious.

I'm there, 'Okay, if you must know, I actually rode the woman in my cor in the Glen of the Downs one night. That's the short version of the story. The long version is that my cor broke down, then my wife showed up and I had to get a tow back to Dublin with Sergei's stepmom hiding in my boot.'

This seems to put their minds at ease. Although it's news to Fionn. His mouth drops open and his eyes go wide.

You can tell he's wondering, will the Rossmeister ever change?

Barry goes, 'So you didn't know what he was up to, like?'

I'm there, 'No, I didn't. And had I done, I would have told you straight away. Because I know what cheating with the girlfriends of your teammates can do to team morale, because I did a fair bit of it myself back in the day. Fionn there will tell you. I could name names.'

There's, like, silence for a good sixty seconds before Preecer goes, 'What are we going to do without him, like?'

I'm there, 'What do you mean?'

'Against Blackrock. We haven't a hope, like?'

I actually laugh in his face.

I'm there, 'Goys, you're not a one-man team.'

Like I said, I can't believe how easy I'm finding it to lie to them.

Nailer goes, 'They hockeyed us before Christmas, like. A hundred points in the first half.'

'Dude, you're a different player to the player you were then. You all are. You're a totally different team.'

Again, they're not convinced.

'Even though he was a prick,' Ricey goes, 'we wouldn't have won any of them matches we won without him, like.'

I'm there, 'I'm calling bullshit on that.'

'It's not bullshit, like.'

'It's total bullshit. You want to know why you lost to Blackrock? Because you didn't believe in yourselves. But I've watched you over the past few weeks and I can't believe how much you've grown as individual players and as a team.'

'But without Sergei –'

'Fock Sergei!' I suddenly shout. 'I don't want to hear his name mentioned again! How can I get you to see that what happened against Michael's, what happened against Clongowes, what happened against Mary's – it wasn't down to Sergei. It was down to you.'

'It's Blackrock, like.'

'And you can beat them. I want you to believe that.'

But they don't. I can see it in their eyes and in their body language. They've, like, given up.

'We've got to go to work,' either Lenny or Dougie goes. They both stand up. One by one, the others stand up as well.

When they've gone, Fionn goes, 'Did you mean what you just said?'

I'm there, 'As in?'

He goes, 'Do you really think they're capable of beating Black-rock College without Sergei?'

And I'm like, 'Not a focking chance.'

'Oh my God,' Honor goes, 'this is *such* a shit cor.'

All I can do is laugh.

I'm like, 'Er, you were the one who bought it, Honor.'

'I know,' she goes. 'That's because I had to make the whole thing believable. But it's still a shit cor.'

She gets in anyway.

I'm like, 'How was school?'

And she's there, 'The usual focking bullshit.'

I spot Roz Matthews getting out of her black Ford EcoSport. I pretend not to see her, but I end up being let down by my need to check her out. I think I'm on the record as saying that she's a less annoying-looking version of Allison Williams, except with a thankfully smaller mouth. But in checking her out, I end up accidentally making eye contact with her. At first, I think – oh, fock, she's going to come over and say something to me. But she doesn't. She just gives me that sad smile that I've seen a million times from other parents – a look that seems to say, I'm just glad she's yours and not mine.

'What the fock is *she* looking at?' Honor goes. 'Yeah, spare us your pitying looks, you stupid bitch.'

I'm there, 'Honor, the window's open.'

'Er, I don't *give* a fock?'

She doesn't. She genuinely, genuinely doesn't.

She shouts, 'Your daughter is a focking sap, Roz – like you.'

I decide it would probably be best all round if I closed the window.

Anyway, sixty seconds later, we're back sitting in a queue of all-terrain vehicles waiting to exit onto Mount Anville Road and it's just like old times. Yeah, no, they reopened the cor pork the other day – no fanfare, no explanation, no apology. The school's experiment with caring about the future of the planet has been quietly put out of its misery, never to be mentioned again. The work of the Mount Anville Climate Justice Committee will continue, with Sincerity as its leader, although its activities will be closely monitored by the school and restricted to running ort competitions and look-ing in the green bins to make sure they don't contain non-recyclable items.

I'm there, 'I hope you're not getting too much of a hord time for what happened, Honor. Because you don't deserve it. And I'm not just saying that because I'm scared of you.'

She actually laughs. She goes, 'Focking spare me, would you? Most people are just relieved that it's all over. They're happy they don't have to get the focking bus any more. And – hilarious – they're all off to focking Pinzolo, by the way, for Easter!'

I laugh along *with* her?

I'm there, 'So can I ask you a question, Honor?'

She's like, 'What?'

'Did you know what you were doing – as in, like, right from the stort?'

'Like I said, at the stort I was just sort of, like, stringing her along, letting her think I cared about the same shit as her, pretending to be as big a sap as *she* is? And then I saw a chance to humiliate her in public.'

'By calling her out in front of the entire United Nations?'

'No, by causing a riot at the Climate Justice Rally. I knew about the formers' protest – that's why I arranged it for that day. That was, like, *supposed* to be my revenge? But then she read that piece in the *Irish Times* and she was suddenly *proud* of what I did? That's how focked-up her thinking is. I thought, "What the fock do I have to do to hurt this woman?" And then the UN thing came up. I just couldn't believe my luck. You know the way she's always banging on about the UN.'

'She does talk about it a lot. I still don't know what it even *does*.'

'I had to pretend I didn't want to fly obviously. I didn't want to look too keen. But I was always going to go. I wasn't going to miss the chance to call bullshit on her in front of all those people – espe-cially her all-time focking hero.'

There's suddenly a tap on the window. I turn to my right and Sister Consuelo is standing there. Shit. I'm wondering could I pre-tend not to see her. But then Honor goes, 'Dad, Sister Fock-Face wants to talk to you,' and I end up having no choice but to acknowledge the woman and open the window.

She's aged about ten years since the last time I saw her. Honor has broken the spirit of stronger people than Sister Consuelo.

'I never thought in all my years,' she goes, 'I'd hear Mary Robinson cry.'

I'm there, 'Er, didn't you already have this conversation with my wife?'

'Your daughter has disgraced herself and she has disgraced this school.'

'Hey, she thought she was worried about the end of human civilization and then she realized she wasn't. As my old man said, there's nothing wrong with changing your mind.'

'She pretended to care about the future of the planet.'

Honor leans across me and lets her *really* have it.

'*Everyone* is pretending to care,' she goes. 'It makes people feel good and virtuous and fills the hole where religion used to be.'

I feel like Ivan Yates sitting in the middle of them. I turn to Sister Consuelo and I go, 'And what's your answer to that?'

She just goes, 'I'm praying for you,' which is a weak comeback and I think the woman possibly knows it.

Eventually, we get out of the cor pork and get on the road. We're halfway home and I'm singing along to the radio when Honor turns around to me and goes, 'You're in a good mood,' and she says it in, like, a *disapproving* way?

I'm there, 'Yeah, no, I'm sorry about that.'

'What are you so focking happy about?'

'I don't know. We're playing Blackrock College in the Leinster Schools Senior Cup final on Saturday.'

'I thought you said you had no chance?'

'I did say that. But that was yesterday. There's always that little bit of you that still believes. Especially as the game gets nearer. You stort to think about driving to the stadium and the crowds of people and the different coloured jerseys and that shiny trophy. You get this feeling in the pit of your stomach that's kind of hord to put into words. But suddenly you don't give a shit about the odds – because it's eighty minutes. And sometimes those minutes go fast and some-times they go slow. But *in* those eighty minutes, Honor, absolutely anything can happen. Don't tell me the sky's the limit when there's footsteps on the Moon.'

'What are you talking about?'

'Yeah, no, it's an old Father Fehily line. He used to say it to us when we we thought we were, I don't know, lacking in belief.'

She thinks about this for a few seconds, then she goes, 'I hope you win your match, Dad.'

I'm like, 'Thanks, Honor. And, hey, none of it would have hap-pened, bear in mind, if you hadn't sent my Rugby Tactics Book to Joe Schmidt.'

She's quiet for a little while then. She's like me sometimes – a deep thinker. You never really know what she's going to come out with next.

Eventually, she goes, 'I'm sorry I caused so much trouble for you.'

I'm there, 'Don't worry about it. Hey, I'm sure Sorcha will even-tually look back on what happened and laugh about it.'

She won't. She definitely won't.

'I don't give a fock whether she does or not,' Honor goes. 'I'm not sorry for what I did. I just wanted to make sure that, like, *we're* still friends?'

I'm there, 'Of course we are! Jesus! *Best* friends!'

'I don't want you to hate me – the same way everyone else hates me.'

'I could never hate you, Honor. Hey, can I let you into a little secret? I'm actually glad you don't give a shit about the future of the planet any more.'

'Really?'

'Yeah, I much prefer you as a bitch – although obviously don't tell your mother I said that. I found that whole caring about global warming thing a bit boring. It's like I've got the old you back again.'

'I'm so glad that *you're* not a focking fraud like her.'

'Thanks, Honor. That's a lovely thing to say.'

'Dad, I feel bad about ruining Christmas for the boys.'

I laugh. I'm there, 'God, I forgot about that. Focking vouchers for hugs. It's a good job Leo didn't have that gun in his hand when we ran into Michelle Obama!'

Honor laughs, in fairness to her.

Then she goes, 'I want to buy them, like, loads and loads of presents and do Christmas for them at Easter.'

I smile at her. I'm like, 'I just wish other people could see the good in you, Honor.'

'I'm going to need, like, ten grand,' she goes.

And I'm there, 'Then ten grand is what you shall have.'

I'm just about to take the turn into Honalee when I see something that causes me to suddenly slam on the brakes. It's, like, a Gorda cor pulling out of our driveway onto the Vico Road.

Naturally enough, I go, 'Honor, is there something you need to tell me? It'd be nice to know if I'm going to go in there and bat for you.'

But she just shrugs her shoulders and goes, 'It's fock-all to do with me.'

I notice Sorcha's old man's SEAT Ibiza – focking two-door – in the driveway.

Into the house we go. I can hear Sorcha sobbing in the kitchen and her old man – at the top of his voice – going, 'It all storted to fall aport when you married *him*. And I begged you not to do it, Sorcha – me *and* your mother.'

Honor rolls her eyes and goes, 'She's such a focking drama queen,' then stomps her way upstairs to see the boys.

I tip down the hallway and I push open the kitchen door. I'm like, 'What the fock is going on? What's this dickhead doing in my house?'

Sorcha goes, 'Ross, the Gords have just been here.'

I'm there, 'Whatever Honor is alleged to have done, Sorcha, I'm saying she definitely didn't do it.'

'They weren't here about Honor. They were here about Leo.'

'Leo?'

'Someone phoned them and told about him shooting the gun in the church.'

'Why are they bringing that up? The old man said he'd pay for the window and whatever other damage.'

'They're curious as to how a five-year-old boy came to be in possession of a gun in the first place.'

'Why didn't you just tell them it was Kennet's gun?'

'Because she did the smart thing instead,' *he* goes. 'She phoned someone who knew something about the law and who told her to say absolutely nothing. *That's* what this dickhead is doing in your house, by the way.'

I'm there, 'I thought you were in the whole family law end of things,' because I love cutting him down to size when he storts doing his hot-shot lawyer act.

'Oh, you're going to *need* a family lawyer,' he goes.

And that's when Sorcha drops a bombshell on me.

'Ross,' she goes, 'they're reporting the matter to Tusla. They're saying we might end up losing the children.'

We take the right turn at Donnybrook Bus Depot and the atmosphere on the team bus suddenly tightens.

You can feel it.

I'm there, 'Remember this moment, goys, because you will never be in this position again. Unless you obviously repeat it.'

Barry storts walking up and down the bus, trying to get the rest of the players pumped, shouting, 'Will of focking iron! Nerves of focking steel! Balls of focking brass! Can I get a "Fock, yeah"?'

They're all like, 'Fock, yeah!'

I'm actually proud of how he's grown as a captain and the mature way he took the news that the love of his life was riding one of his teammates behind his back.

One word. Rugby.

The bus makes its slow way down Anglesea Road. Ballsbridge is – I think it's a word – *aslosh* with colour, although mostly it's the blue and white of Blackrock College that we can see.

Their supporters are already in porty mood. You can see from their smiling faces that they think the cup is already in the bag.

Even Fionn says it. He goes, 'They're not expecting a match.'

When they see us coming, they actually stort waving at us and shouting, 'Good luck, goys!' instead of telling us that we smell of untreated sewage (the Mary's fans), or that Bray is where they send their non-recyclable household waste (the Clongowes fans), or that we come from a town that's still on focking dial-up (the Michael's fans).

It actually gets worse when we turn into the RDS. It's all, like, Rock boys, past and present, standing around to cheer our arrival. Then they form a – *literally?* – gord of honour as we disembork from the bus and head for the dressing rooms.

I hear one or two people go, 'In fairness, Pres are already winners in getting this far' and 'I think we'd all agree that Blackrock and Belvo would have made a far better final.'

It's the most pissed off I've been with Blackrock College or any of its people since Craig Doyle insisted on reverse-porking his white Buick Cascada into the space next to mine in an otherwise empty Frascati Shopping Centre cor pork, then banged my door when he was getting out.

'They don't even hate us,' I tell the goys as they're changing out of their civvies. 'We're not even worthy of their contempt.'

Ricey goes, 'Some fella's after telling me that it was no shame to lose to this side – like we're already beaten, like.'

'Patronizing pricks,' either Dougie or Lenny goes.

I decide to use this to my advantage.

'They think they've already done the hord work in beating Belvo in the semi-final,' I go. 'Having to play you is, like, a massive, massive inconvenience to them. Yeah, no, they'd rather be enjoying their Paddy's Day with a few scoops. Maybe watching Ireland play England this afternoon for the Grand Slam. Instead, they've got to beat Pres Bray, which they've already done once, remember?'

They're all just looking at each other with this sudden expression of – I'm going to use the word – *resolve* on their faces?

'They think you're still that team,' I go. 'The team they scored a hundred points against in forty focking minutes. The team who were too embarrassed to come out for the second half.'

Fionn's there, 'It's up to you to show them that you're not that team any more.'

I'm remembering Craig Doyle pushing his business cord into my hand and telling me – with one of his trademork winks – to 'make sure to reach out to me' if I noticed any dents in my bodywork.

'Focking Blackrock College,' I go. 'We're not here to watch them win. We're here to ruin their focking day.'

They all cheer.

I look around at all the baldy heads in the dressing room, at this group of players who I once thought were useless, but who I now love like they were my own teammates from back in the day. I can't even put into words how much I want this for them.

'I can tell you what they'll be thinking in that dressing room next-door,' I go. 'That we fluked our way to the final. That we caught one or two teams on an off-day. That we had one great player who made us a half-decent team and now he's gone and we're obviously shit again. But I know that's not the case. Because, over the past few weeks, it's been my pleasure – and Fionn's – to watch you grow as people, as players and as a team. I was going to tell you one or two stories about Blackrock College – one of them involving Craig Doyle – but I'm not going to. Because you know what you have to do. So let's give these fockers hell. Let's show them what it means to come from Bray.'

On the way out of the dressing room, I pull Ricey to one side. I have a feeling this is a match that's going to be won by the forwards.

I'm like, 'Dude, did you eat today?'

'Yeah,' he goes, 'I'd a spaghetti bolognese about an hour ago. You said to eat pasta, like.'

'Yeah, no, it's cool. I want you to do something for me. When the first scrum happens, and you're just about to engage, stick your fingers down your throat, then get sick all over the front of the Blackrock hooker's jersey.'

It's a trick that I learned playing front row for the famous Seapoint a few years back. And, while it's admittedly borderline in terms of acceptable behaviour, there's no doubt that it's effective.

Ricey's there, 'Why would I do that, like?'

'Dude,' I go, 'we can't win this match if we stand back and let

Blackrock play their pretty passing game. Our only chance is if we can somehow turn it into a war.'

So we walk out there. The atmosphere ends up being disappointingly *cornival*-like?

Bray has turned out in strength to support us. The Anglesea Stand is, like, two thirds full of our fans, most of them dressed in white, and all of them singing, 'We're Bray, we're Bray, we're Bray! We're Bray, we're Bray, we're Bray!'

You can actually hear the Rock fans going, 'Fair focks to them.'

I spot the old man in the front row of the stand. He's holding up little Hugo and he's shouting, 'Kicker! Kicker! Your little brother says good luck!'

I have to admit, it's a nice touch. But then it's not a *day* for nice?

Brother Ciaran sits down on my left-hand side. He goes, 'Isn't it marvellous? I'm talking about the whole sense of occasion. To see the boys from the two schools getting on so wonderfully well. I've just been chatting to some of the mothers.'

He looks over his shoulder. I follow his line of vision. Not far behind us, the Blackrock College moms are sitting a few yords away from the Pres Bray moms. You can see them looking them up and down in that condescending way of theirs, going, 'Aren't they morvellous all the same, girls? They've even made an effort at dressing up!'

Fionn is sitting to my right. He goes, 'I don't like it.'

I'm there, 'As in?'

'The atmosphere,' he goes. 'It's too cosy. There's no edge.'

I'm like, 'It's all in hand, Dude. Wait until the first scrum.'

The game gets under way. The two teams spend the first five minutes booting the ball back and forth into each other's territory, just basically feeling each other out.

Finals are often like that. There's so much at stake. You make a mistake and you'll have to carry it with you for the rest of your life.

But then Barry *does* make a mistake? He somehow manages to knock the ball on and the referee awards Blackrock a scrum right on the halfway line.

My eyes are fixed on Ricey as our front goys go in for the bind. The two front rows engage. But, as the Blackrock scrum-half goes to feed the ball in, the entire thing collapses like a dropped calzone.

As the players stort to pick themselves up again, I notice that the Blackrock hooker is in an absolute rage. He's got – yeah, no – vomit down the front of his lovely, blue-and-white-striped Rock jersey. They're so proud of their colours, of course. He makes a grab for Ricey, but either Dougie or Lenny gives him a hord shove. Then one or two of the Rock forwards get involved and suddenly a melee breaks out involving every single player on the pitch.

Fionn goes, 'Did you really tell him to get sick on the opposition hooker?' but – in fairness to him – he's kind of smiling when he says it. 'Ross, that's one of the most morally reprehensible things I've ever seen on a rugby pitch.'

You don't prevent Seapoint from being relegated to Division 2C of the All Ireland League without learning a thing or two about the dork orts.

The atmosphere in the RDS has suddenly soured. Both sets of supporters are screaming abuse at each other as they watch the players pushing and pulling out of each other and even throwing the odd punch. I look over my shoulder and I notice that a line of Gords has arrived to form a protective barrier between the two sets of mothers.

I'd call that sensible policing.

Even Brother Ciaran has changed his tune. As the Rock hooker leaves the field to change out of his puke-covered jersey, his coach shouts at the referee, 'What kind of a scumbag would do something like that?' at which point, Ciaran stands up, waves his walking stick at him and shouts, 'Sit down, you blackguard! Or I'll give you a belt of this!'

The incident succeeds in completely destroying the match as a spectacle. It ends up being one of those mean, nasty affairs, full of late challenges, high tackles and desperate, boot-and-bollock defending, while private scores are being settled all over the pitch.

Now, I've seen some shit schools cup finals in my time – a

significant number of them involving Terenure College – but this is undoubtedly the worst I've *ever* sat through?

When the referee blows up for half-time, it's still scoreless. But I'm definitely the happier of the two coaches because we've managed to drag the Blackrock so-called Dream Team down to our level.

There's a row going on when we get back to the dressing room. Barry is having a go at Ricey.

He's like, 'What are you doing, puking on him, like?'

And Ricey points at me and goes, '*He* told me to do it, like.'

Nailer is there, 'It's a war out there. I'm getting battered, like.'

But Fionn goes, 'That's good. A war is what we want. We're not going to beat Blackrock in a free-flowing game of rugby.'

I'm there, 'Fionn is right. Goys, can I just remind you, the last time we came in at half-time against this team, we were a hundred points behind.'

They all just look at each other and the penny finally drops.

I'm there, 'Now, do any of you feel like going home this time?'

'No fucking way, like,' Ricey goes.

I'm there, 'Dougie, Lenny, what about you goys? Anywhere you'd rather be than sitting in the dressing room in the RDS with an evens chance of beating Blackrock College in the Leinster Schools Senior Cup final?'

'No way, like,' they both go.

And I'm there, 'Give me forty minutes more of the same, goys. And I promise you, when that final whistle blows, whether you win or lose, you'll leave this ground without any regrets.'

So out they go again, seriously fired up.

And – yeah, no – the second half ends up being more of the same. One team gains a few yords of ground, then the ball is turned over, and the other team regains the lost ground, plus a few yords of their own – and you know pretty much everybody watching it on TV will have switched it off by now.

But we stort to tire as the minutes wear on. I can see that Ricey is out on his feet. I'm thinking, he could probably use those corbs that he spewed all over his opposite number.

Blackrock are storting to enjoy more and more success in string-ing passes together and they're making progress up the field. As the match enters its final minutes – still scoreless, if you can believe that – it reminds me of an orm-wrestling match, where one person has forced the other person's orm just a couple of inches from the table and you know it's not a case of whether but *when*?

And with a minute to go, they finally break our resistance. And – hand on hort – I have to admit that it's a try worthy of winning a Leinster Schools Senior Cup final. It involves, like, decoy runs, and skip passes, and gear switches, and finally their centre finishes the move – finger pointing in the air before he's even touched the ball down.

'Fock them,' I go.

They celebrate in front of their fans and I watch three or four of our goys hit the deck out of exhaustion and disappointment. I stort screaming at them to stand up.

I'm like, 'What the fock are you doing? On your focking feet!'

When the madness dies down, the Blackrock ten steps up to take the conversion. The conditions are pretty much perfect. There's not even a breeze and it's from as near to directly in front of the posts as even *matters*? It's the kind of kick, in other words, that you don't even bother your hole practising because it's just so boringly *routine*?

The Blackrock kicker does his little pre-kick ritual anyway. He takes four steps backwards, then three to the side, then he sort of, like, crouches down with his orse sticking out like a shitting dog. He looks at the ball, then with his eyes he follows a vertical line upwards to the posts, then back down to the ball, then back up to the post again.

Makes a complete focking meal of it, in other words.

And then, finally, he decides to kick the ball. But at the precise moment he makes contact with it, his standing foot, for no reason, slips. It's only, like, morginal, but it's enough to change the trajectory of the ball's flight, so that instead of going straight down the middle, it veers nervously to the left, like my old dear heading for the hord shoulder when she sees the Gords breathalysing motorists up ahead.

What happens next is so freakishly unbelievable that you know you'll only see it once in your entire lifetime. The ball hits the left-hand post, then flies off to the side and hits the right-hand post. It seems to hang in the air forever and the entire RDS seems to hold its breath as we wait for it to drop.

The question is will it fall *behind* the cross bor or in *front* of it?

And this is the bit that defies all reason. It actually falls *on* the crossbor, then bounces forward, back into play.

We're all just looking at each other, shaking our heads at the sheer randomness of it. And it's not until I hear this sudden rising clamour from the crowd that I notice that Nailer – the smallest man on the field – has the ball in his hands and he's haring down the other end of the pitch with the thing stuck under his orm.

I jump to my feet. So does Fionn and so does Brother Ciaran. I'm just, like, screaming at the dude, going, 'Go on, Nailer! Go on!'

He crosses the halfway line. There's, like, three Rock players in hot pursuit and the Rock full-back twenty metres in front of him. The first player tackles him hord, but Nailer manages to ride it. He very nearly loses his footing. He actually touches the ground with his right hand but manages to correct himself and runs on a few more steps.

Behind me, in the crowd, I can actually hear his old man – the bus driver – going, 'Leg it, Nailer! Leg it!'

Brother Ciaran goes, 'Will he make it?' and he sort of, like, grips my foreorm until it actually hurts.

Fionn's there, 'Why is he running straight *at* the full-back?'

But Nailer seems to *know* what he's doing? Or maybe it's more just good fortune. A second player attempts to tackle him from behind just as the full-back is about to hit him front-on. Nailer feints one way, then goes the other and the two Blackrock dudes collide, taking each other out of the game.

Nailer is, like, twenty yords from the line. The last player chasing back knows he can't catch him. All he can do is force Nailer wide to make the conversion as difficult as possible for Barry. Nailer touches the ball down in the corner and our crowd go absolutely apeshit. And so do our players.

I've never seen anything like it – in all my years of playing and watching rugby. Sixty seconds ago, we were staring certain defeat in the face. We were plucky underdogs who had a go, but came up sadly short. Now – by some freakish twist of fate – we find ourselves somehow level again, with a chance to win the match with what will be the final kick of the game.

Rugby. Sometimes I feel my eyes well up when I just think of the word.

Barry is the only one of our players who doesn't celebrate Nailer's try. He knows he still has a job to do. He takes the ball and he walks over to the sideline with it.

Like I said, the angle is horrible. But he doesn't look even a bit scared as he puts the ball in the cup. He takes his four steps backwards and his three to the side. Then looks over at me and he actually smiles.

'Why's he smiling?' Fionn asks.

And suddenly I know why he's smiling.

I'm there, 'Holy fock – he's not going to do what I think he's going to do, is he?'

It turns out that he is.

There's, like, silence in the RDS. I can hear Brother Ciaran beside me muttering Our Fathers under his breath.

Barry takes a run at the ball. And then, just before he makes contact – I swear to fock – he closes his eyes, just like he used to when I first watched him train.

He strikes it hord and true. From the second it leaves his foot, I know it has the direction – the question is, does it have the distance? Like the rest of the crowd, I stand there in just, like, stunned silence, following the orc of the ball's flight as it rises and then dips . . .

Falling . . .

Slowly . . .

Slowly . . .

Slowly . . .

Until it finally comes down . . .

And clears the bor – by, like, six inches.

All hell breaks loose. Me and Fionn and Brother Ciaran run onto the pitch, as does half the population of Bray. We're all just, like, hugging each other, tears streaming down our faces. It's, like, pandemonium.

I'm being grabbed and pulled by this person and that person. One moment, I've got Ricey hold me by the shoulders and shouting in my face that I'm a rugby genius. The next, I've got Nailer's old man literally weeping on my shoulder, telling me that his wife would be the proudest woman in the world if she'd lived long enough to see this moment.

It's very emotional.

Then Barry goes up to collect the famous hordware – the same tin pot that I lifted exactly nineteen years ago to this day – from his old dear. He keeps his speech short and to the point.

He goes, 'Not many people would have given us a chance of achieving what we achieved today if they'd seen us six months ago, like. But there's a lad here who thankfully saw something in us and he taught us that everything was possible, even if he sometimes had a job persuading us. Ross O'Carroll-Kelly – you made this happen, like.'

I'm crying my eyes out. I'm going, 'No, no – *you* made it happen.'

For one glorious afternoon, I actually forget that my kids could potentially be taken into care.

He's there, 'You're going to be the coach of Ireland one day – I just know it – and we're all going to say we were lucky to be coached by you, like. Our Assistant Coach, Fionn de Barra – let me just say, your courage in facing your illness, and your wisdom, inspired us every day, like.'

I walk over and I give Fionn a big hug.

'Brother Ciaran,' Barry goes, 'our Principal – you always told us that Bray was the best little town in Ireland, like.'

I'm like, 'Hear, hear!'

'You always said that we were every bit as good as the posh fellas who go to Blackrock. Well, maybe this proves that, on our day, we can be even better, like.'

Everyone cheers. I notice a few of the Blackrock players even applauding that line.

Barry goes, 'Say it loud – I'm Bray and I'm proud!' and then he lifts the cup high over his head.

I'm suddenly lifted up onto the shoulders of our fans. Beside me, the same thing happens to Fionn and to Brother Ciaran. Soon, we're being carried around the field, paraded like trophies.

I spot my old man in the crowd, holding up little Hugo, so that I can see him. He goes, 'I can't wait to tell him he was here, Kicker – to see the great Ross O'Carroll-Kelly make history!'

I can put my hand on my hort and say it's the greatest day of my life – obviously after the birth of my children. And, just between ourselves, maybe it's even better than that.

The nurse walks in and connects the tube to Fionn's chemo port for the very last time.

'Is this it?' she goes.

Fionn nods. He's like, 'Yeah, I just have to get through this afternoon and then I'm done.'

'You don't know that,' she goes. 'Some patients have to come back and do a second round.'

'Don't take this the wrong way,' he goes, 'but I hope I never lay eyes on you again.'

I think I mentioned that she wasn't great.

She nods at him and goes, 'Oh, well – you'll know for sure in a few weeks.'

Then off she focks.

Oisinn shakes his head. He's like, 'I still can't believe it. I mean, I *want* to believe it? But Pres Bray winning the Leinster Schools Senior Cup? It can't be real, can it?'

Me and Fionn just smile at each other.

'You know you're going to be in serious demand now?' JP goes. 'There's a lot of All Ireland League clubs are going to be putting you at the top of their wanted lists.'

I'm there, 'Well, I won't be going anywhere without my Assistant here. He's, like, Stuart Lancaster to my Leo Cullen – right, Fionn?'

He just smiles. He doesn't commit himself one way or the other.

Like she said, it'll be months before he knows if the cancer has gone.

'So, er, me and JP have a bit of news as well,' Christian goes. 'I mean, nothing as big as Pres Bray winning the Leinster Schools Senior Cup. But – yeah, no – the pilot scheme to accommodate two thousand homeless people in the hangar near Weston Airport is going ahead. We delivered two thousand beds yesterday and Éadbhard – spelt the Irish way – delivered two thousand Home-drobes. They're already talking about a second phase.'

Oisinn is like, 'Okay, that is getting a fair focks and I don't care.'

And Magnus is there, 'Yesh, fair fucksh, guysh.'

'Plus,' JP goes, 'we're partnering up with Eadbhard – spelt the Irish way – to lobby together to try to change the law relating to minimum aportment sizes. We're just praying that this investigation clears your old man and he's the next Taoiseach.'

I'm there, 'There's not a chance, Dude. He's as guilty as sin.'

And that's when I hear my phone ringing in my pocket. I whip it out and I check the screen. It ends up being Shadden. I answer. I can tell from her voice that she's upset.

She goes, 'Ine arthur been rigging you all day.'

I'm like, 'Yeah, I'm here with my friend. He's having focking chemo, Shadden.'

She's there, 'Ronan's arthur been addested.'

'Arrested?' I go.

'Thee hab him in Doddy Barook.'

'Where?'

'Doddy Barook.'

'Shadden, I have absolutely no idea what you're trying to say.'

'Doddy Barook, Rosser. Doddy. Barook.'

'Oh, Donnybrook! Jesus Christ. Okay, I'm in Vincent's. I'll be there shortly.'

I hang up on her and I tell Fionn that I unfortunately have to go – to find out why my son is in Gorda custody.

He's there, 'Please, go – it sounds important.'

*

Half an hour later, I'm standing in front of some lady Gorda and I'm demanding answers.

'I'm entitled to know,' I go, drumming my index finger off the desk. 'I pay my taxes.'

I don't pay my taxes.

She goes, 'Your son has been arrested in connection with a serious offence. He is being interviewed in the presence of his solicitor.'

I'm not going to comment on her looks.

I'm there, 'I want your name and your rank.'

'My name is Nicola Byrne,' she goes, 'and my rank is Sergeant.'

'Okay, I'm taking a mental note of that.'

'Do you want me to write it down for you?'

I'm there, 'No, I'll hopefully remember,' and I wander over to the seating area and I plonk my orse down on a hord chair.

I end up sitting there for, like, half an hour. Then, suddenly, a door opens and out walks Ronan, followed by – oh, for fock's sake – Hennessy.

They both look surprised to see me.

'Rosser,' Ro goes, 'what the bleaten heddle are you doing hee-or?'

I'm like, 'Shadden rang me. What the fock is going on?'

'Let's conduct this conversation outside,' Hennessy goes walking straight past me. Ronan follows him out through the door.

I turn around to the lady Gorda and I go, 'Thanks, em –' because I've already forgotten her name.

'Nicola Byrne,' she goes. 'Sergeant. Just in case you need it for the Garda Ombudsman.'

What she lacks in beauty, she more than makes up for in being a sassy cow.

I follow Ronan and Hennessy out the door and as far as Hennessy's cor, which is porked outside Marian Gale. They get into the front and I hop into the back.

'Hang on,' I go, suddenly wising up, 'does this have something to do with the gun going off in Foxrock Church?'

Ronan goes, 'Some wooden's arthur grassing, Rosser. Some wooden's arthur tedding them that I got rid of the bleaten thing.'

'Why don't you just tell them the truth and say it was Kennet's gun?'

'With his record, he'll do tedden yee-or insoyut – and he'll do evoddy bleaten day of it.'

'Fock him.'

'He's Shadden's da, Rosser.'

I'm thinking, the sooner he puts distance between himself and that focking family, the better.

I'm there, 'Don't worry about it, Ro. Just focus on your final exams. And then you've got a new life waiting for you in the States.'

He goes, 'I habn't, Rosser.'

'What?'

'Ine arthur been cheerged with posseshidden of a foyer eerm and cubbering up a croyum.'

'Okay – so?'

'I've been ordered to surrender me passpowurt. Ine not going addywheer, Rosser.'

I suddenly feel like I've been kicked in the nuts. In that moment, I just so happen to look at Hennessy. I'm pretty sure I can make out the faintest trace of a smile on his face.

And the mystery as to who tipped off the Gords suddenly isn't a mystery any more.

It comes on the news while we're having our breakfast. Roderic Grainger, the senior counsel appointed to investigate claims that the 2017 General Election was rigged, has found no evidence to suggest a campaign to improperly influence the result.

But Sorcha barely even acknowledges it, except to shake her head and go, 'I really worry about the future of this world.'

'The bad man!' Leo goes. 'The bad man!'

Sorcha's like, 'Leo, eat your breakfast. You too, Johnny.'

What she's really worried about, of course, is the future of our children. Yeah, no, the famous Tusla are sending two social workers to the house next week to talk about the whole Leo-shooting-out-a-stained-glass-window incident and they've let us know, in no uncertain terms, that they're taking the whole thing very seriously.

I'm like, 'What day are they coming again?'

Sorcha's like, 'Thursday.'

'Riiiiggghhht.'

'Why are you saying it like that?'

'It's just that's the day that me and Fionn are supposed to be getting the Freedom of Bray. It's not something you could handle on your own, is it?'

'Are you *focking* kidding me?'

'Hey, it's cool – we'll figure something out.'

'We won't figure something out. You will *be* here. Have you called Honor for her breakfast?'

'Yeah, no, twice. She says she doesn't want any. Hey, she's back doing her fashion vlog, by the way.'

'I'm not interested in anything the girl does.'

'That's, em, understandable.'

'I meant what I said in New York, Ross – she's your daughter now.'

'Hey, that's cool, Sorcha. I think she'll hopefully settle down – now that she's focked you over for sending her to Australia.'

'What if she storts acting up when the social workers are here?'

'Look, I don't think she'll cause trouble. She loves her brothers. Yeah, no, I've a genuine feeling these social workers will come here and see what a hopefully normal family we are.'

'I wonder do we have to tell them about her? We could give her money and send her to Dundrum for the afternoon.'

'Jesus Christ, we can't hide our children from Tusla, Sorcha.'

'Can't we?'

'No.'

'The bad man!' Brian goes. 'The bad man!'

Sorcha's like, 'There's no bad man, Leo! Oh my God, why do they keep saying that?'

For some bizarre reason, I decide that honesty is possibly the best policy.

I'm there, 'I, em, may know what that's actually about,' and I instantly regret opening my mouth.

She's like, 'What?' and she's already angry.

I'm there, 'I, em, sort of let them watch a horror movie.'

384

She goes, 'Excuse me?'

'Yeah, no, it was *Don't Breathe*. I'm just remembering, I think it gave *you* nightmares as well, didn't it?'

'You let them watch *Don't Breathe*?'

'Okay, don't make me regret telling you. I could have gone on pretending I had no idea what was upsetting them.'

'Jesus Christ, Ross.'

'The blind dude in the movie is a ringer for Father Thaddeus. I'm pretty sure that's why Leo tried to shoot him.'

'When did you let them watch it?'

'It was on the flight to New York.'

'But I was sitting right beside them.'

'You were helping Honor with her – yeah, no – speech to the UN.'

I suddenly see this look of, like, guilt come over Sorcha's face.

'Maybe Honor is right,' she goes. 'Maybe I *am* a terrible mother.'

I say fock-all. It's great because it kind of lets *me* off the hook?

She's there, 'Maybe I deserve this. Maybe the kids *would* be better off if Tusla took them from us.'

I decide that I possibly should say something.

'Sorcha,' I go, 'you're an amazing mother. And – not patting myself on the back here – but I'm an amazing father. In a week or two, they won't even remember seeing the movie. They'll hopefully be back to being just normal boys.'

Brian throws a handful of milk-sodden cereal across the table and it splatters across Leo's glasses.

Leo goes, 'You focking prick with ears,' and I smile at Sorcha as if to say, See?

And that's when the doorbell rings.

I go outside to answer it. I can see that it's him even through the frosted glass. I decide to open the door anyway.

'Kicker!' he goes.

I'm like, 'What the fock do you want?'

'You've been listening to the news, I take it!'

'For once, the answer to that question is yes.'

'It seems that I am to be Ireland's fifteenth Taoiseach! The Dáil will be voting this afternoon.'

'Are you looking for me to say fair focks here?'

'I told you our friend would turn up nothing! Is your good lady wife at home?'

'She's in the kitchen.'

He doesn't wait to be invited in. He steps past me into the gaff.

I hear him shout up the stairs, 'Good morning, Honor!'

And Honor goes, 'Hi, Granddad! Congratulations!'

And he's like, 'Thank you, Dorling! The wheels of justice turn slowly, but grind exceedingly fine! Etcetera, etcetera!'

I'm about to shut the door when I notice Fyodor standing there. I actually laugh.

I'm there, 'So you found something on Roderic Grainger, I take it? Some dirt?'

He smiles. 'Yes,' he goes, 'we find dirt.'

Poor Roderic. Although it'll be nothing compared to what Fyodor will do to me if he ever finds out that I rode his wife. Still, that's a worry for another day.

I'm like, 'How's Sergei? Have you heard from him?'

'He is good,' he goes. 'The boy is better with his mother. He is sad for trouble he cause.'

'Er, it was kind of *you* who *caused* it, Dude?'

'But he is happy that Pres Bray wins the cup.'

I reach for my chest and I grab the coach's medal that's been hanging around my neck since about half an hour after the final whistle. I take it off.

I'm there, 'Give him this next time you see him, will you?'

Fyodor takes it from me. He goes, 'Thank you. Is good of you,' and then he walks back to the old man's stretch Merc.

I shut the front door and I go back to the kitchen.

The old man is holding Leo in his orms and he's going, 'I'm going to do wonderful things for our country, Sorcha!'

Sorcha's there, 'So you said, Chorles. I just don't know why you're telling *me* all of this?'

The old man goes, 'Because I want you join me, Sorcha! At the Cabinet table!'

'Chorles, I'm not even a TD.'

'You can be one of my nominees to the Seanad! The rules of the House allow a Taoiseach to appoint up to two Senators to ministerial positions! How does Minister for Climate Action sound to you?'

'Climate Action? Chorles, you don't even believe in global warming.'

'Well, you can spend the next five years persuading me! Sorcha, I want you on my team!'

I'm there, 'Tell him to fock off, Sorcha.'

Sorcha goes, 'Ross is right, Chorles. This *isn't* a good time for us. We've got social workers coming here to talk to us about what happened in the church.'

The old man's there, 'I'll get rid of them for you!'

'What?'

'Just say yes, Sorcha, and I'll make the problem go away!'

I'm thinking, no focking way. They've already got leverage on Ronan. Now they're trying to pull the same trick on Sorcha.

I'm there, 'Tell him to shove it up his hole.'

But Sorcha's like, 'Make it go away? Are you saying you could actually do that?'

And the old man just smiles at her. 'I'm Chorles O'Carroll-Kelly!' he goes. 'I think it should be obvious by this stage that I can do anything!'

Epilogue

The old man runs his hand through his hair slash wig and goes, 'It's a day for the ages! Quote-unquote! Little Hugo will be reading about this one day in his history books!'

'Unless he plays Senior Cup,' I go. 'Then he won't have to worry about shit like that.'

He's there, 'Quite true, Ross! Quite true! And after witnessing your recent exploits, I'm sure he will – play rugby, I mean!'

Kennet looks over his shoulder. He's like, 'What's the stordee, T . . . T . . . T . . . T . . . Teashocked? Are you w . . . w . . . w . . . w . . . wanthon me to thrive up and down the quays wooden mower toyum?'

'No!' the old man goes. 'Let's not torture the poor chap for any longer than is necessary! I think Michael D. has waited long enough – and so have I!'

Yeah, no, we're back in the stretch limo, heading for the Phoenix Pork, followed by a cavalcade of black Mercs and Gordaí on, like, motorbikes with their *sirens* wailing?

We arrive at the gates of the Áras. Some dude in an ormy uniform – the same dude as last time – approaches the cor on the driver's side. Kennet opens the window.

'I've the T . . . T . . . T . . . T . . . Teashocked in the back,' he goes.

The dude knows to mind his manners this time. He just opens the gate and we drive through.

Kennet goes 'S . . . S . . . S . . . Suddem diffordence in he's attitude this t . . . t . . . t . . . toyum, Teashocked, wha'? Ine glad it all w . . . w . . . w . . . w . . . w . . . woorked out in the edend.'

I'm there, 'For you, maybe. Not for Ronan.'

The old man goes, 'Ronan will be fine, Kicker! Isn't that right, Hennessy?'

Hennessy's there, 'Yes, I'm confident of getting the chorges against him dropped.'

'Let me guess,' I go, 'in about three or four months, when that crowd in the States have given the internship to someone else?'

The old man goes, 'Ronan will love working for your godfather, Ross! Can you think of anyone better to mentor the chap than Ireland's next Attorney General?'

He looks over his shoulder to make sure the old dear is still behind us. Yeah, no, she's following in a second Merc, with my brother and sisters. They want them to be here to see this moment, even though they obviously won't remember it.

We pull up in front of the gaff.

'*Datum perficiemus munus*, indeed!' the old man goes.

There's, like, hundreds of people standing around outside – most of them journalists and photographers. Kennet gets out of the cor and opens the back door. The old man gets out first, followed by Hennessy, then the Rossmeister General.

The air is suddenly filled with the sound of cameras clicking and questions being shouted. It's like, 'Chorles, were you surprised that Roderic Grainger found no evidence of overseas election meddling, given some of the leaks that emerged during the course of his investigation?'

He doesn't answer. But Hennessy goes, 'You will address him by the title of Taoiseach.'

The old man opens the door of the second cor and the old dear steps out of it. They kiss for the cameras. Then some, like, Secret Service-looking dudes wearing black suits and shades take the babies out of the back and pop them into three double-strollers.

The photographers keep clicking away. The old dear hooks my orm and pulls me into the shot.

A journalist shouts, 'Fionnuala, what are your children's names?'

She goes, 'They're called Hugo, Diana, Mellicent, Louisa May, Emily and Cassiopeia. And this one here is named Ross.'

I put on a fake-smile for the cameras. Then I spot Ronan and Shadden getting out of the third cor. I walk up to Ro. I'm like, 'Are you okay?'

He just nods. 'Heddessy says he thinks he can get the cheerges thropped, Rosser. It might take him a few munts, but.'

I'm there, 'You're not upset about New York, then?'

'I am. But addy fedda what can get me out of the koyunt of botter Ine in at the moment – he caddent be a bad fedda to leern from, wha'?'

I put my orm around his shoulder and we follow the rest of them into the house.

'Mr President!' the old man goes, shaking the famous Michael D. 's hand. 'I gather you've been expecting me!'

There ends up being a lot of laughter at that line. Even *I* end up laughing.

Michael D. is there, 'Cathal Ó Cearbhaill-Ó Ceallaigh. Congratulations on your election as Taoiseach.'

The old man's there, 'Thank you, President Higgins!'

We're about to move into the next room, where the old man is going to sign, I don't know, whatever needs to be signed, then receive his Seal of Office in front of the cameras.

But then, all of a sudden, everyone's attention is drawn to my old dear, who has a tape measure in her hand and is in the process of – I shit you not – measuring the windows for presumably curtains.

Poor Michael D. is looking at her, obviously thinking, It's a bit early in the day for her to be *that* shitfaced.

Sabina – in fairness to her – tries to make a joke out of it. She goes, 'You do know, don't you, that the job doesn't come with this house?'

And the old dear pretends to laugh along with everyone else. Then she gives the poor woman the serious death stare and goes, 'You have exactly one week to move out.'

Acknowledgements

I would like to thank, as always, the hard-working and talented team of people who are behind every one of these books, especially my editor, Rachel Pierce; my agent, Faith O'Grady; and the artist, Alan Clarke. Thank you to all the team at Penguin Ireland, especially Michael McLoughlin, Patricia Deevy, Cliona Lewis, Brian Walker, Carrie Anderson and Aimée Johnston. And with love and grateful thanks to my family – Dad, Mark, Vincent and Richard. And, most of all, thank you to my wonderful wife, Mary.